MOONSTRUCK AT MIDNIGHT

ALEJANDRA ANDRADE

FIRST EDITION

Book Cover and Interior Design by David Provolo
Cover Art by Sulamit Elizondo

ISBN (hardcover): 978-607-29-2678-3
ISBN (paperback): 978-607-29-2664-6
ISBN (ebook): 978-607-29-2665-3

www.alejandra-andrade.com

For Mariel

March 18, 1986 – January 7, 2007

You taught me many things, but one that stuck to me the most, that inspires me the most—to the day—was your curiosity to try new things and the power of reinventing yourself. You were an ice-skating champion, a painter, a belly dancer, a jewelry designer, a speech delivery expert, a great cook, a track and field athlete. As if that weren't enough, you were well on your way to becoming a great architect. And I know I'm forgetting a few things.

You poured your heart and soul into everything you did; that's why you were so good at it—at everything. And you genuinely didn't care about anyone's opinion. You were you. One of the most talented and creative minds I've ever known.

I've tried a few things myself since you've been gone, mostly out of curiosity, but others because I felt lost. But they all taught me great things. You keep inspiring me to seek within and express myself through different outlets. I'll keep trying new things in your honor, knowing you have my back. My soul sister, my guardian angel. You were, are, and will be forever the greatest friend anyone could ever have.

I wish I could've shared this story with you. I poured my whole heart into it, and I know you would've been so proud. You were a hopeless daydreaming romantic just like me—one of the many things we had in common. So this one is definitely for you.

Love you always.

TABLE OF CONTENTS

CHAPTER 1

Portrait

March 13, 2009

MY FRESHMAN YEAR at Paris College of Arts was nearly finished. Our time in Paris was almost over. It was crazy to think how many things were going to change. But I still had a lot to get done before we left. Cecile was going to sit for my Black and White photography class that day, which was my favorite class ever, but she canceled on me the second I arrived at school. I tried calling Sophie, but she didn't answer my call. She was probably busy at school too.

Nearing panic with no other choices, I turned around and asked my security detail for help. "Could one of you sit for a portrait?" Aaron and Caleb looked at each other with raised brows. "Please? I don't have anyone else to ask, and the class starts in five minutes."

Aaron refused right away, deeming it *inappropriate*, so I shifted my attention to Caleb.

"Caleb, please? You have to help me." I looked in Aaron's direction because I knew he was the one objecting to my request. I knew Caleb would gladly do it, but Aaron had to agree to it first. "Aaron." I widened my eyes at him—a silent plea.

"Okay, Miss Murphy. Just this once," Aaron replied with hesitation. "I'll park the car, and Caleb will walk you to class." Aaron said something to Caleb in Hebrew afterward, which sounded more like a warning than anything else.

"Could you at least take your earpiece off once we're in the classroom?" I whispered to Caleb as we made our way to the main entrance.

"Sure," he replied with a wink. "Aaron won't like the idea, but I don't feel like arguing with you when you always get your way." Caleb was a smart guy. He was right every time, but I *always* got my way with him.

The suit, the tie, the fancy shoes—he didn't need any of it to attract anyone's attention, but it made him stand out even more. Caleb could easily blend in with the college crowd if it wasn't for his elegant outfit.

A small group of girls swooned as we flew down the corridor. *Welcome to the Caleb Fan Club.* And who are we kidding? He *loved* the attention, and I enjoyed teasing him nonstop about it. At least with Caleb by my side, I could count on feeling invisible—all eyes focused on him. Thank you, Caleb.

Portraits were the theme of the week in today's class. And what better face than Caleb's going through my lens? I made a mental note to thank Cecile for ditching me because her understudy turned out to be an excellent choice.

We walked inside the studio classroom and took a seat at one of the high tables. It was surreal having Caleb sitting beside me during class. They usually waited outside.

Our instructor, Miss Genaurdi, finished setting up the lighting equipment and backdrop for the different stations as the rest of my classmates walked in with their models. We were six students in total in that group.

Everyone arrived, and Miss Genaurdi explained the purpose of the day's lesson and how we would take turns with the provided set for the photoshoot. She offered guidance on lighting and camera configuration as each student stepped forward to use the set.

"I'm next after he's done," I whispered to Caleb. "I need you to take your jacket off," I said as I prepared my camera. He raised a brow. "Please?"

"That's not possible, and you know why," he said as he leaned against the table, arms crossed at his chest, legs crossed at his ankles, looking my way.

Of course. Caleb had to conceal his gun. And just reminding myself that he carried one all the time made me shudder. I sometimes forgot that Caleb wasn't just a friend following me around everywhere. He was there for protection—*my* protection. And I wanted the portrait to be as casual as possible, but I didn't have a choice.

"Um—right," I said, pressing my lips together. "Take your earpiece off, then."

"Aaron's gonna be pissed," he replied, keeping his posture in place and showing no intention of removing his earpiece.

"Good. That way, you'll have a real reason to argue instead of the usual UFC fight nights and such," I said, standing on tiptoes to pull the earpiece out of his ear. "This looks really uncomfortable and not at all inconspicuous, by the way."

"That's the point, actually. Security should be obvious," he replied, putting the earpiece back on. "Wait." He clicked on it, said something in Hebrew, and took it off again.

"We agreed you'd take it off for the shoot, so don't look at me like that."

He smiled, amused. "Okay, what else?"

"Um, I need you to lose the tie too," I said with an exaggerated grin. Caleb licked his lower lip and turned away as he loosened up his tie to pull it over his head. "And a couple of these"—he pressed his lips as I undid the top two buttons of his shirt—"because we don't want you to look like a hipster." He searched for my gaze, and I felt how his Adam's apple moved up and down when he swallowed. But he quickly looked away afterward. *Stop making me nervous!*

"Do you need me to take my shirt off, too?" he joked, lightening the mood. I laughed, releasing a bit of tension. That wouldn't have been a half-bad idea. But having his face so close to mine wasn't something I was used to. So yeah, I was tense.

Miss Genaurdi called my name last. It was finally my turn to photograph Caleb. He took a seat on the stool and looked my way with a frown as a bunch of lights hit his face.

I adjusted the lighting, and Miss Genaurdi checked my camera settings to verify if everything looked good. I dashed toward Caleb, undid another one of his shirt's buttons, and ran back to screw my camera to the tripod.

He snorted, and I shot an annoyed face at him, with an *I heard that* kind of gesture. I instructed him to keep a straight face and look into my camera.

And for some *bizarre* reason, my fellow female classmates gathered behind me to see me photographing Caleb. I could hear them whispering. And I had to agree to all of their spot-on observations regarding Caleb's beauty.

Luckily, all of their remarks were said in French, so that meant he didn't understand two shits of what they said—we wouldn't want it to go to his head. *Psh* ... as if he didn't already know what kind of effect he had on women.

I reviewed the photographs on my camera's display with my instructor, and we agreed that I had achieved a favorable result. I unscrewed my camera, and everyone started packing their stuff after the class was dismissed.

Caleb walked out of the classroom, holding his tie over his arm and putting his earpiece back in place. Aaron looked sideways at his disheveled appearance with disapproval.

Caleb immediately placed his tie around his neck and fitted it into a perfect knot in record time. I mouthed "thank you" to him the second Aaron turned around. "You can thank me with a big birthday gift next week," he whispered back with a wink. I shook my head at him. We'd never exchanged birthday gifts before, and I'd love it if we did, but I guess it felt too intimate to do so.

The photographs I shot of him were perfection. And all mine.

Caleb's phone rang, but he muted the sound and placed it back in his jacket's inside pocket, glancing behind his shoulders.

If everyone looked in Caleb's direction, Aaron had the opposite effect on people. He was intimidating—the *proper* one, you could say—and balanced Caleb's bold personality out pretty well. They made a good team but took their job too seriously for my liking.

I had my Introduction to Art and Design class afterward and was done for the day. And since it was Friday, that meant I had dinner plans with Sophie and Cecile. They would usually go to a bar or nightclub afterward. And I could tell you a cute story about how nightclubs aren't my thing, but the truth is I was not allowed to go. Period.

We drove back home, and Caleb's phone rang again while Aaron parked the car, but he didn't take the call and rushed to open the door for me instead.

"Why don't you take the call? It might be important." My suggestion made him nervous.

"Nah, it isn't. I can call the person back later." He was trying to sound casual, but I perceived the exact opposite of that.

I marched toward the Residence's main entrance, and Caleb walked beside me. He wasn't paying attention to what I was telling him, which was unlike him. *Why is he so distracted?*

"And then Mr. Pernot took his pants off at the end of his lecture," I said as we walked up the stairs to the front door.

"That's nice, Red."

I shoved his shoulder in playful protest and replied, "You think it's nice that Mr. Pernot took his pants off?"

"Wait. What?" I now had his full attention.

"What's gotten into you? You're not like yourself," I said, reaching out for the doorknob. He stood beside me and restlessly tapped his foot. "Why don't you call whoever's calling you back. I have an assignment to get to, anyway. I'll see you later."

Caleb nodded and walked back to the parking lot. I watched as he took his phone out of his pocket and wondered *who* was making him act that way—and why.

"Good afternoon, Miss Murphy," Annette said as I walked inside the Residence. She was head of the house staff. "I left a treat for you in the study." She winked at me and excused herself after I thanked her. She knew that's where I usually spent my time after school reading or doing homework.

The study was one of my favorite places here. It had a beautiful view of the gardens—they were breathtaking. My mother would've loved them, especially during spring. And the Residence was practically a mini-Versailles.

I was slowly working my way on a few extra credit assignments for the six classes I took that semester because we were leaving a month shy of the last day of school. The university was informed ahead of time, so they made special accommodations for my particular case.

We were finally going back to New York City. My father knew how I dreamed of going back home. But his time as Ambassador of the United States had come to an end. At least for the next four years—hopefully forever. Culture shock became my currency after almost sixteen years of living like a nomad. We went where my father went—or better said; I did. At least for the last five years, that is. It was just him and me now.

I was tired of not having a real home, but Paris had stolen my heart. Thinking of leaving was challenging, and even though I was excited about returning to New York, I was sad about leaving Sophie and Cecile. They were my two closest friends in Paris.

My father knocked on the study's door. "Kiddo?"

"Come in!"

He walked in and pulled a chair to sit beside me. He usually had a hectic work schedule, so he tried to find small windows of time to talk to me whenever we were both home.

"Any news from the DSS?" I asked. "Perhaps a security detail won't be necessary once we move back to New York." We were waiting for the Diplomatic Security Service to determine if Aaron and Caleb would come to New York or if new agents would be assigned. Or in a crazy world, none at all.

The fact my father wouldn't be an ambassador anymore had to help relax security protocols.

Fingers crossed.

But I can't lie. Without Aaron and Caleb, I'd feel bare. I learned to live my life with a homogeneous mixture of suffocation and safety.

"I think we should play it safe, sweetheart. The investigation about what happened in Mexico City is not finalized yet." I cringed when I heard the word *Mexico*. "I wouldn't feel comfortable having you walk around on your own in New York."

And what about Aaron and Caleb?

If it were necessary to keep having agents following me around, I'd rather have Aaron and Caleb be the ones to do it.

"Gregory, the DSS director, agrees it's convenient to keep things going as usual. We are going to ask Aaron and Caleb if they will move to New York."

Yes!

Suffocated again, but safe.

My father's overprotective nature seemed to yield a bit when he said, "Let's feel things out. Once we're home, we'll see what changes can be accommodated. I know it's unconventional for you to go through life, growing up, under these—circumstances."

Case closed.

My father excused himself to host some dinner event in our Residence, the Hôtel de Pontalba. The place was busier than usual, people coming and going, bringing in beautiful flower arrangements and setting up the dinner tables.

Security was tighter during special events like these since a considerable amount of people were expected to attend. The front gate was bustling with cars and agents.

Talking to my father made me lose track of time. I needed to get ready for dinner.

I jumped in the shower, got ready as fast as I could, and walked out the front door wearing a short black leather skirt with a black, tucked inside long-sleeved blouse. I paired it with nude pumps and a long, dark green trench coat—my favorite. Wearing too much makeup wasn't my thing, but a slightly tinted lip and peachy rose blush was my usual look.

It was almost 8:00 p.m., and there was a lot of movement in the forward area before the front gate. But Aaron and Caleb weren't on site. They would usually have the car waiting for me when they knew I had somewhere to go.

Shoot! I forgot to tell them about my dinner plans.

I sent a text to our Blackberry Messenger group chat and made my way to the west side of the front gate, where they often lingered. I sent another text and heard a distant *ping*! Someone had to be nearby.

The sound prompted me to ask one of the security guards to open the gate for me. I called Caleb, and I could hear his cell phone ringing. I turned right—nothing. I turned left toward the Apostrophe Boutique and ended the call abruptly.

I froze. *Hell no.*

Ping! *Ping*!

Aaron texted me back, and I uselessly tried to silence the notifications when an incoming call from him startled me. I sent it to voicemail to stop the ringtone from breaking my cover. But it was too late.

The *lovely* couple stopped kissing and stared at me from a distance.

CHAPTER 2

Crush

"MISS MURPHY," CALEB SAID, his hands instantly unlocking from Noelle's waist. He pressed his lips together and stared in my direction. I bet he wished he had his phone on vibrate mode—a habit he (and I) acquired after that day's occurrence.

Noelle was an older girl I knew from high school. She studied fashion design at PCA, so I saw her from time to time at the university too.

She greeted me with flushed, peachy cheeks, but I couldn't tell if it was from all the kissing or because I caught them in their secret rendezvous. Probably both. She looked a bit embarrassed. I greeted her back with a Monet smile, hoping it looked better from afar.

"Caleb, I really need to go. I couldn't find you guys. Aaron just texted me, and he's ready to leave too. I didn't mean to intrude."

He nodded.

I said goodbye to Noelle and huffed away from the interrupted love scene. But I couldn't hold in a chuckle when I heard Caleb *chewing* on his French, trying to say goodbye to Noelle.

"Miss Murphy, I'm sorry about the schedule confusion," Aaron said as he opened the door for me.

"No, please, it's my fault. I forgot to tell you about my dinner plans," I replied as Caleb jumped in the front seat, looking agitated. Aaron drove hastily toward the restaurant.

"I can assure you Caleb's not so sorry about the schedule mix-up situation," I teased. "So, you're into blondes, huh?"

Ugh.

Aaron glared at a mortified Caleb, while I secretly enjoyed his embarrassment. "I'm so sorry, Red. I didn't mean for you to see that," he confessed. I'm sure he didn't. "I—I don't know what to say."

"Don't worry. I'm just messing with you." Had Caleb kissed more girls from school? Or just Noelle? I couldn't stop wondering, but I quickly dismissed the thought because the answer was pretty obvious.

The real question was, why did I care?

"Besides, Noelle's really—pretty," I added. She was. A wave of unexpected emotions caught me off guard. One thing is to see girls trying to get his attention unsuccessfully, and another is to see him *French kissing* blonde Noelle from school.

It was more than likely he would prefer I didn't find out about his escapades. It bothered me that he would see *me* as a child but *them* as something else. *Why?* I'm sure he found them way more exciting than dull, book reading, stay-at-home on the weekends me.

The rest of the ride to the restaurant was quiet as the grave. I regretted teasing him about it, especially in front of Aaron, who would call him out on it for sure.

But I always teased him, so why wouldn't I this time?

I caught myself overthinking.

Stop.

Caleb darted out of the car as it was still coming to a stop, *his signature move*, and rushed to open the door for me. He followed me inside, where the hostess greeted me and showed me to my table.

I double cheek-kissed Sophie and Cecile and tried to sound casual when I apologized for being late.

"Good evening, ladies," Caleb said, pressing his lips together afterward, looking guilty. He pulled the chair out for me and walked away to join Aaron outside.

"Is everything okay?" Cecile asked in the cutest French accent ever, following Caleb with her eyes.

"Ah, yes! Just caught Caleb and Noelle smooching outside of the Residence."

"Smooching?" Sophie asked with a grimace.

"Kissing!" I replied with a nervous laugh.

"Wait. Noelle, as in your sister's friend, Cecile?" Sophie inquired.

"I thought she had a boyfriend," Cecile said, lifting the corners of her mouth with a frown.

"Oh, come on, she's been hunting him since high-school," Sophie said. *Basically.* "And Caleb, well, he's a flirt." *Yup.* "He's always loved the attention." *Double yup.*

Our table was beside the window where we had a clear view of Caleb, who had just lit a cigarette—probably trying to smoke his embarrassment away.

"Did it—upset you?" Cecile asked, her eyes locking mine with speculation.

"Psh, of course not."

I peeked over my shoulder again, but Caleb caught me staring at him. He must've known by then that he was the topic of conversation. I swiftly looked away, pretending to sneeze afterward. I don't know why I did it.

"Bless you!" Cecile chirped.

"I see now why he calls you Red, and I don't think it's only because of your hair. I wonder how many times you've blushed like this with him," Sophie teased with a playful smile.

"Sophie, stop!" I laughed. My cheeks were warm. Inflamed. I felt doomed by the newfound, silly infatuation, but I wouldn't *dare* tell a soul. If my father somehow knew about it, he would send Caleb away. And not having him come to New York wasn't an option for me. I *needed* him.

Caleb's presence in my life became an essential element of my sense of security and happiness. He was a friend I couldn't afford to lose. I had to make myself snap out of it.

Besides, he was kissing Noelle, which meant he liked *her*. I mean, he undoubtedly had kissed a bunch of girls by then. It would've been naïve of me to think otherwise.

Cecile stared at me with a puzzled expression on her face. I shook my head as I came out of my daze, completely lost in thought.

"Ah, yes, sorry—what?"

"Ready to order?" she asked, apparently for the second time. The antsy server took our order and left the table promptly. Sophie and Cecile kept talking, but I couldn't keep my focus on their chatters. My mind was elsewhere, thinking about Caleb and Noelle kissing.

Suddenly, I wanted to show Caleb that I could be more than a frightened girl locked up in her room reading. I knew we were in the middle of dinner, but I needed to do this.

I asked Sophie and Cecile if they wouldn't mind if I made a quick call. They didn't. I was determined to call my father but unsure if he would pick up.

"*Dad? Hi, yes, everything's okay … Uh-huh—yes, I know you're busy. I just wanted to ask you if it's okay if I go with Sophie and Cecile to a bar after dinner. It's sort of a farewell party kind of situation … Yes—well, we're leaving soon. They want to bid me farewell properly.*"

Sophie gawked at me with shock-filled eyes. Cecile's face was somewhat similar to Sophie's.

"*Yes, I'll let Aaron and Caleb know, one a.m. … Thanks, Dad … Love you too, ba-bye.*"

This made me wonder how much of me not going out relied on my father, rather than not wanting to go out myself. Perhaps I caught him off guard as he was busy with the event he was hosting, and I didn't give him enough time to process what I asked of him entirely. But he agreed, and I intended to go.

Sophie squealed as I tucked my phone back into my purse. A few people stared at us. Caleb and Aaron must've heard it too, as they were both looking in our direction. I nodded, letting them know everything was fine.

"What's gotten into you?" Cecile asked, sipping on her wine afterward, scanning my face for clues, I guess.

"I can't leave without a proper farewell, can I?"

"I still can't believe you're leaving in less than a month," Sophie said with a pouty face.

"I know. We're going to miss you so much," Cecile added.

"Don't even get me started. I'm going to miss you both like crazy, and you *have* to come to visit." I felt all mushy and teary-eyed all of a sudden.

"Okay, enough with the moping. Tonight, we celebrate!" Sophie yelled—again. "We are going to have so much fun!"

I glanced outside for the millionth time, looking for Caleb's attention, and signaled him to come inside. He rushed to our table gracefully—his long, black coat floating through the restaurant with ease.

"Yes, Miss Murphy?" His thick, sexy accent sent chills down my spine. I've heard him speak for years, but something about the day's events triggered a latent awareness in the back of my mind.

"I just spoke to my father. He agreed to let me go to a bar after dinner with my friends." His hazel eyes widened for a second, giving away his astonishment. "There's a one a.m. curfew, though."

"Yes, Miss Murphy, I'll inform Aaron and take care of any necessary details." He still looked shocked. I thanked him with a sincere smile, and he walked back outside into the chilly evening.

"Paul and a few of his friends are going to be at the bar in Hôtel Costes—we could go there, it's a few blocks away from your home," Cecile suggested.

Very convenient.

We finished our dinner, paid the check, and left the restaurant. Aaron had the car ready and waiting on the curbside. Caleb walked ahead as he raced to open the door for us.

I climbed into the car, sensing a certain wariness from him when he closed the door behind me. He jumped in the front seat next to Aaron, and off we went. Even though it was the first time I would go to a place like this, I knew it was nothing both Aaron and Caleb couldn't handle.

My phone buzzed.

Caleb: I know your father said yes, but there's a bunch of creeps at bars. If you're planning on drinking, make sure to watch your wineglass. Someone could easily slip something into it. I'll make sure that doesn't happen anyway.

Here we go.

CHAPTER 3

Crave

I'M PLEASED TO INTRODUCE to you the other side of Caleb. The one that's overprotective and worries too much. But I knew how to handle him. I was sitting right behind him in the car, and I could see him fidgeting in his seat as he waited for my reply.

Me: Caleb, I'm turning 20 in a few weeks. I'll survive. And I wouldn't mind if you could at least pretend to trust me and give me a bit of breathing space while we're there.

I placed my phone back in my purse because this conversation could've quickly turned into an argument. I could also see myself at the bar texting Caleb all night about this instead of doing what I intended to do, which was … stop thinking about him.

We arrived at our destination, and a surge of cold air slammed my face as we stepped out of the car. A driver from the Embassy was waiting to take the vehicle's keys so both Aaron and Caleb could come inside with us.

"The music here is amazing!" Sophie said as we walked toward the entrance. "You're going to love it."

Two theatrically gigantic men wearing all black stood behind a red velvet rope, evaluating the people who waited to be selected by them. They all looked like decent people. I wondered what it took to get inside a place like this.

A couple of girls, who looked like models, approached the stanchion, and a bouncer automatically let them through. I understood now how things worked in this place. Instinctively, I looked down to evaluate myself—double-checking my overall appearance.

"You look great, don't be ridiculous—we'll get in. Paul and his friends will be here any minute now. We can wait for them to arrive," Cecile whispered, trying to reassure me.

We had been standing there for a minute and a half, and I swear it was the longest minute and a half I've ever had to endure. It was so awkward. I would've rather left than beg to get in.

I could hear a guy shouting in the back, trying to get one of the bouncer's attention. They completely ignored him. It was painful to watch.

A third man approached the entrance from the inside to reckon the access situation. He squinted our way, trying to focus his vision. "Aaron? *Mon ami! Viens ici!*" He cheerfully invited Aaron to approach him.

"Jean-Henri!" Aaron replied as he shook his friend's hand firmly. The exchange looked sincere.

The velvet ropes opened up for us, and we triumphantly stepped inside after Jean-Henri gestured for us to come in. Aaron pulled his friend aside to exchange a few words with him.

A bar employee escorted us afterward to the dim-lighted bar.

My plan was to get my mind off Caleb by attempting to be a typical young woman having fun in Paris. Not to get even. In my mind, I believed I meant nothing to him more than work and a casual friend—someone he could talk to when he was bored or had some free time on his hands.

I really needed to loosen up and have fun for a few hours. I knew my friends could help me with that. And Sophie was right; the music was great. They gave us a small, cozy table, yet something told me it was a prized commodity.

The place was less than half-full, which surprised me because of the number of people outside waiting to get in. You'd think that having a packed venue would be something to look forward to as a bar owner, but they were picky in who to allow inside—that'd been made clear.

We were lucky to have Aaron's acquaintance help us get in faster, or at all.

We took a seat on the red velvety couch that surrounded the table, and a girl who only spoke French approached us with a beverage menu. She had dark brown hair made up in a loose chignon. Her fair skin glowed against her currant-red lips. She was as arrogant as she was pretty.

Was she aware of her job description? Maybe it was all part of the bar's theme.

She swiftly took our drinks order and fled the table.

I had a glass of wine with dinner, and I rarely drank more than two glasses of anything with alcohol. Assuming a safe amount of time had transpired from dinner to the bar, I reset my counter and planned to have two more glasses of wine.

We chatted and waited for our drinks as the bar slowly welcomed more people inside.

Paul arrived with three friends who sat with us, crowding up on our table. We all greeted each other as our favorite server finally arrived with our drinks. Aaron and Caleb idled near, chatting with each other while keeping their gazes locked in our direction.

Paul and his friends ordered bottle service, which prompted our server to yield a subtle smile in return. She pivoted on her heel and marched away in Aaron and Caleb's direction. I saw her eyeing Caleb—flirtatiously smiling at him as she walked by past them.

Business as usual.

The night progressed, and everyone seemed to be having a good time—except me. Paul and Cecile kept dancing to the folk-like beats while Sophie chatted with a guy who approached her.

Two of Paul's friends moved to and from our table to refill their drinks as if it were a gas station, while Paul's third friend was nowhere to be found.

My plan wasn't going as expected. I was bored to *death*. Ordering my second and supposedly last glass of wine was necessary to keep me busy doing something while I awkwardly sat on the couch.

"Look!" Sophie screamed excitedly, walking up to me and clutching my arm.

"What is it?" I looked over both of my shoulders for an answer.

"It's Richard Miller and Tabatha Collins," she whispered in my ear.

"Richard and Tabatha, who now?" I was clueless.

"Come on, *le stars de cinéma*!"

Hollywood was not my forte since going to the movie theater was tricky and not "recommended" by the security advisors. I loved watching a classic now and then, but I mostly kept to my music and books.

"Sorry to disappoint you, Soph." I grimaced.

People couldn't stop staring at the famous couple and their entourage—they all seemed accustomed to it.

Standing up to get my blood flowing was necessary to prevent myself from sadly fusing with the couch. At least the wine was delicious. I took a few sips of it and contemplated a bathroom break when my phone buzzed.

Caleb: Bored?
Me: Of course not! Best night ever.

I looked to my right and saw Caleb replying to my text with a smile. This was the definition of a perfect night-out for him—me alone, bored, and wanting to leave. No *creeps* wanting to talk to me, no *psychos* wanting to spike my drink—everything under control.

Caleb: Do you want to leave?

I honestly was ready to leave. I was typing my reply when someone grazed the back of my arm.

I turned around and saw this tall, illegally handsome guy in front of me with dark-chestnut hair and matching eyes that glistened against his ivory skin.

"Hi," he said, lifting the right corner of his mouth into a cute, crooked smile. He held a short tumbler with an amber-colored drink—probably whiskey.

"I'm Thomas." He introduced himself with an American accent.

"Hi, I'm Guillermina—you can call me Billie."

I peeked in Caleb's direction and saw him tucking his phone back into his jacket pocket. His attention focused on my conversation with the stranger.

"That's a beautiful name, Billie."

My cheeks warmed, and the wine was not helping my case. Thank God for the dim lighting.

Caleb took a couple of measured steps my way, his eyes searching for mine. But I slowly gave my back to him because I couldn't handle the intensity of his gaze. Cecile peered in my direction and turned away quickly, trying not to ruin my interaction with Thomas.

"Can I offer you more wine?" He extended his hand for me to give him my glass, which I did, willingly. I thanked him for what would be my third glass. Or was it my fourth, considering the one I had at the restaurant?

Toughen up.

He took the glass out of my hands and gestured for a refill to someone behind me. A few seconds later, our star server appeared out of nowhere with a fresh glass of wine and presented it to Thomas. His almond eyes kept looking straight through me.

I quickly figured out that men, especially the handsome ones, were the only ones who deserved her five-star express service.

"Here you go." He offered the glass of wine with a flirty smile while casually eyeing me from head to toe. I didn't mind it. At. All.

Thomas asked me if I was in Paris for vacation as he licked his heart-shaped lips right before taking a sip on his drink. Although his lips weren't very full, the shape of them was perfect.

"No, I live here. I'll be going back home soon, though, in about a month." I sipped on my wine, too, mostly out of nerves. "We've been living here for almost four years now."

"Where's home?" he asked, pulling softly at his white shirt's collar.

"New York." I noticed the alcohol really kicking in.

"Your cheeks match your hair." He slowly grazed a strand of my hair with the back of his fingers. My blood raced back to my face again. "And I think it's cute." He smiled, fully aware of the impact he was having on me.

"Do you—live here?" I was hoping he did.

"No, um, I'm originally from Washington, DC. But I'm a sophomore at Princeton now, so I guess we'll be neighbors." He threw a teasing wink at me. An even better response. And that wink melted me.

"My parents are attending an event here in Paris, and since it's spring break for me, I kind of—tagged along. We're heading back home tomorrow," he explained, looking at his empty glass. He moved his thick dark brows up and down swiftly and signaled for a refill.

We chatted for a while. Thomas told me he rowed crew at Princeton and talked about what he did during his time in Paris. I mentioned my passion for photography and how excited I was of going back to New York.

A remix of "Crave You" from Flight Facilities I'd never heard before started playing in the background. Thomas grabbed my free hand, twirled me, and pulled me toward him.

He slightly arched my spine, making our bodies come even closer together as we swayed to the rhythm of the music. I met his gaze once again and got lost in it.

Thomas turned his neck to the side, downed what was left of his whiskey neat, and laid down the empty glass on the table behind me. He jerked his chin at my wine, flashing a smile—an invitation for me to do the same.

I drank the remaining wine and laid the glass on the table.

Our hands were now completely free to roam, allowing us to dance without obstruction. This mysterious intensity and melancholy in his eyes captivated me. All I wanted was to capture his beautiful face with my lens—which was unfortunately back home.

A sudden bump on my back released me from the spell I was under. Thomas grabbed my shoulders and swept me away from the drunk guy who had just collided with me.

"Watch it," Thomas warned the guy with a rough voice. The drunken man half-cursed back at him in French—too intoxicated to speak properly.

"What did he say to me?" Thomas said with a deep frown, seemingly irritated.

Caleb and Aaron were about to intervene, but I quickly shook my head, trying to avoid Thomas knowing about their existence.

Not yet.

"It's okay. I'm fine," I reassured him as I rested my hands on his chest. He refused to look away from the drunk man, who finally managed to recover his balance and wandered off in another direction.

"Do you know where the restroom is?" I asked, trying to remove ourselves from the situation. Subtle anxiety crept on me, wondering if some other girl would snatch him away in my absence, but I couldn't wait any longer.

"Come on. I'll take you." He offered his hand and threaded our fingers together. The blazing anger slowly disappeared from his eyes. Good.

I had previously forgotten about my surroundings, my friends, and even the whole Caleb situation. My plan had worked like a charm.

He led me to the ladies' room door, and to my surprise, he stood there outside waiting for me the entire time, leaning against the wall with his hands inside his pants pockets. He held out his hand with a smile and slowly pulled me toward him.

"I'm sorry I got all—fired-up just before. I think I've had one too many." I suddenly became aware of the extreme closeness between us.

"Don't worry about it," I said, smiling back and combing a strand away from his forehead.

"That face," he whispered, cupping my chin closer to him. "You're perfect." He wet his lips and placed his hands around my waist. My fingers grazed his jawline while I looked from his half-parted chin to his lips.

He came even closer to me, our bodies now completely fixed to one another. I could feel the warmth of his breath against my face. And the delicious scent of bergamot in his cologne surrounded me.

"Uh-hum." Someone cleared their throat to get our attention. I snapped out of the trance I found myself in and saw Aaron standing in the close distance, his hands held together in a tight fist in front of him—the bodyguard stance.

Thomas stared at me, with his hands still firmly placed around my waist. Like me, he was unwilling to let go.

"Boyfriend?" Thomas asked. Caleb appeared next to Aaron before I could answer, holding my favorite green coat, glowering at Thomas. "Boyfriends?" Thomas asked again with a laugh.

Shit.

CHAPTER 4

A Magic Trick

"BODYGUARDS," I REPLIED in barely a whisper. Thomas tilted his head in response.

Aaron approached me and said with his commanding voice, "Miss Murphy, it's past one a.m. We stretched time as long as we could. We need to comply with the curfew."

"Time to go, Miss Murphy," Caleb said in the thickest accent I ever heard coming from him—a small, and probably fake, smile drew on his face. But his full attention remained on Thomas.

I glanced back at Thomas and gently unlocked myself from his embrace. He excused himself for a second, promising to be right back, and rushed through the crowd. I saw him paying the server while Caleb helped me into my coat.

Thomas returned after a few minutes and offered his hand to guide me out of the bar, but I stopped as I remembered I had an open tab at my table.

"It's been taken care of," Thomas replied casually. "Come on, you're running late."

I protested, but Thomas looked back at me and insisted with a laugh, "I've got it, Billie. Don't worry about it."

Thomas led the way to the exit, and I could feel Caleb's glare burning on my back as he followed us out.

Our driver was waiting out front, and Aaron walked past us to open the black Mercedes door for me.

"Who are you?" Thomas asked playfully.

I was so mortified about the whole bodyguard situation. Still, I looked up to him and told him it was nice meeting him, unable to hide the embarrassment in my eyes.

"What do you mean, it was nice meeting me? I would love to see you again when you move back to New York," he said, pulling his phone out of his pocket. "Here—could you type your number down for me, please?" He placed his phone in my hands.

I typed my phone in and casually asked him if he was planning to stay a while longer at the bar. I saw him paying his tab, but you never know. I was curious.

"I'm calling it a night too. We have an early flight back home tomorrow—in a few hours, that is. I'm heading back to meet my parents."

"Do you need a ride?" I asked, giving his phone back to him.

"No, don't worry—thank you. I'll hail a cab out here." He gently kissed my cheek, taking his time doing it. "I'll see you soon." He smiled and released my hand once I got in the car.

Caleb lingered in the distance with deep frown lines between his eyes. He approached us once Aaron had closed the door behind me.

My feet were throbbing inside my shoes—I slipped them off. Fortunately, the ride back was swift, as we were only six blocks away.

There wasn't going to be any small talk in the car, or so it seemed. I texted Sophie and Cecile to let them know I had left the bar. They made me promise to fill them in on all the details regarding my mystery man.

We approached the front gate, and a cab parked behind us. Caleb got out of the car reactively, wanting to see who it was. Aaron followed him, suggesting for me to stay inside the vehicle.

To everyone's surprise, it was Thomas.

He exchanged a few words with Aaron, Caleb, and a couple of

security officers posted at the entrance. He showed them his ID, and an officer took it from him and made a quick call.

A minute later, the officer nodded and handed Thomas back his ID.

Thomas approached my window, which I slid down as quickly as I could. "Hi?" I chuckled.

Looking at him after having just said goodbye minutes before, not knowing if I'd even see him again, was surreal.

"I guess I'm gonna have to accept your ride offer," he joked.

"I don't understand. What do you mean?" I was both excited and confused.

"This is number forty-one Rue du Faubourg Saint-Honoré, right?" He asked as I nodded with a smile. "This is my destination. Scoot over." Thomas opened the door and jumped inside the car beside me. Aaron and Caleb walked through the gate, which closed behind them.

"You know you won't be able to put those back on, right? If your feet are swollen, it's best to keep them off," Thomas said, looking at my bare feet.

The car came to a complete stop. I tried putting on one of my shoes, and a sharp pain made me hiss, proving his theory right. I tried walking barefoot, but needles stung the soles of my feet.

"Okay, close your coat for me," he commanded. I grabbed each side of my coat and closed it tightly in front of me, resting my hands under my crossed arms to firmly grip the coat's flaps.

"Is this a magic trick?" I mocked him.

"Yes, it is." He swept me off my feet in a sudden move, making me gasp as he effortlessly carried me through the parking lot.

"Put me down!" I protested, secretly enjoying it.

"Tricks almost over." He laughed as he made his way up the stairs to the front door. He brought me inside the house where I took a seat on a couch down the main corridor.

"Are you gonna tell me why you're here?" I asked with a laugh. I was used to having people coming in and out of the house all the time. It wasn't really *my* house. I just live here. My guess was he'd probably attended the event my father hosted that evening. Still I wanted to know all the details.

He squatted in front of me and said, "I could ask the same thing, but seeing you here, I can put two a two together. You're Ambassador James Murphy's daughter." I felt defeated because I didn't want him to see me as the ambassador's daughter—I just wanted him to see *me*. My fear was that he would find the whole situation off-putting. Throwing the uncomfortable bodyguard situation into the mix was probably not ideal for him either.

"I can see where you got your auburn hair from," he said, tucking a strand of hair behind my ear. "And to answer your question, my father is a United States Senator. We attended today's event, but after dinner, I excused myself and wandered off on this street until I saw Hôtel Costes and decided to go inside for a few drinks. And then my night got better." He licked his lips and turned to look at mine. He was making me nervous. I wanted that kiss.

"I'm sure you had no trouble getting into the bar." I teased.

"What do you mean?" He laughed, standing up. I'm sure he was aware of how handsome he was. But he probably wanted me to tell him.

I eyed him up and down and said as a joke, "Rowing crew comes with its perks." I directed a haphazard gesture at him, suggesting his statuesque appearance was the answer to his question.

He laughed again. "I'm sure the bouncers cleared the way for you when you arrived," he returned, sitting on the couch next to me. *If he knew we needed to pull some strings to get in …*

He placed one hand on my face and the other on the armrest. There was no way I could escape him now, and I didn't mind one bit. He owed me a kiss.

My head was still spinning. I wasn't sure if it was the wine or just his face that kept drawing near mine. He brushed my lower lip with his thumb, and something ignited inside me, like a sudden blaze that made my body tremble.

"This freckle," he whispered, glimpsing at my lower lip. "Come here." He held my chin and leaned in to kiss me. It was a tender kiss that gradually intensifying its rhythm, and I threw myself entirely into the moment.

Thomas bit my lower lip and released it as our eyes met for a heartbeat, and once again, his soft, perfect, heart-shaped lips searched for mine.

My hands played with his smooth hair, twirling it with my fingers. This was my first kiss ever, and I didn't want it to stop. On the other hand, Thomas seemed to know what he was doing.

The sound of laughter coming from the few remaining guests in the distance made me pull away from him. The event was held on the second floor.

It was now or never.

"I'll be right back," I whispered into his ear. Thomas threw himself back on the couch with a smile. I stood up and winced as my feet touched the floor, but the cold tiles gave them comfort as I walked away to fetch my camera.

I made my way to my room undetected and came back down to meet him with my camera strap hung around my neck and a ten-inch LED ring to help with the lighting. It was the fastest thing I could grab.

"Really?" He grinned.

"Oh, yes, I'm not letting that face leave without having it go through my lens," I replied as I connected the light ring.

"This wall will work." I gestured at the white gilded Rococo style wall. Thomas slid his hands inside his pockets and leaned his back against the wall, taking in the room we were in, waiting for me to finish setting things up.

"Voila!" I turned on the light ring, and Thomas squinted and covered his eyes with the back of his hand, seeking shelter from the intense luminosity pointed at him.

"Sorry about that. Um, could you stand facing me and look through the light ring, please?" I asked. "Try to make no gestures or smiles. Just stand completely still for me." I snapped a few shots of him and checked back on the camera's display screen. His face registered beyond perfection. *That jawline.* "Can you lean your back against the wall again?"

"Of course." He seemed to enjoy my direction.

"Now lift your chin just slightly and follow the camera with your eyes alone." I stood two feet to his right, facing him. He did as he was told.

I wanted to try something I learned in one of my photography classes. I told him to think about someone or something he hated. "Pull that out from the inside and try to project it through your eyes."

He looked at me with narrowed eyes and pursed lips, then looked away as he thought about what I had just asked of him. It didn't take much time for his brows to pull together into a frown.

The camera registered his right side at an oblique angle when I shot his face. His left eye and cheekbone sunk into darkness, transforming Thomas completely as a shadowy veil came upon his features. His eyes followed my lens, filled with resentment—his mouth half-open and relaxed, slightly revealed his top teeth.

Like a bird of prey—patiently waiting. Evaluating. Ready to strike with the full force of his wrath.

A few shots were all it took to capture what I wanted. I hoped he was okay. He seemed upset, and I was curious to know what he was thinking about, but I wouldn't dare ask.

"Thank you." I laid down my camera, switching off the light ring. He stood there quietly in the dark as if deeply trapped in his thoughts.

"Are you okay?" I asked.

"Of course." He forced a weak smile back at me.

"You could always consider a career in acting," I joked, trying to lighten the mood, "since you take such good direction."

He snorted and lifted the corners of his mouth a little more than before, but I could sense he was still trying to pull in his emotions.

I walked closer to him, and he grabbed my waist, slowly tugging me toward him. "What are you going to do with those photographs?" He paused, biting his lower lip. I placed my hand on his face and smiled with a *who knows* kind of shrug.

He shook his head with a genuine smile this time and kissed me. He flipped me around, and I was now pinned against the wall— his hands brushing up and down my waist.

A sudden wave of laughter coming from the second floor startled me.

He withdrew from me, meeting my gaze—our lips moist from the exchange.

"Are you nervous about getting caught?" he asked, brushing a strand of hair away from my face.

"Just a little bit," I replied, pulling him away from the darkness, back into the foyer's illuminated area. We could hear people's voices coming closer.

"I think I should go back. It's getting late," I told him as I grabbed my equipment. His features were neutral again. The rage I saw before was gone now.

Thomas reached for my hand and held it. He whispered, "I'll see you soon." He kissed my cheek, and I walked backward, holding his hand until the distance broke our grip. We both smiled as I turned away to flee back to my room.

A part of me ached at the possibility of never seeing him again. Not that I wasn't used to that feeling.

CHAPTER 5

Twenty

ALMOST A MONTH had gone by since I met Thomas, and still, not a single word from him. I wished it was the 19th century, so his delay in contacting me would be normal and acceptable behavior. But we have cell phones now, and texting is just as essential as breathing. He had my number and had eagerly asked for it.

I guess I was too green on the matter. Thomas was the first guy I met the first time I went to a bar, and here I was waiting for him to reach out to me. I can hear the laughs.

In a poor attempt to achieve peace of mind, I convinced myself that meeting Thomas was merely a one-night fling type of situation and nothing more.

Caleb and I never spoke a word about what happened that day. We went about our days as if I never saw him kissing Noelle, and he hadn't seen my interactions with Thomas.

Delicately swept under the rug.

Yes, we were leaving Paris on Easter Sunday, which unfortunately was a trigger for me. Every year, we celebrated Easter with a huge paella that my mother loved to make. The most delicious paella ever. And after she was gone, we kept the tradition alive with the help of the Embassy chefs.

But this year meant *no paella* on Easter. We would be flying over the Atlantic most of the day. It was impossible.

I sat outside in the garden and lingered on one of the bench swings. I closed my eyes for a few minutes and soaked up the early morning sun. But the sound of fast steps coming down the stairs made me open my eyes. I stood up as Caleb rushed in my direction.

"Happy Birthday, Red! Get in here!" Caleb held his arms out and gave me a long, warm hug that felt great in the chilly morning. He was wearing a gray hoodie, black running shorts, neon orange running shoes, and his curly earpiece that felt so out of place with his outfit. He was my running buddy.

Going out for a run with Caleb was one of my favorite things to do. But I wished it wasn't his job to come with me. I wondered if he would do it either way.

"Ready to go, birthday girl?" Caleb bumped his shoulder against my arm, flashing a smile which I echoed back with a nod.

We walked out the front door, and Aaron was standing by the car. He hugged me and wished me a happy birthday too when we approached him. He then sat behind the wheel and pulled out the Mercedes while we walked out through the gate to start our run.

We followed the usual route, but once we were heading back, I detoured into Tuileries again. He ran beside me while I led him to the *Bassin Octagonal*. Caleb informed Aaron about the detour and current location.

It was still early in the morning, but many people, mostly tourists, wandered about the area. We found a couple of free chairs and took a seat. It was our last day in Paris, and I just wanted that to sink in fully.

"How does it feel to not be a teen anymore?" Caleb shot me one of his playful grins. He was trying to get the conversation going.

"You tell me, old man." I laughed. I covered my face as he sprinkled me with a few drops of water. "Truce!" I lowered my hands. "Ready for New York?"

"Um," he hesitated with a frown. "I've never been to New York before, but yeah, I'm excited." Only he didn't seem excited at all.

"You're not going to chicken out on me, are you?"

"No, of course not," he replied, looking at the water. "It's just—something tells me things are going to be different for you in New York."

"What do you mean?" He was being cryptic and kept looking at me funny.

"I mean, you're all grown-up. You're not a child anymore. It's time you put the past behind you. You owe it to yourself. I'm glad we can come with you and keep you safe, but you're probably going to want to kick us away like the nuisance we are." He snorted, pulling the edges of his lips upward.

"Ugh. I know. I can't wait to throw you out." I nudged Caleb's shoulder with my hand. He probably thought there was some truth in that statement, but honestly, I wanted him close to me.

"Jokes aside, I think you're underestimating my father. You know how he is. Sometimes his overprotectiveness worries me. It makes me wonder if there's anything about the investigation they aren't telling me. I feel like I'm not being informed, and I deserve to be," I said firmly. "Is there anything else you know about—what happened that day?"

"You know I can't talk about it. Besides, we are regularly filled in with certain information, but *you* are my job, and very well cared for. There's nothing to worry about." He tried to reassure me, but his gaze turned to the water once again.

"I wish I could feel normal, someday, you know?" I admitted. My life was different from most people I knew, making it difficult for me to connect with others sometimes. All I wanted was for people to see me as their equal. But the average person doesn't move around with bodyguards in armored vehicles.

"Normal? What's *normal?* Who makes the rules, and why would you want to live by them? Make your own rules," he said. "Never wish otherwise."

Caleb's olive skin glistened in the morning light. There was something about him not wearing a suit, but shorts and a hoodie instead made our exchange a bit more intimate—sincere. It made me feel like I was truly his friend and not just part of his job responsibilities.

"How's Noelle?" I asked, unable to hold in a laugh.

Caleb looked at me with a *really?* face and rested his forearms over his knees. "Back with her boyfriend," he replied dryly, leveling his gaze with mine—challenging me. *Shoot me with your questions. Is that all you've got?*

"Oh," I replied innocently, coaxing him to expand. My friends told me Noelle was in an on-again-off-again relationship with her boyfriend. Caleb turned out to be merely a distraction. He knew it, too.

"You know, it can get lonely," he said softly, "and you can't always get what you want." We both went back to staring at the water after that confession. But he was right, though, about how it can get lonely. He was always right, see?

"Any word from tall, dark, and handsome?" He dared ask. Caleb wet his lips and rubbed his overnight stubble, looking at me as he waited for my answer.

He knew I was not speaking to Thomas. He could smell it like a hound. But what if I was? I wondered if the idea bothered him or not. My all too revealing face would've let Caleb know otherwise, but I have to admit it disappointed me that Thomas hadn't attempted any contact. He seemed so genuine the day we met, and I couldn't stop thinking about it. About *him*.

Anyway, I opened the conversation door for Caleb, and I had to let him in.

"You find him handsome?" I teased, attempting to dodge his question. He squinted down at me, demanding compliance on the silent agreement we made to talk freely.

I surrendered.

"He's gone—*dark*." I chuckled at the irony, knowing better than to expect any different.

"Well, I guess that just makes him an asshole," he snapped. I snorted, acknowledging his effort to make me feel better about the situation. "But I could tell you liked him, and I wish I could say the same. However, there's something about him … I'd prefer he doesn't contact you again."

Hmm.

He was trained to doubt and suspect everyone around me. But was it just that?

"Did it—bother you?" I asked bluntly. His eyes went wide for a heartbeat, somewhat surprised by the candor.

"Well, you know how I—worry." *Worry.* What an interesting choice of a word. "What bothered me was how you had to see me with Noelle, but I thought it was enough punishment to see you with Thomas later that night."

What? I thought he was only embarrassed about being caught, not that he'd be bothered by it in any other way. Seeing him kiss Noelle made *me* feel jealous, but I wasn't thinking about punishing him. I just wanted to stop thinking about it.

But now I was beginning to think that my interactions with Thomas might've triggered a bit of jealousy in him too. But I didn't have a clue of what that meant, and I wasn't going to start asking him about it. No.

Ultimately, he was part of the few good things I had going on for me. Caleb was a presence that, even in the loneliest of days, never faltered. His friendship was more important than any stupid feeling of jealousy. I couldn't let that jeopardize our special bond.

On the other hand, Thomas had been a surprise. One I *did not* see coming. He caught me off guard, and I clung to the possibility of seeing him again.

Caleb sensed that, too.

I just wanted to make sure he knew his friendship meant a lot to me and that I valued it above my immaturity.

"You know you're not just—work, right?" He stood up and moved his water-facing chair at me. He was making a statement that I had his complete attention.

"Of course, I mean, I like to think you consider me a friend," I replied. "Your most boring friend, that is." He grimaced in response, making his disagreement clear.

"You are anything but boring, and you are one of the few people I can talk to about—*things*," he said, softening his facial expressions. "And after all you've been through, yes, I believe you are mature for your age but never boring." He reached for my hand, which had me breathing a bit faster.

"I just want you to be happy," he said, taking a deep breath.

"Believe me. I do, too."

"Taking care of you makes *me* happy, and I wouldn't risk losing the opportunity to keep doing it." He said it in a tone that informed me the conversation was over. But I wondered what he meant by *risk*.

Caleb pressed on his earpiece while still looking at me as if it was his last opportunity to do so freely, conscious that I was about to close the communication door. He muttered something in Hebrew and stood up, offering his hand. "Come on, Aaron's bringing the car around. You must have a lot of things to do."

I thanked him as he helped me up from my seat.

"You know I'll always be there for you." I smiled.

"I know that," he replied, gesturing for us to resume our walk to the car, "but you can go back to closing that door on me."

I swallowed and considered his ability to read minds highly probable as we walked back to the car in absolute silence.

CHAPTER 6

Gifts

"**THESE ARRIVED FOR YOU**, Miss Murphy," Annette informed me, elegantly cocking her head at a dusty pink peony flower arrangement on the foyer table. Caleb was standing behind me under the threshold with his bodyguard stance firmly in place. Annette handed over a white envelope with *Guillermina* written on it. It had to be from my father or the Embassy staff.

Happy Birthday, Billie!
I would've loved to celebrate your 20th birthday with you. I'm sorry I've gone missing these past few weeks. Perhaps I can explain next week over dinner and make it up to you? I hope you enjoy the flowers and the rest of your day.
Sincerely Yours,
Thomas

Annette pressed her lips together, trying to hold in a smile. "They're beautiful," she said. "That is one lucky guy." She'd read the note beforehand. It was protocol.

Someone needed Annette's attention, so she excused herself and left. My stupid smile must've given away my excitement. I even forgot Caleb was standing behind me.

"Who's the lucky guy, Miss Murphy?" he asked with a poker

face. I mimicked his facial expression and tried to reply as casually as I could that Thomas had sent them. "Is there anything else you need, Miss Murphy?" I guess I didn't try hard enough. If I was thrilled about the flowers, then Caleb was whatever the exact opposite of that was.

"Come on. It's just *flowers*," I said, failing at the *try to act casual about it* thing again.

"I need to talk to Aaron," Caleb said with a forced smile. "I'll see you later, Red." I sighed as he rushed down the steps into the parking area.

Reading Thomas's note got me all giddy and excited. I wanted to jump up and down and let everyone know about it. There was absolutely nothing I could do to avoid the cluster of feelings from leaking out of my face. And I guess Caleb didn't enjoy the fact that Thomas had sent me flowers as much as I did. He had just told me a few minutes before how he preferred Thomas didn't contact me. Was he jealous? Annoyed? I couldn't read him.

I walked up to my room. My legs had that after-run ache in desperate need of a hot shower to soothe them. I blow-dried my hair afterward and climbed into bed wearing my bathrobe, allowing myself to relax for a bit before I left to meet my father at the Embassy for *a surprise*.

Twenty minutes later, I got dressed and walked out the front door, beaming, after having just seen the flowers again. Caleb was now clean-shaven and dressed in his usual black suit—back to being *Mr. Cohen*.

I couldn't keep myself from smiling as we drove around the block toward the Embassy. But curiosity seeped from within as I wondered what happened for Thomas not to seek me out in the previous weeks—not that he owed me any explanation, for sure.

It was sweet of him, though, to remember, as I had only briefly mentioned how I would be leaving Paris on April 12th, the day after my birthday. Unfortunately, I didn't have a way to thank him for the flowers. They were beautiful.

We arrived at the Embassy in seconds and drove through the front gate, where Jimmy, who was a part of my father's lead security team in Paris, awaited us. Caleb got out of the car and shook Jimmy's hand while he explained something I could not hear from the inside of our armored vehicle.

Caleb approached my window and asked me to open it.

"Your father will be out in a couple of minutes, and before you start asking questions, I *do* know where we are going, and *no*, I'm not telling you. It's a surprise for your father to reveal."

Damn it.

I patiently waited for my father, but I got out of the car and hurried in his direction as soon as I saw him. "Happy birthday, kiddo!" He yelled and embraced me. A tear rolled down my cheek. And then another.

Every time I saw my father, I remembered I *still* had a family and that I wasn't alone. Spending so much time on my own, mostly due to the nature of my father's work, would often take an emotional toll on me.

Worrying him unnecessarily about my emotional state was something I tried to avoid at all costs. That's why I kept the full-on, gut-wrenching theatrics to myself.

"What's wrong, sweetheart? Everything okay?" he asked, cupping my chin upward.

"I'm sorry I just missed you, and with Easter tomorrow, my birthday today, and mom and—" My throat burned. I couldn't keep talking, not without preventing any further tears from turning into sobs.

My father hugged me again. "I get it, kiddo. I'm so sorry. I know it's—challenging sometimes. Some days are harder than others. You know I'm always here for you, though. I love you."

I brushed the tears away.

"I have a surprise for you," he said. We got in the car, and he immediately held my hand.

"Where are we going?" I was feeling a little more like myself after shedding a few tears.

"We're only a few minutes away, you'll see." He tapped my knee twice.

We finally approached the museum, and I figured out what the surprise was.

"Louvre?" I guessed.

"I can't have you leave Paris without seeing it one last time." Taking me there was the perfect birthday gift—he knew me so well.

A considerable number of tourists were queued, making their way slowly through museum security, but with the help of Miss Laurent, who was part of the museum staff, we breezed through and made our way to the Denon wing.

"Expect the *Salle des États* to be a bit crowded today. You know how tourists congregate around the Mona Lisa," Miss Laurent said as a friendly reminder.

There were enough people for the room to look packed, but Miss Laurent informed us the Mona Lisa had seen far more congested scenes. Luckily, the crowd didn't overlap the painting I had gone to see—the one right in front of the Mona Lisa.

Nozze di Cana. Louvre's largest artwork depicting Jesus's first public miracle: The transformation of water into wine.

I thought I'd bored my father to death as I rambled on and on about the painting and why I loved it. But he was genuinely interested and entertained with what I had to say about it.

"Now, the million-dollar question, kiddo," he said, grasping my shoulders. "Where do you think this painting should be?" I'd explained how it had been stolen from Venice by Napoleon's troops.

"Hmm. If you were Veronese, would you rather have your

painting be where it was intended to be, which is in a monastery in Venice, or would you prefer to have it displayed here with over eight million people walking by it every year?" I asked. "Now, I don't know how Veronese would feel about most people seeing his painting *accidentally* after visiting the Mona Lisa behind us."

"It's complicated. But I think this painting has found a home," my father replied. "It's been torn and re-sown. Restored and moved around. The *conflict* has also been settled with the exchange of the French painting. And you've told me how it has endured a couple of accidents here at the Louvre. Some things are fragile enough to be better left untouched."

"A *very* diplomatic response." I snorted and smiled. *And an interesting one, too.* "I also believe it should remain here."

Without hesitation, the painting reminded me of my mother, whose faith was unbreakable, and the importance of finding one's place in life. Sometimes you were meant to be in a particular place, but ultimately life puts you where you belong. It's about learning how to deserve that new place, which might be very different from what you expected but perfectly designed for you in every way.

Although I did not share my mother's religious beliefs, she used to tell me the transformation of water into wine suggests how great things can surge unexpectedly and enhance our lives by changing them for the better. I could agree to that any day.

The room was getting crowded, which was our security team's cue to suggest we better start moving out. Miss Laurent was waiting for us right outside the room.

"If you ever need a tour guide, Miss Laurent, you can always hire my daughter," my father joked. I chuckled under my breath with embarrassment.

We thanked Miss Laurent once again and made our way back to the car. Caleb opened the door for me, and a small present with a red bow was waiting on my seat. I squinted at my father, who was standing behind me. "That's your second gift, kiddo."

I was already delighted with the Louvre visit, and honestly, having my father's time was a gift enough for me.

I held the small box in my hand, wondering about its content. My father climbed in the car beside me and jerked his chin at the gift, encouraging me to unwrap it. There was a key inside it. I turned to look at him and silently inquired about the meaning of the present.

"It's a symbolic key to your new apartment." He grinned. "I'll replace it with the real one once we get to New York, yes?" My wide-eyed expression spoke about my inability to respond to such a gift. "What do you think?"

"Thank you. This is—so unexpected. How? Why?" I kept fidgeting with the key. That was such a big step for him to take. For me, as well. I've lived my life surrounded by so many people like Embassy employees, house staff, drivers, and guests, but I always felt lonely.

"You're welcome to come to visit me or stay in your old room as many times as you wish," he said. "I bought this apartment a few years ago as an investment, and I've been renting it for a while. But last January, Mrs. Sullivan, my real estate agent, told me the family living there was not planning on renewing their lease, so I got the *brilliant idea* of having you live there instead."

I reached out to hug my father, thanking him once again. I couldn't believe what I was hearing.

"I'll still be traveling often, so I figured it'd be fair for you to have your own space." He added. "There are a few things we need to sort out beforehand, but we'll have plenty of time for that on the flight back home."

Excitement, nervousness, gratitude, and anxiety were a mix of emotions I felt after receiving his generous gift. I placed the key inside my purse, right beside Thomas's note.

We arrived home and were greeted by the beautiful peonies in the foyer.

"Special delivery?" My father asked Annette.

"Ah, yes, Ambassador, sir. For Miss Murphy."

I should've asked Annette to take the flowers to my room.

"Who sent these? Are they from the Embassy staff?" he inquired.

Annette looked at me with doe eyes, not knowing what to answer, so I stepped in, "No. They're from Thomas Hill. Senator Hill's son. They were here for the dinner you hosted about a month ago. Remember?"

"I wasn't aware of your acquaintance." His eyes narrowed, probably wondering what he'd missed.

"I met him that same day at Hôtel Costes. He ended up going there too after dinner."

"Well, he looks like a good kid," he said, examining the flowers as if trying to decipher Thomas's intentions. "Anyway, it's time for your third gift of the day, and last I swear." He took my hand and guided me out to the garden, where I heard a big crowd shouting: "Surprise!"

The entire Embassy staff, house staff, and friends from school were gathered for a surprise party. "It's both a birthday and farewell party, kiddo," he explained as we walked down the steps to greet the guests. "And there's paella, of course—an early Easter celebration."

My father pointed to a large service table where Chef Bellin and three other cooks were finishing the plates and cutlery setup. Two large paella casseroles and several trays of garlic bread were laid upon the table. The delightful saffron smell filled the air. I couldn't wait to try the food.

My father walked over to greet a few people while familiar faces approached me to hug and congratulate me for my birthday.

"Happy birthday!" Sophie and Cecile cheered at the same time. They hugged me, and then we sat down on one of the tables where we drank wine as I told them about the flowers Thomas had sent me and my father's second gift.

"Caleb won't stop looking at you," Cecile said out of nowhere.

"Well, it's his job to look at me all day, isn't it?" I said with a laugh. I turned to where Caleb stood, but he quickly looked away.

"Hmm." Cecile squinted at him. She didn't look convinced about *his job* being the reason he kept staring my way. And I had my doubts, too. He'd been giving me these strange looks all day. I didn't know what to make of them. I feared he would change his mind at the last minute about coming to New York and flee to Tel Aviv.

I just had to wait one more day to find out.

Sophie got sentimental about how much she was going to miss me. A few tears rolled down her cheeks, making Cecile and me cry too. We stood up for a group hug when a server offered us a plate of paella, salad, and bread. We all turned around to see the food and went from crying to laughing. They knew food was my weakness—*especially* paella.

We accepted the food and enjoyed the delicious meal, knowing it would be the last one we'd share together for a while. It was a great and unexpectedly fun birthday. After a long time of continually feeling lonely, that day proved to me otherwise.

☾

Almost all the guests had left the party, only Embassy staff remained, and they didn't seem to be in a rush to leave anytime soon. But my friends had left, and I was exhausted.

I was walking up to my room when my phone buzzed.

Caleb: This year's paella is better than the last. Chef Bellin finally got it right.
Me: I know, right? But none like my mom's.

Caleb: I wish I could've tried her paella.
Me: You would've loved it.
Caleb: I'm sure I would. Happy birthday, Red.

I stepped into my bedroom and saw a small red box with a red bow sitting on top of my nightstand. There was a little white envelope underneath the box with the word *Red* written on it with red ink. I opened the box first because I knew it was from Caleb.

There was an Eiffel Tower metallic key chain inside. The note read:

For your new key to your new apartment.
We'll always have Paris.

חמש תדלוה סוי

C. xx

CHAPTER 7

Arrival

April 16, 2009

CALEB DID SHOW UP the day we left for New York, just FYI. We arrived home on April 12th, and I stayed in my father's apartment for a few days because mine wasn't ready yet. But it was ready now, and Caleb was driving my father and me there, alongside Aaron, for a change. I was finally going to move into my own place.

Caleb seemed thrilled. His reflection of the rearview mirror gave him away. He kept biting his lower lip, probably hoping to prevent an over-enthusiastic grin from sneaking out of his face.

Aaron was being Aaron: calm, cool, and collected. His navy-blue eyes stared out the window and through the side-view mirrors, casually *looking out*. He always managed to look relaxed yet in control of the situation.

My father refused to let go of my hand. His embrace felt warm and safe, and although we were *home*, I could feel his reluctance to keep his word regarding my second birthday present.

We spent most of the flight back to New York talking through the conditions attached to his gift. We both had to compromise, but finally found common ground after a few rounds of negotiation.

My father asked for three conditions—the first one: a *simple request*. I had already transferred my credits from PCA to Parsons, but my father wanted me to enroll in a summer course there. He didn't want me lazing around all summer.

I agreed. It was a perfect idea actually because I would get to know the school before starting the Fall semester.

His second request consisted of having Mrs. Mullins as my housekeeper.

A trap. I was getting a nanny.

I knew Mrs. Mullins's job would include a weekly report to my father. And again, I was okay with it as long as I could experience a more independent life.

I don't remember, but my father said I met Mrs. Mullins or Mimi (as he called her) when I was a child. And after years of having so many people living with us, I realized it couldn't be that awful to have just one person helping me out.

I grew tired of not having real privacy, and my father knew that, but it wasn't an unknown fact that I *couldn't* cook. For my safety and those in my building, it was best to have Mrs. Mullins handling the cooking for me.

And last but not least, a *third* security agent. Yup. *Necessary and non-negotiable*—that's what my father kept repeating on the flight. The new agent would come directly from the DSS. Unlike Caleb and Aaron, who were approved by the DSS but hired independently.

I had overreacted with this request. It felt unfair, like going backward instead of making progress regarding this specific area of my life. This condition incited a heated debate.

If I wanted to roam *freely* in New York City, I was to agree to that. He explained how I would still have two agents on duty. The third would be incorporated to enable rotation on their schedules. My father supposed I would probably have a more demanding agenda in New York.

I had my doubts.

I was going to attempt for the first time to live a life of my very own. It was frightening as hell, but I needed it. I owed it to myself.

I had felt so trapped for years, unaware of the comfortable cage I lived in.

The first step was to convince myself to get out. Even though Aaron and Caleb did an excellent job keeping me safe and comfortable, I would've thought progress meant having less security and not an additional agent following me around.

The past few months in Paris felt more careless, free. But a glacial sensation still gnawed at my chest and stomach as I tried to block out the memories and trauma about my mother's death.

Four years had gone by since she was gone, but there were days when it still felt like yesterday. The worst part of all was not knowing *why* it happened. My father insisted they were still looking into it, and I bought that for a while, but it was evident that he kept something from me. I didn't know anymore if it was best to stop asking—to not know at all.

But how to stop thinking about it?

I refused to talk about this matter with anyone, which wasn't very useful in helping me process everything that happened. I thought I could do it myself—a few steps back to keep thrusting myself forward.

The car approached the sidewalk. A green canvas sunshade with golden poles sheltered the Midtown East's pre-war building entrance.

"Four eighty-five Park, Mr. Murphy," Caleb announced with his thick sexy accent as he shifted into park.

We were greeted by a couple of door guards: Senad, a tall, slender man, and Bruce, who was shorter and rocked a shaved head and frame-less glasses. They were both very friendly and asked us if we needed any help with my things. But Aaron and Caleb had everything under control.

Mrs. Sullivan, the real estate agent who previously supervised the apartment on my father's behalf, approached us bearing keys and a manila folder. My father introduced us and talked to her while I wandered around the lobby, secretly anxious and excited about everything.

"Come on, kiddo, ninth floor." My father wrapped his arm around my shoulders as we walked to the elevator.

The first thing that came to mind as I stepped into my apartment was: too big, considering I'd be living by myself. It was too big, even if I had a roommate, but cozy compared to the Residence in Paris.

Mrs. Sullivan gave me a brief tour of the tastefully decorated place.

Across the foyer, an empty gallery tempted me to hang a few of my photographs, followed by a living room with the coziest gray lounging sofa and large windows overlooking Park Avenue. We continued into a modern six-person dining room beside the living room. The kitchen was at the far end, just beside a small bedroom and a pair of closets.

"Mimi will use this room as needed. You can expect her to arrive tomorrow afternoon and help you unpack and fix you a few meals. She's already bought some things to eat and drink," my father explained.

"David's coming tomorrow to meet you. He'll be working his first shift with Caleb. I'll ask them to send you their shift schedules each week. That way, you'll know who's going to be following you around." He teased.

"And sweetheart, please, no funny business. Let's make this easy. This transition is new to all of us. I expect you to cooperate with the guys if they advise on anything. They know what's best." He sighed with a defeated air to it.

I nodded and went in for a hug. He was feeling nervous, I could tell.

"Come on, let's go see the rest of the place," I suggested, pulling his arm softly. There was still the other side of the apartment await-ing inspection.

I dropped my backpack and camera bag on the loveseat of the master bedroom and jumped back on the king-sized bed with my arms open and the biggest smile on my face. I couldn't hide my excitement anymore.

"Could you at least pretend to be sad about leaving me?" My father playfully complained, but he was right. I was thrilled.

The doorbell rang.

It was Aaron and Caleb with my things. They placed the suit-cases and boxes in the foyer. I glanced at Caleb, who was eyeing the place around with curiosity and amusement. "Nice view, Miss Murphy," he said proudly. You could tell how excited Caleb was about moving to New York. I was too.

We both knew it was going to be a big change compared to how we lived in Paris. Less protocol, more freedom? I hoped. Perhaps he did too, and that's where his excitement came from.

"We'll see you tomorrow. Let us know if there is anything you need." Both Aaron and Caleb excused themselves and left.

They were living in a smaller apartment on the second floor of the same building. My father wanted them to be available 24/7, just in case.

I took out the Eiffel Tower key chain with the symbolic key my father gave me on my birthday and added the new keys. "I'm keep-ing the fake key," I told him, "as a good luck charm." His lips went into a pursed smile, filled with warmth, and I thanked him again for the hundredth time. I walked him out. We hugged each other and said our goodbyes.

The large window in the living room invited me to step closer and enjoy the view—to stare at how the night came upon the city, lighting it up in a million, tiny, bright lights. And just then, without notice, that gut-wrenching feeling that hadn't overcome me in a while kicked in.

Would I ever stop missing my mother? Unlikely.

The unyielding grief remained challenging to conquer at the most unexpected moments. And after sobbing for an undetermined amount of time, I finally dragged myself to bed and fell asleep. Not a single dream I dreamt that night as if I'd unplugged myself from existence.

CHAPTER 8

Tantrums

April 17, 2009

ONE DAY AT A TIME, I kept telling myself—for *years* now. I got out of bed feeling better, but still dragging some of those difficult feelings from last night, knowing they would surely fade away as the day progressed.

Waking up at quarter to nine was late for what I was accustomed to, but God knew I needed that.

There were days when I wouldn't think about my mother, as if the universe had granted me an oblivion spell. But a part of me couldn't help but feel guilty about it when my mind slid back into awareness.

I grabbed my Blackberry and found a bunch of texts waiting for me on the security detail group chat. No word from Thomas yet. Was he a liar?

Caleb: Good morning, Miss Murphy.
Caleb: Everything ok, Miss Murphy?
Caleb: Let us know if you need anything.
Caleb: Are you in the apartment, Miss Murphy?

They must've been wondering why I hadn't notified them about starting my day, but I had *just* woken up, which, as they also knew, was unusual for me.

Me: Good morning! I just woke up. I was thinking of going out to the park in about 20 min. Caleb, are you ok for a run?

I walked to my messily opened suitcases in the foyer. Ugh. I needed to unpack. But that could wait. I changed into my running clothes, poured myself a big glass of water, and embarked on a hopeful coffee quest.

Bingo.

Hmm, instant coffee, though. I needed to attend to this matter as soon as possible. I'd grown accustomed to the taste of the delightful French coffee that was offered to me every morning in Paris. I wanted to fend on my own, didn't I?

Another text came in:

Unknown: Hi, Billie! I'm Christopher Jewell. I don't know if you remember me. Our mothers used to be good friends. We had a bunch of playdates when we were kids before you guys left for Rome.
Unknown: Anyway, your father gave my mother your number. Would you like to hang out and meet up later today? I go by CJ, by the way. Let me know!

I honestly couldn't remember him, and I felt a little embarrassed because of it. But also, we were tiny. I supposed that he didn't remember me either and felt obligated by his mother to send me a text. And since I didn't know anyone here, I agreed to meet for dinner at eight. I needed to expand my social circle.

A knock on my door.

I gave my coffee one last sip and rushed to see who it was.

"Hey, Caleb," I said with a hint of a smile.

"Good morning." He echoed my gesture with a tad of concern in his eyes. He was in his sportswear, ready for our run. "Are you okay?"

"Um, yeah." I tried smiling more to make my words sound convincing.

"You're a morning person. I found it odd for you to sleep in, and I just wanted to make sure you're okay. I know living on your own now and moving back here might be a lot to take in."

At that moment, I knew I couldn't lie to him because he knew me too well.

"It was just one of those nights." I didn't bother smiling after saying that. Plus, he knew exactly what *those nights* meant. After more than four years of seeing our faces every day … he knew.

"I see. Are you feeling better?"

"I am."

"I gotcha, okay?" He took another step forward that lingered somewhere between my personal and intimate space range. "You know that, right?"

I looked down because I'm wasn't going to start crying again, and I knew I had him, and he knew *I* knew. So I did the best I could to compress and ignore whatever was going on inside me. Finally, I looked up to him and said, "I know," followed by a more genuine smile this time. Which I guess he noticed too and made him relax.

"Let's go run this off. Are you ready?" I nodded. "There's someone downstairs waiting to meet you."

We made our way to the lobby and saw a cheerful brown skinned agent, which I guessed was David. The unmistakable curly earpiece gave him away. He was also in his sportswear.

"Good morning, Miss Murphy, pleased to meet you. Name's David, David Scott. I will be joining your security detail team starting today." He introduced himself and offered his hand to me.

David wasn't as tall as the Israeli duo. Still, he handled himself with a much more welcoming demeanor, which shouldn't be taken literally. There would be nothing *friendly* about the former Marine if the situation justified it.

"Pleasure to meet you too, David. I'm sure both Aaron and Caleb here will be glad to have you on their team." I nodded once in Caleb's direction. "Ready for a run?"

"Yes, ma'am. I'm a runner myself. I just ran the Austin Marathon less than a month ago. I'll be surely enjoying the morning runs," he added.

After finishing up with the pleasantries, Caleb and David broke down the running plan for me.

We ran for about an hour and stopped at a juice and smoothie place a block away from the apartment on our way back, where I bought a green juice.

Senad saw us coming and opened the door. I glanced at him to say hello.

"Miss Murphy, careful!" Caleb shouted, but his warning came too late. My half glass of green juice was now dripping steadily from a woman's beautiful day dress.

She stood in front of me with her pale blue eyes looking down at the damage—her cherry-red lips half-parted with shock.

A young guy with icy-blond hair snorted beside her, trying to hold in a laugh. The woman elbowed him in the side. "Ouch, Mother! That hurt," he replied in between snickers.

"Welcome to the building, my dear." She smiled, looking up at me. I was so embarrassed!

"Oh my God, I am *so* sorry!" I exclaimed, mortified—not knowing what to do with my hands. I desperately wanted to help, but I couldn't reach out and touch the stranger in front of me without feeling intrusive and out of place.

Her son stared at me with his arms crossed at his chest, seemingly amused by my predicament. David had moved swiftly to bring back some tissues and handed them to me. I offered them in an automatic motion to my juice-drenched neighbor.

"It's okay. Please don't worry about it. I can go upstairs and change." She tried to reassure me, waving one hand down in a care-free motion—her other hand uselessly wiped the green *off* her dress. "What's your name, dear?"

"Oh, yes, of course. How rude of me. My name is Guillermina. Please call me Billie. So nice to meet you. I just arrived here yester-day. I'm in apartment 9A."

Caleb's disapproving face appeared in the corner of my eye. That only made me more nervous. He was probably irritated because I'd disclosed personal information to my newly acquainted neighbors. But that didn't stop me. "Um, this is David," I blurted out with an awkward grin, "and this is Caleb. He's also new to the building."

Shit!

I couldn't keep my mouth shut, but I was just trying to be polite.

"Nice to meet you, Billie. My name is Nathalie, and we live on the fourteenth floor. I live with my husband, Sivert, and my young-est son Eric." She motioned at her son, who lifted his hands in a *guilty* kind of gesture.

"My three other sons live in the building too. We're from Sweden but have lived here for years now—practically Americans," she said proudly.

"So, Guillermina. That's a beautiful and rare name. Where does it come from?" Nathalie inquired with an almost imperceptible accent.

"Um—my mom was Spanish, and I was named after my grand-mother. The pronunciation is difficult for most people, so Billie was the obvious alternative for everyone." *Will someone please shut me up?*

Caleb volunteered for the job.

"Miss Murphy, we're going to be late for your appointment."

"Ah, yes. The appointment," I replied, playing along. "I'm terri-bly sorry for ruining your dress, Nathalie. It was so nice to meet you both." I shook their hands with a smile and turned around to leave.

David, who was proving himself as an anticipator, held the elevator's door for us. So observant, one could instantly tell.

"See you around!" Nathalie chirped.

"Later, neighbor," Eric added with a lifted brow.

Caleb and I stepped into the elevator with David, and no one said a word as we went up to the ninth floor.

Caleb rushed out of the elevator as soon as the doors opened before us. He took out a spare key from his pocket, clicked hastily into the lock, and signaled me to go inside.

I glowered at him with astonishment. *This* was their idea of giving me independence? Who else had a spare key to *my* apartment?

"Can we come inside?" Caleb asked with a demanding tone. "We'd like to talk to you."

We? Or just him?

Poor David got dragged into the drama on his first day of work. I could see how flustered he was, trying to follow Caleb's lead. I held the door open. "Let's go sit in the living room," I said dryly, dodging the suitcases spread all over the foyer. "What's up?" Frustration boiled out of those two words as I sat on the couch.

"Miss Murphy, I know it's your first day here. You want to *blend in* with the neighbors and be friendly—keep in mind that we need to maintain communication with strangers to a minimum at first. We don't know who all these people living here are. We will, by the end of the week," he said confidently.

David rested his elbows over his knees, and his hands tightened together. He looked back and forth from Caleb to me—assessing the situation—getting to know Caleb's temper.

Caleb had this effortless way of making me feel like a child sometimes, and I *hated* it. We'd talked about it numerous times. My father was a pro at making me feel that way, and I didn't need him, of all people, to follow his lead.

But that was Caleb. He got all worked up when he felt like my safety was at risk. His tantrums became a daily routine. I was used to them, but I was also growing tired of them as the years went by.

"I don't think it's necessary to make a fuss out of this. I understand what you're saying, but the woman and her son looked harmless." I fought back, feeling defeated already. "Besides, you know where to find her. She's on the fourteenth floor, you heard her."

"Don't be too trusting of everyone. You know we're just trying to keep you safe. That's what we're aiming for." He grumbled with an exasperated tone.

"Okay, don't worry, I'll try to be more careful." I took a deep breath and looked away from him, turning my gaze at David, who was in full observation mode. I stood up, walked to the foyer, and opened one of the boxes, looking for my small acrylic case where I kept my stationery.

There it is!

"David, I need a favor from you since you know your way around the city pretty well. Could you go to a nearby bakery and buy something for Mrs. Nathalie? Muffins, maybe? And—if you could add this note."

I sat on the couch again and leaned into the coffee table to write a note on a cute shiny card. I love notes, writing them, and giving them away. Not that I had many chances to use them.

"Of course, Miss Murphy. You can count on it. I'll get to it as soon as possible." He seemed glad we were done with the last conversation—ready to move on to the next assignment.

"Could you drop them off on my behalf?" I asked. "I'm sure I'm not allowed to do it myself."

"Yes, we will," Caleb interjected as we all walked back to the front door. He was probably trying to go back to being the amiable Caleb—the one I preferred.

And as much as I hate to admit it, he was right. There was a protocol to follow, and there was nothing I could do to avoid him from trying to abide by it. Even if I felt like my neighbors weren't a threat.

Caleb and David walked out of the apartment, and just before I shut the door, I addressed the newcomer, "Oh, and David, I know you'll be working the night shift with Aaron. Could you tell him to get the car ready at seven-thirty, please? I'm having dinner with Christopher, a friend of mine." He nodded in agreement, and I closed the door behind them.

I heard Caleb swearing in Hebrew from across the door—he had taught me a few words over the years. I assumed he didn't like the idea of staying in and imagining how the night would go while I had dinner with some guy he didn't know. But he needed to understand that my life would be different here. I wanted him to yield a bit and start trusting me more.

I was walking back to the living room, and there was a knock on my door, but I already knew who it was.

"Hey," I said, leaning against the door frame.

"Who's Christopher? I don't think he's authorized," Caleb said with a deep crease in between his eyes.

"My father gave Christopher's mom my phone number, so … I'd say he's authorized. But you can call my father and verify it if it'll give you peace of mind," I said victoriously. Winning an argument against Caleb wasn't an everyday occurrence. He was always right, but not today he wasn't.

I could see how pissed off he was about not having any information on Christopher, on who he was, what he looked like, what he had for breakfast that morning. They liked being thorough, especially him.

He pressed his lips and snorted, seemingly annoyed by the whole situation. "I'll talk to your father," he said because there wasn't much for him to say. He hated not being right about *everything*. But it wouldn't hurt him to let me win an argument every once in a while.

"Sure. Enjoy your night off," I said with a proud smile. He took a few steps back, shaking his head.

"Are you rolling your eyes at me, Cohen?" I said with a laugh.

"Of course not, Miss Murphy." He finally yielded a small smile and left through the stairs.

Caleb's temper tantrums were amusing and even cute sometimes, but if teasing him was an Olympic sport, then I was a high-performance athlete. That's what friends do, right?

CHAPTER 9

Dinner Plans

IT WAS PAST NOON, and all I had in my organism was that half glass of green juice and a hastily chugged down instant coffee. I took a bath while thinking about my next meal—something simple for sure, but my stomach was demanding sustenance.

Taking my time in the shower helped me wash away the frustration from the earlier debate with Caleb. They knew how to handle things, and I understood that. But it was frustrating to feel like I was being scolded, especially by Caleb. Our *complicated* friendship could interfere with the required dynamic.

Me: Hi. Please remember to add David to the group chat. Thanks.
Aaron: Right Away.

Caleb Cohen added David Scott to the Group.

Me: Hi David! Could you give me a heads up when you've delivered the muffins to Mrs. Nathalie? Thanks.
David: Of course, Miss Murphy. I will let you know as soon as it's done.

Changing into my pajamas and staying home for the rest of the afternoon seemed like the best idea. It would give me time to organize my stuff since I had nothing better to do than wait to get ready for my *rendezvous* with CJ.

Suddenly, I heard a loud noise outside my bedroom. Caleb wouldn't dare come into my apartment unannounced like that, would he?

I stepped out and walked to the living room to find Mrs. Mullins closing my suitcases in the foyer. Of course, I'd forgotten about her—another person, another spare key.

"Mrs. Mullins? Hi, I'm Billie," I greeted her with a smile.

"Oh, halò, Billie!" she exclaimed as she regained her posture. "I'm soo glad to see ye again—it's been years since I last saw you. Yer so grown-up and beautiful. Look at that gorgeous hair, just like yer father's." She stood up and walked in my direction. "Are ye hungry, dear? Ye look a wee bit pale. And please, call me Mimi."

"I'm starving," I countered. "I haven't had a bite to eat since I woke up. Just coffee and juice."

"Well, I willnae alloo that dear, not on my watch," she replied, making her way to the kitchen. I obediently followed her without protest. Mimi was a talented cook and loved nothing more than to feed and take care of people. That brought comfort to my heart. Staying away from the kitchen as much as possible was the smart thing to do.

Mimi was a slender woman, very well conserved, with a few silver strands here and there, wanting to give away her almost sixty years of age. Her peaceful expressions made you want to be around her. "Houdae chicken noodle soup sound for ye?" she asked, opening the fridge to gather the ingredients.

My appetite had *really* kicked in.

"That sounds perfect. Thank you so much. Do you mind if I excuse myself? I'd like to get a head start on those suitcases. I'm sorry you had to see that when you got in."

"Oh, nawt to worry aboot, dear. I was gaun to help ye, but I'm suspecting it's most useful to feed ye first," she said, moving around the kitchen with ease.

Once my clothes and shoes were unpacked and neatly organized in my closet, I stored the empty luggage in the walk-in closet by the entrance. My phone buzzed in my pajama pocket while I heard a knock on my door.

"Come in!" I said, unlocking my phone.

"Chicken soup's ready. I have the table all set for ye. Come on, come on," she encouraged me. I sat down in the dining room and finally read my text messages while eating the most delicious chicken noodle soup I've ever had.

David: Miss Murphy, a box with cranberry muffins was delivered to Mrs. Nathalie.
Me: Thank you so much, David.

CJ: Hey, Billie! Ready for tonight? How do you feel about Lebanese?
Me: I love it!
CJ: Great! See you at ilili then. 236 5th Ave.
Me: Perfect. See you at 8.

I forwarded the restaurant name and address to the security group chat. I poured myself a second plate of chicken noodle soup while Mimi unpacked my books from the boxes and placed them on the living room bookshelves.

The delicious meal made me sleepy. I excused myself to take a well-deserved nap. That morning's run proved to me I was still tired from the move. The delicious white, fluffy duvet cover invited me to crawl inside and shut my eyes without setting the alarm to wake up.

C

My phone buzzed on my nightstand while I was sound asleep. At first, the sound intertwined with my dream, but it slowly brought me out of my slumber. Half-asleep and disoriented, I took the call—my head still rested comfortably on my pillow.

"Hello? … Yes, it's me … Oh, Thomas, hi!"

I left any remaining drowsiness from my nap on the warm, empty pillow. I sat cross-legged on my bed as I carried on with the conversation.

"I was, but I needed to wake up anyway … No, please. Don't worry about it … I did receive them, thank you so much. They were beautiful … I know I'm glad to be back in New York … Um, I'm so sorry. I have plans tonight … Sure. Tomorrow works … Of course, I will … See you soon … You too … Ba-bye."

Thomas's deep, masculine voice ignited all these feelings inside me—flashbacks from the night we first met, the way he held his hands around my waist, his perfect heart-shaped lips pressed against mine.

The thought of canceling CJ's dinner plans had been tempting, but I thought it best not to do so. Besides, Thomas had me waiting long enough for him to call me, so it wouldn't do him much harm to wait a day to see me.

Naps had never been my thing, and after two and half hours of sleeping, one would think I'd be fresh as lettuce, but I woke up feeling cranky and disoriented instead.

I threw my head back on my pillow, hoping to snap out of the uncomfortable after-nap sensation, and texted Sophie and Cecile to fill them in about Thomas *finally* reaching out.

C

ALEJANDRA ANDRADE

Aaron and David waited outside and allowed me to go inside the restaurant without escorting me to my seat as they usually did.

As the hostess led me to the table, I felt normal. For a moment, I was just another girl walking to her table at a restaurant. There was nothing weird or striking about me coming in. There were no big guys with scary faces looking around for potential dangers.

Just me.

Ah! It's the little things.

We finally approached a table in the far end, and CJ was already waiting for me. A brunette sat beside him. "Billie?"

He squinted his eyes at me. The lighting at the restaurant was dim.

"Hi! Yes, it's me, so nice to meet you." I greeted them with double-cheek kisses. CJ had the friendliest face ever.

"This is Nina," he gestured at her as I took a seat on the table.

"So nice to meet you, Billie," Nina replied. She had perky lips, dark brown eyes, and lovely tanned skin.

They both kept complimenting my hair, and Nina wondered if my auburn locks were natural. I opened my mouth to speak but got cut off by CJ, "It is. I remember her father. Same color."

"Well, it's beautiful," Nina said.

"So—are you, um…"

I pointed at them back and forth.

"Oh, no, no, no!" They replied almost in unison. CJ growled with a burst of wicked laughter. "Let's say I have a—divergent sense of taste," he said once he composed himself from laughing.

"He's *quite* gay." Nina pressed a kiss on CJ's cheek.

"See? Nothing." CJ pointed his index finger at his cheek, and we all laughed. "I'm starving." CJ lifted his hand to get the server's attention. "I hope you are too because I'm ordering everything on the menu."

He ordered pita bread, hummus, falafel, brussels sprouts, labneh,

65

duck, and beef shawarmas. "That's enough," Nina interrupted. I thought CJ would never stop ordering. "It's always the same with him. He comes to dinner famished, orders *everything*, and I end up eating more than I'm supposed to."

"She's *definitely* going to need wine," CJ said to the server with a flirty smile, jerking his chin at Nina.

"Three glasses?" he asked. He was cute and smiling back at CJ.

"Um, sorry, not for me, thank you," I replied. CJ was a year older than me, and I assumed Nina was somewhere around his age.

"With that face … you're sure to get carded," CJ said, sipping on his water.

"What's wrong with her face?" Nina grimaced.

"Well, nothing's wrong—she has a pure, innocent-looking face. On the other hand—"

Nina snorted and warned, "Choose your next words wisely."

"Well, you look, experienced, wise, and—intriguing."

Nina stuck her tongue out at him.

We kept talking and getting to know each other as plates filled the four-seat table quickly.

Each dish was better than the last. It was an extraordinary meal altogether—a definite winner. By the end, I was so full I couldn't breathe, but it was worth every bite.

"Those brussels sprouts are glorious," I said to no one in particular, as the server cleared the table. I huffed a long breath out through my mouth.

"I'm telling you, Billie. Next time come to dinner wearing a loose dress. I always end up unbuttoning my pants." Nina snorted. "I swear I don't know where all his food goes to—he's so slim."

CJ stuck his tongue out at Nina this time and asked, "Yoga tomorrow?"

"You know I'll be there," Nina replied. "Billie, you should come too. Do you like yoga?"

I'd never done yoga in my life, but I was willing to try it out. Nina proudly explained that her boyfriend, Juan Pablo, owned an integral, holistic center where he taught yoga, amongst other activities I didn't fully understand. I was curious, though, so I told her to count me in.

They brought dessert to the table, and CJ ended up eating the whole plate by himself. It was impossible for Nina and me to even look at it. We were full, and then some.

CJ promptly asked for the check once done with the last spoonful of what looked like a sugary sin.

We walked outside, and Aaron had the engine going. David kept his bodyguard stance in position—his arms relaxed, and his hands held in a loose fist in front of him. "Good evening," David said with a discreet smile, acknowledging my new friends.

"Good evening, indeed." CJ purred with a mischievous smile on his face, eyeing David from head to toe. I elbowed him gently in the ribs.

"Are these—" Nina started, but CJ cut her off with a glare, suggesting she didn't ask questions. I suspected CJ knew about what happened to my mother. Surely their parents had told him about it if our mothers used to be good friends.

I've dealt with my fair share of sympathy looks and uncomfortable unfinished sentences throughout the years. It'd been a while, though, since I last had to deal with them. I planned to tell them myself about what happened, just not today.

"Do you guys need a lift?" I offered instead. Nina declined, but CJ whined about how he was still breaking into his new Pradas. "Are you sure you don't need a ride?" I offered one last time.

"We're fine, Billie. Seriously. I *really* need to walk this meal off, or I'll have to sleep standing up. We'll see you tomorrow at nine for yoga," she insisted, clutching CJ's arm and encouraging him to walk. I thanked them both for the evening and confirmed I'd see them the next day for yoga as David opened the door for me.

I was so glad CJ had reached out to me because I had so much fun getting to know them. I knew we could become close friends.

New York was starting to feel a lot like home.

My home ... at last.

CHAPTER 10

On Yoga and Other Sensibilities

April 18, 2009

IT WAS EARLY SATURDAY MORNING, a week after my birthday. A week after I'd received those beautiful flowers from Thomas. I smiled as I drank my morning—still instant—coffee and reminded myself I would see him that night. Butterflies fluttered with excitement in my stomach as my mind wandered, reminiscing about the day I met him for the hundredth time.

I ran on the apartment building's treadmill for thirty minutes before heading to the yoga studio. The gym was small but had the essential equipment to have a decent workout.

We got there ten minutes before the class started, and Nina and CJ were already there, setting their yoga mats on the floor.

"Good morning! Was I supposed to bring my own?" I asked.

"Hi, Billie! No, I mean—people are usually picky about the type of mat they use, so they bring their own, but feel free to grab one from the rack on the left," Nina replied as she stood up to hug me.

CJ followed her lead and hugged me too. I suspected Nina had heard the entire story by now, and they wanted to coddle me. I honestly didn't mind. I loved hugs.

"Hi Billie, why isn't David with us today?" CJ grasped my shoulder with one hand and played around with my ponytail with the other. He was *so touchy*. It was an extension of his personality.

CJ stared unceasingly out the window and said, "Sweet. Merciful. Lord." I'm sure he meant Caleb.

I unrolled my mat beside them with a snort, thinking about Caleb's universally appealing beauty. "Where do you find these— men, my God." CJ fanned his flushed face with his hand to make a point.

"I can introduce you to Caleb after class." I laughed. "But he's straighter than straight. They both are. At least Caleb and Aaron."

"And what about David?" CJ asked with hopeful eyes. "Is he gay?"

"David? Who knows—maybe on Fridays?" I joked.

CJ hollered and clapped his hands twice. "I'm sure it'd be my favorite day of the week." The three of us laughed.

"He's—something else," Nina whispered, looking at Caleb. That's when the yoga instructor, Nina's boyfriend, made his appearance.

Juan Pablo was tall, somewhat lean, and sported shoulder-length, ice-tea brown waves with caramel highlights. His eyes were two dark bottomless pits that rendered his pupils undetectable and totally freaked me out. His wide, ultra-white smile heavily contrasted the blackness of his eyes.

He wore a bandana to keep the slightly long locks off his face, black yoga leggings, and a loose sleeveless t-shirt with a couple of what seemed like Mala bead necklaces.

To be completely honest, I did judge him by his appearance. I braced myself for what I expected to be a new age, inspirational quote-filled-class—he didn't disappoint.

C

"Amazing, right?" Nina nodded with a grin once the class was done. We were reincorporating ourselves from a five-minute Shavasana. I couldn't say it was a terrible experience, but it hadn't been *amazing*.

Juan Pablo focused the class on his words, which distracted me from doing the poses. I hate lies, and I hate lying even more.

Sometimes when you risk hurting someone's feelings, is it justifiable to lie? Or should we remain completely impeccable? Food for another day's thought.

"It was a relaxing class. Thank you, Nina," I lied, trying not to make eye contact with her as I dropped my mat back on the shelf. I feared my eyes would give me away.

She pulled me in Juan Pablo's direction, who was enthusiastically talking to a woman who had just taken the class too. The woman slowly nodded with wide eyes as she attentively listened to what he had to say.

Nina grabbed Juan Pablo's puffy but not entirely defined arms and introduced me to him. "Hi, Billie! Nice to meet you." He greeted me with an accent, offering a handshake. CJ was looking at himself in the mirror, combing his curls with his fingers. *Get in here!*

"Did you enjoy the class?" Juan Pablo asked.

"Yes, I did, thank you." I coaxed a smile in return.

"Hmm …" he mumbled, closing his eyes and touching his right temple with his index and middle finger. I turned to look at Nina for answers, but she mouthed, "don't worry."

We stood there for a few heartbeats, waiting for him to snap out of whatever trance he found himself in at the moment.

"A kindred spirit—heart to heart—true mate to the soul. In title behold, as time has come," he said with his eyes still closed. *Okaaaay.* I glanced back at Nina, widening my eyes. *Wait,* she spoke with her eyes. I waited.

"Stature and grace, of confusion, beware." Juan Pablo opened his eyes and directed the blackness of them straight at me. I held my breath for a second. "The heart wants what it wants." He sighed and closed his eyes again.

I realized a few people were circling us, clearly entertained with the spectacle Juan Pablo was putting on for everyone. It was probably included with the class fee.

I held a blank expression, trying to be respectful, but I hoped he would just *stop*. But he didn't. And boy, was he making me feel very uncomfortable. Mostly about being placed in the spotlight like that.

Only once in my life had I used the SOS beacon. It was in Paris, at a friend's party. I was uncomfortable and wanted to leave but had no energy to make up an excuse. It could be handy for these types of situations.

Juan Pablo continued with the show. I slyly grabbed my phone to activate the emergency beacon, texting SOS on the security detail group chat.

"Your mother—" Juan Pablo was about to say something but got cut off by Caleb, who bolted inside to inform me about a "security concern," advising it was best to leave right away.

CJ hurried to my side when he heard Juan Pablo mentioning my mother. "Come with me." I implored with my eyes. He nodded in agreement.

I apologized for having to leave so abruptly and thanked Juan Pablo for the class. "Don't worry, Billie! Thanks for coming!" Nina yelled as we fled the studio.

The nerve of the guy. It should be illegal to meddle like that in other people's business. I assumed Nina had told Juan Pablo about my mother, so he tried to dazzle us with the oracle act.

I got in the car, sulking. It was unusual to find myself in a foul mood or easily angered, but something about that guy didn't click with me. It felt like a violation for him to trespass on something so personal. CJ mouthed back, "sorry," and joined me inside the car.

Although the riddle was bizarre and made little sense to me, what angered me was that he was about to mention my mother. And not only was it scary and weird, but I refused to believe whatever he had to say about it. I was getting a *"your mother is here, and yes, she wants to talk to you"* kinda vibe.

Nope.

"You gotta love the thrill of the SOS beacon," Caleb said as he hopped in the front seat, rubbing his hands enthusiastically. Aaron glowered at Caleb with disapproval. "Hi, I'm Caleb." He introduced himself to CJ, offering his hand.

"And that's Aaron, the normal one," I joked, while Aaron lifted his hand in acknowledgment, keeping his gaze on the road.

CJ extended his hand to Caleb in slow motion. He seemed in awe with the vision in front of him. Yup.

Caleb straightened back on his seat afterward as I whispered to CJ if he needed a napkin to wipe off his drool. CJ laughed while I opened the small bag I carried with me to grab my body splash.

"Can I steal you for brunch?" I asked, spraying a bit of the vanilla-jasmine scent behind my ears and on my wrists. I was all sweaty from the yoga session.

I heard how Caleb took a sharp sniff and looked over his shoulder for a second. "Sorry about that," I said, feeling a bit embarrassed. The car was now filled with my fragrance. Oops.

CJ agreed to have brunch and immediately suggested a place. I was equally starving and annoyed but hopeful about food being able to restore my mood.

Caleb seemed restless on his seat and cocked his head left and right a few times—looking uncomfortable. "You can open the windows if the scent bothers you." I apologized again. Aaron replied it wasn't unpleasant and how the windows should never go down as a safety precaution. True.

The SUV approached the curbside, and Caleb opened the

door a wink before the vehicle came to a complete stop and climbed out.

As President of the Caleb Fan Club, I welcomed CJ with open arms after he witnessed *The Move*. He closed his eyes, took a deep breath, and stepped out of the car with a sigh. So dramatic. I chuckled and shook my head as I followed him, already feeling less ill-humored.

"You smell good," Caleb whispered in my ear as CJ talked to the hostess.

Oh. My. God. I was paralyzed.

I finally found my voice. "Um, thanks," I said, looking at him with a twitchy smile, trying to avoid direct eye contact. He clicked his tongue and shot me one of his triumphant grins. The kind he used when he teased me. But he'd never teased me like *this*.

"Billie! Table's ready," CJ said, gesturing to go with him. I shook my head twice, trying to snap out of whatever that was, and followed him to our table.

We sat on the restaurant terrace, ordered *real* coffee, and an excessive amount of food CJ promised to consume, as expected.

"I'm sorry we had to storm out like that," I apologized as I bitterly buttered a piece of bread from the basket, "but something about Juan Pablo made me uneasy. He was about to mention my mother. Did Nina tell him anything about what happened to her?" I was still holding on to my anger, but Caleb had distracted me with his I'm-going-to-make-you-nervous-and-I-don't-give-a-rat's-ass kind of comment.

"Look, there's nothing to be sorry about, Juan Pablo's—intense. I honestly didn't think he would pull that shit on you, at least not today. And no, he knows nothing. I mean, we didn't tell him anything about you. Nina asked a few questions yesterday after dinner. She was—curious about *them*." He bobbed his head at Aaron and Caleb. "I told her your father's a diplomat and that something had happened with your mother, but that I'd let you explain the rest of the story. I didn't think it was my place to talk about it."

I lifted my gaze behind CJ's head and caught Caleb glancing my way. *Look away*! He usually did once I caught him or vice versa. Those were the rules of the game. But he wouldn't this time. I guess I was also breaking the rules, wasn't I? Luckily, CJ was preparing his coffee, so he didn't notice my awkwardly obvious exchange with Caleb seconds before.

"And man, I don't know how he does it. But he seems to have this—sixth sense or something." CJ continued and sipped on his coffee. "He does have a bizarre way of communicating such things, as you experienced today. It makes me uncomfortable too, so I get you. Nina's so proud of—*that*. I'd say she's even a little dazzled by it, maybe?"

Dazzled, for sure.

I couldn't have chosen a more suitable word myself for what he was trying to accomplish. "So, you're saying his *abilities* are sincere?" I asked incredulously.

"Well, he has predicted certain—events, and I honestly don't know how he does it. He claims angels and other beings 'whisper' things to him," he explained, putting his cup down. That wasn't creepy at all.

True mate to the soul. In title behold, as time has come …

He couldn't know I was seeing Thomas that night. Was he referring to him? *Stature and grace, of confusion, beware.* He *is* tall and handsome. I felt disgusted by my thoughts and considered signing up as a member of Juan Pablo's following.

For an overthinker like me, it was best to dismiss those ideas and avoid dwelling upon them altogether. I wouldn't forgive myself for believing something if Juan Pablo turned out to be a fraud.

"Anyway, where's he from?"

"He's from Argentina, and apparently, he had a pretty rough

childhood," he explained, buttering a toast. "Juan Pablo comes from a background of poverty and domestic violence, which I guess was what initially made him get into the whole—holistic, healing, yoga scene. But, regarding how he first came to the U.S. or managed to stay here, that I don't know."

And now I felt like shit.

I probably did judge him too quickly. It seemed like he was the type of guy trying to get himself out of a sticky situation. Still, I wasn't going to be okay with him meddling in my business or entertaining himself with his so-called *sensibilities*.

My phone buzzed on the table, and the notifications prompted an instant smile on my face.

"Do you mind if I take this really quick?" I asked CJ, whose mouth was full and couldn't reply. He gestured to go ahead.

Thomas: Can't wait to see you. Ready for tonight? How does 8 sound?
Thomas: And could you send me your address? I'll find something near your place for dinner. I'd love to walk with you.

I finished reading his texts and felt my stomach tingle with excitement.

"Was that your soulmate?" CJ teased, still working around his plate as I replied to Thomas's texts.

"That's not funny!" I kicked him playfully under the table. It was.

"Ouch!" He squealed, not able to hold in the laughter. "Oh, come on! Your face is completely flushed. Who's the guy? And is he *gracious*?" CJ laughed again. "I bet he is."

I stared at him, lifting the corners of my lips, keeping myself from grinning. And yes, I was sure he would approve of him. "I told you," he bragged, pointing at me with a piece of bacon. "Juan Pablo knows his shit."

Ugh. I *kind of* wanted Juan Pablo to be right, but I didn't want to believe these sorts of things either. I guess *the heart wants what it wants.*

CHAPTER 11

A Neighborly Introduction

WE DROPPED OFF CJ at his place and headed back home. I was nervous and excited about my date with Thomas. I wanted to shower and take my time deciding what I was going to wear. It was important.

Caleb opened the door for me with a flirty smile as soon as the car came to a complete stop. He noticed he'd provoked a reaction out of me when we arrived at the restaurant, and he was proud of it because his face told me so. *Stop*! Or don't. It was a fun and innocent little game.

I stepped out of the car and saw my neighbor Eric and another guy walking in the distance toward me, carrying beer and a few grocery bags.

"Hey, Billie!" Eric said with a hearty grin. "This is my brother Tobias."

"Nice to meet you, Billie. I'd shake your hand, but …" Tobias held the six-packs up to show me his hands were busy. "I've heard so much about you, though." Eric shoved his shoulder against Tobias's in protest, but Tobias just laughed.

I shook my head with a smile. Eric was cute, but he was a teenager. Tobias seemed a few years older than me. He was handsome, with light-brown wavy hair and those big blue eyes that could bewitch anyone in his radius. Eric and Tobias had similar features, but Tobias didn't look like a boy. Not one bit.

The three of us strolled inside the lobby as we chatted. Aaron and Caleb followed us inside and stood a casual distance away, talking among themselves.

"So why do you smell so good when you look like you've exercised? Aren't you curious?" Tobias asked, looking at a flushed Eric, waiting for him to reply. His pale skin was bright pink now.

Eric stammered, trying to find words to respond to that, and I could tell all Tobias wanted was to tease his little brother.

"I'm just messing with you, man," Tobias said with a laugh. "But you *do* smell good."

Aren't you slick?

"Thanks." I tried changing the subject. "So, what are you guys up to?" I jerked my chin at their groceries. Tobias carried a couple of Heiny six-packs, and from what I could see, Eric held a few bags with chips, among other snacks.

Senad dashed inside the lobby and disappeared off into a corridor at the far end past the elevators as Bruce, the other door guard, held the door open.

"Billie!" Tobias shouted in my direction, but he wasn't looking at me, and he wouldn't yell like that when I was standing right in front of him. I looked over my shoulder toward the door that had been left wide open and saw a black town car parked right beside the apartment building's green shade.

A young driver in a black suit unloaded a couple of suitcases from the trunk while this other tall, well-built guy with blond hair grabbed a backpack and a couple of brown paper bags from the back seat. I blinked fast a couple of times and tried looking away, but I just couldn't.

Who's that?

Senad rushed back out with a service cart to help with the luggage.

"That's William, our brother," Eric said, basically reading my mind.

Oh, he meant Billy!

"We're just going to have a few beers now that Billy's back," Tobias said, placing the six-packs on the floor. "He's been away for work, so we're going to get him hammered." He laughed.

I took another peek in William's direction. *What the ... heck are kids being fed in Sweden?* My God. He was even taller than his brothers. And that velvety sun-kissed skin with the hair spun out of pure gold ... I don't think I've *ever* seen anyone like him *ever* before. Did I say ever twice?

I glanced at Caleb, and he was looking my way with his resting, vicious-hound face. No. He wasn't even looking at me. He was looking at William.

An alpha male reunion.

Because William seemed like a freaking alpha something with that deep frown in between his brows and the way he carried himself. He refused to look our way—apparently, too busy doing his thing to be bothered.

"Douche alert!" Eric yelled with a laugh as William placed the bags on the cart and walked toward us. He was wearing tortoise Ray-Ban wayfarers, jeans, and a plain white t-shirt that highlighted his broad back and the corded muscles in his arms. He was sent down to Earth straight from Valhalla by Odin himself.

A thin thread pulled at the nape of my neck just slightly, sending a heavily charged electric current down my spine as I imagined what kind of perfection might lie beneath that simple yet alluring piece of white fabric. *Stop.*

He stood next to Eric and pushed his sunglasses down just a bit. "Aren't you supposed to be at school or something?" William said to Eric with a deep voice, smelling like fresh oranges and other mouthwatering spices. He messed up Eric's ultra-blond hair with his hand and pushed his Ray-Bans back in place.

Eric protested and took a step back, trying to fix his hair. William tapped Eric's back twice and moved on to greet Tobias.

"Hey, man." They shook hands with a clap, then went in for a hug with a few pats on the back. William's body language indicated he was happy to see his brothers, but his face registered a bit testy to me.

"Billy, this is Billie," Eric said, laughing at the coincidence.

William took his sunglasses off and tucked them on his shirt's collar. He looked at me with his annoyingly dreamy blue eyes for the first time since he arrived. His eyes were the same color as Tobias's, but William's had a mysterious spark to them.

His gaze swept me up and down in a quick move, and his frown got deeper.

What is his problem?

"Nice to meet you," I said, taking a step forward to offer my hand out to him. Senad rushed in with the service cart, and William placed his hand on my shoulder and pushed me out of the way. Senad apologized for nearly running me over.

"Watch it," William said to *me* with a bite.

I noticed my hand was still half-way sticking out in his direction. But I lowered it down immediately, as I realized he wasn't going to shake it.

"Um. I'm sorry. I didn't see the cart coming my way," I apologized with a frown for absolutely no reason. That hadn't been my fault, and I didn't understand why that irritated him. But William's face was creased up since he stepped out of the car anyway. He was probably having a bad day or something.

"You have to excuse him," Eric continued. "He'll probably be in a shitty mood for a while since—"

"Eric," William cut him off with a glare. He softened his features a bit and turned to look at me, offering his hand. "Nice to meet you."

I shook it with hesitation and persuaded my lips to offer a small smile.

"You're new, right?" William asked, brushing a few strands of hair off his forehead.

"Ah, yes. Apartment 9A."

"9A," he replied, lifting the corners of his mouth just slightly for a few seconds. His frown reappeared in between his eyes quickly after that.

That was my cue to leave. William was making me uneasy with all the gesture roller-coaster thing he had going on. I couldn't read him, and even though I was curious, I had things to do.

"Well, I guess I'll see you around," I said to them with a close-lipped smile. "Have fun."

"Bye, Billie," Eric and Tobias replied in unison. William nodded.

"I'll walk you, Miss Murphy," Caleb said with a glower, scanning the brothers up and down as he walked in my direction. Ugh. I turned around and walked away from the Sjöbergs.

"Lighten up, Caleb," I whispered as we stepped into the elevator. He stood next to me, looking at how the doors closed, holding his bodyguard stance in place like his life depended on it. "They're just my neighbors."

"Yeah, I don't know. We arrived just a few days ago, and I'm not comfortable yet seeing you talking to strangers. It makes me uneasy," he said, placing his hands inside his pockets.

"They don't look dangerous to me." I shrugged. *They looked gorgeous.* I stepped out of the elevator, and Caleb walked me to my doorstep. Even with his grouchy attitude, William stood out to me the most.

My mind drifted away into thought—wondering about him.

Anyway, who was I kidding, a guy like that? He was undoubtedly like a new restaurant with a long waitlist—simply unavailable.

"Red?"

"Ah, yes. Sorry," I apologized. Caleb said something before, but I was distracted and didn't listen to what he was telling me.

"What time are you leaving for dinner tonight?" he asked—probably for the second time—gnawing on his lower lip, looking anxious and annoyed.

"Oh, um, Thomas said he'll stop by at eight, and we'll walk someplace nearby." I smiled and turned around to unlock my apartment.

"I don't like him," he said out of nowhere. *I know*. He'd only seen him once, but he'd seen enough to dislike him. I guess he liked Thomas as much as I liked Noelle.

"Oh no, I'm shocked," I said with a dull tone, turning around to face him.

He snorted. "What?" he asked with a smile.

"You don't like anyone. That's what. I thought you liked me, but just by looking at your face right now ... I have my doubts," I joked. Of course, he liked me, and I liked him back. We were friends. But even though I could tell he was excited about New York, he wasn't himself right now. He'd always been overprotective, just like Aaron, but this felt excessive, and he knew it.

"Just for the record ... I do like you," he said with a laugh. "But you're a little rebel. Going out on dates on your first weekend here, telling your strange neighbors what apartment you live in." He raised his brow. "I heard that."

I puckered my lips to the side. "Sorry?" I laughed. He shook his head with a tight-lipped smile.

"We'll be downstairs," he said. "And don't wear that—thing you sprayed in the car for your date tonight. It smells too nice." *Is he joking?* He didn't smile or laugh after saying that.

I looked in my bag and grabbed the body spray. "This?" I splashed his chest, holding in a laugh, waiting for his reaction. He really needed to loosen up a couple of notches.

"You're going to get me fired!" he grumbled. I could see him trying his best not to yield a smile. He brushed his chest with his hands, but that wasn't doing much to help remove the scent off his jacket.

"Then you better go change because my father loves that vanilla body splash. He tells me every time I wear it. You wouldn't want to bump into him smelling like that, now would you?" I laughed again. A little lie to tease him. Not only was my father probably out of town, but I was sure he was unaware of what body splash I used. Besides, I loved perfumes so much that I had more than a few.

And I knew exactly which perfume I would wear for my date with Thomas. I was convinced Caleb was going to *hate* how good it was.

"We'll be downstairs." He shook his head and turned around to leave.

"Don't you roll your eyes at me!" I caught up with him and sprayed his neck.

He looked over his shoulder, rubbing his neck, and said, "You *do* want to get me fired."

If he only knew ... that's the last thing I wanted.

CHAPTER 12

A First Date

I WAS ALL DRESSED UP and ready for my date with Thomas. It was 7:55 p.m. when I heard a knock on my door. It was Caleb, and he didn't look too pleased.

"Thomas is downstairs," he said, raising his brow. "And I still can't take that vanilla thing off my nose. That jacket's going straight to the cleaners." He frowned as if it were a tragedy.

"Well, don't worry, I'm not wearing that body spray. Just as you requested."

"I can smell your perfume alright. It's even worse now," he replied, eyeing me up and down, his lips going into a tight line as I walked out of the apartment. *Ha!* I knew it.

I was going to lock my door, but Caleb jumped in. "I've got it."

He locked my door as I sauntered to the elevator, and out of nowhere, William's face popped up in my head—again. The image of him was stuck in my frontal lobe like double-stick tape. I uselessly tried shaking him off my head as we stepped inside the elevator and descended to the lobby.

Focus. You're going on a date with Thomas.

"Everything okay?" Caleb asked. "You can still turn around. I'll handle him."

"Ha, ha. Just a bit nervous," I lied, poking his chest. He snorted.

We stepped out of the elevator, and there he was, patiently

waiting for me in the lobby, looking as handsome as he did on the day I met him.

"Hey there," Thomas said with a smile as I approached him. I recognized the smell of his cologne. He was wearing dark blue jeans and a brown leather jacket over a white V-neck t-shirt.

What's with all the white t-shirts? And why did they all look so good in them? I would never see a white t-shirt in the same way again.

He pulled me softly to him, and the butterflies paid a visit to my stomach. My cheek burned after the kiss he gave me.

"You look beautiful," he whispered close to my ear as he offered his hand. "Feel like walking? I can always carry you home if your feet get swollen."

And how could I forget about that?

We walked to a nearby Italian restaurant. Aaron and Caleb followed behind a safe and casual distance away.

"Does it bother you?" I asked Thomas regarding my bodyguards.

"Of course not," he replied firmly. "I know what happened, Billie. My parents told me something about it. But we don't have to talk about any of that unless you want to."

He turned to look at me, and I nodded in appreciation. I did *not* feel like talking about it.

Not today.

We took a seat at a cozy table in the indoor dining area. The night was a bit chilly to sit outside on the lovely terrace. Candlelights that had dripped on themselves over time decorated the small restaurant and created a romantic atmosphere.

Caleb followed us inside, and once we were seated, he stood a few feet away with his back against the wall. I cleared my throat, trying to get his attention. Was he planning to stand there the whole time? He ignored me.

"Caleb?"

"Yes, Miss Murphy," he replied, keeping his bodyguard stance firmly in place. He was rooted to the ground. He didn't seem like he was going anywhere. I excused myself and walked over to talk to him.

"Would you like to take a seat at the table?" I asked sarcastically in barely a whisper. Caleb snorted and met my gaze with a slow blink. "I would like some privacy."

"This is your first date, right?"

"Um, yes." My reply came out more like a question.

"I think it's best if I stay just to make sure everything goes smoothly."

"Smoothly?" I looked over my shoulder and saw Thomas waiting like a normal non-menacing person. I didn't see the imminent danger he saw. "Is this protocol or—"

"Of course," he replied without looking at me.

"Suit yourself." I shot a fake smile at him and huffed my way back to the table.

"I'm sorry about that. I was—trying to shoo him away," I explained as I took a seat. "I'm afraid it won't be possible."

Thomas laughed and turned to look at Caleb for a second. "Don't worry about it. He looks like a statue. I don't think we'll even notice him there." *Speak for yourself.*

I took a deep breath. I didn't want Caleb to ruin my first date with Thomas, and the fact that my last meal had been brunch at noon with CJ wasn't helping my overall state of mind. But a small glass of wine could help me relax.

A young and spirited server approached us to take our drinks order. That's when I remembered this wasn't Paris and I couldn't order wine. I was miffed. "Ginger ale, please," I ordered instead.

Thomas laughed. "You're so adorable when you're mad. One more year and we'll be able to order wine for you too." One whole year. He'd pictured himself with me in a year.

That did *not* miff me.

The bubbly server came back after a few minutes with our drinks and a basket of bread and butter, grinning at Thomas.

"I think she likes you." I teased, grabbing a piece.

"And I think I like *you*," he replied, tucking my hair behind my ear, "but I *love*—that you're eating bread with butter because I love it too." He grabbed a piece from the basket and buttered it.

My conversation with Thomas flowed naturally. He told me about his life at Princeton and how much he loved rowing crew. I told him about the Summer Intensive Photography Program at Parsons that I wanted to sign up for and how excited I was about it. But I'd been waitlisted. The school told me someone could cancel at the last minute, so I was hopeful.

We ordered our food. Thomas gave me a quick kiss on the cheek and excused himself to the restroom. The sensation of his lips on my cheek lingered on and drew a smile on my face.

Caleb followed Thomas's every move with his eyes, then approached my table.

"Don't you want to SOS it and call it a night?" He teased with a crooked smile.

"Aren't you bored?" I replied, placing my elbows on the table, leaning my chin against the back of my fingers. "Don't you have anything to argue about with Aaron or something?"

"Bored?" He snorted. "I'm gathering material for today's report. Your father is going to want to know *all* about your new—boyfriend."

"He's *not* my boyfriend," I whispered.

"If he's smart, he'll seal the deal by the end of dinner. At least his transcript says he is." *Did he say transcript?* Caleb walked back to his shadowy spot to continue *gathering material.*

I wondered how in-depth the background check on Thomas had been. If I was allowed to come to dinner with him, that meant they okayed him. I'm sure that's what bothered Caleb. He wanted to find something awful about Thomas, and he didn't. I shook my head in his direction.

Thomas returned and sat beside me. "I've been meaning to talk to you about why I disappeared on you," he said, placing his velvety, perfect-shaped lips on the wineglass to take a sip. "I have a somewhat complicated relationship with my father, and it only gets more complicated as time goes by." Thomas looked down into his plate, holding his wineglass in front of him.

"I had a brother, Joshua. He was three years older than me." He looked at me, and I could see the pain and the rage in his eyes—the same I'd captured with my lens in Paris. I held his gaze and allowed him to continue talking. He had my complete attention.

"Joshua was gay, and he knew it from a young age. My father had a tough time accepting it—accepting *him* for who he was. He never respected him and constantly tried to change him—to convince him otherwise as if it could be done." He took a longer sip of his wine and asked for a refill. Heck, I'd want a refill too.

"My father pushed and pushed. He would regularly compare us and even got to threaten him. Being a politician, he only cared about the optics and how that might affect his career. But one day after a—*nasty* argument, Joshua wanted to storm out of the house, like he usually did, so he ran down the stairs and fell."

Thomas cleared his throat for what seemed like the fifth time since he started talking and paused for a few seconds, rubbing his forehead. I could tell he was having a hard time talking about his brother and all the horrible things he went through.

Our server brought him a fresh glass of wine and left quickly afterward, probably sensing the vibe. Thomas took a sip and continued. "He hit the nape of his neck with the edge of a step and died from the impact. My mother she—hasn't been able to forgive my father ever since. And my father, well, I guess his problem was solved when Joshua died. He was only eighteen years old, and I was fifteen," Thomas said with an empty stare.

His eyes began to glaze when they met mine once again. He licked his bottom lip as if to hold in the emotions that wanted to leak out of him. I reached out for his hand, and he held it with no objection.

Still, I said nothing. I wanted to make sure he was done talking.

"Paris was one of my father's attempts to parade us around like the happy family he wishes to portray to the public. He doesn't want my mother's forgiveness—he knows he won't—can't have it." Thomas's voice went a little grave and continued, "But he does fear for her, for her mental health mostly. And I … I'm just stuck somewhere in the middle of all that chaos, and honestly, I was glad about leaving D.C. and coming to Princeton. But I still can't brush off the feeling of guilt. Of leaving my mother alone—with *him*," he growled as he uttered the last word.

"Anyway, things got complicated when we flew back from Paris. There are things I still can't share with you. Not yet. But I wasn't in the best headspace. I thought about you every single day, and I kept thinking if dragging you into this—mess was fair to you. I'm sure you've dealt and might still be dealing with your fair share of messiness. So, I kept busy with school and rowed myself to exhaustion, trying to convince myself you were better off without me. We had met just once, anyway. And I thought maybe you'd forgotten all about me." He said the last part making no eye contact, putting his wineglass down.

I felt for him. I felt his loneliness, his pain. I'd been there too. I'd felt that anger, grief, rage, the void inside my chest—the injustice of it all.

"I thought about you every single day, too," I managed to say with a dry throat, "and I'm glad you sought me out, sent me those flowers, and that we are *here* right now. Thank you for sharing this with me." He offered me his hand, our foreheads found each other, and I whispered, "I'm sorry you had to go through all that. That you still are."

He lifted my chin slightly, aligning his eyes and mouth with mine. His warm breath collided with my lips as he parted his mouth, just a dab. "I told you the day I met you, Billie. I'm not letting you out of my sight," he whispered. "I meant that—if you'll have me."

I nodded in response. He was so close to me that I wasn't sure if I was even breathing. He finally pressed his warm lips against mine. It was a soft kiss that didn't lack intensity and slowly caught up with a rhythm that lured me to cancel out every thought and sound around us.

His delicious wine-tasting tongue searched for mine while he held my hands with both of his, making me feel safe—cherished. He stopped for a second, our moist, wandering lips still grazing. "This face will be the death of me," he whispered, slowly shaking his head, and once again, he leaned in to kiss me.

For the first time in my life, I felt like someone could understand me and what I'd gone through completely. He also knew about grief of the same magnitude.

He had faced death, eye to eye, just as I did. He knew about loss and loneliness, and I was tired of feeling alone, and so was Thomas. I didn't want to pretend anymore—or feel like I had to be strong and carry on. Sometimes you need to fully disarm yourself and allow the weakness to seep out of every breath and every heartbeat till there's no more left inside of you.

Thomas made me feel like I could do that with him—that I was safe.

We broke away from the kiss, and our food had been magically placed in front of us.

"We should eat. You're probably starving," he said with a small smile. He seemed lighter now that he'd opened himself to me.

"I am," I replied with a faint laugh. I looked up and saw Caleb staring at me, but he quickly looked away when he saw me looking his way. *Shit.* He obviously saw me kissing Thomas, and I was more than sure he didn't like it one bit. I could see it in his face.

☾

At some point during dinner, Aaron went back to the apartment and brought the SUV to the restaurant. They didn't want us to walk back home so late at night. We were only a few blocks away, but that's how they are.

"Do you need a ride home?" I asked Thomas when we stepped out of the car outside my apartment building.

"No, that's okay. I'll walk for a bit and grab a cab or something."

How I wish I could do that someday. Just walk around—alone—grab a cab, go places.

"Thanks for dinner. I had a great time tonight," I told him. Thomas took a step forward and grazed my jaw with his knuckles.

"I did too," he said, looking into my eyes. "Can I call you tomorrow? I'd love to see you again."

I nodded, and he took my mouth in a shamelessly passionate kiss, his tongue sweeping against mine. It was a great kiss. And I wish we were alone so that I could lose myself in it.

But I could feel my back burning, and not only was Caleb standing there but Aaron too. And I don't know why, but knowing Aaron was there made it feel like my big brother was watching—if I had one. Not a comfortable feeling. At all. And Caleb witnessing it—well, I don't know what to compare that with.

Thomas had this effortless way of swooping in without warning. And how was I to refuse his perfect lips? Caleb watching—that's how. I knew Caleb and I were just friends, but I didn't feel comfortable flaunting kisses in front of him when I'd daydreamed about kissing *him* more than a few times already. For more than a few years. Damn it.

Our friendship was … complicated. I know that.

I found the strength to pull away from Thomas and said, "Um—sorry. It's just that—" I jerked my head at my security detail.

"I get it," he whispered with faint laugh, kissing my cheek. "I'll call you. Good night."

I hoped he *would* call me the next day because he ghosted me for a month the last time I saw him. So, you never know.

Thomas wandered away, and I walked inside the apartment building as I avoided making eye-contact with Caleb. I looked over my shoulder, and he was talking to Aaron. He didn't offer to walk me back as he always did. I guess I deserved it. I probably wouldn't want to walk me back either if I were him.

My phone buzzed as I waited for the elevator.

Thomas: I know I said it a few times already, but I had a great time tonight. Maybe we could go to the park tomorrow, and you can bring your camera?
Me: I'd love that. I had a great time too.

The elevator doors opened as I was putting my phone away, and out came William, Tobias, and Eric. They were drunk, as promised. I didn't know how old Eric was, but surely not old enough to drink like that.

"Billie!" Eric cried and went in for a hug. *Oh, okay.*

"Um, hi!" I said, trying not to look uncomfortable as I pulled away from Eric's embrace.

William held a beer in his hand and took a few sips as he stared at me with lowered lids—that same intoxicating cologne flowing my way. He kept looking at me as he did earlier when I met him. He was making me nervous.

"You look pretty," Tobias said with a grin. I pressed my lips and thanked him with a nod. "We're gonna get some pizza. Do you want to come?"

"Actually, I just had dinner. But maybe some other time?" I replied.

"Miss Murphy," Aaron interrupted. He took a few steps closer to me and nodded at the brothers. "Mr. Hill left his wallet in the car." He gave it to me and walked back out to join Caleb.

I placed the wallet in my purse, and my phone buzzed. It was Thomas calling me. I excused myself to take the call, but the three of them just stood there in front of me.

"*Thomas? … Hi, yes. Aaron just gave it to me, don't worry … Are you sure? Don't you need money for the cab? … Oh, I see … Okay, tomorrow then … You too. Good night.*"

I hung up with a smile on my face.

"Who's Thomas?" William asked, his voice all husky and dark, fading my smile a beat later.

"Um …" I trailed off as I struggled with the question. He wasn't a friend, but he wasn't my boyfriend. Yet. "A friend." Final answer. But my reply came out more like a question.

William shot me a smug look, seemingly aware of my predicament. He drained his beer and turned around to dispose of it in the trash can beside the elevator.

"And he leaves his wallet to secure another date?" he asked, walking back with a smirk drawn on his face. "Sneaky little fellow."

Little fellow …

"I don't think that's what happened."

William was obviously drunk, but what the hell was his problem?

"Billy, come on. Back off, man," Tobias said to him with a shove to his arm. "Let's go. I'm sorry, Billie, have a good night."

"I warned you, Billie," Eric said with a chuckle, raising his brows. "He's—"

"Eric," William interrupted him again, shaking his head. He placed his arm around Eric's shoulders and started toward the doorway.

"Ignore them," Tobias said with a grin, pointing at them with his thumb. "Later, Billie." He walked away, and I shook my head with a snort.

William looked over his shoulder, shot me a two-finger wave, and said, "See you around, 9A."

CHAPTER 13

Premonitions

June 3, 2009

A MONTH AND A HALF had gone by since my first date with Thomas. We became inseparable ever since. His father owned an apartment in the city, and he used it when he came for work. It was also used by Thomas's mother when she visited him—which wasn't often. That meant Thomas was free to use it on the weekends on an almost regular basis.

He had a complicated schedule with school and rowing crew. His training regime was grueling. A typical training week for Thomas would be Monday through Saturday, from two to four hours a day. Coming on Fridays to the city was challenging for him. There were times when he couldn't come to see me.

And I have to be honest—it was tricky. I would miss him so much during the week. We would text like crazy during the day and have our mandatory phone call at night before going to bed.

Although I wished Thomas could stay over at my place during the weekends, that was impossible. I had one too many eyes watching and reporting my every move to my father. I did not want to start my new *independent* life abusing my father's trust. He'd have me go back to my old room in his apartment in a heartbeat.

We did fool around—a *lot*. Our hormones raged through the week and found release on the weekends when we finally saw each other. But I was still a virgin, and Thomas knew about it and respected it. But we were waiting until I felt comfortable and ready to take that next step.

I honestly didn't feel like delaying it that much longer. Thomas had me drooling, but every time the opportunity presented itself, I'd chicken out. I told myself over and over again, *next time*.

There was another issue still pending in our relationship.

I hadn't opened up myself with him regarding my mother's death. Since that was one of the most vulnerable parts of me, I was still reluctant to share my burden with someone else—especially with Thomas. He was going through a lot already.

Trust wasn't the issue. It had more to do with my capacity to take that leap into full and undisclosed vulnerability. He had been so open and vocal with me from the beginning regarding his brother's death, but I was still afraid of showing myself entirely out of, well, fear.

Being capable of completely letting yourself go like that and showing yourself to someone—that's powerful. I had many opportunities to talk about it. Still, having so little quality time to spend with Thomas in person, I never wanted to ruin those moments by turning the conversation about me and my traumas. It felt selfish for me to do so.

Thomas was finally done with exams, and I had him all to myself for the summer.

Well ... almost.

He still had to train since his team was attending an important international summer competition in August. But that was plenty more time than the usual once or twice a week we'd been accustomed to.

Thomas mentioned how he would typically go back to D.C. for a few weeks during the summer. It was not his favorite season of the year, but he did it for his mother. He hadn't decided yet when and for how long he would be leaving. He even considered not going at all, and I didn't get it. I'd go see my parents if I were him. But I didn't want to meddle when he hadn't asked for my opinion.

And speaking of going ... Thomas and I were meeting my friends for lunch for the very first time. I texted him to let him know we were picking him up and were a few blocks away from his apartment.

Caleb still didn't like Thomas. He insisted he didn't trust him. I usually just ignored him or told him that I didn't want to talk about it. He had no reason to feel that way about Thomas. He worried too much, as always.

CJ and I had stayed in touch regularly and met for coffee or lunch, but I hadn't seen Nina since that yoga class in April, and I had liked her a lot. I was trying to avoid Juan Pablo altogether, which I thought was a shame.

The only problem was that he was coming with her for lunch. If I wanted to be friends with Nina, I had to learn how to coexist with her boyfriend.

I hadn't talked to Thomas about Juan Pablo. But I thought I could give him the heads up I wished someone had given me before I met him.

"Hey, gorgeous." Thomas grinned as he got in the car, looking handsome as he always did.

"I missed you." I pressed my cheek against his chest and hugged him.

"You look beautiful." He gave me a quick, soft kiss on my lips.

Let's say I never found a way to stop Thomas from kissing me and saying all these nice things to me while Caleb was around. So yeah, Caleb and I weren't as close as we used to be when we lived in Paris. We had these intervals where we talked for a bit and laughed like we used to, but then there would be days where he would take twenty steps away from me.

This was one of those tricky days.

"There's something I need to talk to you about regarding today's lunch," I said to Thomas.

"What's wrong?" he asked, scanning my face for answers.

"Nothing's wrong, don't worry. I just wanted to talk to you about my experience meeting Juan Pablo. Nina's boyfriend."

"Ok, I'm listening," he replied, reaching out for my hand.

"Look, I've only met him once, but he acted super weird that day. He's a yoga instructor and owns a studio and everything. It just happens that he, well"—I was having trouble finding the right words to describe him—"has a certain … gift, of sorts?"

"What kind of gift? Like a medium?" Thomas lowered his thick, dark brows.

"I don't know what to call it, but he claims to listen to certain *messages* and information about people he interacts with. Things got really weird the day I met him. He looked at me and said some kind of—rhyme or riddle. He then mentioned my mother, but I excused myself and left."

"He dared mention your mother?" He looked disgusted by the fact.

"I didn't hear what he was about to say, but it really freaked me out. *He* freaks me out, and I'm not telling you this to make you feel the same way that I do about him. I just wanted to warn you, so if he tries anything like this today, you'll be prepared because I wasn't."

"I mean, you know he's full of shit, right?" Thomas challenged the idea, trying to dismiss it altogether.

"It's definitely hard for me to believe him, yes," I admitted.

We were ten minutes early and the first to arrive at the restaurant. Thomas and I sat down to wait for the others to arrive. Caleb stopped his silly practice of standing beside us whenever we went out to a restaurant. He gave up. He saw how Thomas treated me. I didn't need to be protected from my boyfriend.

Thomas grabbed my hand and said, "I know my schedule has been a bit complicated, and it's been hard for me to juggle everything. I'm so sorry about that, but—I'll be leaving in two weeks for a regatta in Canada." His mouth twisted to the side. I couldn't tell if he felt guilty about going, but I knew for sure he loved regattas. What's the point in busting your ass the whole year training if you can't compete?

"How many days will you be away?" I asked with an exaggerated sad face. He smiled at my reaction.

"I leave on the 17th and will be back by the 22nd of June." He paused for a few seconds and rubbed my back. "We weren't sure if we were going, but our coach confirmed to us a few hours ago that it's official. That's why I didn't mention it before. I'm so sorry."

I knew he loved the sport, and I knew he would have a great time, so there was no reason for him to feel guilty about leaving. Besides, it was only going to be for a few days. And I didn't mind. "You know I'll miss you. Thank you for letting me know." I cupped his cheek with my hand and gave him a quick peck on the lips.

"Anyway, I heard back from Parsons," I said with a grin. "I'm officially enrolled in the three-week Summer Photography Program. It's from July 6th to the 24th. I'm so excited!"

"Congratulations! I'm so happy for you. I'm sure you're going to love it," he cheered with genuine excitement.

"The program will include analog photography, which you know I've been curious about, so I'm looking forward to it too." I nodded and pressed my lips together into an upturned smile. Since I arrived in New York, I felt like I hadn't been doing much aside from exercising. I needed to start doing something productive.

"That means ... we need to go camera shopping," he said, raising both of his eyebrows a few times.

"My thoughts exactly."

"Is this the perfume I gave you?" He lowered his face to my

neck and slowly inhaled, which made my body tingle all-around.

"It is."

"Well, it's delicious on you," he whispered to my lips, kissing them. It was one of his slow kisses that I loved, and neither of us was willing to pull away from it. I wasn't the biggest PDA fan, but Thomas always made me feel like there was no one else in the room but the two of us.

"Ex-cuse-me!" CJ laughed, clapping his hands with every syllable. Thomas and I winced, and our lips unlocked automatically. Apparently, he arrived seconds after we started kissing. I looked up at CJ and laughed.

Thomas didn't seem too pleased about being interrupted, but I gave him a bouncy peck on his lips to cheer him up. Thomas knew all about CJ's bubbly personality. I made sure to fill him in on that too.

"CJ, this is Thomas, Thomas, CJ," I introduced them.

"So glad to finally meet you, CJ. I've heard so much about you."

"Likewise." They shook hands, and I caught CJ scanning Thomas with a raised eyebrow as Thomas took a seat. I wasn't surprised about that either.

Juan Pablo and Nina arrived. He was wearing a pair of baggy, low-seam colorful pants with a simple white t-shirt, a bunch of necklaces, and nude sandals. His long waves were made up in a high bun this time. Nina looked gorgeous. She wore a lovely floral print summer dress with her hair down.

"How's everyone doing?" Juan Pablo asked with an overly cheerful smile. Thomas stood up and extended his hand, but Juan Pablo went in for a hug. "You must be Thomas." Juan Pablo heartily patted Thomas's back.

"That's right. Nice to meet you, Juan Pablo," Thomas replied as he broke away from his embrace. "Nice to meet you too, Nina."

We all sat down, and Juan Pablo immediately took the floor.

"Okay, Billie." He stared at me with his panther-black eyes, holding his hands together on the table in front of him. I took a deep breath and squeezed Thomas's hand under the table. He squeezed it back to let me know that he was right there with me.

"First of all, I want to apologize. I know that I probably scared you the last time I saw you, and for that, I'm sorry." He held his hands up in the universal gesture for *I surrender*. "I will not share anything else that you don't want me to, okay? I can't control when certain messages come through, though," Juan Pablo added, lifting an eyebrow. "But if I close my eyes, just ignore me. Sounds good?"

That sounded *more* than perfect.

"Oh, sure. Please, don't worry about it. I mean, to be honest, you did catch me a bit off guard, you know." I snorted. "But I completely understand, don't worry." I didn't understand his *gift*, but there wasn't much left to say on my part. I was glad that he had noticed my discomfort.

"Perfect! Let's eat!" Juan Pablo chirped, clapping his hands once.

We ate and talked about a lot of things. It was actually fun. Juan Pablo behaved like a normal human being, and he never once closed his eyes to *listen*. I'd say that lunch was a success.

As we walked out of the restaurant, I saw Caleb and David standing beside the car. Nina was looking at Caleb from the corner of her eye because why wouldn't she, right? But she quickly turned away and grabbed Juan Pablo's hand. Maybe as a self-reminder that she had a boyfriend.

We all decided to go for ice cream to a nearby place. And I caught Caleb staring at Nina when she walked by past him with Juan Pablo. Ugh. But he realized I saw him, so he looked away harshly, as if condemning himself for looking her way. *Yeah, that's right.*

I rolled my eyes on the inside and kept walking. Caleb followed us on foot, and David took the car there.

We arrived at the ice cream shop, and I excused myself to the restroom after asking Thomas to choose a surprise flavor for me. Anything except strawberries. I know I must be the only freak in the universe who doesn't like them, but it's the only thing I won't eat.

When I came back, I saw Nina and CJ sitting on a table eating their ice cream and laughing, while Thomas and Juan Pablo lingered near the cashier. Thomas held an ice cream cone in each hand, his gaze directed at the floor. He nodded intermittently, while Juan Pablo whispered to his ear.

That did *not* look good.

"Hey!" I said cheerfully, trying to interrupt the exchange intentionally. Juan Pablo stopped talking when he heard my voice. "Everything okay?" I asked with suspicion, holding on to Thomas's arm.

"Ah, yes!" Thomas replied, handing the pistachio ice cream cone to me. "We were actually done here." He returned a half-legitimate smile in my direction.

Damn it. I knew Juan Pablo couldn't keep his *notions* to himself.

"Let's take a seat," Thomas ordered dryly. Juan Pablo followed us to the table, but Thomas's face was blank while he monotonously licked his dark-chocolate ice cream cone. But the translucency of his eyes spoke words to me. There was anger, irritation, and even sadness in them.

"Do you want to leave?" I murmured through clenched teeth.

"No, I'm fine," he replied without looking at me. I wondered if his anger was directed at me. And that just flipped my switch.

Hold my cone.

I gave my cone to Nina and texted the security group chat.

Me: SOS Light mode. 5 - 10 min.
Caleb: Yes, ma'am.

I turned to the window, and Caleb stared at his phone with a huge grin on his face. It seemed to me like the SOS beacon made him snap out of the bad mood he'd been carrying around all day.

I acted naturally, chit-chatted with my friends, laughed at CJ's jokes, and pretended that I didn't want to jump across the table and shove my ice cream cone into Juan Pablo's nosy face.

Caleb walked in the shop, pressing on his earpiece—full-on theatrics. Nina and CJ gasped when they saw him displaying himself in his element.

"Miss Murphy, I'm so sorry to interrupt," Caleb said in his thick accent, "but your father called, and he wants us to take you to his apartment right away. There's something he needs to talk to you about. It's a pressing matter."

"Is everything okay?" I asked, playing along and trying to sound concerned.

"Yes, everything's okay. But it would be best if we start heading out," he urged, looking at his watch. "We'll wait outside." He turned on his heel and left. Nina followed Caleb with her eyes—cheeks on fire. Juan Pablo squinted his eyes at her and made a funny side-pout to go with it. I wondered if *the voices* would inform him that Nina found Caleb to be hot as hell—because she obviously did.

I couldn't blame Juan Pablo for all the gesturing. I probably made the same face he did after seeing Nina shamelessly blushing for Caleb. Luckily, Thomas was busy looking inside his head that he didn't notice any of the awkward interactions in front of him.

I searched for Thomas's absent-minded eyes and said, "Come on. Let's go." He stood up. We promised to get together more often and said goodbye to my friends.

"Everything okay, Miss Murphy?" Caleb asked, both concerned and amused.

"Yes, everything's fine. Can you take me home, please?"

"What just happened?" Thomas was visibly confused about the whole situation.

"You tell me," I replied, feeling annoyed by his behavior at the ice cream shop. I didn't understand why Thomas had an attitude with me instead of just telling me what happened with my least favorite person in the world.

"We'll talk when we get to the apartment," he snapped back at me.

Excuse me?

He had *never* spoken to me like that before, with that edge. I ignored him the entire way back home and enjoyed what was left of my ice cream cone.

We got home, and I took my shoes off with a sigh. I sat cross-legged on the living room couch beside Thomas. "Can you now *please* tell me what happened with Juan Pablo?"

"Yes." He turned to look at me, and something told me it would be our first fight. "When we were alone, Juan Pablo had a moment, he … closed his eyes and grasped my shoulder. Then, he opened them, looked directly into mine, and asked me if I wanted to *know*." He crossed his arms in front of his chest as he explained everything. "I said yes." I remained silent, forcing him to keep expanding.

But why, why, would he say yes?

"He began with something like 'Avoid and love, but love and avoid—no regret on mistakes that aren't made.' Then he added, 'I was surprised to see you.' He then told me something that absolutely *no one* knows. I can't stress that enough, Billie. I don't know what to think, but it's messed up, so I figured Juan Pablo might be right about everything," he fretted with a broken tone, letting his head hang.

"What is *everything*? I can't even understand his riddles, or if you do, please enlighten me. You can't seriously tell me you believe every word that comes out of his mouth."

"He made it seem as if you and I aren't meant to be together." He sighed, looking intently at my eyes while squeezing my hands.

"What did he tell you the day you met him? I need to know if you truly want to be with me."

When he said that, I quickly realized that he was feeling insecure in the relationship. That somehow, what Juan Pablo told him made him feel uneasy—made him doubt.

I remembered perfectly what Juan Pablo had told me, but there was no use in telling him any of it. What mattered was how *I* felt about *him*. I didn't want Thomas overanalyzing Juan Pablo's words. It wasn't important.

"What are you talking about? These past few weeks have been amazing, and I've enjoyed every minute of them with you." I sat on his lap and placed my arms around his neck. "I warned you about Juan Pablo. He meddles too much, and I know you allowed him to tell you all those things, but that doesn't mean that they are real, valid, or that whatever you think they mean will somehow change how I feel about you." I pressed my cheek between his neck and his shoulder. "I love you."

And I really meant it. I was crazy about him. We hadn't said that to each other, and there I was, opening up myself to him, being vulnerable, not knowing if he would reciprocate the feeling. But I wanted to reassure him, and I was willing to say and do anything for him to feel at ease.

He grabbed my waist and pulled me on top of him in a swift move. We were now facing each other, my knees straddling his hips. He kissed me as he'd never kissed me before—with urgency. He pulled my waist even closer to him, and my fingers brushed his dark-chestnut hair with hunger, giving him exactly what he was giving me. His hands slipped under my blouse and slid against my bare skin, making it react. I was craving him.

He abruptly recoiled away from me, but I complained with a low groan and thrust myself at him again.

"I love you," he whispered, making me stop to look at him as he brushed a strand of hair out of my face. "I can't imagine my life without you."

"Then don't." I wanted him to stop worrying and doubting our relationship.

I brought my mouth to his, and we quickly picked up where we'd left off. I took his shirt off to reveal his rock-hard chest and chiseled abs that I adored. He did the same for me and stood up, wrapping my legs around his waist. He took me to my bed, and I let him do the thinking for me.

I was ready to give myself entirely to him, and I wanted him to know that I was his.

He removed whatever garments still left between us. I patiently enjoyed every second of his hands softly grazing my skin as he did it.

His eyes met mine, and a simple nod from me—an answered invitation—assured him that I was ready for him to keep deciding for me. And he did, so I allowed myself to burn and melt as I felt him for the first time.

CHAPTER 14

An Invitation

June 17, 2009

I HEARD A STRONG KNOCK on the door—the kind of knock that wants to get noticed. I peered through the peephole and saw Eric's unmistakable platinum blond hair.

"Hey, neighbor!" he said as I opened the door. I greeted him back with a broad smile. I liked him. He was holding a white envelope in his hands. "So, um—Billie, we're having a party this Saturday. We're celebrating Midsummer upstairs on the rooftop, and we invited a couple more neighbors." Eric cleared his throat. I could tell he was nervous. "We were wondering if you would like to join us." He took a step forward and handed me the invitation.

I chuckled under my breath. It looked like they printed it at home and made it last minute. It was cute, though, and I appreciated the effort. "It's been a while since I had an actual paper invitation given to me," I said, amused, skimming through it. "I'm actually free this weekend, so I'd love to come."

Thomas was in Canada, and it sounded like a family-oriented event and an excellent opportunity to meet the rest of my neighbors. Eric seemed genuinely excited after I accepted the invitation.

I asked Eric about the dress code because I'd never been to a Midsummer party, and I didn't have a clue of what to expect.

"Well—we do like to dress up," he said, lifting his brow. *Note taken.* "And don't worry, Billy will be in his best behavior."

I scrunched up my nose for a few seconds, remembering how my last interaction with William had been. He was drunk and teasing me about my date with Thomas, but I hadn't seen him ever since, so I thought there was no reason to worry.

Just knowing he was going to be there made me feel a bit anxious and a lot nervous. He had a very imposing personality.

"Oh, psh. Of course," I replied, trying to be casual. "I'll see you guys on Saturday. Thanks again!"

"Sure thing." Eric tapped the wall beside the door twice with a grin, trying to seem cool. "Later, Billie!"

☾

June 20, 2009

I needed to be ready by noon, and Mimi was helping me with my hair. I wanted to wear it up with a braided headband. She was so good with braids, and I thought it would match my outfit and the party's theme well.

I wore a blush pink, knee-length tulle and lace dress with sheer elbow-length sleeves. It was as *Midsummery* as it was going to get. I wished that Thomas could come with me and see me all dressed up.

The morning went by quickly, and it was ten minutes before twelve. I thanked Mimi with a big warm hug and headed to the second floor. I knocked on Aaron and Caleb's apartment, and Caleb answered the door barefoot, wearing shorts and a sleeveless hoodie. I bit the corner of my lower lip when I saw his arms sticking out all—*muscly*.

He looked confused, probably wondering why I was all dressed up and knocking at their door.

"Hi, Caleb." I greeted him with a flirty smile that made me feel guilty right away. But I needed everything in my arsenal to get their approval to go to the party on my own. And it's not like it was a challenging task to flirt with him.

Anyway, I got lucky that Caleb opened the door instead of Aaron.

"Hey, Red." He pursed his lips as if speculating my intentions.

I got distracted looking at his arms again, because *wow*, but I shook my head and said, "Um—I wanted to let you know that I'll be upstairs on the rooftop. There's a party, and the Sjöbergs invited me." He leaned against the wall with a small smile as he heard my case.

"Okay, so you want to go—by yourself?" He raised a brow, aiming those hazel things straight at me. I wasn't sure if he'd agree to my request or not. But I had to at least try.

"Well, I didn't see the need for you to bore yourselves to death on the rooftop. I mean, I'm technically still at home," I replied. "See it as an opportunity to take the rest of the day off."

He narrowed his eyes at me. "I don't know, Red."

"Oh, come on." I shoved his arm in a swift move. His eyes followed my hand as I did it.

"Nope." He balked.

"Caleb!" I complained with a laugh. I was doing my best to convince him, but it wasn't enough for him. And there wasn't much more I could do.

"Why don't you kick Thomas to the curb, and I'll reconsider." He teased with a laugh. He really did hate him. I widened my eyes for a second. I didn't know what to reply to that. "Nah, I'm just messing with you." *Was he?*

I crossed my arms in front of me and stared at him with an *I'm not moving until I get my way* kind of posture.

He sighed. "Fine, I'll talk to Aaron," he said, his words colored with exasperation.

I took a small pocket perfume I had in my bag and sprayed his chest.

"Hey! I just showered!" he complained with a smile.

"That's for rolling your eyes at me again," I said, tossing the perfume back in my clutch.

He shook his head with a smug smile on his face.

"I'm sure you won't miss me," I added with a chuckle, turning around and walking toward the elevator.

"You're lucky your boyfriend's out of town," Caleb said, catching up to me. "There's no way I'd let you go to a party alone with him."

I wasn't going to get into an argument with Caleb about Thomas, so I said nothing. Caleb summoned the elevator for me and waited for it to arrive.

"Text us when you're back at your apartment," he said as I stepped inside the elevator. I clicked on the fourteenth-floor button and took a deep breath.

Yay! My first party alone.

"You look great, by the way." He smiled and the elevator doors closed before I could reply.

Thanks.

Damn it.

CHAPTER 15

Midsummer

I STEPPED OUT of the elevator onto the fourteenth floor and walked up a flight of stairs to the rooftop.

Hell, I was shaking. I didn't really know anyone but Eric, William, and Tobias. But Eric was the only one that actually talked to me. I'd bumped into Tobias a few times, and he would smile, say hello, and keep about his business. And so did I, in all honesty. And William, well, I hadn't seen him since the day I met him. Luckily, Eric was near the rooftop access as I walked in.

"Hey, Billie! You look—really good," he said with a big smile. He looked excited. I walked up to him and greeted him with the accustomed double cheek kiss I used when meeting my friends in Paris. Tobias quickly walked up to me and introduced me to Joel, who I'd never seen before. William was nowhere to be found— probably late. *Is he showing up at all?*

I greeted Nathalie, and then Eric introduced me to his father, Sivert, the neighbors I hadn't met, and Lily, Joel's girlfriend.

Lily had silky butterscotch hair, and her eyes matched it almost perfectly. So strikingly beautiful. She looked familiar, but I couldn't figure out why.

"Hi, Billie! So nice to finally meet you." She grinned as I double cheek-kissed her too. "Come, sit. We're making flower crowns. I'll teach you how to make one." Lily pulled me to the table where a bunch of flowers, twigs, and threads were used to make the crowns.

The rooftop was beautifully decorated with several flower arrangements. A foliage-coated pergola covered a white, wooden, farm-style table filled with various plates and bowls with food, sauces, dips, and fruits. The delicious smell of dill, chives, and other spices emanated from the platters.

A Swedish flag waved proudly at the far end of the rooftop, and lounge music played in the background. Everything looked gorgeous, and everyone seemed happy—it was contagious. My nerves were beginning to settle down.

Twenty minutes went by, and I had almost finished making my flower crown when I heard the rooftop access door close with a thud.

"Chef's here!" Sivert shouted, raising his beer. We all inevitably turned to look at William as he walked in, making quite an entrance.

He came in looking ridiculously handsome, wearing a white V-neck t-shirt, jeans, a navy-blue blazer, and his tortoise Ray-Ban wayfarers. None of his brothers wore jeans, but he probably knew he didn't need much to look good. He could wear a freaking white t-shirt for the rest of his life and still look better than most people.

He walked in like he owned the place—like a bathed and shaved Viking ready for a garden party. I caught myself staring for too long, so I made myself look away and kept to my crown as he greeted his family and neighbors. If I were a cartoon, I'd be whistling, pretending to mind my own business.

I sat at the other end of the table with Lily and his mother, so I was going to be the last one on his greeting path.

William grabbed a beer as he walked beside the table that served as a bar and dashed straight to us like a bullet. He stood behind his mother and kissed her cheek. He then approached Lily and me .

"Hey, Billy!" Lily stood up and hugged him. I stood up too, because I didn't want to seem disrespectful. Hearing people calling him *Billy* kept startling me.

"9A," William said, looking at me. I smiled and leaned in for a double cheek-kiss. His mouthwatering cologne was intoxicating as per usual, but he slightly recoiled after I greeted him, taken aback. I felt my face warming up after observing his reaction.

"You—don't do cheek-kissing?" I was mortified. But that's just how I was used to greeting people I already knew in settings like these. It was automatic.

"Believe me. I'm not going to *ever* argue about that." He smiled playfully. *There goes my blood up to my face again.* At least he seemed in a better mood than the last time I saw him.

"I just double cheek-kissed the entire party," I whispered, then covered my face with both of my hands.

"I don't think that anyone will object to that either." He laughed. "Don't worry about it—it's fine. I just didn't know that you were going to kiss me twice."

Kiss him twice, huh. They were more like air kisses, but okay.

"All done," Lily said, setting the flower crown on my head.

William kept staring at me, at the flower crown, at my dress. It made me feel uneasy, so I pretended not to acknowledge his stare and turned to Lily to thank her instead. "The flowers are beautiful," I told her.

William stood beside me and sipped on his beer—his eyes still focused on me.

"That's a very nice dress, Billie," Tobias said out of nowhere. "Can I get you something to drink?" I turned to look at him and accepted, but William was gone when I looked the other way.

Where did he go?

And why should I care?

Tobias gestured an *after you* hand wave, and we slowly moved toward the table that served as a bar. "What would you like?" he asked.

"What do you usually drink on these occasions?"

"Lots of aquavit … and beer." He smiled naughtily. I'd never heard of aquavit before, but whatever it was it sounded like I wouldn't be able to stomach more than a couple, and I didn't like beer at all.

"Is this the aquavit?" I asked, grabbing one of the bottles from the ice bucket. Tobias nodded. "I've never tasted it before. Do you do shots with it, or how do you drink this?"

I was curious.

"Shots, spritzers, straight out of the bottle. You name it." He laughed. "Let me fix you a spritzer. Girls usually like them."

"I'm not twenty-one yet," I confessed. This new alcoholic beverage made me doubt if I should drink or not. I'd only drunk wine before.

"Well, I won't tell a soul," Tobias whispered in my ear. He grabbed a glass for me and poured ice into it. He looked so elegant and handsome too.

"I've got it," William uttered behind me, casually shoving Tobias away. He started preparing the cocktail before I could even say yes. I wondered how many drinks he'd fixed to girls before and how that was absolutely none of my business. Tobias walked around William and stepped beside me. He wasn't intimidated by his older brother.

"That looks really good," I said as William smashed different berries with a wooden muddler.

"Here you go." He offered the finished cocktail to me. I took a sip—*mmm*—it was delicious.

"So, what's the verdict?" Tobias asked.

"This is different. Fresh. I like it." I was about to thank William for my drink, but he was gone … *again*. He was chatting with his father on the far end of the rooftop.

Tobias and I walked back to the table, and I took a seat next to Lily.

"Why do I feel like I've seen you before?" I asked Lily.

"Um, maybe we've bumped into each other in the lobby?" she replied nonchalantly.

"She's a supermodel, that's why." Eric chuckled. "She's trying to be humble about it, but her face is everywhere."

Of course. Guys that looked like *these* could easily get away with dating supermodels. And there's a ton to pick and choose from in New York City. But still, I'd seen her before, and I thought I remembered where. "Did you, by any chance, attend the Michael Kors event at the Ambassador's Residence in Paris last March? During fashion week? I feel like I saw you there," I told her.

"Yes! I did, actually. Were you there too?"

"Yes, I was."

"Are you a model?"

She must be joking. I'm not even tall enough. "No, no, no. I'm actually a photographer, well, I'm studying photography. My father hosted the event, so I was—a guest, too."

"So, your father's the United States Ambassador of France," Joel affirmed. Not a question. Everyone turned to look at me.

"Was, for the past four years." Thank God Caleb wasn't here. I'm sure he would kill me if he listened to me talking about this matter. But I couldn't live in hiding. The conversation unfolded naturally, and I didn't see any harm in that.

"So *that's* where you learned how to double cheek-kiss everyone around, huh?" William mocked me. *How long had he been standing behind me?*

"Exactly." I snorted with a weak laugh.

"And you're a photographer?" William walked around the table and faced me. I stammered through my response as I explained how I was still studying photography.

I finished what was left of my cocktail in the hopes that it would help soothe the ever-increasing nerves. I was tense about having disclosed more personal information and about William's interrogation, or was it because of his presence alone? I don't know, but I was nervous.

"Why don't you bring your camera up here?" Lily suggested. I agreed. It seemed like the perfect excuse to try out my new camera and take a few seconds to compose myself as I left to get it.

"Do you want me to come with you?" William asked with that sexy and grave voice of his in front of the entire freaking party.

"No, thanks," I replied, standing up. But my answer came out a bit rougher than I expected. What was I to say? I didn't know how to act around him.

"Ohhh! Burn!" Eric yelled. *Damn it, Eric, not helping*! A few laughs were heard after Eric's unnecessary remark, and William didn't seem pleased at all.

Fuck! He wouldn't stop staring at me with a disgruntled expression on his face.

"Let's go grab that camera," Lily said, standing up too. William ran his tongue over his teeth and shook his head a few times. "I'll go with her and make sure she returns because *you* guys are creeping her out."

Eric laughed, and William walked away to the bar and grabbed himself another beer.

"No, I—of course not, that's not what I—" I trailed off mid-sentence, unable to explain myself. But William was now talking to his father and Mr. Clark from the sixth floor.

"Come on, Billie." Lily gestured for me to follow her.

We were walking to my apartment when I told her, "Lily, I didn't mean to sound so crass up there. William seemed pretty serious after I said that. I'm so embarrassed. It's just that I—"

"You have a boyfriend, right? I get it. Don't worry about it. Eric's a jackass, and William, well … he's not been much like himself lately. He's been going through a rough patch, but he knows you have a boyfriend. He's just not so used to being rejected, if you know what I mean."

"How does he know I have a boyfriend?" I'd told them Thomas was just a friend the last time I saw them. That's why it surprised me that they knew we were dating now.

"Eric's seen you with him in the lobby a few times. You know, he has this teenage crush on you or something." She laughed as I unlocked my apartment door. "Thomas, right?"

My eyes went wide with surprise. I nodded in response.

Nosy little neighbors!

"Well, Eric assumed he was your boyfriend."

"He assumed right," I replied with a small smile. "Please, come in. I'll be right back." I gestured for Lily to come inside the apartment. She stepped into the foyer, and I went to my bedroom to grab my camera. I had been playing around with it, but I still needed a lot of practice.

"Is this Thomas?" Lily asked, looking at Thomas's portrait. I nodded. "Did you shoot it?"

"I did."

It was a front-facing black and white portrait. I absolutely loved it. It was the one I took in Paris the first night I met him. He looked *so* handsome. I swooned every time I walked inside and saw it hanging on the gallery wall. Thomas was thrilled when he saw it for the first time.

I asked Lily if she liked it. I supposed that as a model, she must've had plenty of incredible photographs of herself. "I love it," she replied, still studying the image.

"I'd love to photograph you one day."

"That would be amazing! We could have Joel's and mine printed out in this same material and hang them in our apartment. Is this acrylic?" she asked, touching the borders. I nodded as confirmation. "Let's go back before you change your mind and decide to stay here. Come on." She grabbed my arm and pulled me out of the apartment.

We went back upstairs and opened the rooftop access door to find everyone singing to the top of their lungs, including the other neighbors.

Snapsvisor," Lily told me. I didn't know what that meant. "It's Swedish drinking songs. It's tradition. They sing a song and take a small shot of aquavit, or snaps. That's what they call them. And don't get me started with the little frog dance." She laughed. "Lucky for you, we don't have a Maypole here. We usually spend holidays like these at the cottage in Sagaponack, but William wasn't feeling up for it this year. It's the first time we've celebrated it here in the city."

I wondered if William was okay. Lily mentioned before that he wasn't acting like himself lately. I was curious about what was wrong, but I didn't dare ask. Didn't want to meddle.

"Hey!" Everyone shouted in unison when they saw us come back.

"Come sing with us!" Tobias yelled in our direction while Joel offered aquavit shots to everyone. That meant I had to drink a snaps. I'd never done a shot of anything before in my entire life. They explained how I needed to sing along, even if I didn't know the words. I had to mumble whatever I could make of it, then down the shot on their cue.

We gathered around in a circle. William was laughing with Eric. I was still feeling embarrassed about my reaction when he offered to get the camera with me. But he seemed like he didn't care anymore, so I shook the thought away and accepted one of the shots that Joel was passing around instead.

We sang a song called Helan Går, well I mumbled it, of course, and then we all downed the small shot. Thankfully, people sat down to eat after that. I needed food if I was to survive these small but surely sneaky shots.

I tried every dish on the table. They were all so tasty.

"We're lucky to have Billy as our personal chef. He cooks for us every year," Tobias said, pointing at William with his fork.

Oh.

William's food was *delicious*, and somehow, I couldn't imagine him in the kitchen. It must've taken him hours to prepare everything.

William turned our way when he heard his name being mentioned. I praised him for the meal and told him the potatoes were my favorite dish. I was trying to make up for the awkward exchange we had before. He lazily met my gaze and curtsied with a nod. "Glad you liked it."

If he was going through a rough patch, as Lily said, I was sure he appreciated a few kind words for his effort. I knew what hiding pain looked like, and it was not pleasant.

We kept eating, talking, and laughing for a while. The party continued, and I took pictures of everyone, mostly candidly, hoping the camera settings were correct. I feared I would develop a film made of white-out or blotchy prints.

Lily asked me to take one of her and Joel against the rooftop railing with the New York City skyline behind them. I shot a couple of pictures of them and walked back toward Lily.

"Camera," William said behind me. I turned around, and he was extending his hand out to me. You could tell he was *very* relaxed. I removed the camera strap around my neck and gave it to him. He quickly hung the camera around his neck—at least he was reasonable. I didn't want my new camera to slip off his fingers and shatter against the floor.

"Lily." He directed with a limp hand, suggesting we stand for a photograph. He stared at the camera, trying to figure out how to work around it. I told him to click on the silver button and explained that everything had been set up.

He snapped two pictures and walked back in our direction. "You weren't in any of the photographs." He placed the camera strap around my neck and said, "But you are now."

William looked up at the sky and smiled. "Look at that. Waning crescent. You know, my grandmother used to tell me stories about the moon during the Midsummer nights we spent in Sweden when we were younger." William rested his forearms on the railing, and I stood beside him. "'Out with the old, in with the new,' she always told me. 'Let fate run its course.' I don't actually believe in all that crap, but the crescent moon's my favorite moon."

I smiled back—it was a cute story.

"I'm in the mood for something new," he whispered. "Aren't you?" His face drew dangerously near mine. I took a step back, and the rooftop access door suddenly shut with a thump.

"Well, there you are!" A gorgeous brunette with perfect shoulder-length hair snickered in our direction. William winced at the sound of her voice, and we both turned around to see her.

All you could hear was the music playing in the background.

No one dared to utter a single word.

CHAPTER 16

Never

THE ONLY ONES LEFT at the party were the four brothers, Lily and me. The rest of the adults had left by then. William marched in the brunette's direction and dropped his beer on the table as he walked by past it.

"What the hell are you doing here, Erin?" William asked through his teeth.

"You haven't been returning my calls. What was I to do?" she replied cynically, and loud enough for everyone to hear.

William walked off the rooftop, and the brunette followed close behind. I kept quiet while everyone stared at each other.

"Awkward," Eric said, breaking the silence.

"I think I should leave." It was getting late, and I was tired. I'd been there since noon, and the aquavit snaps were swimming through my bloodstream and making me sleepy. I drank a few, but they were small. You needed to drink several to make up a regular-sized shot. Still, I maintained myself collected as usual.

"You can't leave yet," Eric told me as he reached for my arm. "Pick seven flowers from anywhere you want as long as they're different." I turned to Lily, asking with my eyes if I should do it.

"Sure, it's *tradition*." She laughed. "I'll be picking mine, too." She stuck her tongue out to Joel, who pinched her waist in return.

"Put them under your pillow tonight while you sleep," Eric

instructed. "It's—for good luck." He was dead serious about it, and I hesitated for a second but walked around and gathered the seven flowers anyway. I mean, they were just flowers.

"I had so much fun getting to know you." Lily approached me for a hug. I said goodbye to everyone and stepped off the rooftop. Walking down a flight of stairs to the fourteenth floor to take the elevator, I found William arguing with the brunette just beside the elevator buttons. They both stopped talking as soon as they saw me.

I quickly apologized and told them I was about to leave. I tried to walk around William to summon the elevator, but he wouldn't move.

"Oh, I see now," she hissed, scanning me with disgust. "Is this your new pet?" She seemed like the kind of person you didn't want to mess with—furious and territorial.

"She lives here," William snapped back at her. That deep frown of his that he carried around the day I met him was back in between his eyes. I was beginning to understand the reason behind it.

"Oh, that's sweet, so she's moved in?" she asked with a venomous smirk.

Moved in? What is happening?

I was waiting for William to deny it. It wasn't my place to speak. Besides, she looked so angry, and William was drunk. I didn't belong anywhere near this conversation.

William took a step forward, and I was finally able to click the elevator's button.

"That is none of your business," William told her instead. *Oh, come on!* "It stopped being your business a few months ago, or do I need to refresh your memory?"

Why isn't he telling her that I'm just a neighbor?

"Well, I've tried to explain myself to you several times, but you're not returning any of my calls. I know how you like to play hard to get." She chuckled, closing the distance between them with a teeth-less smile.

Why is the elevator taking so long?

"There's nothing left to explain, Erin, now get the fuck *out*." William fumed as he walked up the stairs back to the rooftop. Luckily, the elevator doors opened, and I fled. Once inside, I swiftly clicked on the close door button, trying to avoid Erin from stepping inside with me.

I walked into my apartment and dropped the flowers and my purse on the foyer table. I changed into my pajamas, washed my face, and brushed my teeth. I was going to grab a glass of water when I heard a knock on my door. I rushed to see who it was and saw William through the peephole, holding my camera bag. He had brought it down for me.

Why him?

I was wearing a long pajama bottom and a tank top without a bra on, so I ran to my bedroom and quickly pulled a hoodie over my head before opening the door.

"9A," William said with a smile, but it seemed forced. "You forgot your camera." He scanned my lame pajamas a few times with sleepy eyes. "Did I wake you?"

"No, you didn't," I replied, taking the camera bag out of William's grasp. "Thank you."

I didn't want *him* to see me in my pajamas. *Thank you … now leave!*

"I—sorry about earlier," he said with lowered brows.

"Why didn't you just tell her I'm your neighbor? Who is she? She looked pissed."

"My ex. I guess she did think you were with me." He looked exhausted. Or was he just drunk? A mix of both states, for sure.

"That's because you didn't tell her otherwise." I was super annoyed by that.

"She assumed you were living *with* me when I told her you lived here. So, I ran with it." He laughed weakly—his lids heavy. "I know it's not funny. It just felt good to get to throw a punch back at her after what she did." I wanted so badly to ask what had happened, but it was not my place.

"Well, I hope she won't be waiting for me outside one of these days, wanting to punch me next." I joked. But I also wanted to hear his thoughts on that.

"She won't. I swear." He looked over my shoulder and saw the flowers behind me in the foyer. "I see you picked out your seven flowers."

"Um, yeah," I replied, looking back at them for a second. "Eric told me it's a Midsummer tradition for good luck." He smiled and shook his head, running his fingers through his silky-smooth golden hair. "Did he?"

Stop being sexy!

I felt like a cheater just by looking at him, and it was so unfair that I looked like a hooded-up Care Bear. He needed to leave, and I needed to go back inside. *Now.*

"They don't work if you don't put them under your pillow, you know? I hope they give you lots of good luck," he added, biting the tip of his tongue.

"Thank you."

"I don't know what to call you," he said as I turned my back at him. I was ready to call it a night. "I'm not calling you Billie." I realized that not once had I ever heard him call me *Billie*. He kept calling me 9A.

"And why is that? Do you want to be the only Billy in the building?"

"Guillermina," he muttered. He did an excellent job rolling his r's.

"Present," I replied, crossing my arms at my stomach. I figured Eric told him what my name was. I considered pulling out a chair, wondering if he planned to leave any time soon. I was so tired of standing by the door and having him look like … *that* while I looked like *this*.

"Guille." He pronounced it *Ghee-ye*.

That's how my mom used to call me. It felt too intimate, and it reminded me of her, so I took a deep breath and chewed my bottom lip, hoping it would hold all of my emotions in place. All I wanted was to get into my apartment and go to sleep, but William just stood there.

"Guille is fine." But was it? I thought about how I never saw him anyway. Agreeing was the fastest way to end the conversation.

"Thanks for bringing the camera over. Have a good night, William." It was hard for me to call him Billy, too. I don't know why it just felt weird.

I noticed his silence and turned around to walk back into my apartment, assuming he was ready to say goodbye too. But he twirled me by the shoulders and crushed his lips against mine. I recoiled immediately by pushing his chest and slapping him in the face.

Hard.

He cupped his left cheek, where I'd struck him, and shot one of his cocky smirks at me. He seemed to enjoy the slap even more than the stolen kiss for some reason. "Don't you *ever* try something like that again, William. I have a boyfriend." I warned him.

"If you say so," he replied, smug face and all. "I don't recall anyone pulling away from me before."

Asshole! Arrogant, asshole!

"Really? I find that hard to believe," I said with a bite. But I believed him. *Look at that ridiculously perfect face!* Who was going to pull away from him?

"Never." He grinned. I snorted and shook my head with incredulity.

"Well, consider this a first." I angrily swung the door, but he stuck his foot before I could shut it in his face.

ALEJANDRA ANDRADE

"I'll be taking care of the rest of your firsts once you're done with Thomas," he said with his gruff voice through the small opening of the door.

Thanks for the heads up, you jerk!

The *nerve* of the guy. And there I was, thinking he was nice and feeling sorry for his troubles. "Well, good luck with that." I kept pushing the door, trying to shut it.

"Guille, come on, open up."

I was done with him.

"Just stay away, William." I pushed his foot out of the way and sealed the door shut.

"Never!" he shouted. I swear I heard a laugh.

I grabbed the seven flowers and felt tempted to throw them out, but I placed them under my pillow, hoping that my luck would improve after that Midsummer Night's *Nightmare*.

CHAPTER 17

Out

June 21, 2009

I WOKE UP FEELING parched, and my hair looked crazy. The braid that went over my head like a headband was still messily in place—a reflection of how things ended the night before.

It was eleven in the morning, and I couldn't recall any time in my life when I've awakened so late. I had a few text messages from Thomas waiting for me.

The overwhelming guilt kept eating at my thoughts as I went over and over that stolen kiss in my head. But I decided not to say a word to Thomas about it, fearing his reaction. The important part was that I pulled away from William's unwelcome advances.

Thomas: Good Morning, gorgeous.
Thomas: We got silver.
Thomas: I'm finally done with the event.
Thomas: Call me when you wake up.
Thomas: Everything ok, babe?

I decided to call him instead of replying to his texts. He was probably worried about not being able to get a hold of me.

"*Hey, babe! Congrats on the silver! ... I know. I'm sorry I slept in ... My neighbors invited me to their Midsummer party on the rooftop.*

The whole building was invited ... I'm sorry I ... Hmm, at around eleven, I suppose ... I did ... Thomas, what's wrong? ... No, of course not, you know I love you, and I miss you ... I'll have someone pick you up at the airport ... Okay, text me your flight details ... See you tomorrow ... Okay, love you too ... Bye."

I felt Thomas's uneasiness about my attendance at the party without him, and I didn't blame him. He was a bit insecure, which was fine as long as he kept his jealousy in that sort of cute mode. I had been excessively controlled, monitored, and observed all my life to have my boyfriend become my fourth bodyguard.

I grabbed the crushed flowers that laid under my pillow and threw them out. I hoped I'd sucked all the good luck out of them, but I doubt I did because I dreamt of William that night. Somehow, he kept haunting me in my sleep.

I jumped into the shower and hoped the cold water would cleanse my guilt and William's stupid cologne out of my mind.

☾

June 22, 2009

"I missed you!" I said, throwing myself into Thomas's arms. He had just arrived from the airport looking exhausted but still so handsome as always. He gave me a quick peck on the lips and rolled his suitcase inside my apartment. "Are you moving in?" I joked.

"Don't tempt me." He grinned and dropped his things on the floor. "You always smell delicious. I missed that too," he whispered in my ear and kissed me.

I really missed him. When I was with Thomas, I thought of nothing and no one. He had that power over me—to fully envelop me with his presence.

Thomas squatted and grabbed a change of clothes from his suitcase. "Let me take a quick shower, and I'll see you in a few minutes."

Mimi left containers with food for me in the fridge. I heated some spaghetti and meatballs in a pan and transferred it to a service bowl feeling like a certified chef.

"Wow! Something smells great," Thomas said when he came out of my bedroom, running his fingers through his wet hair to dry it off. He wore nothing but gray sweatpants. No t-shirt. His body looked—amazing.

"Are you—hungry?" I asked while I set the table for two.

"You bet." He snatched me away and carried me over his shoulder.

"Food's gonna get cold!" I protested and laughed at the same time. He held me with one arm, which was enough to immobilize me as he walked down the hall to my bedroom.

He grabbed my waist and laid me on the bed with a thrust. "We can reheat that later." He grinned. "I thought we could jump straight to dessert instead."

He threw his warm, citrusy-smelling body that I'd missed so much against mine with a groan. There was no way I was going to object to that. I've always had a sweet tooth.

☾

"That was heaven," Thomas said as he helped me pick up the plates from the table. "I wish I had a Mimi." He laughed.

"Well, you know you're more than welcome to come to eat anytime."

My new doorbell rang. I rushed to see who it was.

"Hi, Billie!" Lily greeted me with a hug. "I was wondering if you want to grab a coffee or something. I don't have your number yet."

Thomas approached the door and froze when he saw her.

"Thomas, this is Lily, my neighbor. Lily, this is my boyfriend, Thomas."

"Hi Lily, so nice to meet you." His voice came out all weird and pitchy. I mean, Lily was just drop-dead gorgeous.

"Nice to meet you too, Thomas. I didn't realize you had company."

"Well, I—"

"No, no, no, you should go get your coffee." Thomas jumped in. "I have to run some errands anyway." He stood beside me and kissed my temple.

"Meet you downstairs in twenty, then?" Lily suggested.

"Perfect. See you there."

"Nice to meet you, Thomas."

I closed the door, and Thomas slowly whispered, "That's Lily Young," as if afraid that she would somehow have bionic hearing abilities. "She's a *supermodel.*" He whispered again when he said the last word.

"I recently found out, yes," I whispered back just to tease him. I thought it was cute that Thomas felt smitten by her presence. Thomas never gave me any reason to feel jealous or insecure.

"My friends are not going to believe me." He was beaming. Thomas grabbed my hands, cornered me against the wall, and leaned in to whisper in my ear, "But *you* are the most beautiful girl in the world." His lips brushed against my ear, making my skin react, and my knees feel week. "I love you," he whispered, tilting his head to kiss me.

"I love you too." He slowly unlocked his embrace from me and gave me one last peck on the lips.

"I'll call you later."

"Do you need a ride home?" I offered.

"That's all right, thanks. I'll grab a cab outside. Have fun, okay? Text me when you get back." I nodded and blew him a kiss as he left the apartment.

Me: Hi. I'm going out for coffee with Lily, my neighbor. Can I see you in the lobby in ten minutes? Thank you.
Aaron: Of course. David and I will be accompanying you today.

I brushed my teeth and headed downstairs to meet Lily. She was already waiting for me when I arrived. "Ready to go?" she asked with a smile.

"Ready! So, where do you want to go?"

"I thought we could walk. There's a nice coffee shop a few blocks away."

Aaron and David followed us on foot.

We went inside the cute coffee shop and sat at a small table for two. A few people stared in our direction. It was so weird. They obviously recognized Lily.

"I'm sorry," she whispered. "I know this can be awkward." It was, but I wanted to hang out with Lily and get to know her better. I reassured her by saying it was fine and that she shouldn't worry about it.

"Anyway, um … I heard about what happened after you left on Saturday." This time my blood left my face for a change. I was going to have to add extra sugar to my coffee.

"You did?" I asked with a defeated tone.

"I'm so sorry, Billie." She looked embarrassed.

"Why would you be sorry? It's not like it's your fault."

"I know I mentioned this on Saturday, but Billy's not like this at all. He's been drinking more than he should since he ended things with Erin." She was trying to excuse William's behavior.

"He's the one who should be apologizing, not you, Lily. I get that you feel terrible for him and whatever it is he's going through, but he seems old enough to take responsibility for his actions, don't you think?" I didn't know William's age, but I could tell he was a few years older than me. "Does anyone else know about this? I would prefer it if Thomas didn't find out."

"Oh, no, no, no. He only told Joel and me about it. Joel was pissed when William confessed to what he did. It didn't seem like he was sorry, though. I wouldn't expect an apology from him. That's why I wanted to talk to you about it. I wouldn't want you to think that's normal behavior in the family. I don't want Billy to make you feel uncomfortable around the rest of us either."

"Honestly, I wasn't expecting an apology. I just hoped I wouldn't bump into him anytime soon." I laughed, but it somehow came out forced. "Anyway, how old are you guys?"

"Joel's the oldest. He's 28. William's 26, Tobias is 23, Eric's 15, and I'm 22," she replied. "How old are you?" I told her I turned twenty last April.

"I'm sure you think Billy's an immature asshole." We both laughed.

"The thought crossed my mind several times," I confessed in between laughs.

A couple of bright lights coming from the outside startled me. I turned to look at the window and saw three men with huge tele-photo lenses. They were arguing with Aaron while David made a call. A paparazzo snapped a few more shots as David walked inside the coffee shop. People were now *really* staring at us.

"Miss Murphy, sorry to disturb you. Caleb's on his way with the car. It's best if we leave. Walking is not an option. We don't want these men to follow us back to the apartment and see where you both live." I nodded, and he excused himself but remained on the inside of the coffee shop near the entrance. Aaron kept trying to get the paparazzi to leave.

"Lily, are you okay with leaving?" I was flustered.

"Oh, of course. This is uncomfortable. I'm now considering getting a couple of these guys for myself." She laughed.

"I'm sorry. It feels like we got cut short. Is it always like this for you?" I asked while we waited for Caleb to arrive.

"It wasn't. I mean not before—" she broke off.

"Before what, Lily?" I pressed.

"Um, before I—landed a big modeling contract," she said, but I felt like that wasn't what she was about to say.

"Miss Murphy, Caleb's arrived. Please follow me." He nodded at both of us.

We walked out of the coffee shop, and one of the cameras hit my left cheekbone. Hard. David got in between the paparazzo and me, and before I even had a chance to cower, he knocked the guy down. Aaron grabbed my arm and placed me inside the car. Lily jumped in a second after me with David, who shut the door behind him.

"Red, are you okay?" Caleb said, looking at me through the rearview mirror, driving away from the scene. He didn't care about the formalities. He seemed worried and upset.

"I'm fine. Just a bit startled."

"Billie, I'm so sorry," Lily whispered. "This is all my fault."

"It's okay. It doesn't hurt." It did. My cheek was throbbing with pain, but I didn't want her to feel responsible about it because it wasn't her fault at all.

Caleb circled around a few blocks just to make sure no one was following us and then dropped us off at the apartment building entrance. He tossed the keys to Aaron and escorted us inside.

The elevator doors opened in the distance. William came out with a small rolling suitcase, wearing workout clothes and head-phones around his neck.

"Hey, lover," William whispered with a smirk as he walked beside me. My blood boiled at his cynicism. But Lily was right; he would never apologize.

"Billy! Where are you going?" Lily shouted, but he didn't stop. "I need to talk to you!"

"Out!" he replied dryly, without looking back. Senad opened

the door for him, and he walked out of the building. His driver took William's suitcase, and he jumped in the back of the car.

"I think he's been permanently damaged," Lily uttered to herself. "I'm sorry, Billie." She looked worried and ashamed.

"Lily, you need to stop apologizing for him. It's okay. I can take care of myself."

"I bet you can." She chuckled. "His cheek was blazing red when he came back from your apartment on Saturday. We could still see your fingers branded on his face. That's why Joel questioned him in the first place. I don't think that any girl has ever slapped him before."

Damn it! I was sure that Caleb heard that.

I whispered how I never intended to slap him, that it was the first time I've ever done that in my entire life.

William's words came flashing back to me. *I'll be taking care of the rest of your firsts once you're done with Thomas.* I was furious again, and Lily must've seen it on my face.

"Billie, did something else happen that night? You can tell me. I need to know if he—"

"No! Nothing happened," I whispered and pulled her away. I didn't need Caleb to find out about the drama that went down on Saturday.

Lily looked at me with incredulous eyes. "You know you can trust me, right? I'm leaving tomorrow for a few days, but I'll call you when I get back so that we can hang out." She took her phone out. "Here, could you type your number for me?" I typed it down as we walked inside the elevator.

"I'll walk you, Miss Murphy." Caleb stepped in with a letter-sized white envelope and a scary face. We all went quiet as the elevator made its way up.

"I'll text you, okay?" Lily said when the doors opened on the ninth floor. Caleb held the door for me.

"Okay. Thank you, Lily. I'll see you soon." I hugged her and walked out with Caleb. I didn't want to make any eye-contact with him. That's how he read me.

"This was in your mailbox." He gave me the white envelope with my name written on the front, *Guillermina Murphy*. I thanked him and turned around to unlock my apartment door, hoping that was the end of our interactions for the day. But it wasn't.

"What happened on Saturday?" he asked sharply. *There you go.* "I heard your conversation with Miss Young. Who slapped who? Did that asshole say or do something to upset you?" He stared into my eyes, letting me know that he wasn't backing down from this.

"He was a bit drunk. His girlfriend showed up and made a scene. He's not in a good place; at least that's what his family keeps telling me." I tried escaping into my apartment.

"Red, come back here," he snapped. I stopped, took a deep breath, and dropped my bag and envelope on the foyer table.

"Nothing hap—"

"I need to know," he insisted. "It's my job to take care of you, and I can't do my job if you don't talk to me." *A job.* I *hated* it when he said that. He was probably looking for stuff to put on the boring reports they prepared for my father.

"I bumped into him and his ex arguing when I was leaving the party. She—slapped him for some reason."

"Are you sure that's it?"

"Mhm," I hummed calmly.

"If I find out that he hurt you …" His burning gaze promised retaliation. William was for sure getting blacklisted. I could see his name right there beside Thomas's.

"Caleb, you need to calm down. He did no such thing, and you need to *listen* when I talk to you. Nothing happened. I'm fine."

He looked uneasy.

"I knew we shouldn't have allowed you to go on your own," he said, rubbing his forehead and looking away.

"Caleb, I had a good time, and nothing happened, okay?" My insides churned as I kept lying to him.

"No more going anywhere alone, especially if you hang out with—*them*. If your father found out that we weren't there with you on Saturday—"

"But he won't," I interrupted. "And you're not going to tell him, so there's nothing to worry about because *nothing* happened."

Caleb finally backed down. He took a deep breath. "I should've been with you at the coffee shop today, I—"

"It was nobody's fault. And David's a total badass." I chuckled as I remembered the photographer landing on his butt. Caleb snorted, unwilling to yield a smile.

"I hate to see your face like that," he said, lowering his brows.

"It doesn't hurt." I lied. Again.

Caleb pressed his lips into a line, looking defeated. "We'll be downstairs. I'll need to report the paparazzi incident to your father. I don't know where those pictures are going to end up, so he needs to know beforehand just in case they show up somewhere."

I nodded. "I understand. Thank you." I smiled, but he didn't. He turned around and left. I knew he genuinely worried and wanted what was best for me. But I hated lying! And not only did I lie to Caleb, but I also had to leave things out when talking to Thomas about the party.

I blamed it all on William and his stupidly perfect face that I wished I could slap again.

CHAPTER 18

Älskling

I SAT IN THE LIVING ROOM to open my newly arrived mystery correspondence. There were two smaller envelopes inside. Each had a number written on it, 1 and 2.

There was also a snack-sized Ziploc bag with two film rolls in it. I followed the exact instructions and opened the envelope with the number one on it first. There was a handwritten letter inside that read:

Guille,
You're on the right track to becoming a great photographer, älskling. But I think my shots were way better, so I made you a copy of the best photograph I took last Saturday. In case you want to learn a thing or two about how to take a good picture.
W.S.
P.S. I have a copy, and it looks great on my nightstand.

William sent it, and I couldn't shake the thought of what would've happened if I opened this in front of Thomas. He would surely think the worst. I probably would, too, if I were him.

What does älskling mean?

I moved on to the second envelope, and there was a photograph of me inside it. When William took my camera, I saw him clicking twice. This was a zoomed-in photograph of just my face, smiling. Lily had been cropped out of the frame.

The doorbell rang, and the sound of it startled me. "Billie! It's Thomas!" he shouted over the door. I quickly threw everything back inside the envelope and shoved it underneath the sofa.

"Coming!" I shouted back.

"Babe, your cheek is red. What happened?" Thomas said as soon as I opened the door.

I was so caught up reading William's letter and agitated about having to hide it underneath the freaking couch that I forgot about my face. I hadn't even looked at myself in the mirror.

"Oh, that. Um, these photographers were taking pictures of Lily at the coffee shop, and one of them hit me with his camera when we were leaving."

"What? Who was on duty?" He wanted to blame someone, but it wasn't anyone's fault but the photographer's. David couldn't have been standing any closer to me when it happened.

"They handled it pretty well. It doesn't matter. It doesn't hurt."

Thomas ran to the kitchen and brought back a small bag of peas. He lightly pressed it on my cheek. I hissed. "Ow!"

"I thought you said it didn't hurt. Let me take care of you."

"Aren't you cute?" I smiled. "Speaking of cute ..." Lily mentioned how Thomas was cute and seemed like a nice guy, so I relayed her evaluation to him. He couldn't hide his endearing excitement nor his genuine surprise. I thought it was adorable, though, and thought nothing of it other than what it was—he was starstruck.

"I think I'm getting a bit jealous now," I toyed around with the idea as he held the frozen peas against my cheekbone.

"I think *you're cute* when you're jealous," Thomas replied, pulling my chin up, looking down into my eyes.

"Well, in that case, I'm *very* jealous," I stretched out the joke.

He threw the frozen pea bag on the floor and lifted me. I

wrapped my legs around his waist and my arms behind his neck.

"I'm a bit jealous, too." His tone suggested he was veering away from the innocent game we were playing. "I'm always jealous." He kissed my neck.

That threw me off a bit.

He carried me to the living room and threw himself back on the couch in a seated position. I landed on top of him with a gasp. I took his cap off and ran my fingers through his messy hair. I couldn't fully understand what could make this beautiful person in front of me, making me drool, feel insecure. All I wanted to do was kiss him and have him kiss me back, but his eyes were gloomy.

I straight out asked him what made him feel this way, wondering if I would regret asking such a question. But his eyes were begging me to ask, and I would usually find it hard to deny him.

He took a deep breath and slowly exhaled as if organizing his thoughts to answer. It was making me feel like there wasn't something specific he had in mind but an overall sense of doubt that made him feel this way.

"I don't know. I keep thinking about that party you went to on Saturday." He lowered his brows. Well, I guess that was specific, and he wasn't kidding. I wanted to know what he needed to know to help him put his mind at ease.

We had previously talked about this, so I thought we had cleared the party already, but Thomas wanted more details. And I hated that I was probably going to have to lie to him regarding a few questions if he made them.

And just so, he started *grilling* me on the specifics of the event: Who attended, who I hung out with, who I hung out with *the most*.

I moved to sit beside him and answered thoroughly and with no hesitation. I enumerated the guests by their name and apartment number and explained how I hung out with Lily most of the time, having admitted that I got to talk to everyone. I told him it was important for me to meet my neighbors. Still, he wasn't satisfied; he wanted more.

He continued with what felt like a full-on interrogation. He asked again if I had drunk any alcohol—a question he knew the answer to. That, too, had been previously discussed. "I did, but only a spritzer and a few shots." I innocently shrugged.

"Shots? Since when you drink shots?" He was getting pretty fired up. After his reaction, I immediately regretted having answered that question the way I did—even at all.

I tried explaining how they weren't normal-sized shots but tiny glasses that didn't hold much alcohol in them and how it's part of a tradition where they sing different tunes and drink the shots afterward.

I smiled a little as I reminisced on the events of that day. I had a lot of fun. And the feeling of freedom of not having my bodyguards with me made it even more special. That reminded me how I hadn't mentioned that *little* detail to him, and I hoped his cross-examination wouldn't lead there.

"So, you were drunk?" he asked. I denied it because it wasn't true. Thomas sighed with exasperation and straightened himself in his seat. I wasn't *drunk* in the way he was asking. I was fully aware and in control the whole time. It's as if he wanted me to tell him I was super drunk so that he could have an actual reason to make a fuss out of nothing.

His speculations were annoying, and my answers were slowly dripping with indignation—hoping he'd notice it and turn it down a few notches.

"At least Aaron and Caleb were there to take care of you," he said with ironic relief.

But of course, he would go there!

In a dramatic turn of events, I decided to give myself up instead of getting away with it by simply nodding—essentially cuffing myself and throwing away the key.

"I went on my own," I confessed to the *crime*. Thomas shook his head slowly, looking at the floor as if he were discovering a new-found ability that consisted of willing things to combust on themselves. A deep frown drew between his eyes.

"I don't like this, Billie. I don't like this at all."

I didn't understand what the problem was. Thomas had made it clear he didn't like or approve of it. But again, why? Did he only date girls with bodyguards? How did he cope with situations like these before?

Shameful guilt slithered around me as I remembered how William threw himself at me because *I did* wonder what that kiss might've felt like if I hadn't pulled away. One too many times—more than I should've.

Maybe Thomas was right, and I was in dire need of twenty-four-hour surveillance in the interest of being a complacent girl-friend. But I did pull away from that *menacing, threatening, imminent kiss*, and that ought to count for something, right?

Having drifted away into thought, I ushered my mind to come back online. *For how long has Thomas been staring?*

"I don't like you going to parties on your own and getting drunk with dudes."

I stared back after having winced almost imperceptibly—*that tone.*

"I don't think you're listening," I replied with a lazy frown, introspecting, after realizing that our conversation was redundant. Nothing he said was new to me, and he was making me feel like shit too.

"Damn it, Billie!" Thomas shouted and banged his hand on the coffee table, making me shy a few inches away from him. He then rested his elbows over his knees and angrily ran his fingers through his hair. This exaggerated reaction was unlike him, and I pondered for a few seconds on other factors that might be triggering his behavior.

The envelope hiding right beneath Thomas's seat had a beating heart of its own. With every throb and pulse resonating inside my head, I somehow feared it would grow feet and crawl from underneath him to reveal itself. It wouldn't surprise me if it were programmed to do so.

"Promise me you won't go anywhere without me." His gaze begging every word to me.

"I—don't understand what you're asking, Thomas," I asked for clarification because after seeing him react, I couldn't keep assuming things. I needed to know *exactly* what he meant and what he needed to be at peace.

"I can't lose you." He grabbed his cap and placed it backward on his head. His response led to my initial suspicion: he was feeling jealous and insecure.

I kept uselessly insisting on how it was *one* party I had gone to on the rooftop of the building I lived in and questioned him why on Earth he would lose me to *that*? Why the lack of trust?

"I love you." I really did, and he needed to hear that—to remember that.

"I'm sorry. I love you too. Come here." He stood up and opened his arms for me, an invitation to embrace him. I rose from my seat and slowly walked into his arms, making sure that the storm had passed.

"I'm sorry, babe. I'm just bushed from the trip. You know I trust you." He continued apologizing as he held the hug.

"Is everything okay at home, Thomas?" I pressed my good cheek firmly against his chest. "You know you can talk to me." His heart fluttered from the previous agitation.

I could tell he was having mood swings and frequently displaying an unhealthy amount of jealousy. In my opinion, his reaction was *not* normal. There had to be something going on for him to snap like that. He startled me when he hit the coffee table. That got me speculating on what his reaction would've been like if he knew what went down with William.

"It's my mom. She's not been doing so well lately," he finally admitted. "She's been asking me to come home for the summer. I told her about how I'd rather stay here with you, but she keeps insisting, and I've been trying to avoid going back altogether."

"I'm so sorry to hear that." I was genuinely worried. "As much as I'd love for you to stay here with me, I wouldn't mind if you went to see her. She might need you. What are you going to do?"

"I don't know yet. I could go for the three weeks that your summer course lasts. I have a single scull in D.C., so I could train while I'm there too, which would be convenient." He reached out to embrace me once again. "I'm not sure if I want to leave you yet."

If my mother would still be alive, I'd want to see her, especially if she were begging me to go. His family situation was complicated, but it made me think about how we tend to take people and things for granted.

"If you don't go now, you won't see her until Thanksgiving, and that's a long time. I think you should seriously consider going, even if it's only for a few days."

"I guess you're right. I'll talk to her tomorrow, but right now, I want to hang out with my girlfriend if that's okay with you."

"Sounds good to me," I replied with a wearied smile.

Thomas left a couple of hours later, and I immediately ran to the living room and retrieved the white envelope from underneath the cushion. I wanted nothing more than to build a bonfire and burn the entirety of its contents. Instead, I placed the photograph and film rolls in my nightstand drawer, read the letter one more time, and tore it into a million tiny pieces.

I had left my phone in my purse the entire time Thomas was

with me, so I changed into my pajamas and laid on my bed to check on my messages.

Thomas: I'm so sorry about today, babe. I feel awful. I'll make it up to you, I swear. I love you.
Me: Don't worry. I love you too. GN.

I spotted a text by an unknown number, so I assumed it was Lily.

Unknown: Hej älskling.

You've got to be kidding me. When I read the text, I assumed it was William. And yes, I assumed right.

I needed to look up the meaning of that word as soon as possible. It made me nervous to see that he fired this text when Thomas was still in my apartment. Luckily, I'd left my phone in my purse. It wouldn't surprise me if someday Thomas asked me if he could go through my messages, or worse, did it without my consent.

Me: Where'd you get my number?

William replied to my text a few seconds later.

Unknown: I see you've received my special delivery.
Me: I still don't know what älskling means, but yes, I did, and you're a thief btw.
W.S.: You're a smart girl. Look it up. I borrowed your film and returned it. That's not stealing.
Me: Seriously, where'd you get my number?
W.S.: Lily gave it to me. It wasn't easy, though. I told her I wanted to apologize for everything, so that did the trick.
Me: That's the worst apology I've ever heard.

W.S.: That's because I'm not apologizing.

Me: I can imagine it's not something you would know how to do.

W.S.: I will never be sorry for kissing you.

Me: We did NOT kiss. You launched at me, and I slapped you away. Know the difference.

W.S.: Fun, wasn't it?

Me: Jerk.

W.S.: I know.

Me: Stop texting me.

W.S.: Never.

Ughhh! I was tempted to throw my phone out the window.

I had another text from a new contact. This one was actually from Lily. She sent it before William did, trying to let me know she had shared my contact with him.

Unknown: Hi! It's Lily.

Unknown: William asked for your number. I didn't want to give it to him at first, but he insisted. He mentioned how he wanted to apologize. I think that's progress. I just wanted to give you a heads up.

Me: Hey Lily! Don't worry about it, but he didn't apologize. He did the exact opposite. I think I'm just going to block him.

Lily: What? What happened?

Me: Long story short. He "borrowed" Saturday's film from my camera. He must've grabbed it on his way to return my bag. He returned it to my mailbox and wanted to make sure I received it AND let me know he wasn't sorry at all.

Lily: OMG!!! This is getting out of hand. I'll talk to Joel.

Me: Please don't. I think it's best if we just all ignored him. He's probably just bored or something.

Lily: Hmm. Maybe. I'll talk to you soon.

I opened Google Translate and looked up the word: älskling. I bit my lower lip and shook my head at the screen after seeing the translation result.

SWEDISH	ENGLISH
älskling	darling

A smile wanted to draw itself on my face, but I forced it to vanish. After seriously considering changing my phone number, I thought it would only raise more questions with Thomas and Caleb. I knew Caleb reported back to my father.

I grabbed my phone and clicked the block button ten times in a row instead, hoping William would feel it all the way to wherever "*out*" was.

Never my ass.

CHAPTER 19

Jealousy

June 26, 2009

THOMAS AND I were enjoying his summer schedule more than ever. He knew what I liked, how to pamper me, and now that we had more time, we loved spending it just the two of us, alone—savoring and enjoying every moment. I felt so happy and lucky to have him. We loved taking long walks in Central Park, where I would always take my camera and take pictures of everything I saw, but most were of him.

Our typical Friday routine of going out for dinner was changing this weekend. We were invited to Michael Taylor's birthday party, one of Thomas's best friends from Princeton.

I was excited about finally meeting his friends for the first time because I thought it would allow me to know Thomas better. His schedule had been so hectic that we usually spent the little time we had just the two of us.

Thomas arrived at my apartment. He looked so handsome, wearing black jeans and a white dress shirt with a few top buttons undone. I kissed him and rushed back to my bedroom to put my shoes on.

I stepped into the foyer feeling like a million bucks. My cheekbone was still bruised from the blow, but I covered it with makeup—you could barely see it.

"I'm ready." I smiled, waiting for the usual compliment.

Thomas lifted one of his brows, stared at my legs, and said, "Is *that* what you're wearing?"

Uh, yeah.

I wore a simple, elegant little black dress—nothing too fancy or revealing. It was perfect for the occasion, and I honestly didn't understand what he meant by *that*. I've never owned or worn tacky clothes.

I looked down and examined myself, trying to figure out what the problem was.

"It's too short. Go change," he said, rubbing his jaw and looking away.

Excuse me! It really wasn't.

"Thomas, this is not short at all. I've worn shorter skirts with you before. I'm *not* changing. This is *not* too short, and we're running late."

He stared at me, as if trying to decide what to say next. "Everyone's going to be looking at your legs, and I'm not sure if I'm comfortable with that."

I couldn't believe what I was hearing! Not once did my father ever say such a thing to me. I was so upset by both his remark and the tone he used to express it. He didn't mind short skirts as long as I only wore them with him?

Red fucking flag.

"I'm not changing. If you don't like what I'm wearing, then you can go to the party on your own." I wasn't backing down. I would *not* change my outfit because he *thought* my legs were showing too much.

It was completely absurd! Despite that, he didn't reply. I took his silence as a response and turned around to *change* into my pajamas.

He grabbed my arm and apologized, but I brushed his hand off. I was furious!

"Babe, come on." He insisted and offered his hand to me, but I took a few seconds longer than usual to reach out for it.

He made me feel cheap, and I've never been the one to wear the shortest skirt or dress *ever*. It just wasn't my style. I was confident that the dress looked perfect on me.

He begged for a few minutes, and I agreed to go to the party, but I couldn't shake off the frustration. Thomas seemed to notice that because he immediately placed his arms around me when we were on our way to the party and whispered in my ear, "I didn't say I didn't like the dress." His finger slowly brushed down my arm—trying to distract me, but I couldn't help but worry. His jealousy wasn't *cute* anymore.

David and Aaron were on duty that night, but Caleb did a last-minute switch on David, so we were going to have a classic Aaron–Caleb combo for the party.

Hurray.

Caleb had been true to his word. No way he would let me go to a party alone with Thomas. He wasn't kidding. Caleb wanted to be there himself. And I would lie if I said it didn't make me feel safer to know he was coming.

I kept quiet most of the time and even considered dropping off Thomas there and head back home afterward. I sensed my silence made him feel guilty and uncomfortable. "Babe, come on. You look beautiful. You know that's not the problem. I know *I'm* the problem. Please, just say something."

I could see Caleb's reflection in the rearview mirror. He was undoubtedly listening to Thomas's apologies, most likely wondering what had gone down.

I looked away—such a busybody.

"I've told you a million times before. There is nothing to worry about. Sometimes I feel like you don't trust me or something," I whispered.

"I'm sorry, of course I trust you. I just hate the idea of someone else looking at you. There's going to be a bunch of guys from school, and it drives me crazy. Please—let's have a good time. I swear you look beautiful. I know I was a jerk before."

It was safe to say that Caleb had overheard our conversation because Thomas had *not* whispered his reply at all.

Thomas and I had a full week to ourselves before he left for three weeks, and I didn't want to spend the night sulking. I had to attempt to have a good time. He seemed genuinely sorry.

Caleb parked the car, tossed the keys to Aaron, and followed us toward the building. We had previously agreed that they would wait for us outside as we attended the party. Clearly, he'd changed his mind at the very last minute. I asked Thomas if he could let me have a word with Caleb before going in.

"Caleb, what are you doing?" I muttered through my teeth.

"I'm coming inside. It's Friday. I'm in the mood to join your party," he said with an annoyed expression on his face—so festive.

"Stop. You promised you'd wait outside. Besides, you're leaving Aaron out here alone? It's going to be a few hours," I kept whispering.

"I wouldn't do that. David's on his way. He'll stay out here with Aaron, you know, to keep him company. It's going to be fun. Come on, your boyfriend's waiting." He started herding me toward Thomas.

I balked and insisted on how coming inside with us wasn't necessary.

"It is when I can see you're clearly upset about something, and I can hear your boyfriend begging for forgiveness. I'm not letting you out of my sight. It's in my job description, now let's go."

I knew I wasn't going to win this argument, and I *definitely* didn't want to get into any more details with Caleb about my relationship with Thomas. "Just keep your distance, okay. I'm meeting his friends, and I don't want it to be awkward."

I was about to turn around to walk back to Thomas when Caleb whispered, "*I* like your dress, and *he's* insane." I bit on the inside of my cheek, trying to prevent my face from giving away any reaction to his comment.

"Everything okay, babe?" Thomas asked.

"Sure, just going through the logistics." I looked over my shoulder, and Caleb smiled proudly, so I stuck my tongue out to him.

Michael's parents' apartment was amazing. A large black and white sculpture greeted us in the foyer, and the floor to ceiling windows overlooked the Hudson River. The walls were lined with artwork after artwork. It looked like an art gallery.

You could hear the music getting louder as we approached the gathering. "Michael! Happy birthday, man," Thomas said, hugging him with a few pats on the back. "This is my girlfriend, Billie."

"Hi, Billie, so nice to finally meet you. This is Dana, my girlfriend," Michael said with his pearly-white million-dollar smile that contrasted beautifully with his dark brown skin. He was tall and athletic like Thomas. They rowed crew together.

Dana was short and had curly blonde hair. They made a cute couple. "So nice to meet you," I replied to both of them. Thomas kept close to me, with his hand on my waist.

"Tommy!" yelled someone behind us. "You've had me waiting." I turned around and saw a guy with flawless buttered-toast brown hair, eyes to match, wearing designer clothes and shoes. I've never heard anyone call him *Tommy* before. I felt like the nickname didn't suit Thomas.

"Billie, this is Nicholas. Nicholas, this is my girlfriend, Billie," Thomas said, tightening his grip on my waist.

"Tommy, she's *hot,*" he said, scanning me and taking a sip of what looked like whiskey. "I didn't know you were into gingers now. I guess it's always good to mix it up, right?"

Asshole! Hot? Mix it up? I was surprised that Thomas didn't have anything to say to that, considering how volatile he could be. But I could sense his uneasiness, and Nicholas made me extremely uncomfortable too.

"Tommy and I have some quick catching up to do. Why don't you get drinks for the ladies, Michael?" Thomas mouthed the word "sorry" to me as Nicholas placed his arm around his shoulders and took him away. I guess parties were not my forte.

Thomas had never mentioned Nicholas before. I wondered how close they were.

"Would you like something to drink?" Michael offered as a distraction. I nodded with wide eyes, making Dana laugh. I guess she completely understood my need to take the edge off.

"Nicholas doesn't have a filter. He always speaks his mind, and we usually just ignore him." It was kind of her to try to reassure me. "More people are arriving, Michael. Why don't you go greet them? I'll help Billie with her drink."

Dana was drinking red wine, so I just asked for the same. No more shots for me this time. Maybe ever.

Thomas came back after a few minutes. He wasn't gone for too long. I felt relieved since I didn't know anybody, and although Dana seemed friendly, I didn't want her to feel the need to babysit me.

Thomas grabbed an old-fashioned glass and poured some whiskey in it. He downed it, poured himself another, and took my hand. "Everything okay?" I asked. It seemed to me like he was on a mission to get drunk.

"Of course!" he beamed. "Let's have some fun."

Thomas introduced me to most of his friends. They all seemed nice—unlike Nicholas. I hoped I didn't have to talk to him again for the rest of the night.

Dana and I sat on a couch and got to know each other a bit more while Thomas talked to some of his friends. She told me how she also went to Princeton and met Michael there. They've been dating for over a year now. She was also a sophomore like Thomas and Michael.

I was drinking my second glass of wine, and Thomas had refilled his whiskey more than a few times already. I saw Caleb walking around in the distance and looking our way, ignoring a couple of girls who tried to approach him.

Thomas pulled me up from my seat and introduced me to another friend of his who had just arrived at the party.

"This is Billie." He clutched my face and kissed me. I carefully pulled away from him with a bit of a scrunched-up face. That was the weirdest introduction ever. His lips tasted like alcohol.

He placed his hand on my waist and *accidentally* drifted too low for my liking. I didn't mind him doing that, just not at a party in front of all of his friends.

Thomas pulled me to the bar. He wanted to refill his drink, but I didn't think it was a good idea. "Thomas, you're drunk already. Take it easy, okay?"

He kissed my hair and smiled at me. "I'm good." I couldn't smile back. I was worried.

My phone buzzed. A text from Caleb. I read it while Thomas refilled his drink for the millionth time.

Caleb: He's drinking too much. I can see you're uncomfortable. Do you want to SOS it?
Me: No. It's okay. I'll take care of it.
Caleb: Red, come on. Look at him. He's gonna fall asleep standing up any second now.
Me: He's not THAT drunk. Don't worry. I'll ask him if we can leave in a few minutes.
Caleb: I'm not comfortable with his behavior around you while he's drunk.

I couldn't have agreed more with Caleb. But I wasn't going to unleash him on Thomas. I was worried enough as it was, and I didn't need him all over me about it either.

Me: I'm not comfortable either. Let me handle it.

"Let's dance." *Oh, no.* Thomas downed the rest of his whiskey and pulled me toward the center of the apartment, where a few people danced. He grabbed my hands and placed them around his neck. "This reminds me of Paris," he mumbled. I mean, it did if you thought about the whiskey and the dancing, but he wasn't hammered then so no. It didn't remind me of Paris. At all.

It even felt less like Paris when he fondled me in front of everyone as he danced with his body attached to mine. "I can't wait to take that dress off of you."

Sure, he was hot as freaking hell, and he was my boyfriend, but I didn't feel comfortable with his behavior. He wasn't himself.

Nicholas kept staring at us in the distance, and I tried looking for Caleb, but I couldn't place him. He was stealthy, as I had asked him to be, but I knew he was watching.

Thomas was *so drunk* that he didn't even care or notice when I pulled away from him uncomfortably. Instead, he excused himself to go to the restroom and half-stumbled on his way there. I blinked twice, and Nicholas appeared in front of me. *Fuck.*

"It's always the shy ones," he said, lifting his brow.

"Excuse me?"

"The shy ones are always the naughty ones," he whispered in my ear.

Nicholas thought that I was a floozy because of Thomas's drunken behavior while we danced. If he was so intently looking our way, he must've seen how I kept trying to pull away. But why should I care about Nicholas's opinion anyway? Screw him. He was just trying to get under my skin.

I didn't want to spend any more time talking to Nicholas, of all people. But he grabbed my arm when he saw my intention to leave. "I'm just kidding, ginger. How's your evening going?" His eyes were bloodshot. I didn't answer. I didn't want him to feel welcome to a chit chat.

"You need a refill. Let me take care of it for you." Nicholas was talking to himself because, for all I knew, we weren't having a conversation.

"Come on, loosen up a bit," he said, placing his hand on my shoulder and gripping it. "You've had like one. But you don't seem like you need much to—"

"No, thanks." I cut him off, brushing his tedious hand away from my shoulder.

Where's Thomas?

I finally saw Caleb stepping out of the shadows and sauntering toward the living room. There were more people around us, but Nicholas made me feel extremely uneasy.

"I'm just going to grab some water," I said, walking away.

"Dance with me," he said, pulling my arm. "I know Tommy doesn't mind sharing with me every once in a while." I angrily shoved Nicholas's hand off my arm, and Caleb blasted off in our direction, clicking on his earpiece.

No!

"Sir, I'm going to ask you back off," Caleb ordered with a calm tone as his hands rested in a single and relaxed fist in front of him.

"Caleb, I've got it. Thank you." I *clearly* didn't have things under control. I was having trouble making that jerk leave me alone. Nicholas was that annoying buzzing mosquito you keep flapping around, but it keeps coming back to get you. But I didn't want to make a scene. People were starting to stare once Caleb joined us.

I took a deep breath when I saw Thomas making his way back to me.

Finally.

"Damn!" Nicholas snickered. "Tommy didn't mention you had a security detail and shit." He looked amused; his glare reciprocated by Caleb's.

"What's going on?" Thomas asked.

"I see you finally got yourself a decent girl here, Tommy. Daddy must be proud." He patted Thomas's back a few times with an exaggerated grin.

I glanced at Thomas, wondering why he wouldn't shove this prick away because Caleb was a second away from doing it if he didn't. Aaron and David walked in and stood next to Caleb.

"Backup!" Nicholas hollered with a hysterical laugh. He drained his whiskey and left the glass on a cocktail table behind him. "I see the appeal, Tommy. Not that she didn't come here looking like a whole snack. Is she a good la—"

"Shut the fuck up," Thomas said, pushing him away.

"Don't fucking touch me," Nicholas replied, echoing Thomas's shove. "You're already walking on thin ice." *What?*

"Mr. Hill. Let's go," Aaron said in a commanding voice as Nicholas and Thomas kept pushing at each other's chests.

"That's it. We're leaving." Caleb grabbed my arm and started toward the front door. I looked over my shoulder and saw Thomas landing a blow on Nicholas's jaw. *Shit!*

Nicholas struck back at Thomas, but Aaron and David split them in two seconds. I walked out of there with tears running down my face. Caleb followed close behind.

"Damn it. Aaron's got the keys," Caleb said when we stepped outside of the apartment building. "Hey, are you okay?" I wasn't. Not even close. I couldn't stop the stupid tears coming out of my eyes. "Come here."

Caleb hugged me, and I rested my cheek on his chest. He knew how to make me feel safe.

"We're downstairs. She's with me," Caleb said, pressing on his earpiece, his arms still tightly placed around me. "They're coming back. It's best if we—"

"Oh, of course," I replied, breaking away from his embrace. He brushed the tears off my face. "Ow." My cheek was still a bit bruised where the camera struck me.

"I feel like I'm failing you," he said, pressing his lips and shaking his head. "I hate to see you hurting."

"I'm okay," I said—my voice trembling. I reached out for his warm hand, and he held it, taking a quick look behind his shoulder. I could tell he was uneasy about Thomas coming back with Aaron and David. But Thomas didn't seem to care about me tonight. All he cared about was getting drunk. "And you're doing the opposite of failing me. You're always here for me. Thank you."

Caleb nodded. And I had to bite my lips to keep myself from crying again. We stood there in silence, just staring into each other's eyes. All I saw was kindness. My heart ached a bit. I loved Thomas, but did he love me? All those things Nicholas said, I couldn't stop thinking about them and what they meant.

Aaron and David appeared behind Caleb, escorting Thomas, who ambled in our direction with a bleeding lip. I quickly dropped Caleb's hand. I don't think anyone saw us. And Thomas could barely open his eyes, anyway.

Aaron opened the door for me. I got in, and Thomas hopped in behind me. Caleb walked around the car and sat next to me.

"I'm so sorry," Thomas whispered, cupping my cheek. I recoiled from his touch and said nothing. It was becoming a pattern—a repetitive, never-ending Möbius loop kind of pattern. And I was trapped there with him.

Tiny crimson drops trickled on his bright white dress shirt.

He looked away and threw a punch at the car's window. He looked pissed. I instinctively flinched away from him and grabbed Caleb's arm, but I quickly let go of him. It'd been an automatic reaction.

Luckily, the SUV was armored, and it took more than Thomas's drunken fist to do any damage, but it was enough to get on everyone's nerves.

"Mr. Hill, sir, I'm going to have to ask you to calm down." Aaron roared from the driver's seat, making Thomas's mouth twist to the side. He held his hands up, trying to placate the situation. I was so disappointed in his behavior.

Caleb placed his hand on top of mine and squeezed it as if trying to let me know that everything was going to be okay, that he was right there for me. He always was.

Thankfully, nobody said a word for the rest of the drive back to my apartment because I was saving all my words for later. And Caleb's hand gave me all the comfort I needed.

CHAPTER 20

Explanations

CALEB ESCORTED US all the way to my door, which he only did when I was alone. "I'll be here if you need anything, Miss Murphy," he said, looking at Thomas. His voice sounded more like a warning. He seemed rattled and planned to wait outside until Thomas left.

We were all upset, but Thomas's lip didn't look great. I wanted to help him get it cleaned up and attempt to have a conversation, if possible, hoping the adrenaline rush from the fight might've toned down his level of intoxication.

I walked back to the living room with a small first aid kit I kept in the foyer closet and saw Thomas sprawled across the sofa. He objected as soon as he noticed my intentions. "Your lip is still bleeding. Look at your shirt." It was blood-stained here and there. "Let's hope you don't need any stitches."

I knelt beside him to check on his lip, and he winced as I slowly tapped it with a small disinfectant cloth, but he allowed me to finish cleaning the wound. I gave him a clean napkin and told him to apply pressure on the cut, hoping it would start clotting as I fetched a couple of glasses of water from the kitchen.

I wanted to know everything about Nicholas. His relationship with him, for how long he knew him, how close they were. The nickname *Tommy* made me guess they went way back, probably childhood friends.

Everything Nicholas said at the party shocked and affected me. It made me feel like there was another Thomas I didn't know—one that was already starting to do a terrible job at keeping his true self in hiding.

Thomas sat up straight to answer my questions. "We have a complicated friendship, but yeah, he is my childhood friend from D.C." Complicated—you don't say! Besides, he didn't seem *friendly* at all. Nicholas's suggestive remarks had hurt me, and my eyes welled up as I became unable to discourage myself from crying.

"What did he say to you when I was away? Did he touch you?" Thomas wiped my tears away with his thumb.

"He said enough."

"Please, just tell me." His voice sounded lethargic.

He said, please, right? Okay. I just hoped he could keep up.

"He implied that I was *naughty* after seeing us … dance. He touched my shoulder and told me to *loosen up*. I brushed him away. He wanted to dance with me, so he grabbed my arm. I shook him away again. He said you didn't mind *sharing* every once in a while. What's up with that?" I'd been so consumed with Thomas, just him, that I didn't know anything about him besides whatever he chose to tell me.

"I'm going to fucking kill him," he said, his knuckles turning white.

"Please stop cursing. It makes me nervous when you talk like that." I wasn't against curse words, but the way he said them and the tone he used when he said them made me uneasy.

"What did Nicholas mean when he said that thing about sharing once in a while?" Thomas kept shying away from answering my questions. But I insisted until I got what I needed, just as he had taught me.

He sighed. "I went out with a girl a while ago. I really liked her. And he—snatched her away." *What?* To me, that sounded like the worst possible friend someone could have. I couldn't understand why he kept him around.

"What about '*mixing it up*' and me not being your type? What's your type, Thomas?" I never thought I had to worry about my hair color or any other physical attributes until now.

"He's just trying to mess with me. It's not like I have a type or something. I've never dated a redhead before you, that's true. But that doesn't mean anything. You're the most beautiful girl I've ever seen. You know I love your hair, your face, everything about you," he said, befuddled. I hated to see him like this, drunk with a split lip and a blood-stained shirt.

My mind reminisced about how we met. Maybe Thomas thought his politician father might like him dating an ambassador's daughter. I mean, our parents knew each other. Was Thomas with me for me? I never thought he'd care about what his father thought anyway.

I needed answers. I asked about Nicholas's comment on Thomas "finally getting himself a decent girl" and the bit about "making his father proud." If his father gave his brother a hard time about being gay, maybe he pressured Thomas into dating only a specific type of girl. From what Thomas had mentioned, his father did sound like the controlling type of person.

Thomas took a deep breath and exhaled slowly out through his mouth, making a *whoo* sound. "I won't lie to you and say that my father didn't like that you're James Murphy's daughter. But that's absolutely *not* the reason why I'm with you. You know this. When I met you in Paris, I didn't know anything about who you were. I was drawn to you immediately."

Were all the times he said, "I can't lose you," about wanting to keep pleasing his father? I knew they had a complicated relationship. But if anything, a child always wants to please their parents, whether they admit it to themselves or not.

I didn't know what else to say. I just had too many questions and doubts in my mind. "Please, say something, don't push me away." He gently brushed his finger down my cheek, but it was still tender from the blow. I flinched away. He frowned, looking sad, not upset as I would've expected.

Nicholas didn't add any value to him as a friend, and I couldn't believe Thomas wasn't aware of it. I kept thinking about how there must be a reason for him to keep Nicholas around. That worried me, so I voiced my concern to him.

"I've told you. We go way back. We go to the same university. If I get on his bad side, it will only make things worse. I'm not afraid of him, but I know how difficult he can be. Today was just too much for me. I couldn't stand him near you. I've never hit him before, though."

He sipped on his water through a straw. His lip had clotted but still looked tender. "That's why I was a bit nervous going into the party, and why I asked you to change. I didn't want *him* to look at you. That dress looks spectacular on you."

Thomas apologized repeatedly and promised to fix things. He begged me to trust him, but I started crying again instead.

Could I believe everything he said to me? My main issue was how fast I could forget things and move on. I didn't want this to become a pattern, but I was *exhausted* and emotionally drained.

"Okay, let's call it a night. I want to go to bed. We'll talk tomorrow." I stood up and invited him to do the same.

"Let me spend the night, let me make it up to you, please," he begged, pulling me closer to him. He placed his hands on the small of my back and slowly brushed my back up and down. Luckily, his lips were off-limits because I knew I wasn't strong enough to back away from a kiss.

I was doomed. Thomas knew how much I loved him and how to make things go away.

"Caleb's outside. You can't spend the night." He glanced at the door, and his lips settled into a grim line. "I'll walk you downstairs and have them drive you back home."

"I'll get a cab, don't worry about it," he replied.

I insisted. I feared Thomas would go back to the party looking for Nicholas or something of the sort. I wanted him to go home and sleep it off.

He finally agreed and threaded his fingers with mine as we stepped out of my apartment. Caleb leaned against the wall to the left. He looked at me, but I refused to hold his gaze. He still looked furious and annoyed by the whole situation. I asked him if someone could take Thomas home. He quickly pressed on his earpiece and said something in Hebrew while escorting us downstairs.

Thomas hugged me in the lobby and gave me a soft peck on the lips.

"Ow," he whispered with a subdued smile. "I'll see you tomorrow."

He turned around and started toward the exit. The few tears that kept drowning my eyes trickled down my cheeks like a freaking broken faucet you can't get to stop from dripping.

And as I stood there like a crying statue, watching how Thomas left, William and Tobias waltzed in with three girls. They were all laughing, having a good time, it seemed.

William looked at Thomas, at his blood-stained shirt, then at me. He slowed his pace to almost stopping in front of me, but one girl, a pretty one, pulled him to the elevators.

There wasn't anywhere for me to go. I couldn't walk out of the building or step into the elevator and share it with them—*no way*. So just I stood there with an empty stare, hoping they would quickly disappear.

But Tobias stopped to ask me what was wrong. "Billie, your face," he said with wide eyes. "Was that your boyfriend?" He pointed toward the door with a frown, probably thinking the worst. The bruise on my cheekbone was visible again from all the crying. The scene looked like something else entirely. William kept looking my way, as if trying to decipher what was wrong.

I didn't answer. I was trying hard to keep the tears from turning into sobs. You know how it is when you're trying to keep it together, but someone asks you what's wrong, and it all goes to shit. *Why won't you leave?*

"Billie," he said, trying to find my eyes. "Did he hurt you?" He looked dead serious.

"No, of course not," I managed to say. "Please, Tobias, just leave."

And yes, Thomas had hurt me, but not in the way Tobias was thinking.

The elevator arrived, and the three girls rushed in, as if fearing they would be left behind. William held the door with his arm, reluctant to go inside but unwilling to ask for himself why I was crying. The deep frown settling in between his eyes told me he was worried.

"Tobias, come on!" one of the girls shouted. He walked away, realizing there was nothing left for me to say. William kept holding the door and looking at me even after Tobias had stepped inside with them. I turned around and gave my back to him, hearing how the elevator doors snicked shut behind me a few seconds later.

Caleb slowly approached me and placed his hand on my shoulder. "Come on. I'll walk you home."

CHAPTER 21

Rooftop Shenanigans

CALEB STOOD BESIDE ME with his hands firmly tucked in front of him as I summoned the elevator to go back to my apartment. Neither of us spoke a single word. Enough had been said for the night.

I opened my apartment door and turned to look at him.

"Thank you. For everything," I said to him. He nodded, looking a bit more at ease now that Thomas was gone—for the day.

"Do you have any cigarettes?" I asked, trying my best to sound casual.

"I—do. Why?" He raised a brow in return.

"Can I have one, please?" My eyes were welling up again. I thought he would refuse, but he must've felt sorry for me because he handed me the entire box. There were only three cigarettes left and a lighter. *That'll do.*

"Menthols?" I asked with a feeble snort.

"I like them. They're fresh." He smiled for the first time in hours.

"My mom used to smoke these," I replied, examining the box. "I'll just smoke one on the rooftop before going to bed."

I'd smoked once before with Sophie and Cecile in Paris, but I didn't pick it up. I just needed to relax, and I remembered how my mom used to sneak out at night to smoke. I think that's why she did it too.

"I'll come with you. We can talk," Caleb said, taking a step forward, scanning my face. I swallowed the lump in my throat, taking in the closeness of his face with mine. Talking to Caleb was always helpful, but he had already helped me more than he knew. I just needed a break.

I licked my lips and said, "I think I need to be alone right now. I'll um—listen to a few songs on my iPod and come back down."

He nodded and took a step back. "Text me when you get back, though." He looked up and down at me. As if trying to make sure that I was okay to be left alone. "And take it easy with the cigarettes."

He left, and I changed into leggings and a tank top, washed my face and made my way to the rooftop. Luckily it was empty. I took a seat on one of the sunbeds and lit up a cigarette. I coughed at first, but the smoke went through smoothly after a couple of hits. I laid back on the sunbed and listened to one of my favorite playlists.

My mind kept reliving the events of the night. Thomas was hiding something from me. I could feel it. And not just one thing, but probably a few. There was this other side to him that he wanted to keep locked up and out of my sight. And how I wished for him to open up to me, but I wasn't sure if he would.

He answered all of my questions, but something inside just didn't click for me. All the things I heard that night were confusing and disappointing—nothing felt right. I was back to square one.

I knew he loved me. I could feel it. But his outbursts were becoming more constant—worrisome. I wondered about what his true nature would be like if he'd unleashed himself from the restraint that I knew he was imposing on himself.

The three weeks he would be away were going to be helpful for the relationship. They had to be.

I lit up a second cigarette and promised myself that I'd be done with smoking forever.

The sky was clear, and I wondered if my mother could somehow see me as I kept staring at the moon. I wished for her so badly to feel her arms around me. She'd know exactly what to tell me to make things feel right.

"Waxing crescent," a voice whispered behind me, making me flinch in my seat.

"You scared me to death!"

William took a seat on the empty sunbed beside me. "Sorry."

He does *know how to use that word.* I laid back again on the sunbed, took a long hit of the cigarette. *What do you want?*

"Isn't the crescent moon the best moon?" he asked, looking up. He saw me looking at it just before he sneaked up on me and tried giving me a heart attack.

William extended his hand and pulled my right earphone off. He placed it on his left ear. "Regina Spektor?" I nodded. He held his hand out, looking at the iPod. I placed it in his hand. "Aren't you a 90s girl? Cranberries, Alanis Morissette, Dave Matthews Band," he said as he browsed through my playlist. This wasn't my idea of relaxing, but it was surely distracting. "Radiohead? You've got a varied taste in music."

"I like good music."

"I can see that. I know Dave. He's a good friend," he said casually.

"Matthews?"

"Ah, yes."

"What? How?"

"From work," he replied. That was vague. William had probably cooked for him or something since he was a chef. "So, what's your favorite Dave Matthews song?" He extended two fingers my way, asking me to pass my cigarette to him. He gave it a puff and returned it to me. I offered the cigarette box, and he took it out of my hands.

"Crash Into Me."

"Great song. Mine's Say Goodbye." He smiled with an arched brow and opened the box, still looking at me.

"That's—a great song too." Just thinking about the lyrics got me feeling all weird inside.

"I didn't imagine you'd be a smoker," he said.

"I'm not."

"Those things will kill you."

I snorted. "Like you care."

"I won't let you die alone." He pulled the last cigarette out of the box. Caleb had turned it around to have the filter face down on the bottom of the box. "Lucky cigarette. Sure, you don't want it?" I wasn't going to smoke three cigarettes. He could have it all to himself.

"I'm done with luck. Starting with those silly midsummer flowers I placed under my pillow—they've only brought misfortune."

"How so?" He sat up straight to face me, and the earphone fell off from his ear. His eyes were filled with curiosity.

"William, if you're here to torture me, just know there's nothing left for you to torture." I placed the hanging earphone back on my right ear and turned away. He rested his forearms on his knees and shook his head slowly as he removed my left earphone.

"I want to know all about your bad-luck midsummer flowers," he said, lifting the corners of his irritatingly perfect lips into a subtle smile.

"Well—for starters, they made me dream about you, so it all went downhill from there," I said, trying to discourage a smile, but William's cheerful expression vanished from his face. Who knew all it took to wipe out that cocky smile of his was to tell him I had dreamt of him? I'd make sure to write that down somewhere for future reference.

"What kind of dream was it?" he asked, his tone analytical. I didn't know if I regretted having said that, but *fuck it*. I wasn't in the mood for caring about William's opinion. Not tonight.

"Don't get your hopes up. It wasn't *that* kind of dream. It was really stupid. Drinking alcohol that night might've made me thirsty or something, and somehow, I translated that into my dream. You appeared out of nowhere, gave me a glass of water, and left. That was it." I lowered my chin and looked up at him, making sure he understood it was not a big deal. Plus, it was the truth.

He looked away and snorted with a big smile that lasted a second, but his face went grim again. His gaze fell from my eyes to my cheekbone. "Did he hurt you?"

"No, of course not." I shook my head and pressed my lips together. "He wouldn't hurt me like that."

"So, he would, just not physically?"

"That's not what I meant I—"

"Then why is your face bruised?" He wouldn't stop staring. His tone made me nervous and add that deep, rugged timbre of his to the mix … damn it. I couldn't look away either.

"Remember four days ago when Lily and I bumped into you at the lobby?" He nodded with one of his wicked smiles. Of course, he remembered. That's the day he sent me the envelope with all the goodies and called me lover when he walked by past me. "Well, Lily and I went out for coffee, and a photographer hit me with his lens when we stepped out."

"So, a pap did it?" he asked with flared nostrils. I nodded. "Fuck." He looked away, shaking his head.

"I'm fine."

"You're fine." He snorted with a smile. But he didn't seem happy. "There are plenty of ways to hurt someone without touching them." I guess we were back to talking about Thomas. And he was right. I *was* hurting, but in a different, non-physical way.

What do you want me to say? I looked away because I *wasn't* fine. I bit the inside of my lip, trying to hold the tears that threatened to stream down my face. *Again.* It was my night to shine.

"Guille?"

My chest collapsed, and my throat closed up on me when he called me Guille. I wanted so badly to hear my mother's voice calling my name.

The real tears I'd been holding in all night came splashing down like a river escaping a dam. I felt so lonely.

I curled up into a ball on the sunbed and allowed myself to cry, unmoved about William being there, looking at me break down completely.

He sat on his heels beside my sunbed, facing me.

My sobs became trembling pants that forced me to close my eyes and shut myself out from reality. William laid his hand on my face where it was bruised, and I slapped it away.

He tried again, and I sat up and pushed his chest. He sat next to me, grabbed my shoulders, and pulled me closer to him. I kept trying to shove him away, but the more I fought him, the harder his grasp became to pull away from.

His embrace finally gained in on me, refusing to let go. There was no strength left in me to resist him. I finally surrendered and settled myself on his warm chest, waiting for the tears to run dry.

When my mother died, I mourned, but it was mostly a feeling of numbness. Processing her death was a challenging effort, but when I felt like I needed her the most, the feelings of grief became overwhelming. Allowing myself to cry with anyone was rare. Let alone like this.

William refused to let go of me, and I had completely lost track of time. I never knew I needed this—for someone to hold me while I felt like drowning.

I hadn't been strong enough to deal with these feelings on my own, and Thomas had never asked me again how I felt about my mother or if I wanted to talk about it. I knew he was giving me space, respecting me until I was ready to talk. But the moment never presented itself.

Thomas was mourning, too, suffering for his brother's loss. I thought I had to be strong for him, but I wasn't strong enough to deal with his burdens and my own. I'd unconsciously chosen his— an unsustainable practice.

William's arms fulfilled their purpose. I slowly broke away from his embrace. He brushed one last tear away from my face with his thumb. "Better?"

I nodded.

Crying always made me feel better—momentarily.

I decided it was time to at least try to make the pain go away for good. And for some strange reason, William seemed like the kind of person willing to listen.

CHAPTER 22

Pivot!

"**MY MOTHER USED TO** call me Guille," I confessed. "She died when I was fourteen." I took a deep breath. The words came out naturally. "She was shot and killed while waiting outside of school to pick me up one day. I got caught up talking to a friend after school, and that's when we heard the screams.

"The burst of bullets was so intense that it finally got through the armored windows of the vehicle. It was all so fast. My mother and the Embassy driver were killed.

"Aaron ran in my direction when the gunshots were heard for the first time. I didn't know what was happening, but he took me into a classroom and started to make a few calls with agitation. Police and ambulance sirens began to wail in the distance, but he wouldn't tell me anything."

The permanently stationed knot on my stomach untangled itself gently, and the lingering pressure on my chest evaporated into a mist of nothing. The answer was obvious. Talking about my mother's death to someone willing to listen was incredibly therapeutic. And William gave me all his attention.

"More Embassy cars arrived, my mother was taken away in an ambulance, or so I was told, and I was finally taken back to the Embassy. My father was in the hospital. Aaron was the one who broke the news to me." I took another deep breath and exhaled slowly out through my mouth. William's face was solemn, and his eyes had lost their spark that characterized him.

"Where did this happen? Do you know who did it and why?" He had the same questions I had, but unfortunately, I didn't have all the answers.

"Mexico City. There's supposed to be an ongoing investigation. That's what they keep telling me. Every time I ask, I keep getting that same answer." I found it odd they couldn't figure out what had happened after all this time.

"Is—your life in danger?" William asked, offering an uncomfortable look on his face.

"Well, after this happened, it had to be assumed it might be. We moved to Norway, and I didn't leave the residence much—hardly ever. I had a personal tutor because I didn't feel like going to school or doing anything, really. I was just—numb, so I mostly kept to my books."

William fidgeted in his seat but kept his gaze directed at me.

I explained to him how I didn't think my life was in any danger at the moment, but still, certain precautions were taken, mostly for my father's peace of mind.

"Is your father still abroad? You live alone, right?"

"My father lives here in New York, but he travels for work often. He thought I would appreciate a more independent lifestyle after growing up the way I did. So, we're giving it a try." It felt so good to let it all out.

"I'm so sorry you went through all of that. I didn't know any of this. None of us knew." His frown stationed in between his eyes. "I can stop calling you Guille if it—"

"It's okay," I cut him off. "I like it. It's nice to keep hearing it, and I can handle it." I could feel William studying my responses. "Just, don't look at me like that. Like you feel sorry for me or something, please don't."

"I would never feel sorry for you."

"Um, thank you for staying," I said with a tight smile. "I know you could be downstairs instead with—your brother. I'm assuming there's a party you need to get back to."

"I wanted to know if you were okay."

Tobias must've been more than happy to be alone with the three girls. Maybe more girls had arrived by then—who knew? But I was sure at least one of them was anxious for William to return. And for some reason, a part of me didn't want him to go back to his afterparty.

Imagining him in his apartment with those—*girls* triggered an unusually warm sensation in my stomach, almost as if it were absolutely empty. But I tried to squash the feeling by focusing on my conversation with him and remember I was in a relationship with Thomas. I had to accept William's extracurricular activities were *none* of my business with big, bold, capital letters.

Frustrating.

"How did you know I was here?"

"Well, since someone *blocked me* …" He laughed, shaking his head with incredulity. By his reaction, I assumed that no one had ever blocked him before. Because who was I kidding? Who would dare deny *him*? Apparently, I'd been the chosen one for such a heroic task. "I had to go knocking on your door, but there was no answer. I took a chance and came up here."

I wondered if his annoying tendencies permeated equally amongst other girls he knew or if he'd seen me as an easy target to pester. Probably the latter, but he behaved differently this night— normal, and even kind, I dare say. His ridiculously beautiful face did nothing to help my case.

"I'll reconsider." I chuckled under my breath. *Not happening.*

My fear was that if I unblocked him and Thomas saw any message from him, something catastrophic would happen no matter how meaningless it could be.

Unblocking him would have to wait.

If William needed anything, he knew where to find me.

"That's okay. I deserved that. But still not sorry." He lifted a brow and shot his signature smug face my way. But his features hardened up again quickly after that. *That freaking frown*! "I'm not trying to hurt or *torture* you as you keep saying. I'm just—don't worry, I'll—" He trailed off, and for some reason, I got the feeling like he wanted to get out of my way.

Please don't!

I didn't want to push William away, but we weren't friends either. He was my neighbor, and that was it—my annoying, infuriating, *charming* neighbor.

I wanted to tell him I didn't care! That he could keep annoying me for as long as he wished to, but there was no proper way to voice that request. So I kept quiet, allowing the silent defeat to navigate through my body instead—provoking my frustrated lips to pucker, my disappointed brow to furrow, and my blameless stomach to go into a big, fat knot.

Say something! He needed to finish that sentence.

He smiled, as if having made up his mind about what to say next. "Even if I'm blocked, you know I've got other methods of getting my messages across." He winked, smirk back and all.

Whew!

I lightly pushed his shoulder in a relieved way that made my body relax once again.

"You must be tired," he said. You should probably get some sleep."

I was exhausted.

"Am I being dismissed?" I joked, crossing my arms in front of me.

"Oh, I have all night." He played along, laying back on the sunbed beside me with his arms behind his neck.

"No, you're right. I could use some sleep."

He extended his hand, looking at the earphones. I unraveled the cable and gave one to him.

"Okay, one last song on shuffle, and then we leave. Let's see what you've got."

I shuffled the songs folder in my iPod, and *Una Furtiva Lagrima* from the Opera *L'Elisir d'Amore* started playing. He looked at me with wide eyes and a slight grimace.

"Is this opera?" He sounded surprised. I gestured for him to stop talking and listen to the song instead. "Hmm. So bossy." He gave me a lopsided smile and kept silent afterward, looking up at the sky.

Four and a half minutes later, he handed me back the earphone, and I rolled the cable around the iPod.

"It felt like a sorrowful song, but I guess all operas are tragic like that," he said.

"No, no, no. Elixir of Love is anything but tragic. Nemorino just took a 'love potion'"—I air quoted—"because he's in love with Adina, and he desperately wants his love to be reciprocated. But little does he know, the love potion is cheap red wine." I chuckled.

"He then stops talking to her, waiting for the potion's effect to kick in. And Adina wonders why he's not talking to her anymore, and his silence does the trick. Not the cheap wine, of course." I smiled, and he smiled back. "This is one of those few operas with a happy ending, and that's why I love it."

"Hmm. I guess it's interesting once you know what the story is about. Have you seen this opera?"

I stood up and replied as we both slowly made our way to the rooftop access door. "I have, once, in Vienna—four years ago. My father was invited to the event, and I went with him. Rolando Villazón, who played Nemorino, finished the aria we just heard, and people gave him a prolonged standing ovation. And you're talking about Austria. It's—a tough crowd. The orchestra couldn't continue playing because the clapping and cheers overpowered it. So, he did an encore. It was exciting to witness that. It must be an incredible feeling to get that recognition as an artist."

He brushed a strand of hair off his forehead and said, "You're full of surprises, Guille."

"And you must be bored to death, let's go, you have a party or"—I looked at my watch to make a point—"afterparty to get to."

"Hopefully, everyone will be gone by the time I return," he said as we walked down the flight of stairs to the fourteenth floor.

"Yeah, right." I wasn't going to buy that.

He offered to walk me back to my apartment, and I agreed this time.

"You're a good neighbor," I said.

He laughed.

"Oh, I've got plenty of good reviews. I've only gotten *one* complaint." He lifted his index finger and poked my nose with it. "But I'm working on getting it resolved right away."

"Do you want to hug it out?" I smiled. He listened to me when I needed it most and stayed when he could've easily left to carry on with his party. I wanted to thank him and start over.

He took a step forward, hugged me for a few seconds, and then slowly kissed both of my cheeks. I felt my face warming up into an inevitable blush.

Why do you have to smell so good?

The way he hugged me felt all kinds of—interesting. Like he really meant it. Protective even. And those kisses weren't the casual check-on-cheek type of kisses. I could feel the warmth of his lips on my face when he did it. And the shameless *mwah* sound in the end after each kiss ... *God help me.*

"That's how you do it, right?" He teased. "I'm only respectful of your customs. And your cheeks look delicious in that color." *Damn it!* My face had probably gone into a not-delicious-anymore-neon-red flush after his remark.

He grabbed my ponytail and pulled on the hair tie. "I like your hair down," he said with that deep voice of his.

"Hey!" I protested. His fingers teased my hair to make it fall beside my face. I swallowed, feeling how my breathing got a little faster. *Please, stop.* But his fingers felt great in my hair, and I was paralyzed, so I just stared at him while he took his time doing it.

But I eventually took a few steps back to make him stop.

"That's mine," I said, faking self-confidence, putting my hand out for him to give me my hair tie back, but he placed it around his wrist.

"The day you unblock me, I'll give it back." He pulled at the tie and let it snap on his wrist.

"Nice try. I have plenty." Only I didn't. Not only was it green, which is my favorite color, but it had two cute golden stars in it. For some reason, we women tend to be territorial about our hair ties, or is it just me?

"Are you walking me to my apartment or not? Let's go," I ordered playfully, mostly to change the subject. I also needed to lock myself up in my room, for sure.

"No one's ever bossed me around like this, but I'm here for it," he replied, his smile sincere and amused.

"You're crazy. But if you like it so much … take me home, now," I played along with a laugh, summoning the elevator.

"Yes, ma'am." William tapped his forehead once with two fingers.

He started singing Say Goodbye in a low voice, as if he were singing to himself, but I could clearly listen to him.

"Stop." I laughed. He needed to stop, or I wouldn't be able to sleep from the guilt of listening to him sing those words. He shook his head and kept singing, skipping through the lyrics to the parts he knew would make me react.

He laughed as he sang, and I turned away laughing too because

I couldn't look him in the eye when he sang *that*, even if it was a joke. The most interesting joke ever.

"We're *not* friends," I joked, when he sang the part about going back to being friends after a one-night tryst.

"I know," he replied. "And I don't want to be." He kept singing under his breath and clicked on the already illuminated elevator button a few more times. *This guy.*

William was right, though. I didn't think we could be friends. We had to stick to neighbors.

He stopped singing and laughed when the elevator doors opened. Out came walking Tobias carrying a bottle of something with alcohol and the three girls from the lobby holding small tumblers.

Ugh.

"Hey, Billie!" Tobias looked drunker than before. One of the girls clung to him like a tick. Another one with short blonde hair hurried up to William and grabbed his hand, quickly threading her fingers with his. My eyes widened for a heartbeat. She whispered something to his ear, and he laughed, pulling her closer to him. "Do you want to join us? We were just heading up to the rooftop," Tobias offered.

"Thanks, but I'm a bit tired. I'm headed back to my apartment." I refused, looking away from William's too-uncomfortable-to-watch-grip on the girl's waist. "Have fun."

That son of a bitch was flirting with me a second before!

William released the girl when I stepped into the elevator, and said matter-of-factly, "Guille, I'm walking you back."

Like hell you are.

"I'm good," I chirped. He stared at me as the elevator doors shut in front of him. I clicked on the number nine a million times to the point of almost fading it, hoping it would somehow teleport me to my apartment and away from that ghastly scene.

CHAPTER 23

Whispering

June 27, 2009

A KNOCK ON MY DOOR woke me up early in the morning. I made my way to the front door as quickly as my body allowed me to. All I could see through the peephole was a bunch of red roses. I assumed a flower delivery guy stood right behind them.

"Coming!" I walked into the guest bathroom to throw some water on my face before swinging the door open.

"Oh—hi, Caleb!" I tried hiding behind the door as I was still wearing my pajamas, but it was useless.

The sight of him holding flowers threw me off.

"I've come bearing bad news, I'm afraid." His eyes gave away his exasperation as he handed the rose bouquet to me. "These are from Thomas, and you forgot to text me last night. At what time did you get back to your apartment?"

Shit! I completely forgot. I apologized and blamed it on exhaustion.

He didn't look convinced. But when did he, anyway? Sometimes I wondered if my father gave him a bonus for doubting my every response. I left the bouquet on the foyer table and grabbed his lighter.

"Here, this is yours," I said, sticking my hand out to give the lighter back.

"You smoked all three of them?" It sounded more like an accusation than a question.

"Ah, yes. All gone. But don't worry. I'm not interested in picking it up." I was sincere about that last part. It was a better option for him to believe I'd smoked the three cigarettes than get into the details of how William was there with me and smoked one of them.

"Your father will kill me if he finds out."

"He won't. I promise."

Caleb pressed his lips against each other with skepticism. There wasn't much he could do but trust me. "We'll be downstairs," he said with reluctance as he turned around and left.

Sorry! I kept lying to him. It became a habit, and I hated it.

I shut the door and went back to my room. I unlocked my phone and texted Thomas to thank him for the flowers he sent me.

Thomas: Hey, babe. Glad you liked them. I'm so sorry about yesterday. About everything. I couldn't sleep just thinking about it. I love you.
Me: I love you too. I wish we could talk some more, though.
Thomas: Sure thing. I've got an entire day planned for us. Can I meet you at your place in an hour?
Me: Sounds good. How's your lip?
Thomas: Better. I have a sexy nurse who took care of it yesterday ;)
Me: I hope you're referring to me.
Thomas: Who else, silly? See you in an hour.

Thomas could sweet-talk me out of *anything*. He knew he was my weakness. He could kiss me and make it all go away. That was my biggest fear.

☾

Thomas arrived at my apartment, and I was curious about what he had planned for the day.

"It's a surprise. It's a ten-minute walk from here. Do you feel like walking?"

"Absolutely, let's go."

Aaron, Caleb, and David came with us that day. They were probably still worried about the night before. Aaron and Caleb followed us on foot, and David took the car to the final destination. Thomas had previously informed them about his plans, so they prepared accordingly. Caleb, as usual, wasn't in his best mood; one could easily tell.

We walked south on Park, then West on 53rd street.

"MoMa?" I smiled. I'd asked Thomas multiple times to come with me, but we could never find the time to do it.

"Yup." He placed his arm around me as we kept moving. "I think it's about time I brought you to see the Matisse you've been telling me about."

We walked throughout the museum and stopped in front of some artworks that stood out for me the most. We finally got to the fifth floor and found Matisse's *Red Studio*. I took a seat on the bench, and Thomas stood behind me, holding my shoulders.

"Do you want to tell me why you like it so much?" He gently kissed my neck. There he was, making it all go away one kiss at a time.

I tapped the empty seat on the bench beside me, inviting him to join me. How was I to focus on the painting when he was distracting me like that?

I told him all about why I liked it. What drew me to it—how something that seems to have no order finds its way of creating its personal reality. I explained how it's simple and apparently flat but full of life and how it draws you into the space.

"I like that it's mostly red," he whispered to my ear, pushing a strand of loose hair behind it. He kissed my hair afterward. "I should've brought you sooner."

I gave him a careful peck on the lips and stood up. His bottom lip was still puffy and red. "Come on. If we don't leave now, I can stay here all day." I laughed because it was the truth, and I knew museums weren't his cup of tea. He was doing it for me.

"Well, in that case, let's get going." He echoed my laugh and clutched my hand to pull me up from the bench.

We made a quick stop at the gift shop before leaving. As I looked around the shop, I noticed Thomas talking to a guy who was part of the museum staff.

I walked up to them, and he gave the guy six-hundred *freaking* dollars.

"What on Earth are you buying?" I was shocked to see him spending so much money on the gift shop.

"Hey! Don't sneak up on me like that!" He grabbed my shoulders, turned me around, and motioned for me to walk away. "Go look around the store or something," he ordered playfully.

I kept turning around, trying to figure out what he was up to. That was a lot of money. I wanted to know what he'd bought because I didn't know if I felt comfortable with it if he spent that money on *me*.

"It's a surprise, now scoot."

"For me?"

"Of course."

"Thomas, that's too expensive. I can't—"

"Please let me get this for you. Besides, it's five seventy-five, not six hundred," he said, lifting his brows.

I didn't want Thomas to start buying stuff for me to make up for what happened. I'd prefer it if he would sit and talk to me instead of spending that much money on a gift. It was unnecessary. And who carries that amount of cash with them, anyway?

ALEJANDRA ANDRADE

"It'll be delivered to your apartment in a few days. It's done. You'll love it. Let's get something to eat." He smiled. "I know just the place."

We walked two blocks north on 6th Avenue, then East on 56th Street.

"Ramen?" he proposed. I nodded. We went inside and sat at a small table for two.

The food was delicious, and we overate. But it was worth it. Thomas promised to bring me back soon.

He suggested we buy a bottle of wine and drink it at my place. I hoped that meant he was willing to talk to me about what happened last night over a few glasses of wine.

We were walking down the street looking for a liquor store. Thomas started whispering things in my ear, which made me doubt if what he intended to do at my apartment was talking. I didn't mind his suggestions, but again, diversions. We needed to address a few things before any of ... *that*.

I looked over my shoulder, and Caleb shook his head while lighting up a cigarette. He disliked Thomas beyond measure, and seeing him acting so lovey-dovey with me after the events of the night before, probably didn't sit well with him.

We found a liquor store, and Thomas bought a bottle of wine. We were still a few blocks away from the apartment, and my feet were killing me.

David brought up the SUV and drove us back to my place.

I took my shoes off in the car and hissed. I had a big blister just above my heel. "Ouch. I think we walked too much."

"Well, now I get to be your nurse," he whispered in my ear. "Maybe we can—incorporate that." I laughed and said nothing else. In this case, silence meant consent.

We parked in front of the apartment building, and I was about to put my shoes back on when he stopped me, "No, no, no. Grab this." He handed over the bottle of wine and stepped out of the car. "This is *our* thing, remember? Now come here." I approached the door, and he swept me off my feet and carried me inside.

Thomas tickled my waist and whispered things in my ear to make me laugh as he carried me inside the lobby. William, Tobias, and Eric had just stepped out of the elevator and walked straight in our direction. Tobias and William were both wearing baseball hats and sunglasses, probably trying to hide their undeniable hangovers.

"Hey, Billie!" Eric and Tobias exclaimed in unison as they walked in our direction. William turned the other way and kept silent. Thomas didn't even acknowledge them back. He was focused on me, making me laugh.

And in all honesty, I probably overdid it once I saw William. Why not help him understand I couldn't care less about his *friends* from last night—that I usually kept myself very busy too.

So just to put in a little extra effort into it, I whispered back something into Thomas's ear and covered my mouth when I did it.

William walked past me and intentionally rubbed his shoulder with mine as if trying to stop my interaction with Thomas.

"Guillermina," he finally said dryly.

Guillermina? Ugh! He pronounced it *perfectly*, which was even more annoying.

I looked over my shoulder while Thomas summoned the elevator. William had turned to look in my direction, too. He pushed his Ray-Bans down a bit and met my gaze for a fraction of a second. He lowered his brows and quickly walked out of the building.

Why did I bother to play games with a player?

"Neighbors?" Thomas asked. I nodded and kissed his cheek.

Of course, Caleb observed the strange exchange between me and William, which caused him to raise an eyebrow while he bobbed his head up and down slowly with a smirk to go with it. It was an I-saw-that-what's-up-with-that kind of smirk.

What did he expect? An explanation? He knew better than that. But he had to let me know, in the only way he could, that he was always on to me.

Luckily the elevator arrived, and Thomas took me away to my apartment, where he delivered on every single thing he whispered to my ear.

CHAPTER 24

The Tattletale

July 5, 2009

THOMAS AND I had a great week together, but we kicked the dirt under the rug. We never discussed the things I wanted to, which I think was his plan since the beginning. His presence was intoxicating to me. His kisses, the way he looked at me, and how he tried so hard to show that he cared made me want to do nothing else but be with him all day and savor every moment.

I didn't want to ruin our last few days together with another discussion.

Thomas left for D.C. and planned to return three weeks later on the 25th. My photography course started the next day, and my father called to meet up for dinner. He traveled a lot for work, but we tried to keep in touch and see each other at least once a week. Thomas had joined us for dinner a few times already, and my father enjoyed his company.

My father arrived at my apartment for dinner with a long face, seemingly upset.

"Hey, kiddo, how's everything?" I tried to reassure him with a hug and told him that everything was okay. I made sure to carefully conceal the bruise on my face for his peace of mind. It was practically gone, anyway, just a few greenish spots here and there.

We ordered Italian, and as soon as we sat in the living room waiting for the food to arrive, my father voiced his concerns to me.

"Look, sweetheart, Aaron sent me the report from last weekend," he said, looking straight at me. He meant Michael's party, where Thomas got into a fight with Nicholas. "I'm uncomfortable with what I read. First of all, I want to know if you're okay."

"Of course, I'm okay. It was just a silly argument between friends." I didn't want him to worry about that or think less of Thomas because of it.

"Well, it doesn't seem silly to me when Thomas walks out with a split lip and a bloody shirt," he replied with a stern voice. I didn't know what else to say because he was right. It was not silly at all.

"Caleb has mentioned on several occasions that he's seen you, well, distraught, and arguing with Thomas. He mentioned how Thomas seemed violent on your way back from the party—he struck the car's window." He sighed. "Caleb doesn't trust him. Is this something you've often been experiencing with him?"

Caleb!

"Absolutely not. You know Thomas. He's just been stressed about some family issues. He left today for D.C., but I'm sure he'll resolve them once he's there. He'll be back in three weeks. That means there's plenty of time for him to figure things out." I mean, that's what I wanted to believe, and although I wasn't sure if that would happen, I hoped it helped soothe my father's apprehension.

"Okay, well, it makes me feel more at ease that you're taking some time apart," he said, but his face remained unchanged—gloomy. "It'll give you some perspective. Besides, your photography course starts tomorrow. Thomas being away will do you good. You'll be more focused." He seemed relieved to see Thomas gone, and that saddened me. Caleb's opinion on the matter hadn't helped one bit.

My father needed to understand that Thomas leaving for three weeks didn't mean we weren't still together or planning to talk every day. It's not like we were on a break or something.

Thomas checking on his mother had to help resolve the issues he was having with his family. I wished he would tell me what the problem was! I didn't know if I could fix things for him, but having someone to talk to about things is always helpful. Maybe together, we could figure out a solution to whatever the problem was.

My father urged me not to take any offense to Caleb for dutifully reporting to him. He reminded me it was their job to do so and that it was all for my safety and protection.

I insisted on how Thomas would never hurt me. I told him all about his obnoxious friend, Nicholas, and how if Thomas didn't hit him, I was afraid I would anyway. One way or another, Nicholas was meant to get punched that night. And I don't doubt for a second that the thought went through Caleb's mind more than a couple of times, too.

We laughed, and the mood felt lighter.

"How's your face doing? I can't see the bruise anymore."

"Much better." I smiled.

"I can't tell you how worried I was when I found out a camera struck you. I've already given them the instruction to reinforce security when you hang out with them. I'm sorry, kiddo. It's for your safety."

I sighed. For some reason, I couldn't seem to make any progress in that area. My father would never back down. Sometimes I felt like he would give me small windows to breathe and feel free, only to have security get tighter afterward.

I'd daydreamed plenty of times about walking out of the building alone and see what happened. But the truth is, I was a coward. I was terrified of breaking the rules. And it was unlikely I wouldn't get caught.

I still couldn't brush off the feeling of Caleb betraying me. We were supposed to be friends, and it was enough to hear him telling me over and over again how he thought Thomas wasn't right for me, but to say that straight out to my father? What the hell?

On the other hand, I hoped Thomas would gain full clarity regarding his mother's concerns. I feared his burden would only get heavier to deal with if he didn't. There was nothing I wanted more than for him to be happy.

The doorbell rang. I rushed to open the door and saw Caleb holding our food.

Hmm.

"Your food, Miss Murphy," he said with a wink. I bit my lower lip, anger boiling inside me. There he was, winking at me, all jolly and shit, after having turned my father against Thomas.

"Thanks," I said, taking the bags out of his hands.

"Red, what's wrong?" he whispered, analyzing me.

I shook my head. I couldn't talk to him about this with my father sitting in my living room. "Not now," I mouthed back.

"Red," he muttered. I looked over my shoulder and saw my father texting on his phone.

"Thanks for bringing the food up." I closed the door in his face and walked back to my father with a big, fake smile on my face.

My phone buzzed a couple of minutes later:

Caleb: Just tell me what's wrong.
Me: Congratulations. My father hates Thomas now.

Caleb didn't reply to my text. He was probably celebrating.

CHAPTER 25

The Monster Under the Bed

July 6, 2009

I WOKE UP VERY EARLY on the first day of my photography course. Thinking about going for a morning run to the park and being ready on time for school would be tricky. I needed to find another time to run during those three weeks.

An option consisted of running in the park in the afternoon after school, only if there was still light. Running at night was frowned upon by my security detail.

The second choice consisted of using the apartment building's treadmill at the second-floor gym. That was the boring choice, but probably the most viable one.

We arrived at Parsons fifteen minutes before nine. I was nervous and excited about my first day, and I didn't want to be late. Thankfully, Caleb wasn't on duty. I was still angry at him. It's one thing to report an incident like the fight to my father, which I already expected, and a whole other to pass judgment on my boyfriend's character. So no, I didn't feel like looking at Caleb's face.

I found my classroom and took a seat on one of the five empty tables with that first day of school anxiety sending a weird sensation to my stomach.

More students walked in as the minutes went by. Soon, the clock hit nine, and the instructor, a man in his late forties wearing black-framed glasses, entered the room, leaving his things on the desk.

"Welcome to the Summer Photography Program," he said, passing out sheets of paper among the attendants. "My name is Glenn Beckett, and I'll be your instructor. We will have a final assignment due by the end of the third week. You'll work on this project in groups of three." People stared at each other, wondering if they should make the groups. You could tell nobody knew each other.

"The groups have already been assigned by your last names. If you look in your course syllabus, you'll find your group at the end of the page."

There were fifteen of us, which meant there would be five groups.

"You'll be graded both individually and as a group on this final assignment. You only get to miss two sessions for the whole three weeks, so your assistance is of the utmost importance. Now, please, take a few minutes to find your partners and choose a table to share with them. We'll start today's session in five minutes. Have your analog cameras out, please."

I looked at the list, and I was assigned with Benjamin Miller and Nolan Murray. Everyone stood up to find their partners.

"Billie and Ben?" I could hear someone asking around the classroom.

"Hi! I'm Billie. You must be Nolan."

"Yes, I am. Nice to meet you, Billie," Nolan said with a smile, pushing one of his dark, wavy strands away from his forehead. He wore a short-sleeved denim button-down shirt over a white t-shirt and black jeans.

"Hey, guys. I'm Ben. Nice to meet you." His outfit matched the cheerful smile with which he approached us. He wore jeans and a soft, cream-colored, short-sleeved, button-down shirt with a dinosaur print in different green, yellow, and orange shades. The bright colors accentuated his deep golden-brown skin.

After we introduced ourselves, the three of us took a seat on one of the five tables and took out our cameras. Mr. Beckett walked back into the classroom and began his lecture. It was mostly a technical session about film cameras with a bit of history too.

We were sent to lunch for an hour at noon. David and *Caleb* were standing outside in the distance. Aaron was nowhere to be found. Odd.

When it came to Caleb, I never held back. If I wanted to say something to him, I would do so straightforwardly. Last night I couldn't talk to him since I was with my father, and I definitely didn't want to go about it through texts. But I was ready to talk, so I walked up to him and asked him if we could have a quick word.

"Sure, let's talk," he said as we walked away from David toward a bench, looking for privacy. I bit my lower lip and looked down, trying to organize my thoughts.

"Where's Aaron, by the way?" Caleb liked to switch shifts on me. I wanted to know why he did on this occasion.

"He had some personal matters to attend," he informed me. "I know why you're angry. But I can explain."

"I'm sure you can."

"This is about the report we sent to your father about the party, right?" he asked. I nodded. "Well, technically, Aaron was the one who drafted the report, but yeah, it needed to be done, you know that. Is that why you're upset?"

"Not exactly. I understand you have to report everything. I expected it. But why did you have to voice your opinion to my father about Thomas? He's now unnecessarily worried about my relationship, and he questioned me about a lot of things yesterday. Why would you put me on the spot like that?" I was hurt. That's why you shouldn't be friends with your bodyguards.

Caleb kept silent for a few seconds before answering. "I didn't tell him anything I haven't mentioned to you before. I've been honest with you since the beginning. When you met him in Paris, I told you I didn't trust him. I didn't know why then—it was mostly a feeling. But now I can start to see he has somewhat of—a temper."

"And you don't?" I asked rhetorically.

He snorted. "Well, I know I'm not one to talk, but I'm not the one who's dating you. Plus, it's different. I would *never* hurt you like he has." He stared at me and gave me a few seconds for me to process that.

Okay, go on. "And secondly, it's my job to keep you safe, so I'm sorry if I don't trust Thomas. But it's not like I called up your father to talk about this. He started asking questions after the report, and *he* called me specifically to ask my opinion. I couldn't lie either. I'm sorry, Red."

I groaned and stood up. "Okay." He was right, as always, but I wasn't in the mood to accept it. "I'll see you later. I'm going to grab something to eat."

As I walked with my tray looking for a place to sit, Nolan put his hand up, gesturing to join them. He sat with Ben and another girl from class.

"I'm Heather. It's nice to meet you," she said with an accent. Her light brown hair was long and wavy. She had a bunch of cute freckles on her nose and wore chunky tortoise frame glasses.

"Nice to meet you too, Heather," I replied, putting my food tray on the table. "Where are you from?"

"I'm Australian." Ben couldn't keep his eyes off her smiling face.

"I guess you're stuck with us for the next three weeks, huh?" Nolan chuckled as he slid his hands into his pants pockets. "Have you taken any photography courses before?"

"I'm transferring from PCA in Paris. I just finished my first year there. But I'm new to analog photography. How about you?"

Ben, Heather, and Nolan told me they were enrolled in the Photography BFA program but signed up for the summer course for credit. Nolan had also just finished his first year at Parsons. Ben and Heather were a year ahead. I was curious to know how they liked it so far.

"It's been great. It's demanding. There's always a lot of work to do. But it's been fun so far," Heather explained. Ben *definitely* had a crush on her.

"I see you almost made our team," I said to Heather, whose last name was Martin.

"I know! That would've been fun, right?"

We talked and got to know each other a bit better over lunch, and I genuinely liked everyone. They all seemed friendly.

We walked back to the classroom, and Mr. Beckett picked up where he left off before lunch regarding the day's lecture. Just before the class was about to end, he explained a few more things concerning the final project.

"We will have a daily lecture and practice in class. And you will take what you learn here and apply it to your group project. You'll be able to start brainstorming on the concept and ideas for the final presentation as soon as you wish. There will be an allotted time to go through any progress or ideas you'd like for me to review during each session.

"You will have to work after class almost every day, so make sure you make enough time for it. These three weeks will go fast, so try to keep up with the work and don't leave everything to the last minute," he advised. "I'll see you all tomorrow."

Mr. Beckett left, and I exchanged phone numbers with Ben and Nolan. Ben created a group chat for the three of us. There wasn't much group work to get done though, mostly individual practice on the analog camera. We agreed to keep talking about the project the next day.

Caleb leaned on a wall nearby as he waited for me to be ready to leave. I ignored him and kept making my way out of the building. He clicked on his earpiece, probably signaling David to bring the car around. He increased his pace to walk beside me and inquired about my first day.

"Weren't you supposed to be invisible or something?" I replied with exasperation.

"Who cares if you have a security detail," he said, looking over his shoulder. "Your new friends are looking this way. I'm sure if they haven't figured it out by now, they will by tomorrow."

It had more to do with me not liking people feeling curious about me. I just wanted to blend in without attracting any unnecessary attention.

"It's going to be okay, Red. It always has been. Don't worry about stuff like that." He tried to reassure me as he opened the door for me.

Ben sent a couple of texts to the group chat to make sure we were receiving them. That reminded me to give David and Caleb a heads up about how I'd be working with two classmates almost every day after school. I wondered if I had to inform Thomas about it too. He wasn't going to be thrilled about my team consisting of two guys and me.

"Okay. We're just going to need their full names, Miss Murphy," Caleb replied. He still refused to call me Red in front of David. I thought it was funny because it's not like David didn't know he did or hadn't heard him before.

I called Thomas on my way back home to tell him about my first day. I found it odd he hadn't reached out to ask me about it.

"Hey, babe, how did the first day go?" he asked with a dull tone.

"Well, it was interesting. I mean, you know how first days are—mostly getting to know everyone. There's a big project due at the end. I think it's going to be a lot of work, but I'm excited," I replied.

"I'm sure you're going to do great." He sounded uninterested and quickly changed the subject. "Babe, I need a favor. I forgot a folder with documents from school, and I need my parents to sign them. I left it in my apartment. Could you get it and mail it back to me?"

I couldn't say I was overjoyed with his lack of enthusiasm regarding my first day of school, but maybe he was worried about something else or stressed about forgetting the documents.

I always found a way to excuse him.

"Um, sure. But I don't have a key. How am I getting in?"

"There's a key safety box outside of my apartment. I'll text you the code."

I offered to go right away, so I tapped on Caleb's shoulder, gestured to pull over, and asked Thomas to text me the D.C. address.

"Thank you so much, babe. You're a lifesaver."

David drove downtown to Thomas's apartment. They knew where it was since they had given him a ride a few times before.

Caleb insisted on coming up to get the documents with me, and David stayed behind in the car. We breezed through the reception with no problem. Thomas had informed the security guard about our visit.

"Shoot. I don't know his apartment number." I looked at the elevator buttons, not knowing which one to click.

I pulled my phone out of my purse with the intention of texting Thomas, but Caleb clicked on the sixteenth-floor button and said, "16 C."

Okaaay.

I glared at him, but he ignored me and bobbed his head to the rhythm of the elevator music. I was sure they didn't get that information from Thomas directly.

The code Thomas texted me worked and revealed the spare key to his apartment. Caleb waited outside while I fetched the paperwork.

Thomas's place was an open space studio with a small kitchenette on the left. The bed was neatly made on the far end beside a big window. The folder rested on top of it. But the key slipped out of my hands as I reached out for the documents.

I dropped to my knees and peeked under the bed. *Fuck*! I gasped and sat on the floor. *No, no, no.* My blood drained to my feet as my breaths became pants. I inhaled slowly and deeply, trying to stop the drilling sensation in my stomach.

Thomas is cheating on me. Thomas is definitely *cheating on me.*

CHAPTER 26

Assumptions

TWO EMPTY CONDOM PACKAGES.

It was the first time I'd ever set foot in Thomas's apartment, so there was *no way* he could claim to have used them with me. Besides, I was on the pill. I took another deep breath and kept looking for the key, but I couldn't find it. Tears of desperation slid down my face because all I wanted was to get the hell out of there.

A million disturbing thoughts flooded my mind like a whirlwind:

He wouldn't do that to me. There must be an explanation. No, he's cheating on me. Could they be his father's? How many times has he done this? They must be his father's. But what if they're not?

There were only two options to choose from: either his father was cheating on his mother, or Thomas was cheating on me. But someone, either way, was a dirty cheater.

"Everything okay?" Caleb asked over the door, lightly knocking on it.

Damn it! Where's that goddamn key!

I kept frantically looking for it, which caused Caleb to come inside and dart in my direction after I didn't answer.

"What's wrong?" he demanded.

"The key, I can't find the *fucking* key!" Tears kept streaming down my face.

"Hey, it's okay." He placed a hand on my shoulder and looked for my eyes. "I'll help you find it." He must've thought I was PMSing or something, because who cries for losing a key?

He dropped to his knees before I could tell him not to. I didn't want him to see what I'd seen, but it was too late. Caleb peeked under the bed, then glanced back at me with a fiery gaze. He could obviously put two and two together.

I crouched on the floor and cried my eyes out while Caleb searched for the key.

"I found it," he said a minute later. "Now, let's get the fuck out of here." Caleb grabbed my arm and pulled me up. I stood there like an ice statue, staring out the window as Caleb grabbed the documents. "Come on, Red, let's go. *Now.*"

We walked out, and Caleb locked the apartment door behind us, placing the key back on the lockbox afterward.

They can't be his, I kept wishing.

"I fucking knew it," he uttered a few times while we made our way to the car. "And you wonder why I hate the guy? He's a cynic and a—"

"Caleb, stop. Please, just stop." I begged with a stuffy nose. I couldn't pull any air in. "This is his father's apartment. He often comes for work and stays here. Your assumptions are not helping." I couldn't deal with my thoughts *and* Caleb's contagious speculations. It was making me anxious, and I needed to think straight.

"When's the last time his father came to New York?" he mused.

"I don't know, okay! I'll figure it out. It's *my* problem. And you better not say a word of this to anyone. Especially to my father. I'm *begging* you to stay out of it." Caleb's hands shaped into fists so hard that his knuckles turned white. If he could, I'm sure he'd go to D.C. in this very instant and track Thomas down.

I stepped into the car, forwarded the D.C. address to the security group chat, and asked David to find the nearest FedEx.

"You're still going to send—"

"Stop!" I shouted. David kept a straight face, but I could see the confusion in his eyes as he probably tried to understand what had happened. "David, FedEx. Please."

I wished we were in Paris so I could put the car divider up. The SUV didn't have the option to do so, and I wanted to keep Caleb as far away from me as possible. I knew he was worried and trying to protect me, but I didn't need his wrath right now. I needed silence.

We arrived home after sending the documents, and I changed into my gym clothes. Running always helped with clearing my thoughts. It had to.

Something as simple as going for a freaking run on my own— that's all I wanted! But it wasn't a possibility in my world. I needed to be alone, and the apartment building's gym was the closest I would get to such a prized commodity.

Pathetic.

Forty-five minutes into my run, a tall, dark-brown skinned muscular guy wearing a neon green sleeveless shirt came walking in carrying a large duffel bag. He had short dreadlocks on top and shaved sides that made him look like a real badass.

He looked friendly and immediately waved his hand to say hello to me with a smile. I waved back at him and continued running.

Boxing gloves, pads, and bandages came out of the guy's bag. I'd never seen him before, but I was entertained watching as he got his stuff ready to work out—anything to distract me from thinking was welcome at this point.

There were five minutes left on the treadmill when Joel walked into the gym. He waved hello to me, then greeted the friendly stranger. They shook hands and patted their backs with grins on their faces.

The stranger bandaged Joel's hands, and a few minutes later, William waltzed into the gym precisely when my treadmill went into cool down mode. *Shit.*

He greeted the stranger which I assumed was their personal trainer, and placed his hands on the treadmill's handrail. I spotted my green hair tie with the two cute golden stars around his wrist. He pulled an earphone off my ear and said, "Hey Guille. You're looking a little pale, are you okay?" I wasn't.

A heartbeat later, my knees buckled, and William pushed on the emergency stop button, making the treadmill come to a complete stop. I fell on my knees and took a deep breath. I had pushed myself too hard.

"Grant, could you—exactly!" William said to his trainer, who brought a paper cone with water. William squatted beside me and offered it to me. "Just like in your dream," he whispered with an annoying wink that made me scowl at him. I took the water anyway because I needed it so badly. "Do you need help standing up?"

"No, thanks."

Attempting to stand up was foolish—my knees were still weak, and my last meal had been at noon, which wasn't helpful either. I took a deep breath and stared at my reflection in the mirror. My bloodless lips were fading out by the second.

"Stay put," he ordered. William placed his arm around my shoulders, lifted me with ease, and led me to the bench by the door. My stomach felt hollow, but I shut my eyes and concentrated on my breath.

William said something to Joel in Swedish, and then my phone buzzed on the treadmill. I opened my eyes, and William had fetched it for me. The caller ID read *Thomas*. I sent it to voicemail and tossed the phone beside me on the bench. William crossed his arms and lifted his eyebrow with an amused smile. Unfortunately, I didn't have the energy to wipe it off his face.

"Trouble in paradise?" he asked, looking delighted.

I lifted my index finger and closed my eyes for a second, then ran to the women's bathroom and threw up pure bile.

"Guille!" William cried as he knocked on the bathroom door. "Let me help you. Open up." There was no way I would let him inside and see me in this condition. Throwing up made me feel better, though.

Although my lips were starting to draw themselves back on my face, the mirror showed no improvement in my face's coloring. I washed my hands, threw some water on my face, rinsed my mouth, and stepped back into the gym.

William stood outside the door, waiting for me to come out.

"You're not—pregnant, are you?" he whispered. I punched his arm, hoping it sufficed as an answer. He laughed, of course.

"Girl's got a killer right hook, man! I like her already!" Grant exclaimed with a laugh. William snorted in disagreement.

"Hey Billie," Tobias said, walking in with a Coke. "I was told you weren't feeling okay. Take a few sips of this." He took a seat next to me on the bench. I thanked him while doing as he suggested. The Coke was ice cold, and it immediately did wonders for my blood sugar. William turned around, and Grant started to bandage his hands. Joel had his gloves on and seemed eager to start training.

My phone buzzed again. Caleb. I took the call.

"*Yes? ... I'm at the gym ... I know, I was running ... No ... I'm literally beside your apartment ... What? Are you afraid I'll run off? ... I'll make sure to try it next time ... I'm fine.*"

Two seconds later, Caleb walked into the gym, and the space felt too crowded all of a sudden. There were now six of us there, and the gym wasn't huge.

"Hope you feel better, Billie," Tobias said, touching my shoulder. He stood up, and William thanked him as he stepped out.

"You look pale. You should go rest. I'll walk you," Caleb said.

"I'm okay," I replied dryly, withdrawing from his touch. Looking at him reminded me of what we've seen at Thomas's apartment, and I didn't want to remember. I didn't want him meddling in my relationship, and I did *not* feel like talking about what happened earlier with him.

"Come on, let's go. I need to talk to you," he said more gently.

"She said she's okay, man," William said from afar while getting his hands bandaged.

Stay out of it! Why was everyone so nosy?

Caleb shot a glare at William—flames and all. But I just had it with the alpha male energy around me. I wanted to leave, but not because Caleb told me to do so. I felt like everyone was ordering me around all the time.

"Let us know when you're back in your apartment." Caleb turned around without making eye contact with me and left. He looked pissed and then some.

William walked in my direction, but I was done with him too. I stood up and said, "Thanks for the Coke." I was ready to leave. "Nice to meet you, Grant. Goodbye, Joel."

"You can thank me by unblocking me," he whispered, then walked backward with a laugh. I sighed and shook my head on my way out. "I'll make it worth your while!" He actually *shouted* that part for everyone to hear, but I didn't care to look back.

He kept laughing as he always did when he knew he got on my nerves, but I was learning how to make that laugh of his go away. He wasn't laughing much when he saw me with Thomas in the lobby. I didn't know what William wanted, but I knew what he didn't like.

Unblocking him would happen whenever I felt like it, not when he asked me to do so.

I was *done* taking orders.

All I could think of was Thomas and how to approach the situation. I hated he was away and that we couldn't talk about what happened face to face. There was no way to know if the condom packages were his or his father's. I wanted to trust him and what we had. I wanted nothing more but to think he wouldn't do that to me. But wanting wasn't enough. I needed to hear him say those weren't his.

Jumping to conclusions or accusations would do nothing but hurt the relationship beyond recovery. But I didn't feel ready to talk to him just yet. I texted him saying I had an upset stomach, and that I was calling it a night. It'd give me more time to think about what to do and how to approach it—to sleep on it. Besides, it was true.

A part of me wanted to go back to Thomas's apartment and turn it upside down until I found something else—something that would give me some clarity. But then I remembered this saying: "*If you want to leave your man, investigate him.*" And I wasn't sure if that's what I wanted.

CHAPTER 27

Wishing and Hoping and Slapping and Punching

July 15, 2009

WE WERE HALFWAY through the summer photography course. I decided not to mention anything to Thomas about the condoms. I wanted to trust him, and something inside me told me he wouldn't cheat on me. I clung to that thought.

He was acting weird, but I could sense his visit to D.C had stressed him. He kept insisting on how much he missed me. There had to be an explanation for the condoms under his bed.

I didn't want him to feel like I was accusing or attacking him; that's why I decided not to bring it up while he was away. I didn't want to be the insecure, nagging kind of girlfriend.

Once he got back, I would think about a way to bring out the subject. Like right away.

That being said, it didn't mean the situation wasn't affecting me. I shoved plenty of feelings to the side, which was totally different from acknowledging them.

With Thomas away, I had more time to see my friends on the weekends. I would usually hang out with CJ and Nina. They, too, were concerned about me, but I just kept denying that there was something wrong and tried to keep a brave face.

My summer course served as an excellent distraction. I was learning a lot and enjoying myself. But apparently, I wasn't doing a great job in hiding my concerns because Ben and Nolan kept asking me if I was okay all the time.

We would work every day after class, either at school or in my place. We'd gone to Central Park a few times to practice with our analogs, too.

Our final project would focus on vintage style shots, something outdoors. We had the whole concept worked out and approved by Mr. Beckett. But we needed a model for the shoot. I thought of Lily and promised to talk to her to see if she was available that weekend.

"Is she hot?" Nolan asked, moving his eyebrows up and down with a grin. I laughed. I didn't want to tell them *who* my friend was. Nolan would probably pass out from the excitement.

It could be possible that Lily wouldn't be able to make it. She was usually either traveling or working most of the time. I needed to check with her first.

"She's gorgeous, Nolan. But very much taken," I warned playfully.

"If she can't make it, we can always ask Heather. I'm sure she'd love to help us out," Ben said, trying to sound casual. That was a solid plan B. I agreed to let them know as soon as possible if Lily could help us out for the shoot or not.

It was almost seven, and Nolan needed to start heading out since he worked a part-time job at a Greek restaurant. Ben left at the same time Nolan did, and I rushed to the gym afterward.

Grant trained William and Joel every day at eight. I usually left before they arrived for their session. It was best to avoid bumping into William every day.

"How's it going, Billie?" Grant said as I started stretching.

"Oh, hi! You're here early."

"Yeah, we're now going to train at seven-thirty. William wants to start earlier from now on."

"Hm. Does he, now? Well, I hope I don't hinder your training."

Grant laughed. "Of course not. It's always nice to have you around." Grant's training looked like fun, especially the part where you get to punch things around.

"Grant, I was thinking. Would you have time to train me three days a week at seven?" I asked. I thought boxing might help me channel the storm in my chest aside from all the shit I had going on in my head. "That way, you're free by seven-thirty to train William and Joel."

"I'd love to. With boxing, you'll work with strength and cardio too. Running's great, but it's important to mix it up."

I asked if we could start the following Friday, and he agreed.

"Hey guys," Joel said, walking in.

"Hey Joel, is Lily home?" I asked. I wanted to talk to her about the shoot and see if she was available.

"Yeah, she just arrived from L.A. a few hours ago."

I thanked him and climbed on the treadmill.

Grant was getting Joel's hands ready when William walked in. I wondered why he'd switched his training schedule.

He smiled at me, jerked his chin, and sat on the bench to tie his shoelaces. He opened a water bottle he'd brought with him and poured some kind of powder out of an individual packet, shook it fast, and chugged it down in record time. Probably a pre-training supplement or something of the sort.

He stood up and removed the light hoodie he was wearing, slightly pulling the t-shirt underneath with it. His *ridiculously* chiseled abs and part of his chest were revealed for me to see.

Oh. Sweet. Mercy.

He pulled the t-shirt back down and caught me staring at him. *Shit!* I quickly looked away—my hands wet, my face warm, and other indescribable feelings that don't even have a name spiraling up and down my spine.

What is wrong with me?

He walked away beaming with full bragging rights for eternity and approached Grant to have his hands bandaged. I nervously bit my lower lip and increased my running speed, trying to pretend like I hadn't gawked at him like a crazy stalker.

But how to look away from the Sjöberg brothers? They were all genetic lottery winners with their ridiculously out-of-this-world DNA.

Joel looked a lot like William, but his hair was light brown instead of gold, just like Tobias's. William was the tallest of the four brothers, but Joel was only an inch or so shorter than him, and their facial features were very similar.

And that pink supplement William took was *definitely* working because his arms seemed more muscular than the last time I saw him. They were both absurdly good looking.

But William ... simply unreal.

They started training, and I tried to focus on my run. But having a mirror in front of the treadmill made it hard for me to look at anything else but William's reflection on it. I could see the tiny drops of sweat flying around each time he punched on the pads.

Grant seemed satisfied by the intensity with which William was training and kept encouraging him. I was also satisfied with his commitment.

There was a minute left on my run, and as soon as the clock hit zero, I pushed on the emergency stop button to override the cool down mode. I stepped off the treadmill and walked to the bathroom to wash my hands and face. A little ice cold water on the face never hurt anyone.

"Friday at seven!" Grant yelled as I stepped out of the restroom.

"Of course!" I replied, trying to sound natural as I fled the scene. "See you around." I didn't look back. Not when I'd already been staring for the past half hour.

I was still embarrassed about William catching me salivating over his stupid abs. I mean, they were right there in front of me! And William gloated like the conceited fool he was. A mouthwatering, drool-inciting, sexy fool. *Stop*!

I knocked on Lily and Joel's apartment. She opened the door a few seconds later. "Hi, Billie!" she said with a hug. "Do you want to come in?" I stepped inside, and Lily offered me a glass of water.

I couldn't get William's body out of my head. I felt my face warming up again as I relived the image of him taking his hoodie off at the gym.

"Your face is red, are you okay? Joel told me you almost fainted at the gym the other day." I almost fainted today too, but for a totally different reason.

"I just stepped off the treadmill. I need a minute to recover."

"You look a bit thinner than the last time I saw you, too. Don't push yourself too hard. Is everything okay?" She seemed concerned about my recent weight-loss. I admitted to having neglected my diet due to stress, but I assured her I was fine.

I wished I could open myself up to her about Thomas. There wasn't anyone I trusted enough to discuss my relationship issues.

"You know, being a model is stressful, and I'm no stranger to eating disorders. I'm sorry about worrying, but I get nervous when I see a friend losing weight or overdoing themselves at the gym."

"I understand. Thank you for worrying, Lily. I swear I'm fine," I said with a forced smile. Lily narrowed her eyes and went to the kitchen. She came back with a small plate with pretzels, prompting me to have some.

"So, how are things with Thomas?" she asked casually, trying to get to the bottom of whatever was bothering me.

Was it that obvious?

"Um—well, he's in D.C. right now. He'll be back by the end of next week," I said, biting a pretzel.

"Mhm. So, are you going to tell me what's wrong?"

"What do you mean?"

"Come on. Spill. You can talk to me."

I took a deep breath and exhaled slowly out through my mouth.

"Okay. But promise me you won't say a word to Joel." I feared Joel would go to William and tell him about my situation, and I didn't want him to know a thing about it. Lily promised I could trust her, and I was so desperate to talk to someone that I took the opportunity to vent.

"I think I'm about to go out of my mind any day now." I rested my elbows on my knees and my hands on my forehead. I tried to find the courage to tell her what had happened, what I'd seen.

She remained silent, waiting for me to continue. I told her about how and why I went to his apartment and *what* I saw underneath his bed. I sipped nervously on my water and kept explaining how things were tricky since his father also used the apartment from time to time for work.

I told her how the condom packages could belong to his father and how I didn't remember Thomas telling me that his father was coming to town.

"And you're one hundred percent sure he didn't use those with you?"

"It's impossible. It's the first time I've ever set foot in his apartment, Lily. It's so messed up. I've been trying not to think about it. I want to trust him, but it's been hard. I can't stop thinking about this.

"I talk to him every day, but I haven't had the guts to mention it, least of all over the phone. I want to look at him and his reaction when I ask him about it."

"Okay, and how have things been with him? Is he acting weird or suspicious?" That was an excellent question.

"I feel like he's been under a lot of stress lately. He's been going through some family issues for a while now. And he's been somewhat reactive, but other than that, nothing suspicious whatsoever."

Lily pressed her lips together.

"I've gotta say you've got some real willpower. I would've taken a picture of the evidence and sent it to Joel in that second and probably set his apartment on fire afterward," she said with a bleak laugh. "But I'm just extremely jealous. We've struggled with that. He doesn't give me a reason to feel that way, but it's just hard, you know—" she broke off mid-sentence.

"What do you mean?"

"Um—you know how girls can be," she said, but I felt like there was something she wasn't saying. "Anyway, we're not talking about me. I think you're doing the mature thing about not jumping to any conclusions. That's usually the problem in most relationships. We don't give our partners a chance to explain before assuming the worst," she said, biting a pretzel. "I'm sure there must be an explanation, but I don't think it's fair that you're putting yourself through this when all you really want is to talk to him about it."

The problem was that I wasn't ready to listen to what he had to say. It scared me. What if he *was* cheating?

"It's just like Schrödinger's cat." I snorted. "I'm afraid to open the box and see if the cat's dead or alive."

"Whoa! I think Joel must have some pot if you want to take this to another level," she said with a laugh.

I laughed too and said, "Ugh! I'm sorry, I don't know how to stop thinking about this." Another lie. William's abs had proved to be a significant distracter. Jokes on me, I guess.

I thanked Lily for taking the time and listening to me. It felt so good to share my concerns with someone because keeping everything to myself was killing me.

"Of course, anytime. I know I didn't do anything to help solve your problem, but I think it's something for you to figure out. No one knows your relationship better than yourself. Just trust your gut."

I thanked her again and moved on to the real reason for my visit.

"I wanted to ask you a favor. I know you're always busy, but we need a model for our final project, and I was wondering if you're available this Saturday to shoot. We still don't know where exactly, but we know we want something outdoors with lots of natural light, maybe somewhere outside the city."

"I'm actually free this weekend, so I'd love to help. We could even shoot in the cottage at Sagaponack if you want. It's breathtaking over there. I don't know what you're thinking about exactly, but we have the ocean, lots of trees and greenery, a few ponds nearby. I think you could work with that." She seemed excited.

"That sounds perfect, Lily. Thank you so much. Are you sure it's okay for us to go? I don't want to impose." I understood from what Lily had told me before that the Sjöbergs owned a property there. I just wanted to make sure it wasn't an issue for us to go.

Joel came into the apartment, dripping in sweat.

"Hey, beautiful." He approached Lily and kissed her, but she complained about how sweaty he was. Joel laughed and excused himself to take a shower.

"Joel, wait!" Lily shouted before he disappeared off to their bedroom. "Can Billie and I go down to the cottage on Saturday? She's going to take some photographs of me for a school project, and we could use the natural ambiance."

"Lily, come on, you even have a key. You know you don't need to ask. Besides, no one's going to be there this weekend, so you'll have the place all to yourselves." Joel turned to look at me next. "Billie, you're more than welcome to do whatever you need to do."

"Thank you." I smiled at Joel. His face reminding me of

William's wasn't helpful. I needed to get the image of him out of my mind as soon as possible.

"Thanks, baby," Lily said cutely. "Now go shower."

Joel shook his head, smiling. "See you later, Billie."

I thanked Lily with a big hug. "Of course, Billie, so happy to help." We agreed to talk on Friday to set an hour to leave for our field trip on Saturday. "And don't keep things to yourself like that. You'll go insane if you do. You know I'm here if you ever need to talk again."

I left Lily's and opened the door to my apartment. There was an enormous package leaning against the wall. There was a note on the foyer table from Mimi saying she had received it on my behalf. It was a giant framed poster of Matisse's Red Studio.

It was *amazing*!

I called Thomas to thank him for the gift, but again, he sounded weird over the phone. I regretted having called him. He didn't sound okay, and it didn't seem to have anything to do with me. He was distraught, and I urged him to talk to me, but he refused and hung up on me, claiming he had to get back to the rowing machine.

I'd reached my limit. I couldn't keep overlooking his mood swings. Maybe he was done with me, and if so, why make me go through the ups and downs?

What if everything Nicholas said at the party was true? I couldn't stop thinking about it. Was Thomas with me for me? Or to please his father's expectations? Being around his father for three weeks must've been taxing. I just wished he would open up to me and tell me what the hell was going on.

C

July 17, 2009

Ben and Nolan left early, around six in the evening. We had everything ready for the next day. We were thrilled about the shoot, and

I told them my friend had agreed to pose for the photos, but I still hadn't told them *who* she was.

By six-thirty, I climbed on the treadmill and walked for a few minutes to warm up for my class. Grant arrived ten minutes before seven to set everything up.

"Let me get your hands ready," Grant said, gesturing to come forth. He bandaged my knuckles, and I was so ready to start punching things around. He helped me put my gloves on, and I was good to go.

"Okay, stand here for me." He pointed at one of the small cones. He explained a few things like how to stand up correctly to hold a right guard. We began with basic combinations, and he received the punches I gave on the pads.

Grant was intense. I was sweating like crazy throughout the class. His energy was contagious. "We've got eight minutes left. Let's work on your abs. Lie on your back on the mat." I did as I was told, and he held my feet firmly on the ground to assist me with the crunches.

"Grant, I can't," I said after a few minutes, completely out of breath and not at all used to this type of exercise.

"Don't stop, one more minute left." He kept encouraging me.

William and Joel stepped into the gym together, talking in Swedish.

The last few seconds of the workout were killing me.

"We're done, Billie, great job."

I threw my head back slowly on the floor and laid down to catch my breath. Grant knelt beside me and removed my gloves. I couldn't sit up yet, which he found amusing. "Careful with this one. She's tough," Grant said, laughing.

"Oh, you don't have to tell me. I know she's rather feisty," William said, leaning against the wall behind Grant, watching as he finished removing my bandages. "I've already taken a few punches myself. Well, that depends if slaps in the face count as such."

I looked over Grant's shoulder and stuck my tongue out at William. He raised a brow in return.

"I'm sure he's earned them by pulse," Grant said, making Joel laugh.

Thanks, Grant.

I got up, grabbed my things, and walked toward the exit when Joel said, "Good luck tomorrow, Billie. Let me know if you guys need anything, okay?"

"What's tomorrow?" William asked.

"Don't worry. You're not invited." I winked, just as he always did. "Thank you, Grant! See you on Monday!"

CHAPTER 28

Drowning

July 18, 2009

WE PLANNED TO LEAVE at 8:00 a.m. from my apartment. We were just waiting for Ben and Nolan to arrive. Aaron, Caleb, *and* David were going to escort us to the Hamptons. If I hung out with Lily, the three of them had to come.

"Isn't it a bit excessive?" I whispered to Caleb.

"We need to comply with your father's orders, Miss Murphy." He looked away after replying with a flat tone.

Our dynamic was still awkward since the condom package incident. Caleb was furious with Thomas. And he probably thought I was an idiot for not confronting him—yet. But he didn't know what I was thinking, and I was obviously going to talk to Thomas about it. I was doing things *my* way, which was very different from what Caleb would've wanted.

It was a two-hour ride, that's why we decided to leave early. We wanted to have as much sunlight as possible to play around with different lighting. Lily brought a few changes of clothes for the shoot, and we were all packed and ready to go.

A couple of minutes later, a cab pulled over behind us. Ben and Nolan stepped out with a backpack and a large circular bag, which I assumed carried the light reflectors Nolan said he would bring over for the shoot.

Caleb opened the door for them to step into the car. Lily and I sat in the third row of the SUV.

"Lily, this is Ben and Nolan," I said, pointing at each of them as I said their names. "Ben, Nolan, this is Lily."

"Nice to meet you." Lily smiled, extending her hand to them.

"Likewise." Ben shook her hand with a grin.

"Hi, um, I—nice to meet you too." Nolan's big brown eyes went wide when he shook her hand. I was already expecting him to flip out. I couldn't help but laugh. He had two hours to get his shit together and process the fact that he was riding in the same car as Lily Young.

"Aaron, could we stop for coffee?" I asked.

"Oh, yes, please!" Lily joined in.

I had somewhat of a headache because I didn't get much sleep the night before, thinking about how my last call with Thomas went. I was determined not to think about that for the rest of the day. I wanted the shoot to go as planned and to enjoy myself if possible.

We all chatted for a while but ended up snoozing the last forty-five minutes.

Lily woke me up when she took a phone call from Joel.

"*Hey baby … Yeah, everyone's asleep, but we're about ten minutes away from the house … That sounds great! … I'd love that … Okay, see you in the afternoon.*"

"Was that Joel?" I asked, sitting up straight in my seat.

"Yes. He's coming later today, and we're staying for the weekend. You should spend the night. It could be fun."

Spend the night. Damn, I'd never even been to a sleepover before. I was *that* lame. Besides, I had to take Ben and Nolan back, so I didn't think it was a feasible option for me.

"Yeah, it would. I'd have to check with—" I jerked my chin at David, who sat in front of me.

"Oh, come on! Stay! They can drive Ben and Nolan back to the city. We'll drive you back home tomorrow."

I promised to see what I could do to stay. I thought it would be fun and distracting to do something different. Perhaps the easiest way was to call my father and ask for his permission.

We finally arrived, and the house was spectacular. My jaw dropped to the floor. "When you said cottage, I imagined something different," I told Lily. "Something, I don't know—smaller."

Lily laughed. "Well, it's a modern Swedish inspired cottage. It's amazing, right? I love it here."

The house was on the ocean side of the property. There was a pool in the back, followed by a breathtakingly beautiful garden with different flower shrubs and huge trees that bordered Fairfield pond. The house was two stories and had large floor to ceiling windows.

"Oh, man!" Ben cried, walking around. "This place is legit."

"Very impressive," Nolan said, starting to take stuff out of his bag. "Billie, why don't you help Lily with her clothes while we set up? I think we can start taking a few shots here in the garden with the pond as a backdrop." He sounded so professional. He was probably trying to impress Lily.

"Sure," I replied. Lily and I walked into the house, and Caleb brought Lily's suitcase inside.

"Thanks, Caleb," Lily said with a smile. He seemed nervous around her. Who wouldn't?

Caleb left, and Lily unpacked the outfits she had brought with her. "He's quite the stunner, isn't he?" Lily whispered. "He could be a model. I swear he'd get booked in two seconds."

I laughed. I couldn't imagine Caleb being a model, but I completely understood where Lily was coming from. He was exotic, and well … all sorts of other things.

"So, what do you think?" she said, placing a cute long-sleeve white dress in front of her. I told her it was perfect. "Okay, I'll be right back. I'll give you a tour later." She disappeared into one of the rooms to change as I got my stuff ready for the shoot.

The interior design of the house had a heavy Scandinavian aesthetic, predominated by a neutral color palette. Everything looked so fresh and clean. Most of the furniture was white or gray, with a few subtle burnt orange and navy-blue touches in certain accessories here and there.

All I could see was the massive open-space kitchen, dining room, and two doors on the far end beside the stairs. I couldn't wait to see the rest of the house, and I was curious about the bathrooms.

Lily came out looking gorgeous. "What should I do for makeup?"

"You don't need much, perhaps some blush and a bit of this," I said, taking one of my favorite lipsticks out of my bag. "Just a few taps, so it gives you a rosy tint, that's it."

We walked outside, and Ben and Nolan had everything ready for the shoot. I worried about Nolan's jaw. I feared it would dislocate when he saw Lily walking out of the house.

We agreed to rotate and take a few shots on each location and make a final selection of the presentation's best twelve photographs.

Lily made it so easy for us to shoot her. She didn't need any direction and gave us plenty of ideas. It felt like cheating.

After the garden and pond shots, we moved to the beach. We mostly used the golden light reflectors during that part of the shoot. Lily had this idea of going in the water with her dress on. Those shots turned out pretty amazing. Even Ben, who was the collected one, stuttered after Lily walked out of the ocean, looking like a water nymph.

We took a break, so Lily could dry herself and change her outfit. She slipped into another dress and added a hat.

We ordered lunch from a nearby place and took some extra photographs against a cabbage rose shrub backdrop in the garden while Aaron went to pick up the food. We all ate together at the terrace table by the pool, and Lily opened a bottle of wine, which was a great idea because Nolan finally relaxed.

Lily mentioned something about a nearby wheat field and how it could work for the shoot. We spent a while longer in this location as the ideas started flowing once we saw the marvelous place.

After the three of us had the opportunity to shoot Lily there, we went back to the house and took another break. We were waiting for the sunset to take a few last shots. Lily opened another bottle of wine, and I poured myself a third glass of wine. Oops.

We were honestly having a great time just talking, laughing, and commenting about how great the shoot was going to turn out.

My phone buzzed on the table. It was my father. I fled to the garden to take the call. He just wanted to ask how the shoot was going and make sure if I was okay. He also wanted to know at what time we would head back.

For some reason, I didn't find the courage to ask him if I could spend the night, so I just hung up after telling him we wouldn't stay for much longer.

I walked back, but Caleb intercepted me.

"Hey," he said with his bodyguard stance in place. "I just wanted to see how you were doing. Are you having fun?"

"I am," I replied with a smile. Ugh. Caleb was the sweetest when he wanted to be. And even though a few awkward and unexpected things had happened in the last few days, I knew he cared for me a lot. I cared for him a lot too.

"You look cute when you're drunk." He laughed.

Caleb!

"I'm not!" I replied. "And this doesn't go on the report, okay?"

"Don't worry. But yes, you are."

"I swear I'm not drunk." I stood on one foot and lifted my arms to the sides, showing him how well I could keep my balance.

"I meant cute, Miss Murphy."

Stop! I honored my nickname when there was nothing I could do to stop myself from blushing. But it's not like he wasn't used to it by now. It's been a while though since he last made me blush.

"You're lucky I don't have my body splash with me," I said, crossing my arms in front of me.

"Why? I didn't roll my eyes at you." His hands were still in a tight fist in front of him. He looked so professional. No one would imagine our conversation if they saw us from afar.

"Because maybe that'll get you to stop—saying stuff." I tried to hold in a smile with no success whatsoever.

"Okay. Do you want me to stop, Miss Murphy?"

"Yes. And I also want you to stop calling me Miss Murphy." I snort-laughed. Yeah, the wine wasn't helping. I usually hated it when he called me Miss Murphy, but when he said it *like that* … *Whew.*

"You don't seem too convinced. So, what's it going to be?" he pressed. *Why are you doing this to me*! I didn't know what kind of bug bit him. Or perhaps his brain got over oxygenated out here. But he seemed to be enjoying himself at my expense.

"I think it's best if I head back." This little conversation with Caleb was fun, but it was making me nervous. Good nervous. I think. That's why I needed to leave.

"Take it easy on the wine," he added. "I'll be with the guys if you need anything." He winked and walked away.

Okay.

I sat at the table, and Ben and Nolan played a silly drinking game that made Lily laugh. My phone buzzed again. Thomas.

"Hey." I was *not* in the mood to talk to him. At all.

"Hey babe, how's the shoot going?"

"Great, thanks," I said curtly. I hadn't forgotten about how he'd hung up on me the night before. He sounded calm right now, but I wasn't happy.

Nolan shouted something from the game they were playing, and Lily and Ben burst out into laughter.

"Where are you?" he asked with a demanding tone. *Here we go again.* I told him I was in the Hamptons, shooting. He then wanted to know who I was with, so I explained I was with Ben and Nolan and that we had asked Lily to model for us.

"Hmm."

"Is there a problem?" I asked as Ben shouted something back at Nolan. They were having fun with their game, and Lily was entertained watching them. I could've been enjoying it too, but what are you gonna do?

"I wasn't aware you were doing the project with two other guys." He sounded disappointed. And I found that odd since I was sure I'd mentioned it a couple of times already.

"You don't seem to be paying much attention to what I have to say lately," I told him. The three of them kept laughing in the background.

"Doesn't seem to me like you're working on a school project."

I explained how we had been shooting since ten in the morning and were taking a well-deserved break.

"Have you been drinking? You sound, I don't know—tipsy. I don't like it." His tone got more severe with each question. And so was my impatience.

"I'm currently drinking my third glass of wine, yes. And no, I'm not drunk." He was right. I was *a bit* tipsy, but we were doing nothing but sitting down and talking. There was absolutely no harm in that.

He kept cross-examining me, as per usual.

"Where exactly in the Hamptons are you?"

I wasn't going to answer anything more than exactly what he asked. "Sagaponack."

"Okay, but where? A house? A restaurant?" He pressed.

"A house."

I was aware of how my brief responses might've been annoying to him. But I had spoiled him. He always expected me to over-explain myself, to make him feel at ease. For me, it was an automated thing I did just to avoid him getting mad. I wanted him to understand that the number of questions he asked bordered on the excessive side.

"Whose house are you in?" His hastiness grew—by choice.

"It's my neighbors' house. You know, the ones who invited me to their Midsummer party," I added, purely for theatrical purposes.

"Why would you go there? And drinking with your school buddies? What the fuck? I don't like this." Things were escalating quickly. I stood up from the table and walked away to the garden for privacy again. I could see Caleb and his sixth sense staring my way, but I gave my back to him. He always knew when something was wrong.

"You don't get to talk to me like that, Thomas. There's absolutely nothing wrong with what I'm doing here, and still, I keep answering all of your questions. When are you going to answer mine?

"I don't have many friends, and I can never see them, or when I do, you don't feel *comfortable* with it. I could list a few things that make me feel extremely uncomfortable, yet I've never questioned or doubted you like that."

"Like what?" he mused.

"Like … something's clearly going on with you, but you don't talk to me about it. *At all.* Like how you give me small pieces of truths to put together like an impossible puzzle, so I can have something to hold on to while something else comes up. Like how I'm just so tired of guessing what *you're* thinking. Like how ridiculous it is for you to be jealous and mad about me working on a school project, which I loved working on, by the way, not that you care about any of that.

"And last but not least, like why don't you go home, look under your bed and when you can come up with an explanation for *that*, let me know so I can decide if I like it or not. Something *like* that."

Fuck, fuck, fuck. That was not how I intended to approach the condom situation. The wine was not helping with holding my tongue in place. Backing down was useless now.

"What's that supposed to mean?" he asked defensively.

"Which part, exactly?"

"The last one," he barked.

"That's *exactly* what I want to know."

"I don't know what you're talking about. But I want you to go back to the city. Please leave." He begged.

"I'm so tired of people telling me what to do—especially you. You don't trust me. You're extremely jealous of *everyone* and *everything*. And I have never given you any reason to feel that way. You're so wrapped around your issues that you don't even notice how *I'm* feeling. I constantly worry and have *begged you* to talk to me about what's wrong, and you can't deign to tell me anything. I'm done, Thomas."

"I'm sorry, babe. Wait, what do—"

"That's the problem, Thomas," I cut him off mid-sentence. "You're *always* sorry, and I *always* look the other way, yet somehow we always end up precisely where we started. I really can't do this anymore." I felt defeated. Tired. Angry. Sad.

"Babe, please. I'm sorry," he pleaded. "You don't know what I'm going through with my family right now. The things I've had to deal with while I've been here."

"Okay, then talk to me. Let's figure it out together," I proposed.

Thomas stayed silent for a few seconds.

"I can't."

"That's what I thought."

"I'll fly out tomorrow. We—we'll talk about this."

"You've said enough. Which is not much." My throat closed off.

"Please, let's talk." He kept begging. Why was it that things had to get to a certain point so he would agree to talk to me? And I knew what *talking* meant for him. It meant distracting me so he could try to make things go away for a while to buy himself time. On repeat.

"What do you want to talk about? The used-up condoms under your bed? Or about how sorry you are for not trusting me to have any friends and wanting to control everything I do? Don't change your travel plans."

"Wait. What condoms? I would never—"

"Thomas. It's over." I crouched on the grass and covered my mouth to keep the sobs away from the phone's microphone.

"Babe, I can fix this, please. I'm sorry. I can't lose you. Let me fix this."

"It's over, Thomas. I'm not strong enough to deal with this, I'm sorry. I thought I was," I managed to say, crying. "I have to go. It's almost sunset, and we're not done shooting."

"Billie." He echoed my sobs. My stomach went into knots. I didn't want to hurt him, but this was the right thing to do. The past few weeks had been torture. I'd been drowning in my thoughts. I needed to breathe again. He wasn't satisfied unless I was with him all the time or locked up in my apartment. I couldn't do it.

"I'm sorry, Thomas," I whispered, feeling my heart cracking into pieces. "I really need to go."

I hung up the phone and threw it on the grass. I rested my head between my knees. Lily came running and asked me what was wrong as she sat down and placed her arms around me.

Caleb approached us with a troubled expression on his face and retrieved my phone from the grass. He squatted in front of me.

"Hey," he spoke softly. "Is everything okay?" A part of me wanted to throw myself into his arms and stay there for a while. But the emotions running through my body were so diverse I wasn't sure about what I needed at that moment. "Tell me, what's wrong?"

"I want to spend the night here. I need to stay, please. Take Ben and Nolan back to the city. Joel can drive me back home tomorrow. Please." I begged like I've never begged before.

"Red, I—we can't just leave you here," he whispered. Lily stood up, squeezing my shoulder, and gave us some privacy. "Your father will kill us if we don't take you back tonight."

"Please. I can't go back to my apartment. I don't want to be alone tonight. Lily's offering me to stay, and I want to stay."

"You don't need to be alone. You have me." I knew I had him. But I needed a friend that wasn't—him. I couldn't talk to him about Thomas. He couldn't be objective, and I knew Lily could help me with that.

"I'm sorry. I know. You have me too. But I need to fucking breathe. Everything feels lighter here." Caleb looked disappointed with my response. He didn't get it. He didn't understand I couldn't talk to him about Thomas. It was too hard. And the cottage was so peaceful. I was the one messing with this place's zen.

He pressed his lips and said, "I'll talk to your father. Let's hope this isn't a mistake that'll get me fired tomorrow." I always ended up getting my way, but this time I didn't feel triumphant about it. I could tell Caleb was upset and worried about leaving me here. But I really needed it.

He gave me my phone back and stood up. I was still sitting on the grass, and somehow, that small distance between us stung.

I wanted comfort. Comfort I knew he could give me. A part of me wanted to go back to the city and have him help me through this. The other part of me desired freedom. Staying would provide that even if it was a temporary fix. I needed to figure this one out on my own.

"You won't get fired. Are you kidding me? I need you."

Shit.

The needing him part had always been part of my internal dialogue. I'd never said that to anyone, let alone him. But it was true.

Having Caleb around made me feel safe. That's why I needed him.

Caleb stood there like a statue. He was processing what I just said to him—the needing part. And I just hoped the result of such a process wouldn't blow up in my face. I didn't want him to get the wrong idea or make things awkward between us because of that.

"Tell me what happened. I need to know."

"We broke up," I said, finding his eyes. "Well, *I* broke up with him."

Caleb took a deep breath, and for the first time since we got to New York, I saw the very same look and spark in his eyes he had when we lived in Paris. The old Caleb. New York Caleb was a different Caleb. And now I knew exactly why that was. It was all because of Thomas.

Caleb's lips tipped up slightly into the smallest, most controlled smile I've ever seen in my life. He was glad, I could tell, but he probably didn't want to smile when my face was drenched in tears.

He held his hand out for me and helped me up from the grass.

We walked up to Ben and Nolan and talked to them while Aaron got the engine started. My friends packed their things, and I apologized for missing the sunset, but they thought we had enough material to choose from anyway. They seemed worried about me, and I just kept trying to convince them I was okay, that I would see them on Monday.

"I hate to see you like this, Billie," Ben said, twisting his mouth to the side.

"We had a great time today. Thank you for setting this up. I know we're gonna do great in our final presentation," Nolan added. "And thanks for the ride back." I hugged them both, and they left with Aaron, Caleb, and David.

And the countdown begins.

My freedom spell would end the next morning, but I was already breathing easier.

I walked back to Lily. She sat at the table, waiting for me. I asked for a refill.

"What happened, Billie? Do you want to talk about it?" she asked, filling my glass with more wine.

"I ended things with Thomas," I replied, looking away.

"Oh my God, I'm so sorry," she said, pushing my glass closer to me. She probably thought I was in desperate need of more alcohol.

"It's okay, I—it was for the best. He had a jealous fit about me being here with my school friends, and he noticed in my voice I had something to drink," I said, lifting my glass. "He asked me to leave the Hamptons. To go back to the city. But that just flipped my switch, and I confronted him about the whole condom thing too." I placed my hand on my forehead. My head was spinning. I didn't know if it was from the alcohol, the breakup, the crying, or all of the above.

"What did he have to say about that?" She looked concerned.

"He seemed confused when I mentioned it. Like he didn't know what I was talking about or something. But that was not the reason why I broke up with him. He is choosing to pay attention to all the wrong things, and I just need to breathe. All my life, I've been controlled—monitored. And he's just doing the same with me. I can't deal with that anymore. I feel like I'm suffocating."

Lily extended her hand and held mine for a few seconds.

"I'm so glad you're staying. It'll do you good, you'll see. And we can talk about this all you want. Or, if you prefer, we can keep raiding this place." She laughed and lifted the wine bottle. "There's plenty from where this came from."

I took a deep breath. This is what I needed. A fucking break.

A car's headlights illuminated the way into the driveway—a black BMW M6 Convertible. It was Joel. And. He. Wasn't. Alone.

CHAPTER 29

Tech Support!

"HONEY! I'M HOME!" William shouted as he got out of the car, grabbing a few grocery bags from the backseat. *You've got to be kidding me.* I wanted to seem annoyed but couldn't help myself from laughing at his greeting.

I stood up and drank what was left of my fourth glass of wine. "I'll be right back, okay? I'm a mess," I said to Lily, tying my hair into a pulled-back pony.

I escaped to the bathroom before William and Joel got to us. I blew my nose and washed my face with water. I felt dizzy.

I took a deep breath, stared at my reflection in the mirror one last time, and finally came out of the bathroom. William and Joel sat with Lily outside with beers in their hands.

"Guille." William stood up and kissed me once on each cheek. Lily laughed, which made *me* laugh. I was having trouble pretending to be annoyed by him. It was the wine's fault.

"What? That's how she likes saying hi to people," he said. I sat down and raised my glass to Lily. She poured more wine into it—a mistake.

"Hey, Joel." I glanced back at William and took a sip of my wine. "I recall telling you that you weren't invited." I joked. "Yet here you are." He couldn't seem any less disturbed by my remark.

"Huh. I've never been uninvited to my own home. I'll say that's

… a first, don't you think?" He winked. I hated his winks.

Did I?

I think I hated what they stirred up inside me. I didn't need anything else to be stirred. And now, I was stuck in Sagaponack with this—*stirrer*.

My phone startled me when it buzzed on the other side of the table. Joel passed it to William and William to me. It was Thomas, but I sent the call to voicemail.

I stared at the cell phone's screen, thinking if I should've answered the call or not. I quickly shook my head, trying to disconnect from my thoughts. "Um, sorry about that." I placed my phone back on the table.

Lily and Joel had just walked into the house and plated snacks in the kitchen from what I could see. "Your eyes look a little irritated," William said, lifting an eyebrow—inquiring.

"I know it's—been a long day with the shoot," I stuttered. I wasn't planning on letting him know I've been crying.

"You're drunk, aren't you?" He laughed.

"What? Psh. No!" I was. A little. But it was none of his business.

I should've grabbed my phone and called up Caleb to tell him I had changed my mind about spending the night. That would've been the smart thing. Apparently, wine makes me dumb. Very, very dumb.

"Stick your tongue out." He ordered playfully.

"No!"

"Oh, come on." He insisted. "I won't bite."

I wanted to be angry and sad about breaking up with Thomas, and William was ruining it for me. He was making me laugh, which was a much better idea.

I stuck my tongue out, and he chuckled under his breath. "Oh, yeah, you're drunk. Your tongue is purple."

I mentioned how the wine was delicious, and it was one of the best wines I've ever tried, which was true. But I tried to create a diversion from exposing myself to the real reason I was overdrinking. "I can tell you liked it. You girls are drinking my best wine."

His best wine? My face shrank into thought. I was about to ask if those bottles belonged to him, but my phone buzzed again—*send to voicemail.*

"If you need to pick it up, go ahead," he said, analyzing me. I shook my head. I wouldn't risk answering only to have William's voice overheard in the background. Besides, there was nothing to talk about at the moment. Things needed to cool off.

It rang once again, and I tossed the phone to the side without looking. William burst out laughing. "What?" I asked obtusely.

"Your phone's drowning," he said calmly, sipping on his beer.

"What!" I ran to the pool and saw my Blackberry lying at the bottom of the water. William sauntered my way, and we both watched how the screen glitched until it went black. "Oh, no, no, no, no, no!"

"You might still be able to save it. But you need to get it out of the water. The faster, the better." He lifted the right corner of his lip into a smirk. I was wearing a white tank top and had nothing else to wear afterward, so diving in the water to retrieve it myself was *not* an option.

"Go get it, William! Please!" I begged.

"Nope." He balked.

"But these are the only clothes I have with me. I'm sure you have a closet full of things to wear in there." I pleaded for his help, but he didn't care. "You'll go in the pool and get my phone out," I said, waving my hand in front of his face.

"Did you just Jedi-hand wave me?" He laughed.

"I did. Now go." I couldn't hold in a laugh either. But I was out of options. William took a sip of his beer and stared at me, as if thinking what to do next.

Lily and Joel came out, asking what was wrong.

"Guille dropped her phone in the pool, and I'm going to help her get it out!" William yelled back at them. He placed his hand on my back and pushed me into the pool.

"Oh, my God! William!" I shouted, submerged in the water up to my neck. I splashed water at him, but he took a few steps back, laughing—at me.

I dived, retrieved the phone, and placed it on the edge of the pool.

I jumped out and ran in his direction. I tried pulling him toward the pool with absolutely zero success. I kept tugging as hard as I could, but he wouldn't move an inch. "Don't get yourself tired unnecessarily." He kept laughing.

His eyes strayed to my chest, and I groaned with exasperation, covering myself almost automatically. I wanted revenge, but I was helpless. Instead, I stood behind him and tried pushing, but his feet were rooted to the ground like a tree. Impossible.

He sipped on his beer, placed it on the floor, carried me over his shoulder with ease, and dropped me back in the water. Joel laughed, and Lily came out with towels and placed them on the table, shaking her head with a smile.

I flashed a vulgar finger at William, but I think he actually enjoyed the gesture. I tried to get out of the pool again, but he wouldn't let me. He kept pushing me back every time I approached the edge and tried to pull myself up.

William took his phone out of his pocket and threw it on the grass. He removed his shoes, his shirt, and unzipped his jeans. *Lord Almighty*! I turned around and heard him jump into the pool a few heartbeats later.

Once inside, he reached the edge and pulled himself up slightly to grab his beer. Thankfully, he kept his underwear on. Black boxer briefs.

ALEJANDRA ANDRADE

"Couldn't you leave your jeans on or something?" I said, look-ing away again.

"I wouldn't want them to get ruined with all the chemicals in the pool." He explained.

"Oh, I see. So, my jeans can get ruined, but not yours, correct?"

"Exactly. I mean, you're free to take them off, of course." He was insane. I splashed him.

"Can I get out now?" I was somewhere between laughing, cry-ing, irritated, yet entertained.

"No," he replied, wandering in my direction. I kept walking backward and away from him.

"You're so annoying," I said, trying to sound angry. But I laughed. I was having fun.

"I know," he admitted. "And you're a dorky nerd trying your Jedi tricks on me." He smiled, then shouted something to Joel. His voice sounded so sexy in Swedish—gravelly, if possible.

"I'm not."

Joel brought my wineglass and left it on the edge of the pool beside my wet phone. I thanked Joel and walked around William to grab my drink.

"Yes, you are. And I kinda like it," William said, standing beside me. He grabbed my phone and took the battery out to dry all the parts with his shirt.

Oh, my God! I spotted my green hair tie with the stars around his wrist again. "That's mine, by the way."

"It's definitely not. I'm still blocked, and since you don't even have a phone now"—he kept drying the parts—"there's no way for you to unblock me now."

"I wasn't planning on it," I replied. But he just smiled, com-pletely unperturbed by my remark. But how to shake him? Rattle him? *That's his specialty, not mine.*

"Do you think Joel or Lily might have any cigarettes?" I asked,

235

placing my wineglass back on the edge of the pool. He stared down at me with a frown, pursing his lips just slightly with disapproval—rattled? The cell phone parts were now dry and resting on top of his t-shirt.

William ran his fingers through his hair to pull back the loose strands stuck to his forehead.

Breathe.

I sunk my head into the water, hoping the lack of oxygen would help me forget about his charming face, perfect hair, rock-hard chest. *Stop.*

"Guille." I heard him call me through the water.

"Guille, come on." He pulled me out, and I slowly emerged, looking away. "Okay, something's wrong. The last time I saw you smoking, you were having a terrible day, and you mentioned you never smoked. Is this related to the fact that you'd rather drown your phone instead of answering it?"

"Mhm." I pushed my head back into the water to rinse my hair out of my face and walked to the pool's steps. It was time to get out, and I was getting cold. These Swedish freaks probably thought the water temperature was perfectly warm for their Viking standards.

"I just want to know if you're okay." He insisted as I placed my foot on the first step.

I sighed deeply, slowly, without looking back at him, and muttered, "I was having the shittiest day until you arrived."

Did I just say that out loud? Yup. *Now* I'm *rattled.*

I heard William settling his beer in silence. I caught him off guard. He wasn't expecting *that* as an answer. At least I'd entertain myself waiting while he browsed through his mind for a witty comeback.

But William had gone mute, so I took another step up the stairs. I was ready to walk out of the pool and call the guys to come and get me. I needed to leave.

William grabbed my hand and pulled me back into the water. He placed his hands around my waist and pressed the hard line of his body against mine. He licked his lips and kissed me. He had me pinned against the pool's wall in a heartbeat.

I tried pushing his chest away from me—more than a few seconds later than I should have—but he didn't move much, as expected. William groaned and launched at me again, grabbing my legs and wrapping them firmly around his waist. I cupped his cheeks with my hands as he released my hair from my hair tie and ran his fingers through my wet hair in a frenzy.

My mind was split in two—an ongoing battle. A part of me wanted to give myself into the moment and stay there forever. The other guilt-ridden part wanted to push him away as far as possible. Don't underestimate guilt—it's a powerful feeling.

I pulled my face back slightly and slapped him. He snorted and replied with a bright expression, "You know I love it when you do that, Guille." He leaned in once again to kiss me. This time it was a softer, slower kiss—one I could not find the strength to pull away from.

His tongue brushed against mine, and I completely melted in his arms. My fingers ran through his wet, silk-smooth hair. He was utterly enjoying it. And so was I. But somehow, I managed to unlock my lips from his because I'm *that* stupid.

We kept our foreheads pressed against each other—both panting. I understood now why no one had ever pulled away from him—from a kiss.

I didn't care if he'd kissed a million girls before because if that had taught him how to kiss like that, then praise be.

But I was drunk and hurt. And that was the last thing I should've been doing. I couldn't even think straight, but I wanted to keep going.

"I'm sorry." I placed my hand on William's chest instead, and he sighed with frustration.

"Don't be. Do you know for how long I've wanted this?" he whispered back, stroking my cheek with his thumb.

"This was wrong. I've had too much to drink, and I shouldn't have—" I fell silent mid-sentence, unable to express my guilt.

I had broken up with Thomas a minute ago. But what I said to William was true; as soon as he arrived, he brightened my day. He always did. The last few times I've been down, he somehow managed to be there for me. He always showed up.

"I'm sorry," I said again. I unlocked myself from him and walked up the steps—he didn't pull me back inside this time.

I hugged my upper arms as I walked to the table where Lily had left a couple of towels for us. Thankfully, she and Joel weren't there anymore. It would've been embarrassing if they saw us kissing. But I needed a change of clothes.

I dried myself as much as I could before attempting to go inside, looking for Lily.

"Did he hurt you?" William asked from behind me. I turned around, and there he was, dripping wet in his boxer briefs. His skin glistened with the reflection of the lights coming in from the house, highlighting every single line of his perfect body.

"No," I replied, too fast to sound convincing. I looked away and threw a towel at him. He needed to cover himself up for my own sake.

"You keep looking away," he said to my back. "But you don't have to." I looked over my shoulder and he had wrapped the towel around his waist. I slowly turned around to face him—his gaze so intently directed at me. The sight of his body so close to mine overpowered my senses.

"Are you still together?" he asked, running a hand through his hair and down his neck.

"I'll be unable to respond if you keep doing that." I sighed. *Because that's not distracting.*

"What? This?" he asked, stroking his hair back again slowly with his eyes closed, mocking me, of course. He always found a way to make me laugh, even when I didn't want to.

I quickly frowned after that, looking at the floor, and switched back to a serious mood. "I broke up with Thomas on the phone just before you arrived," I admitted.

William pulled my chin up, trying to find my eyes. "That's—nice to hear."

"Can I borrow your phone? I'm calling the guys. I should leave." It was not a good idea to spend the night, not after all the kissing. I wouldn't want to give him the wrong impression.

"No."

"No?" I grimaced—confused.

"No, you can't borrow my phone."

"So, I'm going to be held against my will?" My teeth chattered. Even though it was summer, the ocean breeze against my soaking wet clothes felt cold.

"Let's get you inside. You're freezing." He placed his hand on the small of my back, guiding me. "Why don't you take a shower in the guest room, and if you still want to leave afterward, I'll let you borrow my phone."

It sounded like a decent plan to me since I *was* freezing, and the thought of a warm shower was tempting. William guided me to the guest room in the far end, leaving a water trail behind us.

"This is the bathroom. I'll leave something for you to wear out here on one of the beds," he said, stepping out. I closed the bathroom door and peeled the soaked clothes off my body.

The warm water felt great on my cold skin as I hopped in the shower.

I washed my underwear afterward and dried them out with a blow dryer I found in one of the bathroom drawers. What was I to do?

So, I did *that* and walked out to the room with a towel wrapped around me and found nothing but a huge white t-shirt that was probably William's lying on top of one of the beds. *Son of a bitch.*

The t-shirt fit me like a mini dress. It didn't even cover my derrière completely, but there was nothing else for me to wear.

I looked in the closet to see if there was anything else I could wear as a bottom because there was no way in hell I would step out like that. And he knew it.

I found extra bathroom stuff for the guests and grabbed a toothbrush and a small toothpaste tube while I was at it. Three drawers awaited my inspection. They were my last hope.

Empty.

Empty.

Bingo!

A navy-blue bathrobe. It was too big for me, but it was comfy, and most importantly, it covered me a couple of inches below the knees.

I walked out of the guest bedroom—my bedroom, if I were to stay.

Should I stay?

I shouldn't.

My body craved a glass of water. William was already in the kitchen and looked like he'd also just taken a shower. Something smelled delicious, and it was not just him for a change. But I could smell him alright.

I sniffed slowly, taking in the mix of delicious aromas, and walked up to Lily and Joel, who sat on the stools in front of William, keeping him company while he cooked dinner.

William moved with ease around the kitchen—slicing, tasting, smelling, boiling, sauteing. I got lost for a second watching him do his thing. He managed to make everything he did seem sexy, while I looked like a wet puppy (that stared a lot) in an oversized robe.

"Hey, where'd you disappear off to?" I asked Lily and Joel, taking a seat on the empty stool beside them.

"We went for a walk on the beach," Joel replied. "We thought you needed some privacy."

Oh God. Of course, they saw us.

I felt my face getting warm, and Lily smiled at my reaction.

"Um, could I please have a glass of water?" I asked. William quickly pulled out a glass, poured water out of the faucet, and placed it in front of me.

"I see you didn't like what I left out for you to wear," he said, looking down at my robe. He dipped the tip of the wooden spoon in the tomato sauce and took it to his mouth.

"You're crazy if you thought I'd be leaving the room in nothing but that." William looked away probably deciding if the sauce was ready or not. He added a pinch of salt and stirred again with the same wooden spoon. "Hey! No double-dipping!" I joked. Lily laughed.

He shot an amused grin at me. "First of all, you weren't so scared of my saliva at the pool." He lifted an eyebrow. I rested my elbows on the marble countertop and covered my face with my hands. I could hear Joel laughing under his breath. "And secondly."

"Stop."

"I bet my t-shirt looks better on you than it does on me." I peeked through my hands and saw him taking a tray of bread out of the oven, giving off a chill vibe, as if Lily and Joel weren't sitting right there beside us hearing him say those things.

I knew I shouldn't have kissed him.

"We can wash your clothes, so they're ready for tomorrow when we leave," Lily offered. "Don't worry about it."

"Thank you, Lily. But I don't know if I'm staying over," I replied, finally coming out of the pathetic hidey-hole I created with my hands. "Can I borrow your phone now?" I looked at William and put my hand out.

"Pasta's ready," he replied, completely ignoring my request. He kept stirring and tasting things. I was *starving*, and everything smelled like something I definitely wanted to eat. "You need to eat. You can call them afterward."

"Well, at least let me help out." I stood up to make myself useful. I was just sitting there.

"Okay, help yourself to a seat at the table," he replied, plating the dishes. He didn't look like he needed any help anyway, so I complied. Joel and Lily sat with me at the table while William brought the plates to us.

"Parmesan?" he asked.

"Yes, please."

"Do you want more wine?" Lily asked.

"Oh, none for me, thanks. I think I've had enough for today. I'm still kind of dizzy." The shower made me feel better, but I needed to stop drinking for sure.

William's pasta didn't disappoint. He kept asking about the photoshoot and my friends from school while we ate. He was curious about everything, as usual.

We finished with dinner, and Lily and I helped with the dishes.

"Want a tour?" William asked.

"No, I want your phone. Or should I ask for Lily's?"

Lily overheard and pulled out her phone from her pocket.

"Lily." William shot a don't-you-dare-lend-her-your-phone type of face in her direction. I assumed he wanted me to stay. And it's not that I didn't want to, but I thought it might not be the smartest thing to do.

"Do you even know what time it is?" William asked rhetorically. "It's eleven p.m. By the time they come back to get you, you'll be fast asleep. It's not a good idea. You're staying." I hated being told what to do, but I didn't mind this time. It was a different kind of ordering around, one that at least took my interests into consideration.

"So, tour?" He insisted.

I sighed with resignation and made sure my robe was tightly tied up around my waist. I felt so ridiculous in it. "Okay." I agreed. And to be honest, I was curious to see the rest of the house.

We walked upstairs. There was a family room with an immense television and a couch that looked extraordinarily comfy with a bunch of throw pillows. We kept walking, and he opened a door. "This is where Tobias and Eric sleep," he said. The room had a wooden bunk bed and a beautiful view of the pond and garden.

We moved on to the next room, which was Lily and Joel's. It had the same view but had a king-sized bed instead.

There was a door in front of those two rooms. William opened it to reveal a much bigger bedroom than the previous two. It had a king-sized bed, a sofa chair with a marble top coffee table beside it, and a large window overlooking the ocean. The whole house looked like something that belonged in Architectural Digest.

"Is this your bedroom?"

"No, it's my mom and dad's room," he replied.

I was curious to see his room. We walked out, and there was another door at the end of the corridor. "*This* is my room," he said, opening the door.

Wow.

CHAPTER 30

Crash

WILLIAM'S BEDROOM was the largest one in the house. It had floor-to-ceiling windows on each end. One overlooked the ocean, and the other side had a view of the pond and garden. There was a king-sized bed with a fluffy, white down-feather comforter and gray throw pillows.

A large dark gray puff beside the window looked soft and cozy. There was a small wooden coffee table beside it with a couple of books laid on top. An acoustic guitar was displayed on its stand in the corner.

"Do you play?" I asked. Is there anything sexier than a guy who can play an instrument?

"Mhm," he replied, grazing the strings.

A large bookshelf leaned against one of the walls beside the door. It was filled with books and a few photographs of William and his family. I thought it was the most breathtaking room I've ever seen in my life. Simple yet cozy and inviting.

"You were so cute!" I said, lifting a frame. William and Joel were dressed up as clowns. They looked like twins. The only way I could tell them apart was by height. "Well, you still kinda are."

"Cute?" he lifted a brow. "I'm a grown-ass man."

I laughed because he was so damn right.

"Um—you know what I mean," I said, putting the portrait down.

"I don't. I know you can do better." He sat on the bed and crossed his arms at his chest with a wicked little smile that always got under my skin.

"I'm sure you've received enough flattery for a few lifetimes." I kept walking around the room, looking at everything.

"Not from you." He wanted me to tell him he's hot and gorgeous, but he already knew that! *Sorry. Not yet.* I looked over my shoulder to where he sat on the bed and smiled in response.

Time to change the subject.

"I've always wanted to play the piano, but I never got into it."

"I'll teach you," he said casually, standing up and making his way to the garden view window. He grabbed a small remote and clicked on it.

"You *also* play the piano?" I snorted with disbelief, looking at how the curtains slowly started closing.

"I do," he replied with a sexy grin. This guy couldn't have been more unreal. "What?" he asked with a faint laugh after I kept staring at him without saying a word.

"Nothing. You don't exist, so I'm going to bed. I'm probably talking to myself right now." I walked toward the door to increase the dramatic effect of my remark.

He grasped my arm and said, "That was cute, but you're not going anywhere."

William pulled on my robe's belt and drew me near him. I was now standing an inch away from him. I'm sure he got the wrong impression at the pool that somehow, I was now eager and willing to submit to his charms whenever he felt like it.

And in a way, to be completely honest, I'd always found him utterly attractive. How could I not? I'd need to disconnect myself from my senses to become unaware and unaffected by his existence.

Another part of me knew the type of guy he was—a charmer.

I witnessed first-hand how he flirted with me, then left a minute later, holding another girl's waist. The memory of that triggered a weird sense of discomfort inside of me.

Was it *jealousy?*

I'd never considered myself to be of the jealous type. Perhaps it had been an uncharted sensibility that hadn't been prompted in this way before. The last time I felt jealous was when I saw Caleb kissing Noelle, but it seemed different this time. More … real.

Where were we?

William slowly placed his hand around my cheek, but I grabbed his hand and slowly took his hand down. I took a few steps back, still holding his hand and sat on the bed. I turned to my left and gasped.

"I thought you were going to miss it," he said.

I released his hand and picked up the framed photograph he took of me on Midsummer. *It looks great on my nightstand*, he'd written. I was surprised to see it here.

"I'm many things, Guille, but I'm not a liar, especially when I joke."

He threw himself back on the puff and grabbed his guitar.

Don't you dare. Put that back!

I returned the framed photograph to its place and stood up from the bed. William grazed the strings once, then started playing a tune. A tune I perfectly recognized. Crash Into Me. Again, he sang the parts he found convenient to fulfill whatever intention he had in mind.

He stopped playing abruptly. "You need to touch your lips. Just like the song says."

"No."

"*Touch* your lips," he said, waving a hand slowly in my direction.

"I'm immune to your Jedi-hand wave."

"I can assure you you're not," he replied. "You *will* touch your lips." He waved his hand again.

I laughed under my breath because I wasn't immune to him or whatever he did. "Ugh." I grazed my bottom lip with my thumb. "Like this?"

He bit his lower lip just slightly. "That's the spirit." He winked and continued.

I was finished. Done. Doomed. Ruined.

He was playing one of my favorite songs ever. He remembered when I told him on the rooftop. He could carry a tune quite nicely too.

He kept playing, and stopped again when he got to the part about *hiking up the skirt*. But he switched it to robe. I laughed hard at that one. "You need to get with the program—hike up your robe."

"You're insane." I pulled my robe up a couple of inches to reveal my knee. He laughed but kept playing.

William wouldn't keep his eyes off mine, and I couldn't look away, either. At one point, he threw the guitar to the side and darted at me.

He pulled me by my robe's belt and kissed me. I was shocked with the eagerness with which my lips took his again. His tongue wandered lazily inside my mouth, incapacitating me completely from acting against my conscience. He walked back as he kept kissing me, but the bed was behind us.

He's good—he knew what he was doing. He brought me up to his room with an excuse of a tour, wearing nothing but his t-shirt underneath the silly robe—that I was fortunate enough to find—and serenaded me with my favorite song. He had me well under his spell.

My mind drifted. Wondering how many girls he had brought up to this room, implementing the same modus operandi. The thought alone was enough for me to find the strength to pull away from him. Besides, after having showered and eaten dinner, I wasn't feeling as drunk as before, only exhausted. That was helpful-*ish*.

"I'm sorry," I said, breaking away from him, slowly this time, without fighting him, as I did before.

"You keep apologizing," he replied, trying to kiss me again. I took a step back and pulled on my robe's flaps as if they could close any more than they already were.

How to say it?

"So, is this your special place where you bring all the girls?" I guess that was a way to voice the discomfort associated with my assumptions.

Straight to the point.

"Oh," he said mostly to himself. "Would it ... make you jealous if I did?" he asked, entertained.

"Never!" I snorted with a smile, shaking my head.

Never ... More like, always.

I hated it when I saw him parading himself through the lobby with other girls, which was more often than I would prefer. I needed to sit down. I was drained—physically and emotionally. It'd been the longest day.

"I told you I'm not a liar. And no, I don't bring girls *here*. It's too far away." He teased, which meant he was telling the truth, but it was still an *infuriating* answer.

I grabbed one of the throw pillows and did justice to their name, but he caught it mid-air. "Today was convenient, though, since you brought yourself here." He stretched the joke. The second pillow I threw at him connected perfectly on his forehead.

I wanted to change the subject. No more talking about girls or having him come at me. It was complicated, and I felt like the worst person as I remembered I had just broken up with Thomas a few hours ago.

I was pretty sure Thomas wanted to talk to me again. He wasn't going to take no for an answer. I knew him too well to know that. Although I found it hard to believe I could get back together with him. It was too complicated. Too exhausting.

"So, why do you get the coolest room in the house? Are you like the favorite son or something?" I asked humorously.

"Um—this is actually *my* house," he replied coyly. It was the first time I've ever seen this type of reaction coming out of him. Almost humble.

"What do you mean? Your house as in—yours?" He found my query amusing.

"Yeah, I mean, I *bought* it, but it's for the family to use, of course."

What!

CHAPTER 31

An Unwinnable Bet

WILLIAM WAS *BEING MODEST*.

"Aren't you like 26 years old? You must be one hell of a chef." Maybe he was a *famous* chef. Like a TV chef, or something. I wouldn't be surprised by my unawareness.

"Well, that's because I'm *not* a chef, and that's strike one. You get two more strikes, and when you fail, which you will, I'm taking you out on a proper date."

A bet. A date. I tried swallowing, but my throat had gone dry. I gawked at him instead, playing along to the game he proposed. "How are you so sure I won't get it right? What do I get if *I* win?"

"I'll give you the keys to my car," he said, almost celebrating his imminent victory.

"So cocky," I replied, squinting my eyes at him. "No guy would give up his car. You really don't think I can win this." I didn't know what else to guess. I'd been one-hundred percent positive he was a chef. But now, he could be anything!

I knew I was probably losing, but I wanted to win. Not to win his car, of course, I would never accept it. But to have the satisfaction of proving him wrong. "I barely use the car anyway."

Perhaps if I was more observant, I could have a fighting chance at winning. But William didn't think so. "You'll end up going on this date with me. Just let that sink in for a minute. And no cheating," he added, pinching my waist. I let out a small cry. "No googling. No Facebooking. Let's keep this clean—no asking around my brothers or Lily, either."

"I don't have Facebook." I shrugged. I wasn't allowed to, not that it sparked much interest, anyway. I'd probably have like five friends in there. I don't think that would classify as a *book* with the required amount of *faces*.

"This is going to be fun," he replied excitedly, jumping back into the big gray puff, rubbing his palms against each other. "This is my happy place." He placed both hands behind his neck and shut his eyes for a few seconds, allowing himself to relax.

"Do you come here often?" I asked.

"Yeah, but not as much as I'd like to. I wish I had more time. There are moments when I'm traveling too much. It's exhausting. I don't know how to stop."

"Hmm … So, where do you usually travel to?" I asked, trying to sound naive.

"I see what you're trying to do. Stop digging for clues." He laughed. "Let's change the subject. I was thinking if … you'd like to sleep here tonight."

I froze.

"Um—what do you mean like …"

He flashed a flirty smile at me, enjoying the sight of me thinking about what to say to his proposal. "What I meant was *you* should sleep *here*, and I'll sleep downstairs in the guest room. I want you to wake up and see the view. You'll love it. Plus, this bed is just the best bed ever."

"Oh. I can't. I mean, this is your—"

"I insist."

I pressed my lips together and took a deep breath through my nose. How could I refuse that face? I accepted his offer under one condition: that he let me borrow his phone. I needed to call Aaron immediately to let him know what happened to my cell phone. If I called Caleb, I knew I would get scolded, and I didn't know his number by memory. Aaron's number was easier. He was easier.

William took his phone out of his pocket and gave it to me unlocked.

Does it end in 33 or 43?

"Everything okay?" William asked.

"Uh, yeah." I was having trouble remembering Aaron's number. I looked away from him, hoping it would help me concentrate.

I dialed the one ending in 33, but a woman picked up the phone, so I hung up. *Shit*! If I didn't call them, this was going to end badly. I dialed the one ending in 43, hoping for the best.

"Hirsch," answered a man with a deep voice.

"Aaron, hi. It's Billie." Aaron cursed in Hebrew. I could hear him talking to Caleb in the background, but I couldn't understand any of it. Caleb took the call.

"Red, we've been worried sick. I've called you a hundred times. You're not answering your texts. David left fifteen minutes ago for Long Island. He was going to check on you physically." *Shit, shit, shit.*

"I'm sorry. I'm fine. I accidentally dropped my phone in the pool. That's why I'm calling you right now to let you know I'm phoneless."

"Your father wasn't pleased about us leaving you there. I shouldn't have listened to you. We have direct orders from him to pick you up tomorrow first thing in the morning. We were trying to call you to let you know about this, but we couldn't get a hold of you. Fuck!" he yelled over the phone.

"Caleb, calm down. I'll take care of it. I'll talk to my father."

William sat next to me on the edge of the bed.

"Whose phone are you calling me from right now?"

"That's none of your business." I felt William's grasp on my shoulder.

Caleb dictated William's phone to Aaron and said, "*Run it.*"

"Caleb!" I couldn't believe him. He was going to track down the number and see who it belonged to. What the hell? "It's William's phone, okay? Don't waste your time. If you need to reach me, call this number. I'll see you tomorrow." I hung up and exhaled slowly out through my mouth before I could even listen to his response.

"I just realized how big of a deal it is that you're alone without those guys," William said.

"I know. It's strange. Like something's missing, but I don't miss it. It's hard to explain, but I feel like I can breathe," I said, throwing myself back on the bed.

"So, what's up with this—Caleb guy? He seems intense." He laid on his belly beside me.

"He's—overprotective. They all are. It's their *job*. They've taken care of me since I was young. Sometimes I think they still see me as a child. I'm so tired of people wanting to control me. When I sent them away earlier, I just … I wish it could always be like this."

"I don't think you'll live like this forever."

I hoped.

"So, what was your mother like?" he asked out of nowhere. *What?*

"Um, well, she—" I trailed off. I wasn't expecting him to ask me that.

"I'm sorry. I'm just curious to know more about her, but I understand if you don't want to talk about your mother," he said, his impossibly blue eyes looking into mine—working their hypnotic thing on me.

"No, it's fine. It's—it's just that no one's ever asked me that question before. But I'd love to tell you about her," I replied. He nodded, as in, *go ahead, I'm listening.* "Well, she had light brown hair and brown eyes." I smiled. "She was just the sweetest but would speak her mind when something didn't sit right with her. She was frank and straightforward like that."

"Who does that remind me of?" He smiled with a raised brow. I poked his nose with my finger and smiled back. He jerked his chin up and down once, prompting me to continue. "She was Catholic and liked to celebrate Easter eating paella—her favorite dish ever. It became one of my favorite meals, too. My father and I try to keep the tradition alive every year and eat paella on Easter Sunday."

"You're in luck because I make one *mean* paella." He laughed.

"I'll have to try it sometime." Having tried William's food before, I was sure it would be amazing. It's as if he poured his entire heart into his cooking. *How is he not a chef?*

"I promise to cook next year's Easter paella for you. Come rain or shine."

"But what if you hate me by then?" I laughed. "Will you still want to cook it?"

"You're un-hateable. And yes. That's what come rain or shine means. Keep going."

"Every year on her death anniversary, I go to church and listen to mass. I'm not religious, but I just feel a little bit closer to her when I do that. And I like buying white flowers—lots of them. And just fill my room with them.

"Well, that's what I did before, but this year since I now live on my own, I placed a few vases with flowers around the apartment."

"Okay, so lots of white flowers. I should probably write this stuff down." He laughed. He was so sweet. "What was her name?"

"María."

"I love how you say it. *María.*"

"You actually roll your r's pretty good. I remember being annoyed by how well you said my name. Nobody really knows how to say it."

"Gui-llerrrr-mi-na," he said, poking my nose back. "I don't know why, but I like your name."

"Probably because it's the female version of yours, and you're not arrogant at all?" I laughed.

"You think I'm arrogant?" He asked with a slight grimace filled with sincere curiosity.

"I did, at some point. But I know there's this other side to you. And you might not always feel comfortable showing it to everyone. You'd rather have people think whatever they want to think instead of showing *yourself*. Am I right?" He licked his lips and stared at me, then snorted after a few heartbeats. "What?" I asked after he decided to keep staring at me in silence.

"I know myself. I don't need to prove myself to anyone. But I'm careful of who I let in, yes. I can't help it. I um—yeah."

"Is this got anything to do with your ex? Erin?" I dared ask. I wanted to ask him about it ever since I saw them arguing. William seemed so emotionally drained that night.

"In part, I guess. But not exactly."

Vague much?

"Did she hurt you?" It was my turn to ask. And I could see in his eyes how my question had made him feel … weird? Uncomfortable? I couldn't read him. But he had asked me that a few times by now. He always wanted to know if Thomas had hurt me—in any way. And now I wanted to know if *she* had hurt him. Which I was sure she did. I just wanted him to open up to me.

A deep frown made its appearance in between William's eyes, and I felt the walls coming up, but hey, I'd gotten myself a sledge-hammer made out of questions to break that wall down and make him talk. Because I really wanted to listen.

"I guess I deserved it," he chose as a reply.

"So, she did?" I pressed.

"She cheated on me," he revealed with heavy eyelids, biting on his lower lip with a shrug to go as in, *you tell me.*

"WHAT?" William laughed at my reaction as I tried to reduce

my eyes' size back to their relaxed, neutral state. At least I made him laugh. But really … *what?*

I kept staring at him, wondering things that were not my business, and I wished I could ask, but I couldn't find it in me to do so. And yes, I was still surprised, but I didn't let him notice anymore.

"I don't think anyone deserves that." *Especially you.* Because from what I saw, as of recently, I knew he had a good heart. And I mean—*look at him.* It was my turn to frown. I couldn't help but think about the doubt that has been feeding off my stomach for the past few weeks regarding Thomas.

"She did me a favor." He smiled, and it seemed sincere, so I was satisfied. He rolled on his back and placed his hands behind his head, looking up. "I'm doing much better now."

I rolled on my belly to be able to see his face, and I believed him. He seemed better now than he did back in Midsummer.

"I might understand you better than you think," I said, pressing my lips together.

"Did that asshole cheat on you?" he asked in a hushed voice, his gaze trained on mine.

"No. I mean, I—I don't know. I'm not sure. Let's say I saw something that's not—encouraging." *And doubt's a hurtful, whiny bitch.*

He lifted his neck and placed a soft kiss on my lips. "Good riddance, then."

I nodded once. I guess he was right, but the feelings were all still so fresh. Raw.

"So, when's your mother's death anniversary?" He probably wanted to change the subject. He had shared more than I expected him to, and I did too. Plus, I knew he liked asking questions, the good kind of questions. And I enjoyed answering all of them for him.

"May 14," I replied. William's smile melted away. "What? What's wrong?"

"Nothing." He pressed his lips into a tight smile.

"What is it?" I insisted. He laid on his side next to me, holding his head with his hand. I slid to my side as well to face him with my hands under my face like a sleeping baby.

"That's my birthday," he confessed.

"What? May 14? You're kidding me," I said, sitting up straight, looking down at him.

"I'm not. It is." He smiled and laid on his back again. "It's crazy, right? I guess you'll never forget my birthday." William reached out for my hand and pulled me down to lay beside him. He turned to his side again, and our eyes were now leveled. "When's your birthday?"

That *was* crazy.

His face was drawing near mine. His gaze on my lips. "Um—April 11."

"Noted," he whispered, brushing my lower lip with his thumb. "Can I kiss you?" I nodded, and he slowly moved his lips to mine. It was the softest kiss ever.

He placed his hand on the small of my back and pulled me closer to him. "You're the first girl I've kissed in this room." He kissed my cheeks. "No. You're the first girl to ever set foot in this house that's not Lily." He kissed my neck. "And there I was thinking I hadn't any firsts left in me, but I guess there are still some for you to claim—if you want to. Because I wasn't lying when I told you I'd be taking care of the rest of yours."

I grabbed his face and kissed him because, I mean, come on. That's a speech if I ever heard one. This guy was killing me. Asking about my mother, opening up himself to me, saying all the right stuff, serenading me with his guitar. My God. He wasn't afraid to go into deep conversations, and I needed that. I appreciated it.

I slowly broke away from the kiss and brushed his lower lip, still moist, with my thumb. I turned away from his face and couldn't stop myself from yawning. "That's my cue to leave," he said, kissing my hair. He stood up and walked toward the door. *Stay!* "It's been a long day. You should rest. I'm keeping you awake, and I can see you're exhausted. I'll go downstairs and wonder how my t-shirt looks on you." He raised a brow with a naughty smile. "Or perhaps you want to hike up your robe a little more?" I sat up straight on the bed while he laughed.

"Never!" I closed my robe's flaps even tighter.

"That's going on my very long list one way or another." He found my eyes and opened the door to leave. "Good night, älskling." I parted my lips, but he closed the door behind him.

"Stay," I said in a breath, wishing I had the guts to have said that before he left.

CHAPTER 32

The Right Headspace

July 19, 2009

A BRIGHT RAY OF SUNSHINE peeked through the window curtains, drawing lines of light in the room. *What time is it?* I sat up in the bed, forgetting for a second where I was. *Ow!* My head was throbbing, my mouth was dry, and I felt a faint nauseating sensation in my stomach. Now, *that* was officially my first real hangover. Both physical and moral.

I couldn't help but feel so much guilt for having kissed William the night before. I knew I had broken up with Thomas, but it felt too fast—too planned, almost. I wasn't aware William was going to show up. And being drunk and feeling hurt didn't do much to help my case.

Trying not to think back on all that kissing was probably the hardest part of all. It'd been perfect. And not just that, but our conversation too. I could've stayed up all night just talking if he wouldn't have left.

I walked to the bathroom and saw my clothes neatly folded on top of a small bench beside my purse. They had been washed and dried. I was sure Lily did it. She was the sweetest. I wondered how my things got in here because I didn't notice anyone coming in while I was asleep.

I took my robe off and smiled at my reflection in the mirror. I shook my head with a snort as I took William's shirt off my back. I changed into my clothes, washed my face, brushed my teeth, and pulled my hair into a ponytail.

I didn't have any makeup with me but a single lipstick, so I dabbed my lips and cheeks with it to look less like a person that was about to faint.

The curtains opened once I clicked the small remote William left for me on the nightstand to admire the breathtaking view. I would spend as much time as I could in this place if I were him.

But not me. I needed to leave.

I made my way downstairs and saw William, Lily, and Joel sitting outside on the terrace table. It looked like they had already finished eating and were just talking and drinking coffee.

The bright light of day was blinding and made my head hurt even more as I stepped outside. I grabbed my sunglasses out of my purse and put them on. The polarized shades instantly relieved my temporarily sensitive eyes.

The sight of the black SUV parked in the driveway made me snap back into reality. The three of them were standing in the distance, waiting for me. I was sure I would get scolded for what happened the day before, and I really wasn't in the mood for it. I could see Caleb staring from the corner of my eye.

"Good morning," I said to everyone. William looked at me with a smile, and I smiled back as the events of last night came flashing back all at once. Seeing him sitting there in front of me made everything feel so surreal but special, too.

"Don't you mean, good afternoon?" Joel said with a chuckle. William stood up, kissed my cheeks, and went inside the house. *Where are you going?*

"What time is it?" I asked. Since my phone was dead, I was clueless. I hadn't brought my watch.

"It's just a bit past noon," Lily replied. *What?* I was impressed

Caleb hadn't gone inside the house looking for me, trying to make sure I was still alive.

William came out a couple of minutes later with a plate in one hand and a small white box in the other. "Food. Phone. Coffee?" he asked, placing the hot plate with eggs and pancakes and a brand-new iPhone on the table in front of me.

I widened my eyes at the phone. *Is this for me?*

"Um—yes, please." I needed coffee. Urgently. I wasn't planning on eating. All I wanted was to leave—after having my cup of coffee, of course. William disappeared inside the house once again.

He had managed to keep throwing hooks at me to prolong my stay.

Call Aaron after having a warm bath in my cozy guest bedroom—you're freezing!

No clothes? Wear my t-shirt. It smells delicious, and it will make you think of me, but that's okay because I planned it that way.

Sit. You need to eat the delicious pasta I made from scratch.

Wait. It's late. Sleep in my comfy bed after I've serenaded and kissed you—a few times.

You can't leave yet! You need coffee. Food. And a brand-new phone.

William came back with my coffee, and I lifted the box with a grimace. "What's this?" I knew he bought it for me, but it was too much. I intended to find out the cost so I could pay him back.

"You kept asking for my phone last night. It seems to me like you urgently needed a replacement. Your food's getting cold," he replied, gesturing to start eating.

I groaned to myself in protest. "But what about my number, my contacts—"

"It's been taken care of," he said, sipping on his coffee. "Your SIM card's been installed on the new phone. Same number, company, everything."

I asked for a receipt, and he laughed. "You're crazy if you think

I'm taking your money. Your Blackberry wouldn't turn on, I tried. I looked at your old SIM card and went to the AT&T store that's three minutes away from here. No big deal."

He wanted to make it seem like it was nothing to grab my old phone, investigate the company, go to the nearest store, buy a new one and transfer everything into it *before* I woke up so I wouldn't object and could start using it right away—no big deal.

"I was very fond of my Blackberry," I replied. I guess I was going to have to get used to the new phone.

"Well, I'm pretty sure you were one of the last people on Earth who owned one."

I tried not to laugh, but he was probably right. "Please let me pay for it. It would make me feel more comfortable," I insisted.

"When have I passed on the opportunity to make you feel uncomfortable?" He teased. I guess he was right. It was his specialty.

I closed my eyes and touched my temples for a second as my head's throbbing sensation came and went for small instances. "Headache?" Joel asked.

"You have no idea."

"Let me get you some ibuprofen."

"If you eat, you'll feel better. Trust me," William insisted. I started to eat some eggs because I was sure he had plenty of experience with hangovers.

"Here you go," Joel said, placing the medicine bottle beside my coffee. "Take two of those."

"Thanks, Joel." I smiled. "Do you know at what time these guys arrived?" I asked William as I opened the bottle and took two pills as Joel instructed.

"I woke up somewhere around nine, and they were already outside. I went up to talk to them to let them know you were still asleep. They wanted to know if you were okay."

"They're making me nervous," I said, looking over my shoulder.

Caleb was looking at me, and he didn't mind looking away. But I did.

"I'm sure they were just worried about what happened yesterday," William said, meeting my gaze. The light of day made his lovely blue eyes shimmer in a spellbinding way. I couldn't seem to be able to look away. I hoped my sunglasses helped in concealing that fact.

"So—we've heard about the little game you guys are playing," Lily chirped.

Oh, the bet! How could I forget? Lily was probably trying to distract me from my restlessness.

"William here doesn't think I can win," I snorted. "But I'm sure I'll be a car owner soon. Who do you think will win?" I asked Lily and Joel.

"Well, that depends," Joel replied. "Give us your top three guesses. They won't count as final answers, of course, unless you feel like burning your second guess right now."

"Lily, don't you dare move an inch," William ordered. "I'm sure you will make a face or a sound and give something away. I'd like to keep my car and torture this one on a date."

Torture. *Where do I sign up for that?*

"Hey! Tell that to your brother! He's the one who's been a second away from blowing it a few times already," she said in her defense. *Already?*

"What do you mean? I thought you just found out about the game." I was confused about her remark.

"This is precisely what I'm talking about, Lily," William replied to her, clearly annoyed.

"Since we all met you, Billy asked us to ... refrain from any comments about what he does for a living," Joel added.

"Oh God, you two are impossible!" William said with an exasperated laugh. He then shook his head and crossed his arms in front of him, looking defeated.

"Are you like … a *drug lord*?" I whispered, covering my mouth away from my security detail. I wouldn't be surprised if they were trained to read lips. They all burst out laughing, which I thought was a good sign because it probably meant he wasn't. I hoped so.

"Is that a final answer? It'll count as your second guess," William said.

"No, no, no!" I shouted.

"Okay then, what are your top three guesses then?" Joel asked with curiosity.

"I don't know. I'm in shock! I really thought he was a chef. Now I don't know what to think. He could be anything!" I replied.

"You're clueless. You better get ready for that date," Joel said with a laugh.

"In your defense, Billy does spend a lot of time in the kitchen, so I get why you'd think that," Lily added. William narrowed his eyes at me as if he were trying to read my mind. But I was the one that hoped I could read his.

"Well, yesterday, he mentioned something about traveling a lot. I guess that'll help me think about a few more options. I really don't know."

My phone buzzed inside the box. I didn't even know it was on. William apologized and said the guys at the store must've left it on after installing the SIM card.

It was Thomas.

I didn't know how to answer the phone, so I looked at William for help. "Swipe right," he said. I did after excusing myself from the table. I thought I could at least listen to what he had to say. I'd dodged too many of his calls since the night before, and I knew eventually, I'd have to pick up.

"Billie? I've been calling you non-stop since last night. You turned off your phone. I was so worried. I even called Caleb, and he said you weren't picking up. I'm at the airport. I'm flying back to

New York," he said, sounding pretty agitated. "My flight leaves in about an hour, so I'll be back in about a couple of hours. Can I see you? I want us to talk."

"Um," I hesitated. I wasn't ready to talk to Thomas right now. What if he did what he always did? Which consisted of wrapping my mind around his words and explaining himself perfectly to make it all go away. I had a weakness for him that needed to be isolated before I could talk to him.

"Thomas, I don't know. I—"

"You can't just break up with me on the phone. After all, we've been through, are you going to throw it all away just like that?"

It's not that I didn't want to talk to him in person. I knew we had to sit down to talk at some point. I just needed a few days. "This was not a decision made on an impulse," I replied.

"Then, let's talk about it, please," he begged. "Please." He exhaled slowly. I've never heard him so disturbed.

"I'm still in the Hamptons, and I don't know at what time I will return. I'll let you know once I'm back, and if it's not too late, we'll talk."

"You spent the night?" he asked in a defeated tone. He knew he wasn't in a position to demand answers anymore but kept asking questions as he usually did. He couldn't help it.

"I did."

"Who else stayed over?"

"Thomas."

"I'm sorry. Okay. Let me know when you get back." There was a silent pause, and then he said, "I love you, Billie. Please, you need to give me another chance." A tear rolled down my cheek.

"Love is not the problem, Thomas. I need to go. I'll talk to you later. Have a safe flight."

This was going to be more complicated than I thought. Suppose Thomas found out William and I had kissed last night and that I didn't pull away this time. I cringed at the thought.

Thomas had a gravitational pull that affected me for some reason. I was still wondering about the condoms under his bed, and the thought of it made my stomach churn. For all I knew, he was a cheater. I wished there was an easy way to face this, but deep down, I knew there wasn't.

I quickly brushed the tears away and walked back to the house. They were now inside, sitting in the living room.

"You're a pilot," I said as I approached them, trying to distract myself from the heart-wrenching call. I took a seat on the sofa, and William stared at me, probably noticing I was hurting.

"Are you sure? If you don't get it right, that means you only get one more shot, and then I'm snatching you away." He was taking the game seriously and enjoying every part of it, just as I was. But when Thomas mentioned being at the airport, it occurred to me that William could be a pilot. He said he knew Dave Matthews from work. Maybe he was a private jet pilot?

I just wanted to take my mind off of things. Playing William's game was fun. And being at his house proved to be a relaxing getaway. I knew once I headed back to the city, things would get real again. I wasn't excited about that. At. All.

"You said you travel a lot and that it's exhausting, so I'm going to take a chance. Pilot. Final answer," I said, feeling sure of myself.

"I'm so happy," he said slowly, "because I'm one step closer to winning." He laughed.

"Damn it!" I yelled with disappointment.

I was so hopeful about my second guess. I needed to get my shit together before getting wrapped up in the game and start going on dates. My third guess had to wait. I had to take my time with it. There was an underlying significance to it, and I couldn't pretend otherwise either. It was more than just a game.

"I think I'm going to head back before I make another stupid guess," I said to them. Aaron, Caleb, and David's presence was uncomfortable and pressured me to leave. Probably that's what they wanted.

"You're free to make another stupid guess right now if you wish," William said with that mischievous smile of his.

"Nah, I'm not on a date-kind-of-mood right now," I replied as I gathered my things.

"I'll ride back with you," he said, standing up. "Someone needs to get you in the right headspace." I knew he was joking, but damn it! He didn't even need to ride back with me. He got me at *right headspace*.

"You don't have to. Really. I know you love it here. It's the weekend. You probably want to stay another night."

"I have stuff to do in the city. Besides, Joel's car is way too small, and poor Lily would have to ride in the back for two hours. Let's go," he said, grasping my shoulder.

Joel stood up and embraced me, which caught me off guard, to be honest. I'm all in for hugs and kisses, but I found it curious as he usually handled himself with a certain distance.

Lily came flying down the stairs. "Aw! You're leaving?" I nodded and thanked her for everything. She had been a lifesaver. I gave her a big, warm hug. William grabbed my hand and lead me to the car. I took a deep breath and readied myself for his unnecessary persuasion.

CHAPTER 33

Wrath of the Gods

DAVID SAT BEHIND THE WHEEL, and Aaron opened the door for us. William and I stepped into the car, and Caleb was already seated in the third row. I huffed air out of my mouth because *really?* He was going to sit behind us for the next two hours? Awkward. I knew how observant he could be. As if he didn't manage to do so even when riding in the front seat, anyway.

Frustrating.

"You okay?" William inquired under his breath. I nodded.

"Thank you for letting us use your house for the shoot and for letting me stay over. You kind of didn't have a choice, anyway." I smiled.

"What did you think of my bed? Isn't it the best?" he asked.

William! He made it sound as if we had *shared* his bed.

Caleb's prying gaze felt like a wave of hazel crashing on my back. He obviously didn't know I slept there alone. He was probably thinking the worst. I hoped he knew to expect better from me.

Stop caring about Caleb's opinion!

"If me waking up at noon didn't say enough, I don't know what will. And the view is something else," I added.

Let Caleb believe whatever he wants to believe.

"Glad you enjoyed it. Do you need any help to set up your phone?" Honestly, I did. Perhaps switching to tech talk would be a better type of car conversation than William's innuendos.

I asked him if he could help me download the Blackberry Messenger app for iPhone. I needed it because of the different group chats I had in there. He helped me download the app, among others he swore I had to have. He was obviously a devout iPhone user.

"Now, there's one more thing left to do." He pulled his cell phone out of his pocket, typed something, and then my phone buzzed. An iMessage came through:

W.S.: New phone, not blocked.
Me: Ugh.
W.S.: Fresh start?
Me: Maybe.
W.S.: You're a tough nut to crack.
Me: You have no idea.
W.S.: I think I do.
Me: Thanks for the phone. I still feel weird accepting it.
W.S.: Relax. I'll find a way to make you pay for it.
Me: I'm sure you will.

I chuckled, which was weird since we weren't talking out loud. It was evident that William and I were having a conversation through the phone.

W.S.: You could start by taking your third and last guess.
Me: Nah, I'm good. I think I'm gonna have to REALLY think about it. It could take weeks or months for me to decide. There's a car at stake.
W.S.: You're funny.
Me: I didn't hear you laughing.

William turned to look at me, nudged my shoulder with his as a sign of protest, and kept typing.

W.S.: I was being sarcastic. Months? Really?

I typed my reply, but William's phone rang. He sent it to voice-mail. "Go on," he prompted. He seemed curious about what my next reply was going to be. He seemed to be enjoying our texts. It was fun. But his phone interrupted us again.

The person trying to get a hold of him was very insistent, and William was not turning off his phone because I'm sure he wanted to keep texting me. The fastest way to deal with that call was to answer it, and he did.

"*What's up? ... I'm busy at the moment ... No ... I don't know anything about that ... You know that's almost three months away, right? ... Have, what's her name ... Ellie, right. Have her talk to Alice about it in a couple of months ... Because I couldn't care less, that's why ... Erin, you need to relax, and you need to stop calling me ... No ... I need to go.*"

Erin.

I wanted to know why they kept in touch if William couldn't stand her. At least he didn't seem too enthusiastic about talking to her. It felt like an annoying business call to me.

W.S.: Sorry about that.
Me: We don't need to keep texting, you know.
W.S.: It's fun. It's like having unlocked a new feature on my phone.
Me: So, does Erin work with you?
W.S.: Yes. But not for long.

I knew it wasn't my business to pry, and I'd gotten the answer I wanted. They worked together. That's it. I switched the mood back to fun instead.

Me: Is she your boss? Haha.

W.S.: She wished.

Me: So, you're her boss?

W.S.: You know you're not getting any answers, right? Or if you want to go ahead and take your third guess, we can talk about anything you want regarding my job.

Me: Boring.

W.S.: Cheater!

Me: Help me practice.

W.S.: How so?

Me: I'll try to guess things about the car I'll own soon.

W.S.: Ask away.

Me: Is it a sports car?

W.S.: Yes.

Me: Is it red?

W.S.: No.

Me: Black?

W.S.: Yes.

Me: Nice! Is it a two-seater?

W.S.: Who have you been talking to?

Me: I'll take that as a yes. Why do I get the feeling you're a German-manufactured car enthusiast?

My father was *quite* the car enthusiast. And since I was his only child, there was nothing much he could do but talk to me about his passion. The irony rested upon the fact that I didn't know how to drive yet. There hadn't been a need for it.

W.S.: I'm sure Lily said something.

Me: She didn't. I swear.

W.S.: Ok, keep going.

Me: I'm torn between Audi and Porsche.

W.S.: You're so annoying.

Me: Well, now you know how I feel most of the time.

W.S.: You're close.

Me: I'm wondering which would be a sexier car. An Audi or a Porsche?

W.S.: You're calling me sexy?

Me: You wish. We're talking about cars. My car.

W.S.: So I'm not sexy?

Yes! You are the sexiest thing I've ever seen, okay? I'm sure it wasn't hard for him to read that fact written all over my face in HUGE bold letters. But then, men could be oblivious sometimes. Or pretend to be—according to their needs.

Me: I'm not sure if you're my type.

W.S.: What's your type?

If you could draw me a man … it'd be him.

Me: Sexy.

W.S.: You're infuriating.

Me: No, that's all you.

I laughed out loud. It was so much fun making William squirm. I understood now why he teased me all the time. I was getting on his nerves—a new hobby. Plus, he needed a humility check. I'm sure he had grown accustomed to being praised and worshiped by women all the time. Not me. Not yet, at least.

Me: I'm going with Porsche. Black, sexy, Porsche. Final answer.

W.S.: If you apply yourself in this very same way, you might win the bet.

Me: My new car's going to be a Porsche?
W.S.: I'm afraid so.

"Yes!" I screamed out loud, raising both of my hands above my head, and laughed again. "We're not done yet," he said, jerking his chin at the phone.

W.S.: I think you're like a Porsche.

He laughed out loud. I figured he noticed how lame that was once he sent it. I just shook my head and echoed his laugh. I'm glad I could see and hear his reactions after he sent his texts. It was easier to understand the context.

Me: This was fun. I won, and you got to learn a new pick-up line. I almost blushed with that one. Might work with someone else.
W.S.: I know how to make you blush. And I know how to get under your skin too, don't forget that.
Me: It's a condition. My face tends to get red around the cheeks. It's very unpredictable.
W.S.: I'm sure it is.
Me: Hahaha
W.S.: I don't hear you laughing. Learn to take a compliment.
Me: Haven't read any.
W.S.: I think you're beautiful and sexy.

An oldie, but a goodie. I found his eyes and said, "Thank you." I had to pretend with all the strength of my being that what he had just written to me wasn't affecting me. But oh, it did. I could feel my pulse accelerating. And that was the inconvenient part of chatting with him side by side. I didn't think that was fair.

Not only did I have to worry about my replies, but I also had to seem cool when *thinking* about writing them. I wondered if William played poker often because he was doing an excellent job at keeping an expressionless semblance while he texted me. Maybe he was a professional poker player.

Me: See? I'm a fast learner.
W.S.: I also think that little freckle on your lower lip is pretty cute. I really liked kissing it.

He was pushing my limits. I bit my lower lip as I drifted into thought, but my fingers froze. I froze. I didn't know what to respond to that. He *knew* how to make me blush—we both knew that. He just wanted to brag about it.

He turned his head down slightly to look at me, searching for my eyes, and confidently smiled once I met his gaze.

W.S.: Your skin condition is acting out. You might need to see a doctor right away.

This time I was the one to nudge his shoulder with mine. He laughed victoriously and jerked his chin at my phone again, inviting me to answer his text. I wrinkled my nose at him and went back to texting. I had to be quick on my feet with William.

Me: I told you, it gets triggered out of nowhere. We still can't figure out exactly why that is.
W.S.: I'm sure I can help with the research.
Me: I'm sure you can.
W.S.: Anyway, I have exciting news. Well, good and bad.
Me: Ok. Tell me all about it.
W.S.: Do you remember the Midsummer "good luck" flowers?
Me: Mhm.

W.S.: Well, the bad news is they weren't exactly for good luck.
Me: I knew it! But Lily said it was "tradition."
W.S.: She wasn't lying. What you did with the flowers is one of many Midsummer traditions.
Me: So, what's the good news?
W.S.: The good news is you are going to be my wife.

I cleared my throat. "I beg your pardon?"

"Keep to your phone," he ordered with a laugh.

What is happening? I echoed his laugh, but mine was more of the nervous kind.

Wife.

W.S.: Allow me to explain. And let me start with the fact that we are VERY superstitious.
W.S.: The tradition consists of picking seven different kinds of flowers and putting them underneath your pillow. It is said that once you do that, you'll dream about your future spouse that night.

Oh, my God. That was so embarrassing! I did dream about him and I told him about it on the rooftop. He was going to bully me for eternity. William laughed again when he saw me thinking about the things he just wrote.

I give up! I didn't know what to say. I looked at him, and he said, "We wouldn't want to anger the Gods, now would we?" His face came a little closer to mine.

"Oh, I'll unleash their full wrath, believe me," I taunted him as I faked self-confidence.

"We'll see about that," he replied, stroking my rosy cheek with the back of his finger as he slowly adjusted his seating position to get even closer to me.

His finger grazed my jaw, and his hand lazily traveled behind my neck and released my hair from the ponytail with a big smile and placed it around his wrist, just beside my green hair tie with the golden stars.

My throat dried. His blue eyes were hypnotic. I couldn't stop staring at them as they drew nearer by the second.

"I think I found a fun new nickname for you," he breathed. His lips were half an inch away from mine. He licked his lower lip. "Wife."

"Never," I said in a breath.

My hands were shaking, and he must've noticed that because he immediately gripped both of them with his free hand. Finally, his warm, rosy lips meld with mine, and his wandering sweet cinnamon-tasting tongue sought mine out. It was a soft and slow kiss, like the ones he gave me on his bed the night before—effortless. I could've stayed there forever.

Talk about getting in the right headspace.

Someone cleared their throat. *Shit*! And if I had to put my money on it, I would have to say that it was Caleb. I became so immersed in my conversation with William that I don't know if I forgot about Caleb or didn't care about him sitting right behind us when William kissed me.

William cleared his throat with a laugh and straightened up in his seat. He took his phone and texted me again. I didn't know if I should laugh or cry, so I grabbed my phone too and tried to bury my face in it.

And now William wasn't the only one texting me.

CHAPTER 34

Hope

Caleb: Having fun with your husband?
Me: It's just a joke.
Caleb: Why is he calling you wife? I don't like this guy. I don't want you to get hurt. He's a player.
Me: We're just texting.
Caleb: Is that what you kids are calling it these days?

Kids. I stared at the screen, trying to come up with an answer.

William nudged my shoulder with his, wondering why I wasn't answering his texts. I didn't know what to reply to Caleb, so I thought it was best to talk to him later in person. I could tell he was upset and probably confused too. I didn't blame him.

W.S.: Are you leaving me on the back burner?
Me: It took me less than a minute to reply to you. You'll survive.
W.S.: Waiting time goes slower than regular time.
Me: So just like the opposite of snooze time?

William laughed.

W.S.: Exactly. I might have to punish you for this one.
Me: Hey! What'd I do?

W.S.: You made me wait. And I hate waiting. But don't worry. I'll make sure you like it.

I swallowed hard. My cheeks were warming up again. I obviously didn't know what to answer to that.

We were a few blocks away from the apartment building, and as I kept thinking of a reply, my phone buzzed with an incoming call. *Saved by the bell,* because I was most definitely under-qualified, mind you, to keep up with such a conversation with William. As interesting as it might've been.

It was Thomas. William met my gaze and searched for my hand. It was comforting. I swiped right to answer the call.

"Hey, Billie. My flight's been delayed. I will be there today, but late. Can we meet tomorrow?" The disappointment in his voice was undeniable.

"Sure, um. I've got school tomorrow. But I'll be free after eight." I had to meet with Ben and Nolan, plus I was training with Grant at seven.

"Okay," he agreed. "I'll see you tomorrow, then." He hung up the phone with resignation. I turned to look at William and found comfort in his calm semblance.

If Thomas knew I was holding hands with William, kissing him, and had slept on his bed last night … I don't know if he would've been so eager to come to talk to me. Even though we weren't together anymore, I still felt guilty about kissing William. But damn, it was so hard refusing him. Starting with the fact that I didn't want to.

We finally arrived. William released my hand and stepped out of the car, looking at his watch. I turned to look at Caleb just before I got out, and he didn't seem happy. He licked his lower lip with a frown and looked away.

William offered his hand to me and helped me step out of the

SUV. "There's a meeting I need to get to," he said, pulling me closer to him.

"Hmm, what kind of meeting would that be?" I asked, hoping to get any insights—wishing it wasn't a meeting Erin would attend.

"The kind that is none of your business," he replied with a smile, poking my nose with his finger. "It's just a boring meeting. I'd rather convince you to take a third guess right now and whisk you away to our first date."

A young driver held the door for William. "Text me if you get bored," I replied, echoing his smile. "Because I'm not taking any guesses right now. And that's mine."

"You can have this one," he said, handing over the simple black elastic tie, leaving the one with the stars on his wrist. I liked it on his wrist, and I didn't mind if he wanted to keep it, but I enjoyed teasing him.

"What about the other one? You're not blocked anymore."

"I changed my mind. But you can always come and get it," he said, crossing his arms in front of him—a challenge, for another day, at another time, when I wasn't being observed with a magnifying glass.

I looked over my shoulder and confirmed my assumptions. The three of them were looking at us in the not so far distance.

"I'll get it off your wrist one of these days."

William shook his head slowly with one of his charmingly crooked smiles. And just before he left, he kissed my cheeks and whispered in my ear, "Don't wait up." He got in the car and brushed his bottom lip with his thumb.

I brushed my bottom lip, too, and smiled for the millionth time. I felt like the bottom-lip brushing was already our thing—our little secret sign.

This weekend at the cottage was the first time I've ever been with William outside of the apartment building, which was crazy.

It felt—weird living in the same building now. I was hoping our dynamic wouldn't get awkward. I just wanted things to feel like they always did.

I was still standing on the sidewalk when my phone buzzed.

W.S.: When the meeting gets boring (it will), I'll keep thinking about how I'm going to punish you.

That whole punishing thing he had going on was giving me a hot flash. Damn. And my curiosity levels were skyrocketing.

Thankfully, William had gone to his meeting because I really needed to get my shit together. Starting with the fact that I needed to talk to my security detail—all three of them. And I knew things were going to be awkward with Caleb after that kiss with William in the car, but there was nothing I could do about it. *What's done is done.*

I asked them if we could have a word and walked inside the lobby. I could reply to William's text later. Perhaps if I made him wait a little longer, he'd get more creative.

"Of course, Miss Murphy," Aaron replied as they followed me inside.

I was sure Caleb told Aaron and David I'd broken up with Thomas, but I wanted to let them know we would probably meet one last time tomorrow. But just in case he showed up today, I wanted to be notified before he came up to my apartment unannounced, as he usually did.

I could see Caleb's power-filled stare from the corner of my eye, but I kept my gaze focused on Aaron and David.

"Would you require extra security around him from now on?" Aaron asked casually. *Way* too casually. I think he probably misunderstood me. I wasn't afraid of Thomas. I just didn't want any more surprises.

"No, not exactly. Look, we broke up. But there's nothing to be worried about. I don't want him to feel comfortable going up to my apartment like he used to, that's all."

"Of course, Miss Murphy," Aaron replied. "We'll take him off the authorized visitor's list." *There's a list?* Of course, there was. And it was probably a very short one.

I apologized for last night. I told them how it wasn't my intention to have them worry like they did. I knew they always had my best interest at heart, and I didn't want them to feel betrayed by my behavior. I assured them I would talk to my father and that this wasn't in any way their fault.

Before I excused myself, I directed my gaze at Caleb. He was still looking at me. I wet my lips and took a deep breath through my nose. What was I to say? That I'd prefer he didn't have to see William kissing me? Of course! That it was a possibility he would never have to see that again? Could be.

I didn't know what to expect from William. For all I knew, he could walk in with a girl on each arm tomorrow. At least, he was free to do that. Not that I would enjoy the sight of it.

I finally excused myself, and Caleb offered to walk me back to my apartment. *Shit.* I didn't need any more drama.

We walked in silence all the way to my doorstep.

"Thank you, Caleb," I said as I unlocked my door.

"Did you sleep with him?" he asked bluntly.

What? I turned around, and his face looked grim. He kept gnawing at his bottom lip, looking anxious. His face was telling me he thought the answer to his question was *yes.*

"That is none of your business, Caleb."

"It *is* my business to take care of you, actually."

"I can take care of myself."

He snorted. "You just told me you needed me."

"I do need you." I sighed. I knew I shouldn't have said that to him last night. I was so stupid. But it was the truth! I needed him. *Please don't look at me like that.*

"Please, I need to know."

Don't you know me at all?

"Caleb, I broke up with Thomas *yesterday*. I wouldn't." *But I did kiss William a few times—in the pool, in his room, and in the car right in front of you.* I hadn't had the time to process if kissing William had been right or wrong, but it felt *so good.* I couldn't stop thinking about it.

He frowned. "I'm just—why would you kiss him in front of me?"

I stared at him, not really knowing what to say because he was right.

Seeing him kiss Noelle had been hard for me. But I had caught them. He would've never kissed her if he knew I was standing right beside them. Right?

I don't know if I could've endured watching him with someone else day in day out as he'd been doing for the past months. Our relationship was complicated as it was, and I was pushing him into having to tell me to stop because he couldn't stomach it any longer.

I had zero doubts now that he'd been the one who cleared his throat in the car. I felt like shit. He just wanted me to stop. And I didn't take the time to think about him. "I'm sorry. I—"

"No"—he held a hand up—"You're right. This isn't any of my business." He seemed so disturbed, and I felt terrible by the second. "We'll be downstairs." He turned on his heel and left.

"Caleb! Wait!" He ignored me and kept walking away. "Caleb!" Fuck.

All I wanted was to take a shower to wash all the confusing feelings away. Things were getting very complicated.

I changed into my pajamas after showering. It was a way of telling myself it was best to stay at home. I couldn't go out without inevitably seeing Caleb. He was on duty for the rest of the day, and I was sure he didn't want to see me.

I sat on my bed and took the photograph William shot of me out of my nightstand drawer. I smiled at the memory of seeing it on *his* nightstand.

When he sent it in the first place, I thought he was teasing me, but he'd been telling the truth. I regretted having thrown his letter away. William was the sweetest, even though he liked to pretend otherwise.

The photograph slipped through my fingers, falling on its front face against the floor. There was a small inscription on the bottom left side of the back of it I hadn't noticed before.

"*The heart wants what it wants, or else it does not care.*"

I read the quote over twenty times before finally placing it back in my drawer. He was quoting Emily Dickinson, and I absolutely adored her poetry and became rather obsessed with it. I even read and studied her correspondence. The quote William wrote was part of a letter written to Mary Bowles that I particularly liked.

It was inevitable for me to remember Juan Pablo's words when I first met him—*the heart wants what it wants*. My mind was blown to Mars and back. Freaking Juan Pablo! How could he know such things? Was he implying William's the one I was supposed to be with? *In title behold, as time has come.* Title. William and I have the same name.

Stop.

It was a rabbit hole, and I was missing the point. Besides, believing those things made me feel very stupid. I needed to stop analyzing Juan Pablo's riddles.

The quote on the back of the photograph was such a thoughtful gesture. The fact that it was handwritten made it even more special. No one writes anymore. But what was William trying to say? And why would he hide the inscription on the back? Maybe he didn't want me to find it right away.

I feared I would pass out as I felt my heart melting, but another side of me had plenty of doubts about him and his intentions. He was an undeniable flirt. It could've been one of his jokes. *Even when I joke, I tell the truth.*

Cause of death: overthinking.

He'd been feeding me truths disguised as taunts with a dropper. Was this his way of being "subtle" while I was still in a relationship with someone else? I would have to wait and see what he would do now that he *knew* I had ended things with Thomas. The bet was one of those things. It seemed to me that William had been planning it for a while. He wouldn't have asked his brothers to refrain from talking about what he does for a living if he hadn't.

All of this ironically reminded me of one of my favorite poems by the same Emily Dickinson that says, *The Truth must dazzle gradually, or every man be blind—*

William liked the chase, the thrill, and if he could provoke me in the process, even better. And to be honest, his method was doing wonders on me.

I knew what I wanted. I needed to formally and definitely end things with Thomas to make space for shinier and brighter possibilities ahead. I didn't know what to expect with William, but I was curious.

Where doubt reigned, now hope prevailed.

CHAPTER 35

Baked

July 20, 2009

BEN SHOWED US the printed photographs we all took on Saturday's shoot after school, and all I could think of was *why hasn't William texted me all day?* We evaluated the 4" by 6" standard-sized prints to make the final selection as I went deep into thought. *He must be busy. He must be at work. Not with Erin, hopefully.*

Probably.

I took on the responsibility to develop the selected photographs in a larger format for the presentation.

He's guarded. His last girlfriend cheated on him. *Of course, he's guarded.* We broke down the walls between us, but he was still standing on the other side of the rubble.

Baby steps, I reminded myself of that. We did text a bit last night, and it was fun and easy and flirty. But I couldn't stop thinking about him today. *Help?*

"You okay, Billie?" Ben asked.

"Ah—yeah. Sorry." I reeled in my focus back on our after-class meeting because that was actually helpful. Anything to get me out of my head was welcome at this point.

Nolan agreed to digitalize the selected prints, and Ben said he'd start to draft the Keynote presentation. We worked great as a team, but we had also become good friends. They were worried about me for what they witnessed two days before, but I talked to them and explained how I had ended things with Thomas. If they knew my mind was elsewhere …

How quickly things can change in a heartbeat. I knew that much.

We finished our after-school session pretty quickly right there on campus. David and Aaron were on duty. I hadn't seen Caleb since he left my apartment the day before—a loose end. And I didn't like the feeling. I hated when things were tense between us. It was almost as if my mind refused to function correctly because of it.

I asked the guys if they could take me to a supermarket because I was determined to bake a cake for my father's birthday. Baking it a day before would give me time to buy one if I ruined it for some reason.

But there's nothing much that can go wrong with a cake mix. You whisk the ingredients and throw it in the oven, right?

Thomas called me early in the morning to set up a time to meet. He planned to arrive at my house at 9 p.m. once I was done training with Grant and had enough time to shower and get ready.

I got home at around 6:30 p.m. That meant I had thirty minutes to change into my gym clothes and start baking the cake before my session with Grant at seven.

Unfortunately, Mimi had left two hours ago. She would've loved to help me, but I wanted to do this on my own. I knew my father would appreciate the gesture.

I followed the instructions word for word, placed the cake in the oven just a minute before seven, and sprinted to the gym. I set up an alarm on my phone to remind myself to go back to check on the cake as soon as I was done with Grant.

William was probably going to be there—our meeting point— and I knew how easily distracted I could get around him.

The box indicated thirty-six minutes of baking time, enough to train and make it back a few minutes before it was ready to take out of the oven.

Grant was waiting for me at the gym. He quickly bandaged my hands and helped me with my gloves.

I got anxious thinking about William showing up. My fear was that things would be different or awkward after the cottage. I hoped not. However, it was obvious that our dynamic was going to change. It couldn't all be the same as before; it had to be better. But I just wanted to see him and make sure for myself. And I missed his face already—too damn much that it caught me off guard.

My half hour with Grant was about to end, and I heard someone coming in behind me. I looked over my shoulder, but it was Tobias.

"Hey, Billie!" he said with a big smile as he walked into the gym. I greeted him back. It was odd to see Tobias as I'd never seen him work out at this time before. William had to be close behind.

Grant took my gloves off, and I lingered a while longer in the gym, waiting for William to show up. I didn't want to ask Tobias about him, so I jumped on the treadmill for a few minutes to make time for him to arrive.

My brisk walk turned into a run as the minutes went by, and still no sign of him. Grant and Tobias had just started training, and my alarm hadn't gone off, so I was good.

I had decided before not to ask Tobias about William, but I couldn't deal with the curiosity. I jumped off the treadmill, washed my hands, and ambled out of the bathroom. Grant was setting up a few of the small cones he usually brought, and Tobias was taking a water break, so he was free for me to ask away.

"I've never seen you train at this hour before." I casually led the conversation to where I wanted it instead of asking Tobias directly about William.

"Yeah, I'm taking up Billy and Joel's training spot for now," he replied, panting. His face was red and sweaty from the workout.

"Oh, I'm sure they couldn't keep up with you, Grant," I said humorously, trying to dig for information. Grant laughed, and Tobias grinned, brushing away the sweat from his face with his forearm. *Come on! Spill!*

"I'm sure they'd find any excuse to skip a class. But you know they started today with that project they're working on together, so I'll be training them at whatever available time they have."

"Project? What project?" I asked, faking dementia. I knew I wasn't supposed to ask around, but maybe I could win our bet.

"You know, the—"

"Hey, hey, hey! No cheating, Billie. I see what you're doing there." William had trained him well. Apparently, he forgot to talk to Grant. I almost got him.

"What bet?" Grant asked with a curious-filled smile.

"Billie has to guess what William does for a living or risk going on a boring date with him. I'd be fishing for information to get out of it too if I were you." He joked.

"Oh, really?" Grant looked surprised.

"Don't react to anything," Tobias ordered. "Look at her. She's analyzing our every word and gesture." I was.

My phone buzzed.

W.S.: Hej älskling. I forgot to mention yesterday I won't be seeing you at the gym for a while. I'm sure you bumped into Tobias. I'm busy right now, but I'll text you once I'm done. I'm gonna need you to take that last guess soon, okay? You know I hate waiting.

I looked at the top left of my screen. *8:15 p.m.*

"Oh my God, the cake!" I shouted. My alarm *never* went off. I quickly checked the alarm settings, and it was set to thirty-six freaking hours! *I hate iPhones!* This would've never happened with my Blackberry!

"Wait, Billie! What's wrong?" Tobias urged. But I ran out and desperately clicked on the elevator button without replying.

The elevator arrived, and as the doors were closing, a shrilling alarm startled me. It was the building's fire alarm system. *Fuckfuckfuck*!

I ran out of the elevator and unlocked the door to my apartment. Grayish smoke flooded out from the kitchen. I couldn't see fire, only smoke everywhere. My first instinct was to fill a bowl with water. I planned to open the oven's door first and then throw water inside it.

My father is going to kill me!

He was surely making me go back to live with him after this. I kept thinking about the firefighters coming in and how *embarrassing* it would be with all my neighbors. Especially with William. He would surely give me shit for burning a simple cake mix through all eternity.

I needed to fix this.

I desperately browsed through the cupboards with a cough that wouldn't cease, looking for something useful that could hold enough water. I rarely used the kitchen, and I didn't know where Mimi usually kept things other than the basics.

I finally found a plastic bowl big enough to work and filled it with water. I grasped it with one hand as I reached for the oven door with the other.

The handle was scorching to the touch. I recoiled fiercely away from it—my hand throbbed with pain—both the plastic bowl and the water ended up on the floor. The smoke was getting denser by the second, I could barely see, and my cough only got worse with every passing second. That's when I saw the flames inside the oven.

Oh, nonono!

I thought about how there must be a fire extinguisher out in the hallway. I quickly turned around to get it, but I lost my balance when my foot stepped in the empty plastic bowl, making me slide and fall on my back.

The air was knocked out of my lungs from the blow, and I couldn't pull any air in. I couldn't breathe. My hand throbbed from the burn.

As I tried to summon short and shallow breaths into my lungs, Caleb's face came into sight through the smoke. His horrified expression was the last thing I saw before passing out.

CHAPTER 36

Perceptions

A CHEMICAL TANG triggered my nose, and my throat itched. I let out a faint cough as I tried opening my eyes with little success. My right bandaged hand stung and burned like crazy.

Ow!

"Billie, hey," a soothing voice called. "It's okay. I'm here."

"Thomas?" *Where's Caleb?* I felt dizzy and couldn't focus on his face. I tried to sit up, but a woman I didn't recognize grabbed my shoulders and pulled me back again on my pillows as I took the place I was in—my bedroom.

"Billie, my name is Lauren. I'm a paramedic. How are you feeling?" she asked loudly.

"What happened? I'm fine." I lied. My head hurt, and I couldn't recall why I was lying here on my bed. I could hear a whispering voice outside my room, asking if I was okay. I recognized that voice; it was Tobias. I was suddenly reminded of the burning cake.

"You burned your hand and fainted. You were found on the kitchen floor. Do you remember this?" Lauren asked.

"I—do, yes." I stammered. It was all coming back to me. I could see Thomas clearly now, standing beside the bed.

"She seems stable. But I would still like to have her come over to the hospital so that—"

"No, no, no. I'm fine. Really." I interrupted her before she finished giving her opinion to Thomas. I didn't want to leave.

Tobias knocked on the open door. "Hi, sorry to interrupt, but a doctor is arriving any minute now. He's our family doctor, and um—we insist he takes a look at her." Thomas acknowledged him with a gentle frown, and Lauren beamed at Tobias with agreement.

"Okay, but if the doctor feels like you still need to go to the hospital, I think you should consider it," she replied, blushing. I shrugged on the inside. I didn't blame her, though. She packed her stuff and dismissed herself, handing her card to Tobias, just *in case* we needed to reach her.

Ha!

"Billie, do you mind if I come in?" Tobias asked, looking at Thomas, probably seeking his authorization. I nodded.

"I'm sorry I ran off like that earlier. I was freaking out."

"I'm sure you were. After you left, Grant and I heard the alarm, so we stepped out of the gym and saw Caleb coming out of his apartment. We told him how you mentioned something about a cake. We assumed the fire alarm was triggered at your place. Caleb rushed to get you and found you on the floor. He carried you out of the kitchen after you passed out. Grant and I brought the fire extinguisher." Tobias looked tense and worried.

Thomas was pacing slowly in my room with his hands inside his pockets as Tobias explained what had happened.

"The smoke was controlled quickly after that, but the firefighters paid a visit. They checked your kitchen to rule out any damage, but everything was okayed. You'll have to get a new oven, though. Aaron and Caleb handled the firefighters and answered all of their questions. So, I stepped out and made a few calls," he said, widening his eyes. "And so—we decided to call our doctor." I felt like he was trying to tell me something, but it was apparent he couldn't speak freely in front of Thomas.

"Thomas, could you bring me some more water, please?" I

needed to know what Tobias wanted to tell me.

"What are you not telling me?" I asked Tobias as soon as Thomas stepped out of the room.

"Billy's caught up at work, he doesn't know when he's getting out, but he's getting on my nerves," he murmured. He paused and looked over his shoulder. "He insisted on the doctor. I hope that's fine with you."

Thomas walked back into the room, so I nodded.

"Anyway, I think I'm gonna get going, Billie. I just wanted to know you were okay. I didn't want to leave without being sure. Let me know if there's anything you need." I thanked him, and he nodded at Thomas before stepping out of the room.

"I was so worried," Thomas said, grabbing my hand and kissing it. This situation was not going to be helpful. I couldn't even open my eyes fully. How was I going to talk to Thomas about seriously breaking up with him? I didn't have the energy to do so.

"Where's Caleb? I want to talk to him."

"He's busy, I think. I'll let him know you want to talk to him."

Busy doing what? I was sure he was out there. He must've been worried sick, and I wanted to thank him for saving my life. I felt like Thomas didn't want me to talk to him.

The door to my bedroom was open, but Caleb knocked on it anyway a few minutes later.

Busy, huh?

His eyes darted from my left hand, being held by Thomas, to my eyes in a fraction of a second. I hadn't even noticed that my hand was being held until he looked at it. I instinctively released myself from Thomas's grasp, and Caleb's mouth went into a tight line. "The doctor's here, Miss Murphy."

I sat up straight and said, "Caleb, I need to talk to you."

"Sure, we'll talk—later," he said, looking at Thomas. "Once you're feeling better."

Thomas moved away to allow the doctor to get near me. "Good evening, Miss Murphy, I'm Dr. Lindström," he said with an accent. He looked amiable, and I assumed he was Swedish because of his last name and the fact that he was the Sjöbergs' go-to doctor. "I hear cooking isn't your forte." He was surely trying to lighten the mood. I laughed under my breath, but it came out forced somehow. I was so worried and embarrassed. "I'm just going to check up on you to see how you're doing, okay?" I nodded.

He took my blood pressure, asked me a few questions, and removed the bandages to check my hand. "Any ringing in your ears? Nausea or dizziness?"

I told him about my burned hand's discomfort, and how other than that, I felt fine, just a little worried about what had happened.

"Mhm. Okay, so would you say you've been under a lot of stress lately?" he asked casually. Thomas standing there, listening to our conversation, made me extremely uncomfortable.

"Somewhat," I replied. "I've been taking a photography course, and it has been a bit stressful." *And I just broke up with my boyfriend two days ago, and he's standing beside you, and once you leave, I'll have to talk to him again about it, and I have the stupidest crush on William. And I don't know what to do about that either. Oh, and Caleb hates me.*

That too.

"Headache?"

"Tolerable."

"Okay, I'd like you to monitor for any other symptoms if they should arise. I'm going to prescribe something for the headache and an ointment for your hand. Try to stay hydrated and make no significant efforts right now.

"Rest as much as possible. You should feel better tomorrow, but I suggest you take it easy. Stay home if you can. I'd like to see you at my office in a week to see how your hand is doing."

"Can I attend my photography course or—"

"I don't think so. I'd prefer it if you take tomorrow off, but I can write you a letter if necessary."

"Okay, thanks, that would be helpful."

"Take this for now," he said, leaving a sample box of medication on my nightstand. "It'll ease your hand's pain and help you relax. I'll leave the prescription and the letter with the big guys outside." He grinned. I knew he would call William once he left. I wished he could be here instead.

"Take good care of her," Dr. Lindström said to Thomas, lightly tapping his shoulder. Thomas looked anxious. "Are you her brother?"

Oh, come on.

"I'm her boyfriend," he replied with a puzzled frown.

Boyfriend?

This is going to be harder than I thought.

"I see." Dr. Lindström raised his brows for a second and started toward the door. Thomas followed him. "Let me know if she needs anything else." Dr. Lindström handed his card over to Thomas as he stepped out the door.

Thomas walked back and sat on the bed beside me.

"That was awkward," he said, opening the small box of medication the doctor left for me. I thought the exact same thing, but probably for an entirely different reason than he did.

There was a single pill inside, and Thomas gave it to me. The doctor said it would help me relax, so I can't stress enough how excited I was about downing that capsule.

"I'm so embarrassed about what happened." I buried my head deeper into my pillows and closed my eyes for a few seconds.

"There's nothing to be embarrassed about. What's important is that you weren't badly hurt," he replied, taking my good hand between both of his.

"So, who's outside? Has anyone talked to my father?" I asked.

"Aaron, Caleb, and David. Your father's flying in tonight. He was supposed to arrive tomorrow."

I kept thinking about how my father would probably ask me to move back with him or convince Mimi to live with me permanently.

Thomas excused himself to take a call, and I closed my eyes for a while.

Twenty minutes later, Thomas came back and laid down on the bed beside me. The pleasant effect of the medication was taking over my senses. The knots around my body untangled, my mind wasn't jumping from thought to thought, and everything felt delicious.

"I miss this … us," he whispered in my ear. The tingling sensation of his breath against my responsive skin was so inviting.

"Mhm," replied my medication to him.

I was zoned out—there but not—surrounded by a happy fog. I was not myself *at all*.

"I'm so glad you're okay. Everything's going to be okay from now on, I promise." He drew a line down my arm with his finger, making me shudder. "I promise."

He leaned in to kiss me, and I allowed him to do it. His soft, familiar lips were comforting, and I foolishly yielded into the feel-good sensation of it. I ran my fingers through his smooth hair. He placed his hand around my neck, pulling me closer to him.

What an idiot! Me, of course. Not him. He knew what he was doing. I was drugged, and he probably took advantage of it. And I never could resist his kisses. They were soooo good.

Someone get me a time machine.

A voice in the distance quickly closed in, but I had immersed myself in the kiss.

My bedroom door was open. I started to piece what the voice began to say as it made its final approach. But Thomas's lips were firmly locked in with mine—unwilling to disengage.

"*Kitchen's off-limits indefinitely. From now on, Guille, you leave the cooking to—*" The voice came to an abrupt halt, and I pulled away from Thomas to see William standing at the threshold. It took me a few seconds to react and understand that William was *actually* standing there with a burning look on his face. My body slowly thawing on the floor.

"I see you're doing much better now. Good as new ... I think I'll get go—"

No, no, no, no, no.

Don't think it! Say it!

"No!" I somehow managed to shout as he turned around to leave. "William, please!" He froze and looked at me over his shoulder. "Please," I said again, mostly to myself. Thomas shot straight up from the bed to his feet.

William turned around to face me but said nothing. His eyes were waiting for me to speak. The medication baffled my brain and made my head feel heavier by the second.

There was so much I wanted to say to both of them, yet I couldn't piece two words together. Starting with wanting Thomas to leave and William to stay.

I sighed. Slowly. And a discouraged tear streamed down my face.

I fucked up. Bad.

Thomas took a quick look at me, then turned around to face William—evaluating us. I couldn't face him now; he'd figure it out. But on the corner of my eye, I saw him ... nostrils flared, scowl in place, and hand curled up into a tight fist.

"I see now," Thomas said, his arms crossed firmly in front of his chest. I could hear William's heavy breathing, loud and clear. I tried to sit up again. I hated being stuck in this bed, watching this scene unfold in front of me like a movie—the kind that's so shitty that you have to stay till the end.

CHAPTER 37

In, Up, Twist, Out

I COULDN'T UNDERSTAND if Thomas was enjoying himself or merely suffering when he started asking questions. It was a masochistic hybrid of both states.

"*This*—is your Swedish neighbor, correct?" Thomas asked me. He said *this* as if he were referring to an object. I nodded. "So, you're into fucking celebrities now? Is that what this is about?"

What is he talking about? I grimaced in response to his allegations.

William's face was scorching red, and his knuckles were white from the strength with which he held a fist in place. His nostrils flared too, his mouth a thin line.

He hates me.

"You better watch your mouth, kid," he said with a grim, dark, menacing tone.

Thomas snorted with a cynical laugh and gnawed at his bottom lip.

"What—I-I don't understand." I looked at William for answers, but he wouldn't speak to me. His face reminded me of a pot with boiling water, crackling at the lid from the building pressure.

"William?" I urged.

"Guille, I—" he said softly, with that dreaded frown of his before being harshly cut off by Thomas.

"Oh, this is only getting better." Thomas clapped once and

placed his hands inside his pockets. He was about to say something. *Let him speak!*

My heart fluttered, and my stomach warmed with the growing anxiety that craved to come up to the surface, but it couldn't find its way out through the medication flowing in my veins.

"She doesn't know, does she?" Thomas asked. William went silent again, his gaze fixed on me. It was so *frustrating*. I wished I could stand up and shake the words out of him.

"For someone who memorizes *words* for a living, you're not doing yourself justice," Thomas said to William, sauntering in my direction. "But don't worry, I'll help clear the air."

"Don't you fucking *dare* tell her," William warned.

Thomas sat on the bed next to me and placed his hands on my shoulders. "Blondie here, you see, is a famous movie star, babe. Not that I expected a girl like you to know such a thing," he said, tucking my hair behind my ear. I flinched away from his touch. "Wouldn't that somehow feel … *beneath* you?" His tone was bundled up in a sarcastic and condescending package left for me to unwrap on my own. "This is William *fucking* Sjöberg!"

Thomas burst out laughing—each gasp oozing with cynicism.

I shook his hands away from my shoulders because *who the hell are you*? I couldn't recognize him. This wasn't the guy I used to date.

Thomas rose to his feet. William's face shifted from mad to dim and back. I couldn't read his expression. But whatever it was, it wasn't good.

"Now, this is what happens when you keep things from each other. Not a good way to start a relationship." Thomas kept going with a smug smile on his face.

"I'm sure you know *all* about that," William replied. He took his time when he said the word *all*. I closed my eyes for a few seconds, trying to process the words being exchanged in front of me.

"Excuse me?" Thomas barked back at him. "Babe, come on.

This is getting ridiculous. I'm sure we can talk things through. Just ask Lothario here to leave so we can fix this."

"Get. Out," I muttered.

"You heard her," Thomas said with a gravelly timbre. I took a deep breath. Thomas was delusional or pretending to be, at the very least. Either way, my message was not getting through.

"Get the fuck out, *Thomas*," I said louder this time. The menace of my tear flooded eyes was imminent. A blink was all it took for my face to become thoroughly drenched.

"Billie, you're not thinking straight. The medication is not allowing you to—"

Louder.

"Get the fuck out!" I cut him off with a scream that made my head feel like a soda can that'd been shaken too much.

Aaron materialized himself a few seconds later inside my bedroom. He took a quick look at both William and Thomas before looking at me. Thomas faced Aaron, and everyone remained silent.

"So, who's getting the fuck out?" Aaron asked with the scariest face I've ever seen him make. I'd never heard him swear in English before. Just a couple of times in Hebrew, but the impact of it was quite different.

Caleb appeared in the back of my bedroom, slowly pacing from one side to another, whistling while he waited for Aaron's cue, enjoying the fact that someone, either way, was getting thrown out.

No one would answer Aaron's question, so I gave him a hint and jerked my head to my right toward Thomas.

"Let's go, Mr. Hill." Aaron extended his hand in Thomas's direction and swiveled his fingers, summoning him to come forth.

"No," Thomas replied dryly with a deathly glare on the side.

Caleb stopped whistling and directed his predator focus on Thomas. My breathing felt ragged, and the walls began to close in on me.

"Why her?" Thomas yelled in William's face, but he didn't even flinch. "You can have *anyone*! Any girl you fucking want. Isn't that what you're famous for too? You only want her because you *can't* have her. But she's mine. So *why her?*"

Mine.

William refused to engage with Thomas. And I was thankful for that.

Caleb said something to Aaron in Hebrew, and they both stepped forward to seize Thomas by his arms. "Don't fucking touch me!" he shouted, trying uselessly to release himself from their grasp.

"Billie!" he cried. I hadn't enough energy to sob as my soul required, so my face went blank, yet tears inevitably kept streaming down my face. "Billie!" he yelled again over his shoulder.

As he was being dragged away, Thomas looked at me not with an exasperated look, nor a discouraged look, but with more of a don't-you-fucking-dare-think-I'm-done-with-this kind of look. And I didn't even know what to expect, but I was already exhausted.

The door snicked shut behind them—the sight of him being hauled out made me shudder.

"William, please let me explain," I said, trying to get up from the bed. I had to focus all the available energy inside me—which was flimsy and scarce—to gather the five words I'd just said to him out of my brain and actually say them.

I took a shaky step in his direction, and he looked away and held his hand up as in *stop, don't bother*. "I thought you were different—that I could trust you. But I was wrong. You're all the same."

He pulled my golden star hair tie off his wrist and tossed it on the floor. It felt like a dagger to the heart—*in, up, twist, out.*

His words, the tone, his hand ripping my tie off of his wrist. *Fuck …*

Everything that happened with Thomas hurt too, but he was my past now. And William was the promise of a future that had shattered into pieces—it vaporized in front of me in the blink of an eye. It was hope that was lost, and the look in his eyes told me I shouldn't hold on to that hope any longer—that it was useless.

His face was a mixture of anger, sadness, disappointment, and guilt. Or perhaps I was seeing my own feelings reflected on his face.

I felt terrible.

I had managed to knock down that heavy brick wall of his, he had opened up himself to me, and I disappointed him. I let him down. And now I felt a new twenty-inch steel wall building between us.

I sat down on the bed, unable to keep myself on my feet any longer, and stared at the floor for a few seconds as I allowed my brain to settle. When I looked up ... William was gone.

I threw myself back on my pillows, feeling completely numb. A dull heaviness buried me deeper into my bed. But I couldn't give up.

I picked up my phone on an impulse and texted William. I didn't care anymore about what was the right thing or the smart thing to do.

Fuck the rules.

He saw me kissing Thomas, and I wanted him to know what had happened. I *needed* to tell him. He must've thought I wanted to get back together with Thomas. I couldn't allow that! Even if William didn't want anything to do with me, I wanted him to know I was done with that toxic relationship—that I messed up. And being freaking *drugged* wasn't helpful either!

I had to try to talk to him, and my body was telling me I didn't have much time before I collapsed into sleep.

Me: You won the bet.

He texted quickly back.

W.S.: No, I didn't. Your boyfriend ruined it.

Me: I told you I broke up with him on Saturday.
W.S.: Didn't seem like it to me.
Me: Well, it's true.
W.S.: I suppose you won't have to keep guessing your way out of a date with me. You must be relieved. Besides, it's not safe for you to be around me. You saw what happened when you hung out with Lily. Those were only three paps, and you ended up with a bruise. You don't know how crazy it can get.
Me: I don't care about any of that.
W.S.: You say that now. You have no idea.

I couldn't fathom the idea of William being a celebrity. And I didn't care. To me, he was just William. My William. *Please be my William.*

Me: Enlighten me.
W.S.: Why don't you go ahead and Google me. You'll see that Thomas is right about everything. You don't know me.

I didn't know what he meant by that or what I was facing in doing such research. But I didn't care, and I didn't want to know. I just wanted things to go back to how they used to be the day before.

Me: I DON'T care because I do know you. Even if you want to hide, you can't anymore. I see you.

He took longer to reply, but after a few minutes of staring into my screen, he finally did.

W.S.: It doesn't matter anymore.
Me: He kissed ME! I didn't know what I was doing. I messed up. Ok? I'm sorry.

W.S.: It seemed to me like you knew perfectly well what you were doing. And as I said. It doesn't matter anymore. I'll be filming for the next three months. That's enough time for you to patch things up with Thomas. I'm getting out of your way. Believe me. It's for the best. I'm sure he'll forgive you for "fucking" a celebrity.

I knew he was hurt. He must've felt something for me too, or he wouldn't have reacted like this. What hurt *me* was that he wasn't giving me a choice. I had no say in this! And I had half of an overwhelmed brain to work with, and the other half was numb with medication. *Could this be nothing but a nightmare?* Maybe I hadn't woken up from when I passed out.

Me: Who said that's what I want?
W.S.: What is seen is not asked.
W.S.: You must be tired. You should be sleeping or something. I'm sure I'm not doing much to help with that either.

But you could! Come to me! Talk to me! Kiss me! Annoy me! Can't you see I want you?

But I couldn't find it in me to say any of those things. Instead, I opened my drawer, took the picture William shot of me out, and re-read the quote behind it a million times and one.

How ironic was it that the first part of the letter was left out? It would've rounded up perfectly the crushing, gnawing, piercing feeling inside my chest at that moment.

I grabbed a pen and wrote just above it:

Dear Mary,
When the Best is gone — I know that other things are not of consequence —

I placed the photograph inside the same white envelope it came in and crossed out my name and wrote above it: *For Mary*. I texted David and asked him to come to my bedroom. He was the perfect person for this assignment—discreet.

He came flying in two seconds later, and I gave him a very specific assignment: deliver the envelope directly to William's hands and say nothing to no one about it.

David left on his quest, and I threw myself back on my pillow, feeling drained. And in the middle of all this chaos, I still felt the desperate need to talk to Caleb, to thank him for pulling me out of the kitchen when I passed out. I don't know what would've happened if he hadn't found me there.

I grabbed my phone, intending to ask Caleb to come talk to me, but the medication finally won the battle and knocked me out into deep sleep.

CHAPTER 38

Birthday Wish

July 21, 2009

WAKING UP THE NEXT DAY confirmed to me that it hadn't all been a dream. The first thing that came to my mind as I opened my eyes was William. He had to give me a chance and listen to what I had to say. Or read it at least. Perhaps he'd slept it off. His thoughts and feelings from last night had to be mitigated. How had everything gone to shit so fast? I refused to believe that all was lost.

I didn't have a headache anymore, but my burnt hand was still throbbing with pain. I grabbed my phone and texted William, hoping he would answer.

Me: Can we talk? Please, just hear me out.
W.S.: Working. Can't talk or text.

I was a second away of peeling the skin off my face. I never knew frustration of this magnitude.

I heard a knock on my door, which reminded me to breathe. It was Mimi.

"Halò," she said, coming in. Looking at her made me miss my mother. And I swore to myself I wasn't going to cry again, but I couldn't keep the tears in any longer. Not without creating irreparable damage to my soul.

"There, there. It's awright." She embraced me, and since the medication's effect was long gone, my emotions came crashing down on me all at once. She held me tight in her arms, and then my father walked in.

"Hey, kiddo."

That's all I needed to hear at the moment. Mimi stood up and excused herself to take care of breakfast. My father took Mimi's place on the bed and held me in his arms.

"I'm sorry. I'm *so* sorry," I managed to say in between sobs. Not only was my life a mess, but I was sure the kitchen was too.

"There's nothing to be sorry about, darling. I'm just glad you're okay," he said in the warmest voice.

"Oh my God, happy birthday, Dad!" I cried and hugged him even tighter. I wiped the tears off my face.

"Thanks, kiddo. I heard you were baking a cake for me," he said, brushing off the tears that kept streaming out involuntarily.

"I was. I'm so embarrassed about it. I really don't belong anywhere near the kitchen. I'll ask the guys to buy a cake for you."

"No need to be embarrassed either. And that sounds great. I've cleared my schedule for the whole day. There's nothing more I want but to spend my birthday with you. When I arrived yesterday, you were sleeping, but I did get to talk to the guys," he explained, brushing his forehead with a slight frown. He was worried, but I could see it in his face that he didn't want me to notice. "I actually spent the night here."

"Oh." That was all I could say. He knew everything that had gone down the day before, and there was no way of avoiding it.

"Caleb looked quite … agitated. He refused to leave last night. He wanted to station himself outside the apartment. I told him it wasn't necessary, and I finally dismissed him," he said, taking a seat on the sofa across from my bed. "So, things got a little out of hand last night with Thomas?"

I explained how we had broken up the previous Saturday when I stayed over at the Hamptons and apologized for having dismissed Aaron, Caleb, and David to spend the night there.

I took a deep breath and told him how Thomas flew in to talk to me since he was having a hard time accepting we were done. "He refused to leave after I told him to, so … well, you know how Aaron and Caleb get all protective," I said, looking down. "I'm not happy about how they took him out, but he was acting like a jerk. He was disrespecting us, and I wasn't going to allow that."

"Us? Who else was here with you?" he asked. His brows moving closer.

Oh, great! Now *they leave things* out *of the report?*

"Uh, yes. William, my upstairs neighbor, was here last night too. He was checking in on me, and Thomas didn't appreciate his presence, so to speak."

"Aha," he replied, narrowing his eyes and raising the right corner of his mouth slightly. "William, the Swedish actor, yes?" I was surprised he knew about William. My father laughed when he saw the surprised look on my face.

"Hmm. I just found out last night that he's an actor," I snorted. "Thomas was the one to break the news. He didn't take it well that William and I are—well, friends." I was shocked Thomas hadn't said anything before, but we'd only bumped into William twice. He never really saw him. The first time, Thomas was drunk and exhausted, and the second time William and Tobias wore hats and sunglasses.

I guess I understand now why they did. They probably didn't want to be recognized wherever they were going. Although William's not too hard to miss in a crowd, no matter what he's wearing.

"How come you didn't know you had a bunch of celebrity neighbors? You know, I did find it odd you'd never mention anything about it. I thought you didn't find it interesting."

"Neighbors? So, it's not just William?"

"Oh, kiddo. They all are, except the youngest one and their mother," he replied. "Why do you think I asked to reinforce security if you hung out with them? I meant all of them. Not just Lily."

What?

I couldn't believe it. I did recognize Lily, and Sivert, their father, did seem familiar, but I could never place him. "And, are they like, super famous or something?"

"Well, Sivert has been an actor for quite a while. I'm sure you must've seen a film with him in it, but you probably don't remember. And from the three brothers, let's say William's right up there. Haven't you walked through Times Square?" He laughed again. "I guess this is my fault. I've probably kept you a bit shut out of the world." His smile slowly disintegrated.

And no, I hadn't walked through Times Square ever since we got back in April. We drove a few times through there, but I never noticed anything. "Is there a big poster of him or something?" I still couldn't believe he was famous. I hoped it was all a big joke, but it wasn't.

"Yes, I believe he has a new movie coming up."

"I see."

I just wanted him to be William—*my* William. But it didn't make much of a difference because he'd never been mine anyway. And you can't lose what you never had and all that crap.

"Are you good friends?" he asked, digging for information.

"Mhm."

A lie. William wasn't my friend. We'd never been, and I honestly didn't care to be *friends* with him. That wasn't an option. It was all or nothing for me.

"And what about Thomas? Do you think you will try to fix things with him?"

He was getting up to date, wasn't he?

I told my father there were more than a few things in the relationship making me uncomfortable. And how after the events of the night before, I couldn't think about getting back together with him.

"I love him, but I don't like him anymore. Does that make any sense?"

When I said that, it hit me. It was just a matter of time before Thomas faded away into a memory. It's challenging to keep loving someone you honestly just don't like anymore.

Was he trying to reign in his true self all this time? It's hard to keep up with a façade. It always ends up crashing down sooner or later.

"And do you think he will … behave? I can't stress enough Caleb's concern about Thomas after what happened yesterday. We'll see how things unfold in the next few weeks. We will probably have to take this into consideration and make a few adjustments to the current protocols for your safety." His tone was solemn. And I knew what *a few adjustments* meant to him. Not promising.

"I don't think that will be necessary. He was upset, and I get that. But I don't believe he would ever hurt me." I wanted to assume things would get cold in the following weeks and that it would all end up being a thing of the past.

I was going to cherish a lot of good memories with Thomas. Even though our relationship hadn't been lengthy, it had been intense. And I still refused to believe he was bad. I was convinced that Thomas's behavior resulted from his poorly dealt with grief, seeing his mother suffering all the time, plus all of the trauma generated by his father.

Mimi knocked on the door to announce the food was ready.

"Whoa." I lost my balance when I stood up from the bed.

"Are you okay to walk?" My father asked as he rushed to my side to help me.

"Yes, I am. I've just been lying down for too long."

I felt more stable after taking a few steps toward the bathroom. My father waited for me to be done and walked me to the dining table, where fresh fruit, eggs, bagels, berry jam, and lots of coffee awaited us. Mimi told us how she used Aaron and Caleb's kitchen to make the eggs because, again, no stove.

Someone knocked on the door, and Mimi rushed to see who it was. A man carrying a huge vase filled with roses came in, and Mimi instructed him to place them on the living room's coffee table.

"Bonnie flowers!" Mimi exclaimed. I hopelessly walked toward the flowers to fetch the card, knowing perfectly well they weren't from William because why would they be? But a girl can dream.

"Mimi, sit, please. At least have coffee with us," my father said. She had already eaten, but he was so fond of her, and they barely saw each other. Mimi took a seat at the table and poured herself a cup of coffee as I sat down to read the card. *Billie,* it read.

I'm so sorry, babe.

Please forgive me.

Thomas

I closed my eyes for a second and took a deep breath. I tossed the card to the side and poured myself some coffee. "Billie, ye can't drink coffee right noo. Doctor's orders," Mimi informed me.

Fuck my life.

Mimi insisted on how I needed to eat something first because I couldn't have those pills on an empty stomach. Eating was the last thing I wanted, but she was right.

I ate some fruit, a spoonful of scrambled eggs, and two bites of a bagel. Mimi wasn't satisfied with the amount of food I'd eaten, but it was more than I would've had if I weren't being scrutinized.

I turned to look at the flowers, and all I wanted was to throw them out. The gesture felt forced. Couldn't Thomas wait at least a couple of days to think about what he was sorry for? His apologies were automated, and I was starting to *hate* them.

"Did Thomas send them?" my father asked.

"Mhm," I hummed, sipping on my caffeine-free juice.

There was another knock on the door, and I was thankful that people were choosing not to ring the doorbell. It always startled me.

Mimi walked up to the front door opened it to let Caleb in.

"Good morning," he said, placing a cake on the table. "Happy birthday, Mr. Murphy." He extended his hand to my father. My father stood up and went for a hug. He genuinely liked Caleb, probably because he was the gossipiest of all.

Just before Caleb turned to look at me, I straightened myself on my seat and ran my hair behind my ears, trying to appear less like whatever it was I looked like, which was not my best.

"Are you feeling better, Miss Murphy?" Caleb asked with a worried, bordering-on-gray sort of tone.

"Ah, yes, thank you, Caleb. Just a bit tired, that's all," I said, lifting the corners of my lips into a modest smile.

I needed to talk to him! But I couldn't find the right time to do it.

"Glad to hear that, um"—he frowned and turned his gaze to the floor—"we'll be downstairs if you need anything." He nodded at my father, glanced at the flowers, and turned on his heel to leave.

"He's soo attentive, inne? By eight in the morning, he'd awready brought yer medication," Mimi commented cheerfully.

"Indeed," my father agreed with the most subtle frown I've ever seen between his eyes.

I excused myself to take a bath. I texted Ben and Nolan afterward about why I didn't show up at school.

My friends texted back, insisting on paying a visit after school to talk about the project. But I felt like they wanted to check up on me, which I thought was sweet of them.

I texted David directly and asked him if he could take the film from Saturday's photoshoot to develop. He came upstairs fairly quickly, and I gave the film to him. My father was sending a few emails from the living room couch. I joined him and grabbed a book as I waited for him to finish with work.

"You see, this is why you didn't *recognize* anyone," he said, closing his laptop and taking the book away from me. "Why don't we watch a movie?"

My father stood up and browsed through my DVDs but couldn't seem to find anything of his liking. "You really need to get Netflix, kiddo. These DVDs will be obsolete soon. The tendency is moving toward online streaming."

He clicked his tongue repeatedly until he finally picked a title. "Roman Holiday?" he asked, trying to please me, knowing it was a favorite of mine.

But no. Too romantic.

Not exactly what I was aiming for. Besides, I'd just recently seen it. Something bloody or haunted would probably get the job done, but I had nothing of the sort.

"Star Wars?" he asked with shock, shuffling the titles on his hands. "All six of them? When did you get these?"

"You've always insisted on how they qualify as classics, so I added them to my collection." I shrugged. "I actually did like them. A lot." I'd never thought I'd be into sci-fi, but I loved the story.

"Which one did you like best?" He seemed very eager to listen to my answer.

"Hmm, from the old ones, Episode V. And the new ones Episode III."

"I think Episode II beats Episode III, but I'll agree on Episode V," he conceded.

"The Duel on Mustafar just won me over."

"Yeah, that's a pretty great scene. So, Episode V, then?" he suggested, taking the DVD boxed set out of the drawer.

"Perfect."

The doorbell rang at around six in the afternoon. David had escorted Ben, Nolan, and Heather up to my apartment.

"Hey, Billie!" They exclaimed in unison with big smiles.

"Hey, guys! Come in, come in."

Heather walked up to me and gave me a big hug. I thanked David with a nod and closed the door behind us. My father was busy in the guest room, making a few calls.

"Whoa!" Ben cried as he saw the flowers Thomas had sent me.

"Someone's *very* sorry," Nolan teased.

I laughed with a smile that quickly twisted into a grimace. "You bet."

We sat in the living room, and Heather was the first to comment on the apartment's smell.

"Is something burning?" She sniffed a couple of times. Ben sat next to Heather and intertwined fingers with her.

Oh, my God! Finally!

I got distracted for a second and then replied, feeling embarrassed, "Oh no, I um—burned a cake yesterday."

"How did it happen, Billie? Are you okay?" Nolan asked with genuine concern on his face.

I told them the whole story and how I would be joining them tomorrow at school since the doctor wanted me to take a day off. They were just glad I was okay.

My father came out of the room and was surprised by the visit. I introduced everyone and offered them cake afterward. The cake Caleb bought was huge, so it was a great idea to share it with them.

We sang happy birthday to my father while he kept chuckling—his way of channeling his shyness from the unexpected situation. We even encouraged him to make a close-eyed wish, and I couldn't avoid laughing at his commitment.

Mimi seemed pleased with the fact that I was eating something. And I just wished I could be the one to make the wish instead.

We talked and laughed for hours, but my father eventually excused himself and left. He had early meetings the next day. My friends left soon after, and I was finally alone in my apartment.

Having people looking out and caring for me made me happy, but I needed some well-deserved alone time too. Alone so that I could stare at my phone in peace—waiting for a message that wouldn't come to magically appear on my screen and pull me out of the abyss I'd voluntarily launched myself into.

CHAPTER 39

Stay

August 14, 2009

THREE WEEKS HAD GONE BY, and I feared William had returned the courtesy of blocking me. I tried calling him on two different occasions, but the call never went through.

Touché!

A fresh flower arrangement arrived every week from Thomas, but I kept ignoring his calls.

There had to be a glitch in the Universe because we were all trying to get a hold of someone who wasn't willing to pick up the phone.

I even made a mental note about placing a fresh set of flowers under my pillow next year on Midsummer because, again—the glitch.

Breaking up with Thomas and having William out of the picture was all Caleb needed to go back to being the best version of himself. I'd never seen him happier, and because of that, I never found it in me to talk to him about everything like I wanted to— afraid I'd somehow ruin things. And well, I wasn't leaving the house much either, so we didn't have many opportunities to be alone and talk freely.

I had finally agreed to have dinner with Nina and CJ tonight. And since I was done with my photography course and I hadn't felt like going out to run in the past few weeks, I—drumroll please—sat in the living room to read a book.

I canceled Grant's training sessions. After the fire, Dr. Lindström asked me to take a break from boxing until my hand healed. But even though I was cleared for resuming exercise, I preferred to keep my distance. I would have to bump into Tobias every day, and the thought of it made me uncomfortable. That meant I had a lot of free time on my hands, which I usually spent inside my head.

Ten minutes into my reading, and I was sound asleep.

C

I woke up feeling disoriented with the book open on my chest, but the twinkling night lights gave me an idea of how late it was. My cell phone indicated it was almost midnight.

Shit. It was much later than I thought.

My phone was bustling with texts and missed calls from Nina, CJ, and my security group chat—all wondering if I was going to show up for dinner or not.

Should I throw my iPhone away? It would always remind me of William.

All the unpleasant memories and feelings came flooding back to me—reminding me of the mess I'd made of things.

All cats are gray in the dark. That much I knew.

Going back to sleep wasn't going to happen. I texted Nina and CJ back instead, apologizing for not showing up. I also wanted to let Aaron, Caleb, and David know what had happened.

Me: Good evening. I fell asleep and missed dinner. I'm going to head out to the rooftop to get some fresh air.
Aaron: Thank you for letting us know, Miss Murphy. I'll meet you up there in a few minutes.
Me: That won't be necessary, Aaron. I'd like to be alone if that's okay. I'll carry my phone and let you know if I need anything.

I needed to breathe.

Did I hope for William to show up like he always did?

I didn't know anymore.

Did I honestly think he would?

Never!

The irony ... We kept saying *never*, hoping for always, and now its meaning had come to life—it was sneering back at me, mocking me—ready to eat me alive.

Almost two months before, I stood on the same rooftop, picking up flowers to place under my bed. To dream of him. What a different night that had been.

I rested my arms against the farthest end of the rooftop for a while. I focused on my breathing and tried to keep my thoughts in check, and my tears locked in place.

In through my nose, out through my mouth.

It was one of those gut-wrenching nights, I'm afraid.

The rooftop door closed with a thump, but I didn't want to look back. I couldn't. I kept breathing in and slowly out through my mouth.

A hand delicately grasped my shoulder. I still refused to turn around.

"Hey, Red."

As soon as I saw him, my sobs ran loose and rushed into the haste of the city's skyline. I disarmed myself because I knew it was Caleb, my friend. Not Caleb, my bodyguard.

He ripped off his earpiece, letting it hang over his shoulder, and pulled me closer to his warm embrace. He intended to hold me until I was done crying—we were going to be there for a while.

"Thank you," I muttered under my breath, looking straight into those warm hazel eyes that took my breath away, reluctant to break away from his arms.

I crushed my face back into his chest and took a deep, gasping breath. "I never had the chance to thank you. You saved my life the day of the fire. I was such a fool, and I'm still so embarrassed I—"

"Hey," he interrupted me, softly brushing my hair away from my face. "Stop. It was an accident. There's no need to feel embarrassed about anything." I was probably ashamed about more than a few things, not just about burning the cake that day.

"I guess you were right about Thomas. You're always right. I—I should've listened to you," I cried, looking up to meet his eyes once again.

Caleb held his grip around my shoulders and shook his head. "That guy is *obsessed* with you. I never liked the way he looked at you, the way he talked to you. I don't like him near you," he said with a scowl. I wiped the tears off my face and kept staring at him afterward. He wasn't done talking.

"He makes me feel … uneasy. But oh, how I enjoyed being able to *throw* him out," he confessed with a pursed smile. "What happened? Did he have one of his jealous fits?"

I knew it must've been one of Caleb's favorite days in his life, but I hadn't enjoyed having to throw Thomas out one single bit. It had caused me pain to hear him say the things he said and see him act the way he did. I was having trouble forgiving him for that.

"Yup. A jealous fit," I replied, unlocking myself from his arms. "Not only that, but he also threw some *big* accusations at William and me."

Thomas had finally shown his true colors. I knew he was repressing a lot of feelings, emotions—words even. And that night, he had the perfect excuse to unleash himself on me. On everyone.

There was no way I would ever take him back, and the sad part was that I'd loved him, but he kept pushing me out and away in his attempt to prevent losing me, which was paradoxical.

"Hmm. So … false accusations?" Caleb asked with curiosity, standing next to me as we both looked into the shimmering city lights. He wanted to know where I stood with William, but there was no ground to stand on.

"*Very* false accusations," I replied firmly.

"What's up with him, anyway?" he asked, wanting to sound casual.

"Nothing's up. You saw it for yourself. He got what we wanted, so he turned around and walked away at the first chance he got," I answered bitterly, unable to swallow down the growing lump in my throat.

"So, he's an idiot, then?"

I'm the idiot.

But I said nothing.

"So, okay." He shook his head, looking anxious. "Look, Red, I've wanted to talk to you for days now," he confessed as my last shred of hope crumbled inside me. *Now what?*

Thomas turned out to be the opposite of who I thought he was. William wanted nothing to do with me. I'd only been a game—a distraction. And by the look of Caleb's intensified frown, I knew whatever he wanted to say wasn't going to be good.

The revelations on the night of the fire made me feel like I didn't need to know anything new for a while. There was too much I still needed to process.

"If you're pulling off the band-aid, don't do it slowly." I persuaded myself to draw a smile on my face.

"I got a job offer in Tel Aviv," he blurted out. *Ouch.*

"No!" I yelled as an automated response. "No! Caleb, you promised."

How can this be happening?

"Ah, it's—it's been challenging—being here in New York," he admitted, rubbing the length of his face.

"But are you actively looking for jobs, or did they seek you out?" I asked with indignation. And this was the part where all my selfishness blazed like a forest fire. I couldn't lose him too, could I? I needed to do *everything* in my power to make him reconsider.

"A bit of both, I guess," he replied. I could see he was having a hard time talking to me about this.

"Stay." I nodded once, locking my gaze with him. "Stay."

"I thought I could, but it's not been what I expected. It's just too much," he explained, running a hand through his short, brown hair.

"What were you expecting?" I demanded.

"I don't know … Paris in New York? But I had a feeling things would change here. I thought I'd be able to stomach it." He sighed, looking away again. He hated Thomas and probably hated each minute he had to see me with him even more.

He'd also seen me kissing William right in front of him, but it wasn't my intention to make him feel uncomfortable—it just happened. I got caught up in William's enveloping presence.

"Well, believe me when I say things will start looking *a lot* like Paris," I declared. Single and deeply relying emotionally on Caleb. "We'll … resume our morning runs in the park."

I knew I could convince him to stay. I had to.

"Don't do this, Red."

He kept looking away because he knew, too, that if he looked me in the eyes while I *begged*, I could get my way like I always did.

"Please, don't do this."

"Then stay."

My hand searched for his and tightened around it. He finally turned to look at me while I kept pressing, "I want you to stay. I *need* you."

Caleb placed his hand behind my neck and kissed me. I wrapped my arms around him and allowed myself to fade away into his arms. His unexpected kiss was filled with longing and nostalgic passion—it was way overdue. On both ends.

All I wanted, and all I dreamed of for years, was for him to kiss me like that. If he would've done so in Paris, would things have been any different?

"Stay," I kept saying in between kisses. Over and over again—until I got what I wanted.

"Okay," he breathed softly into my selfish lips. I sighed with heartfelt relief and leaned in—inviting him once again to kiss me. His hands cupped my face while I stood on my tiptoes and placed my arms tightly around his neck.

"Let me take care of you," he said as he took short, gasping breaks from my lips. "I know how to do it." I slowly broke away from him, our lips trembling. "We've played this game for a while now. I know I've had to endure it, but I will *never* hurt you, Red."

Caleb had been my rock through the years, the only constant in my continually changing world. And now there we stood. He'd saved my life in many ways, not just the day of the fire.

I knew I could love him. I trusted him blindly. And here he was offering to be there for me always—in ways, only he knew how. No one knew me better than he did.

Had everything else been a distraction? An infatuation?

I would need time to let everything else settle, but I knew he could make me happy.

As I peered into Caleb's sincere eyes, I knew deep down he would never hurt me. "Just promise me you'll stay no matter what," I whispered back.

He grazed my cheek with the back of his fingers, "As long as you want me to." His warm, sweet breath collided against my hopeful lips as I allowed myself to believe he could be everything I'd always wanted.

I looked up at the starless sky, begging for answers that wouldn't come, but that *damn* crescent moon taunted me. It whispered back … that I was completely and foolishly moonstruck at midnight.

END OF BOOK ONE

ACKNOWLEDGEMENTS

First of all, I want to thank all of you who picked up the book and gave me a chance to introduce you to Billie's world. Writing this story has been so therapeutic during this past year. A year that has been filled with so many challenging situations for everyone all around the world. I hope that reading it provided a fun distraction during these uncertain times. There's so much more in store for Billie in the next two books in the series, and I'm sure you'll enjoy her journey.

I want to thank my husband Germán for not only believing in me and supporting me but for putting up with me. Writing's a very lonely and demanding venture that can take away from time with family and friends, and I'm so thankful that you supported me throughout the whole process. I love you!

Marianna Andrade: Prims! You're one hell of a rockstar developmental editor in disguise. Thank you for pushing my limits, for your honesty, the selfless dedication, and the support you've given me from the start. You were the one who read the very first words I ever wrote and got to see how the story unfolded. Thank you from the bottom of my heart! This story wouldn't have been the same without you; I promise you that.

Andrea Medina: Thank you for reading one of the first versions of the manuscript. Your color-coded notes and comments were amazing! Thank you for taking the time to do so.

Melissa Ortiz and Andrea Lomelí: Thank you for the endless encouragement. Your support means the world to me. Thank you for always believing in me.

Nolan Abeyta: Thank you for giving me a glimpse into your

world rowing crew at Princeton. You helped me understand Thomas a lot more. I really appreciate you taking the time to do so.

Pedro Valdés Sada: Thank you for sharing your vast astronomical knowledge regarding the moon—the most important element in the story.

Sulamit Elizondo: Your art is not only beautiful and inspiring but feminine and powerful. Just like Billie! Thank you for bringing her to life. I couldn't have found a better artist to convey that for the cover. I'm so excited to see what you'll create for the next two books.

David Provolo: I couldn't have been happier with the beautiful cover you made for me. I'm in love with it.

Bruce and Senad, the doormen of 485 Park, you're the best! It was so fun meeting you guys and thank you for allowing me to include you in the story.

Jennifer Herrington: I don't know where to start! It's been *amazing* working with you. Thank you so much for accepting to work with my story, for your patience, for your incredible suggestions. I feel like we make a great team, and I'm so happy to keep having my manuscripts go through your eyes. Thank you for believing in Billie's story!

Kristen O'Connell: Thank you, thank you, thank you! You're a lifesaver.

My petit Covid comité: Christianne Warschawski, Vanessa Dominique, Daniela de la Fuente. Thank you for keeping me sane, for giving my family and me a sense of normalcy during the past year, for all your support. Your friendship means a lot to me!

Jose Carlos—JC! Thank you for inspiring a great character, my real-life CJ, for doing the Billie landmark tour in NY with me, supporting me, believing in me, letting me crash at your place every time. *For all that it is.*

To my parents: I know that I've tried many things in my endless curiosity, and I'm impressed how in all of them, you've always been there behind me, supporting me, believing in me, and cheering me on!

Katia thank you for taking the time to read one of my first drafts. I'm sorry I made you stop reading it, but I really wanted you to read the finished product!

To all my friends who have encouraged me during this process, it means more than you could ever know. You know who you are. All of you who liked and shared a Moonstruck related post on social media to help spread the word, thank you! It's such an easy thing to do but so meaningful and helpful.

And last but not least to my son, Germán, who can't read this right now, but I hope you do one day. I hope one day when you grow up, you'll see this and feel proud of your mother!

www.alejandra-andrade.com
Follow the author on Instagram: @alejandra__author
to learn more about the upcoming books in the
Moonstruck Series.

Read a sneak peek of Book Two of the Moonstruck Series: *Heartstruck at Dawn.*

Go to: https://cutt.ly/HeartstruckAtDawn

Or Scan:

Made in the USA
Monee, IL
03 August 2022